JEWELS

Jenny B.

JEWELS

Danielle Steel

CORGI BOOKS

JEWELS
A CORGI BOOK : 0 552 13745 6

Originally published in Great Britain by Bantam Press,
a division of Transworld Publishers Ltd

PRINTING HISTORY
Bantam Press edition published 1992
Corgi edition published 1993
Corgi edition reprinted 1993 (twice)
Corgi edition reprinted 1995
Corgi edition reprinted 1996

This book is set in 10/11½pt Linotype Plantin by
County Typesetters, Margate, Kent.

Corgi Books are published by Transworld Publishers Ltd,
61–63 Uxbridge Road, London W5 5SA,
in Australia by Transworld Publishers (Australia) Pty Ltd,
15–25 Helles Avenue, Moorebank, NSW 2170
and in New Zealand by Transworld Publishers (NZ) Ltd,
3 William Pickering Drive, Albany, Auckland.

Printed and bound in Great Britain by
Cox & Wyman Ltd, Reading, Berkshire.

TO POPEYE

There is only one real love in a lifetime, only one, that matters, that grows, and that lasts forever . . . in life . . . in death . . . together, as one . . . sweet love, you are mine. My one and only love . . . forever.

With all my heart,
Olive

Chapter 1

The air was so still in the brilliant summer sun that you could hear the birds, and every sound for miles, as Sarah sat peacefully looking out her window. The grounds were brilliantly designed, perfectly manicured, the gardens laid out by Le Nôtre, as Versailles' had been, the trees towering canopies of green framing the park of the Château de la Meuze. The château itself was four hundred years old, and Sarah, Duchess of Whitfield, had lived here for fifty-two years now. She had come here with William, when she was barely more than a girl, and she smiled at the memory as she watched the caretaker's two dogs chase each other into the distance. Her smile grew as she thought of how much Max was going to enjoy the two young sheepdogs.

It always gave her a feeling of peace, sitting here, looking out at the grounds they had worked so hard on. It was easy to recall the desperation of the war, the endless hunger, the fields stripped of everything they might have had to give them. It had all been so difficult then . . . so different . . . and it was odd, it never seemed so long ago . . . fifty years . . . half a century. She looked down at her hands, at the two enormous, perfectly square emerald rings she almost always wore, and it still startled her to see the hands of an old woman. They were still beautiful hands, graceful hands, useful hands, thank God, but they were the hands of a seventy-five-year-old woman. She had lived well, and long; too long, she thought sometimes . . . too long without William . . . and yet there was always

7

more, more to see, to do, to think about, and plan, more to oversee with their children. She was grateful for the years she had had, and even now, she didn't have the sense that anything was over, or complete yet. There was always some unexpected turn in the road, some event that couldn't have been foreseen, and somehow needed her attention. It was odd to think that they still needed her, they needed her less than they knew, and yet they still turned to her often enough to make her feel important to them, and still somehow useful. And there were their children too. She smiled as she thought of them, and stood, still looking for them out the window. She could see them as they arrived, from here . . . see their faces as they smiled, or laughed, or looked annoyed as they stepped from their cars, and looked expectantly up at her windows. It was almost as if they always knew she would be there, watching for them. No matter what else she had to do, on the afternoon they were to arrive, she always found something to do in her elegant little upstairs sitting room, as she waited. And even after all these years, with all of them grown, there was always a little thrill of excitement, to see their faces, hear their tales, listen to their problems. She worried about them, and loved them, just as she always had, and in a way, each one of them was a tiny piece of the enormous love she had shared with William. What a remarkable man he had been, larger than any fantasy, than any dream. Even after the war, he was a force to be reckoned with, a man that everyone who knew him would always remember.

Sarah walked slowly away from the window, past the white-marble fireplace, where she often sat on cold winter afternoons, thinking, writing notes, or even writing a letter to one of her children. She spoke to them frequently on the telephone, in Paris, London, Rome, Munich, Madrid, and yet she had an enormous fondness for writing.

She stood looking down at a table draped in an ancient, faded brocade, a beautiful piece of antique workmanship that she had found years ago, in Venice, and she gently touched the framed photographs there, picking them up at random to see them better, and as she looked at them, it was suddenly so easy to remember the exact moment . . . their wedding day, William laughing at something someone had said, as she looked up at him, smiling shyly. There was so much happiness evident there, so much joy that she had almost thought her heart would break with it the day of her wedding. She wore a beige lace-and-satin dress, with a very stylish beige lace hat with a small veil, and she had carried an armload of small, tea-colored orchids. They had been married at her parents' home, at a small ceremony, with her parents' favorite friends beside them. Almost a hundred friends had come to join them for a quiet, but very elegant, reception. There had been no bridesmaids this time, no ushers, no enormous wedding party, no youthful excess, only her sister to attend her, in a beautifully draped blue-satin dress with a stunning hat that had been made for her by Lily Daché. Their mother had worn a short dress in emerald-green. Sarah smiled at the memory . . . her mother's dress had been almost exactly the color of her own two extraordinary emeralds. How pleased with her life her mother would have been, if only she had lived to see it.

There were other photographs there as well, of the children when they were small . . . a wonderful one of Julian with his first dog . . . and Phillip, looking terribly grown-up, though he was only eight or nine, when he was first at Eton. And Isabelle somewhere in the South of France in her teens . . . and each of them in Sarah's arms when they were first born. William had always taken those photographs himself, trying to pretend not to have tears in his eyes, as he looked at Sarah with each new, tiny baby. And Elizabeth . . . looking so small . . . standing beside

Phillip in a photograph that was so yellow, one could hardly see now. But as always, tears filled Sarah's eyes as she looked at it and remembered. Her life had been good and full so far, but it hadn't always been easy.

She stood looking at the photographs for a long time, touching the moments, thinking of each of them, gently brushing up against the memories, while trying not to bump into those that were too painful. She sighed as she walked away again, and went back to stand at the long French windows.

She was graceful, and tall, her back very straight, her head held with the pride and elegance of a dancer. Her hair was snowy-white, though it had once shone like ebony; her huge, green eyes were the same deep, dark color as her emeralds. Of her children, only Isabelle had those eyes, and even hers weren't as dark as Sarah's. But none of them had her strength and style, none of them had the fortitude she had had, the determination, the sheer power to survive all that life had dealt her. Their lives had been easier than hers had been, and for that, in some ways, she was very grateful. In other ways, she wondered if her constant attention to them had softened them, if she had indulged them too much, and as a result had made them weaker. Not that anyone would call Phillip weak . . . or Julian . . . or Xavier . . . or even Isabelle . . . still, Sarah had something that none of them had, a sheer strength of soul that seemed to emanate from her as one watched her. It was a kind of power one sensed about her as she walked into a room, and like her or not, one couldn't help but respect her. William had been like that, too, although more effusive, more obvious in his amusement about life, and his good nature. Sarah had always been quieter, except when she was with William. He brought out the best in her. He had given her everything, she frequently said, everything she had ever cared about, or loved, or truly needed. She smiled as she looked out over the green lawns, remembering how it had all begun. It seemed like only hours ago . . . days since it had all started. It was impossible to believe that tomorrow was going to be her seventy-fifth birthday. Her children and her grandchildren were coming to celebrate it with her, and the day after that, hundreds of illustrious and important people. The party still seemed foolish to her, but the children had absolutely insisted. Julian had organized everything, and even Phillip had called her from London half a dozen times to make sure that everything was going smoothly. And Xavier had sworn that, no matter where he was, Botswana or Brazil, or God only knew where else, he would fly in to be there. Now she waited for them, standing at the window, almost breathlessly, feeling a little flutter of excitement. She was wearing an old, but beautifully cut, simple black Chanel dress with the enormous, perfectly matched pearls that she almost always wore, which caused people who knew to catch their breath the first time they saw them. They had been hers since the war, and had they sold in today's world, they would have surely brought well over two million dollars. But Sarah never thought of that; she simply wore them because she loved them, because they were hers, and because William had insisted that she keep them. 'The Duchess of Whitfield should have pearls like that, my love.' He had teased her when she first tried them on, over an old sweater of his she had borrowed to work in the lower garden. 'Damn shame my mother's were so insignificant compared to these,' he had commented, and she'd laughed, and he had held her close to him as he kissed her. Sarah Whitfield had beautiful things, she had had a wonderful life. And she was a truly extraordinary person.

And as she began to turn away from the window at last, impatient for them to come, she heard the first car coming around the last turn in the driveway. It was an endless black Rolls-Royce limousine, with windows so dark, she wouldn't have been able to see who was in it. Except that she knew, she knew each of them to perfection. She stood smiling as she watched them. The car stopped directly in front of the main entrance to the château, almost exactly below her window, and as the driver stepped out and hurried to open the door for him, she shook her head with amusement. Her eldest son was looking extremely distinguished, as always, and very, very British, while trying not to appear harassed by the woman who stepped out of the car just behind him. She wore a white silk dress and Chanel shoes, her hair cut short, very stylishly, with diamonds glittering in the summer sun absolutely everywhere she could find to put them. She smiled to herself again as she turned away from the scene at the window. This was only the beginning . . . of a mad, interesting few days . . . Hard to believe . . . she couldn't help but wonder what William would have thought of all of it . . . all this fuss over her seventy-fifth birthday . . . seventy-five years . . . so much too soon . . . It seemed only moments since the beginning . . .

Chapter 2

Sarah Thompson had been born in New York in 1916, the youngest of two daughters, and a slightly less fortunate but extremely comfortable and respected cousin of both the Astors and the Biddles. Her sister, Jane, had in fact married a Vanderbilt when she was nineteen. And Sarah got engaged to Freddie Van Deering exactly two years later, on Thanksgiving. She was nineteen herself by then, and Jane and Peter had just had their first baby, an adorable little boy named James, with strawberry-blond ringlets.

Sarah's engagement to Freddie came as no great surprise to her family, as they had all known the Van Deerings for years; and although they knew Freddie less, as he'd been in boarding school for so many years, everyone had certainly seen a lot of him in New York while he was going to Princeton. He had graduated in June, of the year they got engaged, and had been in high spirits ever since that illustrious event, but he had also managed to find time to engage in courting Sarah. He was a bright, lively boy, always playing pranks on his friends, and intent on seeing to it that everyone had a good time wherever they went, particularly Sarah. He was seldom serious about anything, and always joking. Sarah was touched by how attentive he was, and amused to find him in such good spirits. He was fun to be with, easy to talk to, and his laughter and high spirits seemed to be contagious. Everyone liked Freddie, and if he lacked ambitions for the business world, no-one seemed to mind it, except perhaps

Sarah's father. But it was also well known to everyone that if he never worked, he could live very handsomely on the family fortune. Nevertheless, Sarah's father felt it was important for a young man to participate in the business world, no matter how large his fortune, or who his parents were. He himself owned a bank, and spoke to Freddie at some length about his plans, just before the engagement. Freddie assured him that he had every intention of settling down. In fact, he'd been offered an excellent position at J. P. Morgan & Co., in New York, as well as an even better one at the Bank of New England in Boston. And after the New Year, he was going to accept one of them, which pleased Mr Thompson no end, and he then allowed their official engagement to go forward.

The holidays were great fun for Sarah that year. There were endless engagement parties for them, and night after night they were going out, having fun, seeing their friends, and dancing until all hours of the morning. There were skating parties in Central Park, luncheons and dinners, and numerous dances. Sarah noticed that during that time Freddie seemed to drink a great deal, but no matter how much he drank he was always intelligent, and polite, and extremely charming. Everyone in New York adored Freddie Van Deering.

The wedding was scheduled for June, and by spring, Sarah was overwhelmed, between keeping track of wedding presents, fittings for her wedding gown, and more parties given by still more friends. She felt as though her head were spinning. She hardly saw Freddie alone at all during that time, and it seemed as though the only time they met was at parties. The rest of the time, he was with his friends, all of whom were 'preparing' him for the great plunge into A Serious Life of Marriage.

It was a time Sarah knew she was supposed to enjoy, but the truth was, as she confided to Jane finally in May, she really wasn't. It was too much of a whirlwind, everything seemed out of control, and she was absolutely exhausted. She ended up crying late one afternoon, after the final fitting for her wedding gown, as her sister quietly handed her her own lace hankie, and gently stroked her sister's long dark hair, which hung far past her shoulders.

'It's all right. Everyone feels like that just before a wedding. It's supposed to be wonderful, but actually it's a difficult time. So much is happening all at once, you don't get a single quiet moment to think, or sit down, or be alone . . . I had an awful time right before our wedding.'

'You did?' Sarah turned her huge, green eyes to her older sister, who had just turned twenty-one and seemed infinitely wiser to Sarah. It was a huge relief to her to learn that someone else had felt equally overwhelmed and confused just before their wedding.

The one thing Sarah did not doubt was Freddie's affection for her, or what a kind man he was, or how happy they would be after their wedding. It just seemed as though there was too much 'fun' going on, too many distractions, too many parties, and too much confusion. All Freddie ever seemed to think about was going out and having a good time. They hadn't had a serious conversation in months. And he still hadn't told her what his plans were about working. All he kept telling her was not to worry. He hadn't bothered to take the job at the bank after the first of the year, because there was so much he had to do before the wedding that a new job would really have been too distracting. Edward Thompson took a dim view of Freddie's ideas about work by then, but he had refrained from saying anything about it to his daughter. He had discussed it with his wife, and Victoria Thompson felt sure that after the wedding, Freddie would probably settle down. He had, after all, gone to Princeton.

Their wedding day came in June, and the extensive preparations had been worthwhile. It was a beautiful wedding at St Thomas Church on Fifth Avenue, and the reception was held at the Saint Regis. There were four hundred guests, and wonderful music that seemed to go on all afternoon, delicious food, and all fourteen brides-maids looked adorable in their delicate peach-colored organdy dresses. Sarah herself wore an incredible dress of white lace and French organdy, with a twenty-foot train, and a white lace veil that had been her great grand-mother's. She looked absolutely exquisite. The sun had been shining brilliantly all day. And Freddie looked as handsome as anyone could. It was in every possible way, the perfect wedding.

And almost the perfect honeymoon. Freddie had borrowed a friend's house and a little yacht on Cape Cod, and they were completely alone with each other for the first four weeks of their marriage. Sarah felt shy with him at first, but he was gentle and kind, and always fun to be with. He was intelligent when he allowed himself to be serious, which was rare. And she discovered that he was an excellent yachtsman. He drank a good deal less than he had before, and Sarah was relieved to see it. His drink-ing had almost begun to worry her just before the wedding. But it was all in good fun, as he told her.

Their honeymoon was so lovely that she hated to go back to New York in July, but the people who had lent them the house were coming back from Europe. Sarah and Freddie knew that they had to get organized and move into their apartment. They had found one in New York, on the Upper East Side. But they were going to stay with her parents in Southampton for the summer, while the painters and the decorator and the workmen got every-thing ready.

But that fall, once they returned to New York after Labor Day, Freddie was too busy to get a job once again. In fact, he was too busy to do much of anything, except see his friends. And he seemed to be doing a great deal of drinking. Sarah had noticed it in Southampton that summer, whenever he got back from the city. And once they moved into their own apartment in town, it was impossible not to notice. He came home drunk, late every afternoon, after spending the day with friends. At times, he didn't even bother to show up until long after midnight. Sometimes, Freddie took Sarah out with him, to parties or balls, and he was always the life of the party. He was everyone's best friend, and everyone knew they would always have a good time as long as they were with Freddie Van Deering. Everyone except Sarah, who had begun to look desperately unhappy long before Christmas. There was no longer any mention at all of his getting a job, and he brushed off all of Sarah's delicate attempts to discuss it. He seemed to have no plans at all, except having fun and drinking.

By January, Sarah was looking pale, and Jane had her over to tea to see what was the matter.

'I'm fine.' She tried to seem amused that her sister was concerned, but when the tea was served, Sarah turned paler still and couldn't drink it.

'Darling, what's wrong? Please tell me! You have to!' Jane had been worried about her since Christmas, Sarah had seemed unusually quiet at their parents' house for Christmas dinner. Freddie had charmed everyone with a toast in rhyme about the entire family, including the servants who had worked for them for years, and Jupiter, the Thompsons' dog, who barked on cue while everyone applauded Freddie's very accomplished poem. It had amused everyone, and the fact that he was more than a little tipsy seemed to go unnoticed.

'Really, I'm fine,' Sarah insisted, and then finally began to cry, until she found herself sobbing in her sister's arms and admitting that she wasn't fine at all. She was miserable. Freddie was never home, he was out constantly, he stayed out until all hours with his friends, and Sarah didn't admit to Jane that she sometimes suspected the friends might even be female. She tried to get him to spend more time with her, but he didn't seem to want to. And his drinking was worse than ever. He had his first drink every day long before noon, sometimes when he got up in the morning, and he insisted to Sarah that it wasn't a problem. He called her 'his prim little girl', and brushed off her concerns with amusement. And to make matters worse, she had just learned that she was pregnant.

'But that's wonderful!' Jane exclaimed, looking delighted. 'I am too!' she added, and Sarah smiled through her tears, unable to explain to her older sister how unhappy her life was. Jane's life was totally different. She was married to a serious, reliable man who was interested in being married to her, while Freddie Van Deering most assuredly wasn't. He was many things, charming, amusing, witty; but responsibility was as foreign to him as another language. And Sarah was beginning to suspect that he would never settle down. He was just going to go on playing forever. Sarah's father had begun to suspect that, too, but Jane was still convinced that everything was going to work out happily, especially after they had the baby. The two girls discovered that their babies were due at almost exactly the same time – within days of each other, in fact – and that bit of news cheered Sarah a little before she went back to her lonely apartment.

Freddie wasn't there, as usual, and didn't come home that night at all. The next day he was contrite when he came home at noon, explaining that he had played bridge till 4 a.m. and then stayed where he was because he was afraid to come home and wake her.

'Is that all you do?' For the first time, she turned on him angrily after he had explained it, and he looked startled by the vehemence of her tone. She had always been very demure about his behavior before, but this time she was clearly very angry.

'What on earth do you mean?' He looked shocked at her

question, his innocent blue eyes opened wide, his sandy-blond hair making him look like Tom Sawyer.

'I mean, what exactly do you do at night when you stay out until one or two o'clock in the morning?' There was real anger there, and pain, and disappointment.

He smiled boyishly, convinced he would always be able to delude her. 'Sometimes I have a little too much to drink. That's all. It just seems easier to stay where I am when that happens than come home when you're asleep. I don't want to upset you, Sarah.'

'Well, you are. You're never home. You're always out with your friends, and you come home drunk every night. That's not how married people behave.' She was steaming.

'Isn't it? Are you referring to your brother-in-law, or *normal* people with a little more spunk and joie de vivre? I'm sorry, darling, I'm not Peter.'

'I never asked you to be. But who are you? Who am I married to? I never see you, except at parties, and then you're off with your friends, playing cards, and telling stories, and drinking, or you're out, and God knows where you are then,' she said sadly.

'Would you rather I stayed home with you?' He looked amused, and for the first time she saw something wicked in his eyes, something mean, but she was challenging his very lifestyle. She was frightening him, and even threatening his drinking.

'Yes, I would rather you stay home with me. Is that such a shocking thing?'

'Not shocking, just stupid. You married me because I was fun to be with, didn't you? If you'd wanted a bore like your brother-in-law, I imagine you could have found one, but you didn't. You wanted me. And now you want to turn me into someone like him. Well, darling, I can promise you that won't happen.'

'What will happen then? Will you go to work? You told Father last year you would, and you haven't.'

'I don't *need* to work, Sarah. You're boring me to tears. You should be happy that I don't have to scrabble like some fool, at some dreary job, trying to put food on the table.'

'Father thinks it would be good for you. And so do I.' It was the bravest thing she had ever said to him, but the night before she had lain awake for hours, thinking of what she would tell him. She wanted to make their life better, to have a real husband, before she had this baby.

'Your father is another generation' – his eyes glittered as he looked at her – 'and you're a fool.' But as he said the words, she realized what she should have known from the moment he walked in. He'd been drinking. It was only noon, but he was clearly drunk, and as she looked at him, she felt disgusted.

'Maybe we should discuss this some other time.'

'I think that's a fine idea.'

He had gone out again then, but returned early that night, and the next morning made an effort to get up at a decent hour in the morning, and it was then that he realized how ill she was. He was startled as he questioned her about it over breakfast. They had a woman who came in every day to clean the house and do ironing and serve their meals when they were at home. Usually, Sarah liked to cook, but she had been unable to face the kitchen for the last month, although Freddie hadn't been home often enough to see that.

'Is something wrong? Are you ill? Should you go to a doctor?' He looked concerned as he glanced at her over the morning paper. He had heard her retching horribly after they got up, and wondered if it had been something she had eaten.

'I've been to the doctor,' she said quietly, her eyes looking at him, but it was a long moment before he glanced her way again, almost having forgotten his earlier question.

'What was that? Oh . . . right . . . good. What did he say? Influenza? You ought to be careful, you know, there's a lot of it about just now. Tom Parker's mother almost died of it last week.'

'I don't think I'll die of this.' She smiled quietly and he went back to his paper. There was a long silence, and then finally he looked at her again, having totally forgotten their earlier conversation.

'There's a hell of a stink in England over Edward VIII abdicating to be with that Simpson woman. She must be something else, to get him to do a thing like that.'

'I think it's sad,' Sarah said seriously. 'The poor man has been through so much, how could she destroy his life like that? What kind of life can they possibly have together?'

'Maybe a pretty racy one.' He smiled at her, much to her chagrin, looking handsomer than ever. She wasn't sure any more if she loved or hated him, her life with him had become such a nightmare. But maybe Jane was right, maybe everything would be better after they had the baby.

'I'm having a baby.' She almost whispered to him, and for a moment, he seemed not to hear her. And then he turned to her, as he stood up, and looked as though he hoped she were joking.

'Are you serious?' She nodded, unable to say more to him, as tears filled her eyes. In a way, it was a relief finally to tell him. She had known since just before Christmas, but hadn't had the courage to tell him. She wanted him to care about her, wanted a quiet moment of happiness between them, and since their honeymoon on Cape Cod seven months before, that just hadn't happened.

'Yes, I'm serious.' Her eyes said she was, as he watched her.

'That's too bad. Don't you think it's a little too soon? I thought we were being careful.' He looked annoyed and not pleased, and she felt a sob catch in her throat, as she prayed not to make a fool of herself with her husband.

'I thought so too.' She raised her tear-filled eyes to him, and he took a step toward her and ruffled her hair, like a little sister.

'Don't worry about it, it'll be all right. When's it for?'

'August.' She tried not to cry, but it was hard to control herself. At least he wasn't furious, only annoyed. She hadn't been thrilled when she heard the news either. There was so little between them at this point. So little time, so little warmth or communication. 'Peter and Jane are having a baby then too.'

'Lucky for them,' he said sarcastically, wondering what he was going to do with her now. Marriage had turned out to be a lot more of a burden than he had expected. She seemed to sit around at home all the time, waiting to entrap him. And she looked even more woebegone now, as he glanced down at the little mother.

'Not lucky for us though, is it?' She couldn't restrain the two tears that slid slowly down her cheeks as she asked him.

'The timing isn't great. But I guess you don't always get to call that, do you?' She shook her head, and he left the room, and he didn't mention it to her again before he went out half an hour later. He was meeting friends for lunch, and he didn't say when he'd be back. He never did. She cried herself to sleep that night, and he didn't come home until eight o'clock the next morning. And when he did, he was still so desperately drunk from the night before that he never made it past the couch in the living room, on the way to their bedroom. She heard him come in, but he was unconscious by the time she found him.

And for the next month it was painfully plain how badly shaken he was by her little announcement. The idea of marriage was frightening enough to him, but the idea of a baby filled him with nothing less than terror. Peter tried to explain it to her one night when she had dinner alone with them, and by then, her unhappiness with Freddie was no secret between them. No-one else was to know, but she had confided in both of them ever since she had told her sister about the baby.

'Some men are just terrified of that kind of responsibility. It means they have to grow up themselves. I have to admit, it scared me, too, the first time.' He glanced lovingly at Jane, and then soberly back at her sister. 'And Freddie is not exactly famous for his ability to settle down. But maybe when he sees it, he'll realize it's not the dire threat he thought it was. They're pretty harmless when they're small. But it might be rough until you have the baby.' Peter was more sympathetic than he let on to her; he had frequently told his wife that he thought Freddie was a real bastard. But he didn't want to tell Sarah what he thought. He preferred to offer her encouragement about the baby.

But her spirits stayed pretty low, and Freddie's behavior and drinking only got worse. It took all of Jane's ingenuity to get Sarah out at all. Finally, she got her out to go shopping. They went downtown to Bonwit Teller on Fifth Avenue when Sarah suddenly became very pale and stumbled as she grabbed blindly for her sister.

'Are you all right?' Jane looked instantly frightened when she saw her.

'I . . . I'm fine . . . I don't know what happened.' She had had a terrible pain, but it only lasted for a moment.

'Why don't we sit down.' Jane was quick to signal someone and ask for a chair and a drink of water, and by then Sarah was clutching at her hand again. There were beads of sweat on her brow, and her face was a grayish green as she looked up at her older sister.

'I'm so sorry . . . Jane, I don't feel well at all . . .' And almost as she said the words, she fainted. The ambulance came as soon as it was called, and Sarah was carried out of

Bonwit's on a stretcher. She was conscious again by then, and Jane looked terrified as she ran along beside her. They let her ride to the hospital with Sarah in the ambulance, and Jane had asked the store to call Peter at his office, and their mother at home. And both arrived at the hospital only a few minutes later. Peter was more worried about Jane than anyone, and she clung to him and sobbed as her mother went in to see her sister. She was in with her for a long time, and when she came out, there were tears in her eyes and she looked at her eldest daughter.

'Is she all right?' Jane asked anxiously, and her mother quietly nodded and sat down. She had been a good mother to both of them. She was a quiet, unpretentious woman, with good taste and sound ideas, and values that had served both girls well, although the sensible lessons she'd taught hadn't done much to help Sarah with Freddie.

'She'll be all right,' Victoria Thompson said, as she reached out for both their hands, and Peter and Jane held her hands tightly. 'She lost the baby . . . but she's very young.' Victoria Thompson had lost a baby, too, her only son, before Sarah and Jane were born, but she had never shared that sorrow with either of her children. She had told Sarah now, hoping to comfort her and help her. 'She'll have another baby one day,' Victoria said sadly, but she was almost more concerned with what Sarah had blurted out about her life with Freddie. She had been crying terribly, and insisting that it was all her fault. She had moved a piece of furniture by herself the night before, but Freddie was never there to help her. And then the whole story had come tumbling out, about how little time he spent with her, how much he drank, how unhappy she was with him, and how unhappy he was about the baby.

It was several hours before the doctors would let them see her again, and Peter had gone back to the office by then, but he had made Jane promise she would go home at the end of the afternoon, to rest and recover from the day's excitement. After all, she was pregnant too. And one miscarriage was bad enough.

They had tried to call Freddie, too, but he was out, as usual, and no-one knew where he was, or when he would be returning. The maid was very sorry to hear about Mrs Van Deering's 'accident', and she promised to refer Mr Van Deering to the hospital if he called or appeared, which everyone silently agreed was unlikely.

'It's all my fault . . .' Sarah was sobbing when they saw her again. 'I didn't want it enough . . . I was upset because Freddie was so annoyed, and now . . .' She sobbed on incoherently, and her mother took her in her arms and tried to stop her. All three women were crying by then, and they finally had to give Sarah a sedative to calm her. They were going to keep her in the hospital for several days, and Victoria told the nurses she would be spending the night with her daughter, and eventually she sent Jane home in a cab, and then she had a long talk on the phone in the lobby with her husband.

When Freddie came home that night, he found his father-in-law waiting for him in the living room, much to his amazement. Fortunately, he had had less to drink than usual, and was surprisingly sober, considering it was just after midnight. He had had a boring evening, and had finally decided to come home early.

'Good Lord! . . . sir . . . what are you doing here?' He blushed faintly, and then flashed him his broad, boyish smile. And then he realized that something had to be very wrong for Edward Thompson to be waiting for him at this hour in this apartment. 'Is Sarah all right?'

'No, she isn't.' He looked away for a moment, and then back at Freddie. There was no delicate way to say it. 'She . . . uh . . . lost the child this morning, and is at Lennox Hill Hospital. Her mother is still with her.'

'She did?' He looked startled, and felt relieved, and

hoped he wasn't so drunk that he couldn't conceal it. 'I'm sorry to hear that.' He said it as though she were someone else's wife, and it had been someone else's baby. 'Is she all right?'

'I believe she'll be able to have more children. What is apparently not all right, however, is that my wife tells me that things have been somewhat less than idyllic between the two of you. Normally, I would never interfere in my daughters' married lives; however, in this rather unusual instance, with Sarah so . . . so . . . ill, it seems an opportune moment to discuss it with you. My wife tells me that Sarah has been hysterical all afternoon, and I find it rather significant, Frederick, that since early this morning, no-one has been able to reach you. This cannot be a very happy life for her, or for you. Is there something we should know about now, or do you feel able to continue your marriage to my daughter rather more in the spirit in which you entered into the union?'

'I . . . I . . . of course . . . would you like a drink, Mr Thompson?' He walked swiftly to where they kept their liquor and poured himself a liberal glass of Scotch, with a very small splash of water.

'I think not.' Edward Thompson sat expectantly, watching his son-in-law with displeasure, and there was no question in Freddie's mind that the older man expected an answer. 'Is there some problem that keeps you from behaving appropriately as her husband?'

'I . . . uh . . . well, sir, this baby thing was a little unexpected.'

'I understand, Frederick. Babies often are. Is there some serious misunderstanding with my daughter that I should know about?'

'Not at all. She's a wonderful girl. I . . . I . . . uh . . . just needed a little time to adjust to being married.'

'And to working, too, I imagine.' He looked pointedly at Freddie, who had suspected that was coming.

'Yes, yes, of course. I thought I'd look into that after the baby.'

'You'll be able to do that now a little more quickly, won't you?'

'Of course, sir.'

Edward Thompson stood up, and he was a daunting vision of respectability as he looked over Freddie's rather dishevelled state. 'I'm sure you'll be very anxious to visit Sarah as soon as possible tomorrow morning, won't you, Frederick?'

'Absolutely, sir.' He followed him to the front door, desperate to see him out now.

'I'll be picking her mother up at the hospital at ten o'clock. I'm sure I'll see you there then, won't I?'

'Absolutely, sir.'

'Very well, Frederick.' He turned in the doorway and faced him for a last time. 'Do we understand each other?' Very little had been said, but a great deal had been understood between them.

'I believe so, sir.'

'Thank you, Frederick. Good night. I'll see you tomorrow.'

Freddie heaved a sigh of relief as he closed the door behind him, and went to pour himself another Scotch before he went to bed, to think about what had happened to Sarah and the baby. He wondered what it must have been like, losing it, but didn't want to ask himself too many questions. He knew very little about things like that, and had no desire to expand his education. He was sorry for her, and he was sure it must have been awful for her, but it was odd how little he felt about the baby, or for that matter, for Sarah. He had thought it would be so much fun to get married to her, parties all the time, someone to go out with whenever you wanted. He had never anticipated how shackled he would feel, how bored, how oppressed, how claustrophobic. There was nothing about being married he liked, not even Sarah. She was a beautiful girl, and she would have made the perfect wife for someone. She kept a beautiful home, cooked well, entertained beautifully, was intelligent and pleasant to be with, and he had even been excited by her physically at first. But now he just couldn't even bear to think about her. The last thing in the world he wanted was to be married. And he was so relieved that she had lost the child. That would have been the icing on a cake he already knew was poisoned.

He showed up at the hospital the next morning, dutifully just before ten o'clock, so Mr Thompson would find him there when he arrived to pick up his wife. Freddie looked somber in a dark suit and dark tie, and the truth was that he was extremely hung over. He had bought flowers for her, but she didn't seem to care; she was lying in bed, staring out the window. She was holding her mother's hand as he walked into the room, and for a moment he felt sorry for her. She turned her head to look at him, and without a word, tears rolled down her cheeks, and her mother quietly left the room, with a squeeze of Sarah's hand, and a gentle touch on his shoulder.

'I'm sorry, Freddie,' she said softly, as she left, but she was wiser than he knew, and just from the look on his face, she already knew that he wasn't.

'Are you mad at me?' Sarah asked him through her tears. She made no effort to get up, she just lay there. And she looked terrible. Her long, shining black hair was a tangled mess, and her face was the same color as the sheets, her lips looked almost blue. She had lost a lot of blood, and she was too weak to sit up. But all she did now was turn her face away from him, and he had no idea what to say to her.

'Of course not. Why would I be mad at you?' He moved a little closer to her, and moved her chin so that she would look at him again, but the pain in her eyes was almost more than he could bear. He wasn't up to dealing with it, and she knew it.

'It was my fault . . . I moved that stupid chest in our bedroom the other night, and . . . I don't know . . . the doctor says these things happen 'cause they're meant to.'

'See . . .' He shifted from one foot to the other, and watched her fold her hands and then unfold them, but he didn't reach out to touch her. 'Look . . . it's better this way anyway. I'm twenty-four, you're twenty, we're not ready for a baby.'

She was silent for a long time, and then she looked at him as though seeing him for the first time. 'You're happy we lost it, aren't you?' Her eyes bore into his until they almost caused him pain, as he tried to struggle with his headache.

'I didn't say that.'

'You didn't have to. You're not sorry, are you?'

'I'm sorry for you.' It was true. She looked really awful.

'You never wanted this baby.'

'No, I didn't.' He was honest with her, he felt that he at least owed her that much.

'Well, neither did I, thanks to you, and that's probably why I lost it.' He didn't know what to say to her, and a moment later her father came in with Jane, and Mrs Thompson was busy making arrangements with the nurses. Sarah was going to stay for a few more days, and then she was going home to stay with her parents. And when she felt strong again, she would go back to Freddie at the apartment.

'You're welcome to stay with us, of course.' Victoria Thompson smiled her welcome to him, but she was firm about not letting Sarah go home to the apartment with him. She wanted to keep an eye on her, and Freddie was visibly relieved that he didn't have to.

He sent her red roses at the hospital the next day, and

visited her once more, and he visited her daily during the week she stayed with her parents.

He never mentioned the baby to her. But he did his best to make conversation. He was surprised at how awkward he felt, being with her. It was as though overnight they had become strangers. The truth was that they always had been. It was just that now it was more difficult to hide it. He shared none of her grief with her. He only went to see her because he felt it his duty. And he knew her father would kill him if he didn't make the effort.

He arrived at the Thompson house each day at noon, spent an hour with her, and then went out to have lunch with his cronies. And he very wisely never stopped in to see her in the evening. He was always worse for wear by then, and he was smart enough not to let Sarah or her parents see him. He was really sorry Sarah was so unhappy over losing the child, and she still looked dreadful. But he couldn't bear thinking of it, or what she might expect from him emotionally, or worse yet, the prospect of another baby. It only made him drink more and run harder. And by the time Sarah was ready to come home to him, he was in a downward spiral from which no-one could save him. His drinking was so out of control that even some of his own drinking buddies were worried about him.

He nonetheless dutifully showed up at the Thompsons' to take Sarah home, and the maid was waiting for them at their own apartment. Everything was clean and in order, although suddenly Sarah felt out of place there. It felt like someone else's home, and she felt like a stranger.

Freddie was a stranger there too. He had only been there to change his clothes since she'd lost the baby. He'd been out carousing every night, taking full advantage of the fact that she wasn't there to see it. And now it was odd and very confining to have her at home again.

He spent the afternoon with her, and then told her that he had to have dinner with an old friend; he was talking to him about a job, and it was very important. He knew she wouldn't object to it then. And she didn't, although she was disappointed he wasn't spending her first night at home with her. But she objected a great deal to the condition he was in when he came home at two o'clock that morning. The doorman had to help him in, and she was shocked when they rang the doorbell. Freddie was draped all over him, and he scarcely seemed to recognize her when he tried to focus on her blurred face, as the doorman assisted him into a chair in their bedroom. Freddie handed him a hundred-dollar bill, and offered profuse thanks for being a good sport and a great friend. Sarah watched in horror as Freddie made his way unsteadily to the bed and collapsed there unconscious. She stood looking at him for a long time, with tears in her eyes, before she left the room to sleep in their guest room. As she walked away from him, she felt an ache in her heart for the baby she had lost, and the husband she had never had, and never would now. She had finally understood that her marriage to Freddie would never be more than a pretense, an empty shell, and a source of endless grief and disappointment. It was a grim prospect as she slid into the guestroom bed alone, but she couldn't hide from the truth anymore. He would never be anything more than a drunk and a playboy. And the worst of all was that she couldn't imagine divorcing him. She couldn't bear the thought of bringing disgrace to herself and her parents.

As she lay in bed in the guest room that night, she thought of the long, lonely road ahead of her. A lifetime of loneliness, with Freddie.

Chapter 3

By the time Sarah had been home a week, she looked healthy and well, she was back on her feet, and out having lunch with her mother and sister. She seemed fine, although both women thought she was still a little quiet.

The three of them had lunch together at Jane's apartment one afternoon, and their mother tried to ask Sarah casually about Freddie. She was still deeply concerned over everything Sarah had told her when she lost the baby.

'He's fine,' Sarah said, as she turned away. As always, she said nothing about the nights she spent alone, or the condition Freddie was in when he returned in the morning. In fact, she barely spoke about it to him. She had accepted her fate, and she was determined to stay married to Freddie. If nothing else, it would have been too humiliating not to.

Freddie sensed a change in her, too, a kind of compliance, and acceptance of his appalling behavior. It was as though when the baby died, a piece of her died too. But Freddie didn't question it, he just took full advantage of what appeared to be Sarah's good nature. He came and went as he pleased, seldom bothered to take her anywhere, made no secret of the other women he saw, and drank from the moment he got up until he finally sank into unconsciousness at night, in their bedroom, or someone else's.

It was an incredibly unhappy time for her, but Sarah seemed determined to accept it. She kept her sorrows to herself as the months went on, and she said nothing to anyone. But her sister grew increasingly frantic about her each time she saw her. And as a result, Sarah saw her less and less often. There was a kind of numbness about Sarah now, an emptiness, and her eyes were filled with silent anguish. She had grown frighteningly thin since she'd lost the child, and that worried Jane too, but she also felt that Sarah was doing everything she could to avoid her.

'What's happening to you?' Jane asked her finally in May. By then she herself was six months pregnant, and she had hardly seen Sarah in months, because Sarah couldn't bear seeing her sister pregnant.

'Nothing. I'm fine.'

'Don't tell me that, Sarah! You're like someone in a trance. What's he doing to you? What's going on?' Just looking at her, Jane was frantic. She also sensed how uncomfortable Sarah was with her, so most of the time she didn't press herself on her sister. But she didn't want to leave her to her own devices now. She was beginning to fear for Sarah's sanity, or her life, at Freddie's hands, and somebody had to stop it.

'Don't be silly. I'm fine.'

'Are things better than they were?'

'I suppose so.' She was intentionally vague, and her sister saw right through it.

Sarah was thinner and paler than she had been right after the miscarriage. She was profoundly depressed, and no-one knew it. She kept assuring everyone that she was fine, that Freddie was behaving. She had even told her parents that he was looking for a job. It was all the same old nonsense, which no-one believed anymore, not even Sarah.

And on their anniversary, her parents tacitly agreed to continue the farce with her, by celebrating their first anniversary with a little party for them at the house in Southampton.

At first, Sarah had tried to discourage them, but in the end it was easier just to let them do it. Freddie had promised her he'd be there. In fact, he thought it was a great idea. He wanted to go to Southampton for the entire weekend, and bring half a dozen friends with him. The house was certainly big enough, and Sarah asked her mother if it was all right, and her mother was quick to tell them that their friends were always welcome. But Sarah warned him that his friends had to behave if they stayed with them, she didn't want them embarrassing her with her parents.

'What a dumb thing to say, Sarah,' he berated her. In the past month or two, he was slowly becoming increasingly vicious. She was never sure if it was due to the alcohol he consumed, or if he had truly begun to hate her. 'You hate me, don't you?'

'Don't be ridiculous. I just don't want your friends to get out of hand at my parents'.'

'Aren't you the prim, prissy little thing. Poor darling, afraid we can't behave at your parents'.' She wanted to tell him that he didn't behave anywhere else, but she refrained. She was slowly resigning herself to her lot in life, knowing full well that she would be miserable with him forever. There would probably never be another baby, and even that didn't matter any more. Nothing did. She just lived day by day, and one day she would die, and it would all be over. The thought of divorcing him never even occurred to her, or never more than fleetingly, in any case. No-one in her family had ever gotten divorced, and in her wildest dreams, she would never have thought of being the first one. The shame of it would have killed her, as well as her parents. 'Don't worry, Sarah, we'll behave. Just don't annoy my friends with that long, sad face of yours. You're enough to spoil anyone's fun at a party.' It had only been since being married to him, and losing the baby, that she seemed to have lost all her color, all her life, all her *joie de vivre* and excitement. She had always been lively and bright and happy as a young girl, and suddenly she seemed like a dead person, even to herself. It was Jane who always commented on it, but Peter and her parents told her not to worry, Sarah would be all right, because they wanted to believe that.

Two days before the Thompsons' party was to take place, the Duke of Windsor married Wallis Simpson. They were married at the Château de Candé in France, amidst a maelstrom of press and international attention, all of which Sarah thought was tasteless and disgusting. She turned her thoughts back to her anniversary party instead, and instantly forgot the Windsors.

Peter and Jane and little James planned to spend the weekend in Southampton for the big event. The house looked beautiful, filled with flowers, and there was a tent over the lawn looking out over the ocean. The Thompsons had planned a beautiful party for Sarah and Freddie. On Friday night, all the young people were to go out with their friends, and they went to the Canoe Place Inn and had a wonderful time, talking and dancing and laughing. Even Jane, who was extremely pregnant, went, and so did Sarah, who felt as though she hadn't smiled in years. Freddie even danced with her, and for a few minutes he looked as though he were going to kiss her. Eventually, Peter and Jane and Sarah and some of the others went back to the Thompsons' afterwards, and Freddie and his close friends went out to do a little carousing. Sarah grew quiet again then, but she didn't say anything as she rode back to the house with Jane and Peter. Her sister and brother-in-law were still in high spirits and seemed not to notice her silence.

The next day dawned sunny and beautiful, and later, the sunset over Long Island Sound was spectacular, as the band struck up and the Thompsons began greeting their guests, who were there to celebrate Sarah and Freddie. Sarah looked remarkable in a shimmering white gown,

35

which clung to her figure enticingly and made her look like a young goddess. Her dark hair was piled high on her head, and she moved through the crowd with quiet grace as she greeted her friends and her parents' guests, and everyone commented on how she had matured in the past year, and how much more beautiful she was even than at her wedding. She was in sharp contrast to her warmly rotund sister, Jane, who was looking touchingly maternal in a turquoise silk dress that covered her voluminously, and she was good-natured about her lack of figure.

'Mother said I could wear the tent, but I liked this color better,' she joked with an old friend, and Sarah smiled as she drifted past them. She looked better, and happier, than she had in a long time, but Jane was still very worried about her.

'Sarah's gotten so thin.'

'She . . . she was sick earlier this year.' She had lost even more weight since the miscarriage, and Jane sensed, although Sarah didn't admit it to her, that she was still wracked with guilt and grief over losing the baby.

'No babies yet?' people asked her repeatedly. 'Oh, you two will have to get started!' Or finished. She only smiled at them, and after the first hour, she suddenly realized that she hadn't seen Freddie since the party started. He had been near the bar with his friends an hour ago, and then she had lost track of them as she greeted the guests, standing next to her father. She asked the butler eventually, and he said that Mister Van Deering had left in a car a few minutes before, with some of his friends, and they were heading toward Southampton.

'They probably went to get something, Miss Sarah,' he said, looking at her kindly.

'Thank you, Charles.' He had been their butler there for years, and he stayed on in the winter when they went back to the city. She had known him since she was a child, and she dearly loved him.

She started to worry about what Freddie was doing. He and his friends had probably gone to one of the local bars in Hampton Bays to have a few quick, stiff drinks, before returning to the gentility of her parents' party. But she wondered just how drunk they would be when they got back, and if anyone would notice their absence in the meantime.

'Where's that handsome husband of yours?' an elderly friend of her mother's asked, and she assured her that he'd be back downstairs in a minute. He'd gone up to get a wrap for her, she explained, and the friend thought his attentiveness was very touching.

'Something wrong?' Jane sidled up to her, and asked in an undertone. She had been watching her for the past half hour and knew her too well to be convinced by the smile she was wearing.

'No. Why?'

'You look like someone just put a snake in your purse.' Sarah couldn't help but laugh at the description. For a minute, it reminded her of their childhood, and she almost forgave Jane for being pregnant. It was just going to be so hard to see her with her baby two months from now, knowing that hers was gone, and she might never have one. She and Freddie had never made love again since the miscarriage. 'So, where's the snake?' Jane asked.

'Actually, he's out.' The two sisters laughed for the first time in a long time at Sarah's comment.

'That isn't what I meant . . . but actually, it's pretty apt. Who did he go out with?'

'I don't know. But Charles says they went out half an hour ago, headed toward town.'

'What does that mean?' Jane looked worried for her. What a headache that boy must be to her, even more than they all suspected, if he couldn't even behave for a single evening at her parents'.

'Maybe trouble. Booze, in any case. A great deal too

37

much of it. With any luck, he'll hold it pretty well . . . until later.'

'Mother will really enjoy that.' Jane smiled as they stood together and watched the crowd. People seemed to be having a good time, which was at least something, even if Sarah wasn't.

'Father will actually enjoy it more.' They both laughed again, and Sarah took a deep breath and looked at her. 'I'm sorry I've been so awful to you for the past few months. I just . . . I don't know . . . it's hard for me to think about your baby . . .' There were tears in her eyes as she looked away again, and her older sister put an arm around her.

'I know. And you haven't done anything except worry me to death. I wish I could do something to make you happy.'

'I'm all right.'

'Your nose is growing, Pinocchio.'

'Oh, shut up.' Sarah grinned at her again, and they went back to the other guests shortly after. By the time they sat down to dinner, Freddie was still not back yet. His absence, and that of his close friends, was instantly noticed as the guests sat down to dinner in their appointed places at tables on the lawn, and Freddie's seat of honor, to the right of his mother-in-law, was visibly vacant. But before anyone could make comment, or Mrs Thompson could ask Sarah where her husband had gone, there was a frantic sound of honking, and Freddie and four of his friends drove across the lawn in his Packard Twelve Phaeton, shouting and laughing and waving. They drove right up to the tables, as everyone stared, and stepped out of the convertible with three local girls, one of them adoringly wrapped around Freddie. As they approached the assembled company, it became obvious that the ladies were not just local girls, but women who had been paid for their services for the evening.

The five young men were blind drunk, and it was evident that they thought the stunt the funniest that had ever been accomplished. But the young women looked faintly unnerved as they looked at the well-heeled, and clearly shocked people around them. The girl with Freddie was nervously trying to convince him to take them back to town, but by then all hell had broken loose around them. A group of waiters was trying to remove the car, Charles, the butler, was trying to remove the girls, and Freddie and his friends were stumbling everywhere, tripping over the other guests and embarrassing themselves, and Freddie was the worst of all. He absolutely would not let go of the girl they had brought back with them. And without thinking, or seeing clearly, Sarah stood up, watching him, tears brimming in her eyes, remembering their wedding only a year before, all the hope she had had then, and the nightmare it had become since her marriage. The girl was only a symbol of the horrors of the past year, and suddenly it all seemed unreal to her, as she stood there in silent anguish and watched him. It was like watching an absolutely ghastly movie. Only the worst part was, she was in it.

'What's the matter, babe?' – he called across several tables to her – 'Don't you want to meet my sweetie?' He laughed at the look on Sarah's face, and Victoria Thompson began to make her way swiftly across the lawn to her youngest child, who looked as though she were rooted to the spot in shock, frozen beyond reason. 'Sheila,' he continued to shout, 'that's my wife . . . and these are her parents.' He waved an arm grandly, as people watched in amazement. But by then Edward Thompson had swung into action. He and two waiters removed Freddie and the girl as firmly and swiftly as they could, and the other young men were escorted away, with the ladies, in the company of an army of waiters.

Freddie was a little more belligerent as his father-in-law led him into the little beach cottage they used to change clothes in. 'What's the matter, Mr Thompson? Isn't this party for me?'

'No, as a matter of fact, it's not. It never should have been. We should have thrown you out months ago. But I can assure you, Frederick, that all of that will be taken care of very quickly. You are leaving here immediately, we will send your things to you next week, and you will be hearing from my attorneys on Monday morning. Your years of torturing my daughter are over. Please do not return to the apartment. Is that clear?' Edward Thompson's voice boomed in the tiny cottage. But Freddie was too drunk to be frightened.

'My, my . . . sounds like Papa is a little upset! Don't tell me that you don't have a few girlies too from time to time. Come on, sir . . . I'll share this one with you.' He opened the door, and they both saw that the girl was just outside, waiting for Freddie.

Edward Thompson began to shake as he grabbed Freddie by the lapels and almost lifted him off the ground with the strength of his fury. 'If I ever see you again, you little piece of filth, I will kill you. Now, get out of here, and stay away from Sarah!' he roared, and the local woman quaked as she watched them.

'Yes, sir.' Freddie performed a drunken bow, offered his arm to his prostitute, and five minutes later, he and his friends and their 'ladies' were gone, as was Sarah from the party. She sat in her bedroom sobbing, with her sister, Jane, insisting that it was all for the best, that it had been a nightmare from the first, that maybe it was all her fault because she had lost the baby, maybe that would have changed him. Some of it made sense, and some of it didn't, and all of it washed up from the bottom of her soul as she clung to her older sister. Her mother came in briefly to see how she was, but she had to return to her guests, and she was satisfied that Jane was handling the situation. The evening had been a terrible fiasco.

It was a long night for all of them. But everyone ate as quickly as they could, a few brave souls danced, and they all very politely appeared to overlook what had happened, and then left early. By ten o'clock, all the guests were gone, and Sarah still lay sobbing in her bedroom.

The next morning in the Thompson home was a serious one, as the entire family gathered in the drawing room and Edward Thompson explained to Sarah what he had said to Freddie the night before, and he looked at her very firmly.

'It's your decision, Sarah,' he said, looking unhappy, 'but I would like you to divorce him.'

'Father, I can't . . . it would be terrible for everyone . . .' She looked around at all of them, fearing the embarrassment and the shame she would bring them.

'It will be much worse for you if you go back to him. Now I understand what you've been going through.' As he thought of it, he was almost grateful that she had lost the baby. He looked at his daughter sadly then. 'Sarah, do you love him?'

She hesitated for a long time, and then shook her head, looking down at her hands tightly folded in her lap, and speaking in a whisper. 'I don't even know why I married him.' She looked up at them again. 'I thought I loved him then, but I didn't even know him.'

'You made a terrible mistake. You were misled by him, Sarah. That can happen to anyone. Now we have to solve the problem for you. I want you to let me do that.' Edward's resolve never wavered for a moment, as the others nodded their agreement.

'How?' She felt lost, like a child again, and she kept thinking of all the people who had seen him make a fool of her the night before. It was almost beyond thinking. It was mortifying . . . bringing prostitutes to her parents' home . . . She had cried all night, and she dreaded what people would say, and the terrible humiliation to her parents.

'I want you to leave everything to me.' And then he

thought of something else. 'Do you want the apartment in New York?'

She looked at him and shook her head. 'I don't want anything. I just want to come home to you and Mama.' Tears filled her eyes as she said the words, and her mother gently patted her shoulder.

'Well, you are,' he said in an emotional tone, as his wife dried her eyes. Peter and Jane held hands tightly. The whole thing had upset everyone, but they were all relieved now for Sarah.

'What about you and Mama?' She looked at them both mournfully.

'What about us?'

'Won't you be ashamed if I get divorced? I feel like that terrible Simpson woman – everyone will talk about me, and about you too.' Sarah started to cry and buried her face in her hands. She was still a very young girl, and the shock of the last months still overwhelmed her.

Her mother was quick to take her in her arms and try to soothe her. 'What are people going to say, Sarah? That he was a terrible husband, that you were very unlucky? What have you done wrong? Absolutely nothing. You have to accept that. You have done *nothing* wrong. Frederick is the one who should be ashamed, not you.' Once again, the rest of the family nodded their agreement.

'But people will be horrified. No-one in the family has ever been divorced.'

'So what? I'd rather have you safe and happy, than living that nightmare with Freddie Van Deering.' Victoria felt her own guilt and pain at not having realized how bad things were for her. Only Jane had suspected how great her sister's distress was, and no-one else had really listened. They had all thought her unhappiness was due to the miscarriage.

Sarah still looked woebegone when Peter and Jane went back to New York later that afternoon, and the next morning, when her father left to meet with his lawyers. Her mother had decided to stay in Southampton with her, and Sarah was emphatic about not wanting to return to New York for the moment. She wanted to stay there and hide forever, she said, and more than anything, she didn't want to see Freddie. She had agreed to the divorce her father had suggested to her, but she dreaded all the horror she assumed would come with it. She had read about divorces in the newspapers, and they always sounded complicated and terribly embarrassing and unpleasant. She assumed that Freddie would be furious with her, but she was stunned when he called her late Monday afternoon, after he had spoken to her father's attorney.

'It's OK, Sarah. I think this is all for the best. For both of us. We just weren't ready.' *We?* She couldn't believe he had actually said that. He didn't even blame himself, he was just happy to be free of her, and the responsibilities he had never bothered to face anyway, like their baby.

'You're not angry?' Sarah was amazed, and hurt.

'Not at all, babe.'

And then a long silence. 'Are you glad?'

Another silence. 'You love asking those questions, don't you, Sarah? What difference does it make what I feel? We made a mistake, and your father is helping us out of it. He's a nice man, and I think we're doing the right thing. I'm sorry if I caused you any trouble . . .' Like a bad weekend, or a rotten afternoon. He had no idea what the last year had been like for her. No-one did. He was just happy he was getting out of it, that much was obvious as she listened.

'What are you going to do now?' She hadn't figured out that much for herself yet. It was all too new and too confusing. All she knew was that she didn't want to go back to New York again. She didn't want to see anyone, or have to explain anything about the demise of her marriage to Freddie Van Deering.

'I thought I'd go to Palm Springs for a few months. Or maybe Europe for the summer.' He mused, making plans as he talked.

'That sounds like fun.' It was like talking to a stranger, and that made her even sadder. They had never known each other at all, it was all a game, and she had lost. They both had. But only he didn't seem to mind it.

'Take care of yourself,' he said, as though to an old friend or a schoolmate he wouldn't be seeing for a while, instead of never.

'Thanks.' She sat staring woodenly at the phone as she held the receiver and listened to him.

'I'd better go now, Sarah.' She nodded in silence. 'Sarah?'

'Yes . . . I'm sorry . . . thank you for calling.' Thank you for a terrible year, Mr Van Deering . . . Thank you for breaking my heart . . . She wanted to ask him if he'd ever loved her, but she didn't dare, and she thought she knew the answer anyway. It was obvious that he hadn't. He didn't love anyone, not even himself, and certainly not Sarah.

Her mother watched her grieve for the next month, and on into August and September. The only thing that had caught her attention in July was when Amelia Earhart disappeared, and a few days after that when the Japanese invaded China. But for the most part, all she could think about was her divorce, and the shame and guilt she felt about it. She grew even worse for a time when Jane's baby girl was born, but she drove into New York with her mother to see Jane at the hospital, and insisted on driving back to Southampton by herself that night after she'd seen her. The baby was very sweet, and they had named her Marjorie, but Sarah was anxious to be alone again. She spent most of her time now dwelling on the past and trying to figure out what had happened to her. It was much simpler than she thought, actually. She had simply married someone she didn't really know, and he had turned out to be a terrible husband. End of story. But she insisted somehow on blaming herself, and she became convinced that if she dropped out of sight, and stayed away, people would forget that she existed, and wouldn't punish her parents for her sins. So for their sakes, and her own, she insisted on literally disappearing.

'You can't do this for the rest of your life, Sarah,' her father said sternly after Labor Day, when they were moving back to New York for the winter. The legal proceedings were going well. Freddie had gone to Europe as he had said he might, but his attorney was handling everything for him and was cooperating fully with the Thompsons. The hearing was set for November, and the divorce would be final almost exactly a year later. 'You've got to come back to New York,' her father urged. They didn't want to leave her there, like a discarded relative they were ashamed of. But as crazy as it was, that was how she saw herself, and she even resisted Jane's pleas to return when she came out to Long Island to see her in October with the baby.

'I don't want to go back to New York, Jane. I'm perfectly happy here.'

'With Charles and three old servants, freezing to death on the Long Island Sound all winter? Sarrie, don't be stupid. Come home. You're twenty-one years old. You can't give up your life now. You have to start over.'

'I don't want to,' she said quietly, refusing to pay any attention to her sister's baby.

'Don't be crazy.' Jane looked exasperated with the stubbornness of her younger sister.

'What do you know, dammit? You have a husband who loves you, and two children. You've never been a burden, or an embarrassment or a disgrace to anyone. You're the perfect wife, daughter, sister, mother. What do you know about my life? Absolutely nothing!' She looked furious, and she was, but not at Jane, and she knew it. She was furious at herself, and the fates . . . and at Freddie. And then she was instantly contrite as she looked at her sister sadly. 'I'm sorry, I just want to be alone out here.' She couldn't even really explain it.

'Why?' Jane couldn't understand it. She was young and beautiful, and she wasn't the only woman alive to get divorced, but she acted as though she had been convicted of murder.

'I don't want to see anyone. Can't you understand that?'

'For how long?'

'Maybe forever. All right? Is that long enough? Does that make it clear to you?' Sarah hated answering all her questions.

'Sarah Thompson, you're crazy.' Her father had arranged for her to take her own name back as soon as he filed for the separation.

'I have a right to do what I want with my life. I can go be a nun if I want to,' she said stubbornly to her sister.

'You'll have to become a Catholic first.' Jane grinned, but Sarah didn't find it amusing. They had been Episcopalians since birth. And Jane was beginning to think that Sarah was a little crazy. Or maybe she'd come out of it after a while. It was what they all hoped, but it no longer seemed certain.

But Sarah remained firm in her refusal to move back to New York. Her mother had long since picked up her things from the apartment in New York and stored them all in boxes, which Sarah insisted she didn't even want to see now. She went to her divorce hearing in November wearing a black suit and a funereal face. She looked beautiful and afraid and sat through it stoically until it was over. And as soon as it was, she drove herself back to Long Island.

She went for long walks on the beach every day, even on the bitterest cold days, with the wind whipping her face until it felt as though it were bleeding. She read endlessly, and wrote letters to her mother and Jane and some of her oldest friends, but in truth she still had no desire to see them.

They all celebrated Christmas in Southampton and Sarah hardly talked to anyone. The only time she mentioned the divorce was to her mother, when they heard a news story over the radio about the Duke and Duchess of Windsor. She felt an unhappy kinship with Wally Simpson. But her mother assured her again that she and the Simpson woman had nothing in common.

When spring came, she looked better again finally, healthier, rested, she had gained back some weight, and her eyes were alive. But by then she was talking about finding a farmhouse on Long Island somewhere, in the remoter parts, and trying to rent it, or perhaps even buy one.

'That's ridiculous,' her father growled when she suggested it to him. 'I can understand perfectly well that you were unhappy over what happened, and needed some time to recover here, but I'm not going to let you bury yourself on Long Island for the rest of your life, like a hermit. You can stay here until the summer, and in July, your mother and I are taking you to Europe.' He had decided it just the week before and his wife was thrilled, and even Jane thought it was a splendid idea, and just what Sarah needed.

'I won't go.' She looked at him stubbornly, but she looked healthy and strong and more beautiful than ever. It was time for her to go back out in the world again, whether she knew it or not. And if she wouldn't go of her own accord, they were prepared to force her.

'You will go, if we tell you to.'

'I don't want to run into Freddie,' she said weakly.

'He's been in Palm Beach all winter.'

'How do you know?' She was curious, wondering if her father had spoken to him.

'I've spoken to his attorney.'

'I don't want to go to Europe anyway.'

'That's unfortunate. Because you can go willingly, or unwillingly. But in either case, you're going.' She had stormed away from the table then, and gone for a long walk on the beach, but when she returned, her father was waiting for her just outside the cottage. It had almost broken his heart to see her grieve over the past year, over the marriage that never was, the child she had lost, the mistakes she had made, and her bitter disappointment. And she was surprised to see him waiting for her, as she came up off the beach, through the tall dune grass.

'I love you, Sarah.' It was the first time her father had ever said that to her, in just that way, and it reached her heart like an arrow covered with the balm she needed to heal her. 'Your mother and I love you very much. We may not know how to help you, to make up to you for everything that happened, but we want to try . . . please let us do that.'

Tears filled her eyes as she looked at him, and he pulled her into his arms and held her there for a long time as she cried on his shoulder. 'I love you too, Papa . . . I love you too . . . I'm so sorry . . .'

'Don't be sorry any more, Sarah . . . Just be happy . . . Be the girl you used to be before this all happened.'

'I'll try.' She pulled out of his arms for a moment to look at him and saw that he was crying too. 'I'm sorry I've been so much trouble.'

'That's right!' He smiled through his tears. 'You should be!'

They both laughed, and they walked slowly back to the house, arm in arm, as he silently prayed they would be able to get her to Europe.

Chapter 4

The *Queen Mary* sat proudly at the dock, in her berth at Pier 90 on the Hudson River. There were signs of festivity everywhere. Large, handsome trunks were still being taken on board, huge deliveries of flowers were being made, and champagne was liberally being poured in all the first-class cabins. The Thompsons arrived in the midst of it all with their hand luggage, their trunks having been sent on ahead. Victoria Thompson was wearing a beautiful white suit by Claire McCardell. The large straw hat she wore went perfectly with it, and she looked happy and young as she stepped on to the gangplank just in front of her husband. This was going to be an exciting trip for them. They hadn't been to Europe in several years, and they were looking forward to seeing old friends, particularly in the South of France and England.

Sarah had made a terrible fuss about going with them, and had flatly refused to go, almost until the end. And finally, it was Jane who had made the difference. She had gotten into an out-and-out shouting match with her younger sister, calling her names, accusing her of being cowardly, and telling her that it was not her divorce that was ruining their parents' lives, but her refusal to pick up the pieces again, and that they were all damn sick of it, and she'd better pull up her socks, and quickly. The motives behind the attack didn't really occur to Sarah as she listened to her, but she was overcome with a wave of fury at what Jane said to her, and the very anger she felt seemed to restore her.

'Fine, then!' she shouted back at Jane, tempted to throw a vase at her. 'I'll go on their damn trip if you think it's so important to them. But none of you can run my life for me. And when I come back, I'm moving to Long Island permanently, and I don't want to hear any more garbage from anyone about what it's doing to their lives. This is *my* life, and I'm going to live it the way I goddamn well want to!' Her black hair flew around her head like ravens' wings as she tossed her head, and her green eyes flashed angrily at her older sister. 'What right do any of you have to decide what's good for me?' she said, overwhelmed by fresh waves of outrage. 'What do you know about my life?'

'I know you're wasting it!' Jane didn't budge an inch. 'You've spent the last year hiding out here like a hundred-year-old recluse, and making Mother and Father miserable with your gloomy face. Nobody wants to watch you do that to yourself. You're not even twenty-two years old, not two hundred!'

'Thank you for the reminder. And if looking at me is so painful for all of you, I'll be sure to move out even faster when I get back. I want to find my own place anyway. I told Father that months ago.'

'Yeah, right, a falling-down barn in Vermont, or a collapsing farmhouse in the wilds of Long Island . . . Is there any other punishment you can find to heap on your head? What about sackcloth and ashes? Had you thought of that, or is that too subtle for you? You'd rather go for the big time, something miserable, like a house with a hole in the roof and no heating, so Mother can worry about your getting pneumonia every year. I have to agree, it's a great touch. Sarah, you're beginning to make me sick,' she raged at her, and Sarah had answered by sweeping out of the room and slamming the door so hard that some of the paint fell off the hinges.

'She's a spoiled brat!' Jane announced to them

afterwards, still fuming. 'I don't know why you put up with her. Why don't you just force her to go back to New York and live like a normal human being?' Jane was beginning to lose patience with her by spring. She had suffered enough by then, and she felt that Sarah owed it to all of them to at least make an effort to recover. Her estranged husband certainly had. There had been an announcement in the *New York Times* in May that he was engaged to Emily Astor. 'How nice for him,' Jane had said sarcastically when she'd heard, but Sarah had said not a word about it to anyone, although her family knew it must have hurt her deeply. Emily was one of her oldest friends, and a very distant cousin.

'What do you suggest I do to make her "live like a normal human being"?' her father asked. 'Sell the house? Take her back to New York in a straitjacket? Tie her to the hood of the car? She's a grown woman, Jane, and to a certain extent, we can't control her.'

'She's damn lucky you put up with her. I think it's high time she pulled herself together.'

'You have to be patient,' her mother had said quietly, and Jane had gone back to New York that afternoon, without seeing Sarah again. Sarah had gone off for a long walk on the beach, and then had driven off in the old Ford her father kept there for Charles, the butler.

But in spite of her determination and stubbornness about remaining apart from society, Jane's words had obviously reached her. In June she quietly agreed to join her parents in Europe. She told them at dinner one night, and tried to pass it off casually, but her mother stared at her in amazement. And her father clapped his hands when he heard the news. He had been just about to cancel their reservations, and give in to her refusal to go with them. He had decided that dragging her around Europe as an unwilling prisoner would have been no treat for anyone, not for them, and certainly not for Sarah.

He didn't dare ask her what had convinced her finally. They all credited Jane with Sarah's change of heart, although, of course, no-one said a word to Sarah. As Sarah stepped out of the car at Pier 90 that afternoon, she looked tall and slim, and very serious in a plain black dress, and a very severe black hat that had once been her mother's. She looked beautiful but austere, her face pale, her eyes huge, her dark hair pulled tightly back, her perfect features free of makeup. And as people looked at her, they noticed how beautiful she was, and how sad she looked, like a strikingly pretty, much-too-young widow.

'Couldn't you have worn something a little happier, dear?' her mother said to her as they left the house, but Sarah only shrugged. She had agreed to go to humor them, but no-one had said she had to have a good time, or look as though she were going to.

She had found the perfect house on Long Island before she left, an old deserted farm, with a tiny cottage sorely in need of repair, near the ocean, on ten untended acres. She had sold her wedding ring to put a deposit on it, and she was going to speak to her father when they got back about buying it for her. She knew that she would never marry again, she wanted her own place to live, and the farmhouse in Glass Hollow suited her to perfection.

They had ridden to Pier 90 that morning in silence. She was thinking about the trip, wondering why she had agreed to come. But if going with them made them feel that she had at least tried, then maybe her father would be inclined to help her buy the little farm when they returned. If that was the case, then it was worth it. She loved the idea of fixing up the old house anyway, and she could hardly wait to do it.

'You're very quiet, dear,' her mother had said, gently patting her arm in the car. They were so pleased that she was going with them. It had given them all hope, mostly because none of them had an idea how determined she was to resume her solitary life as soon as she got back. Had they known, it would have saddened them deeply.

'I was just thinking about the trip.'

Her father smiled, and chatted quietly to her mother about the telegrams he had sent to friends. They had a busy two months planned, in Cannes, Monaco, Paris, Rome, and, of course, London.

Her mother was still telling her about some of their oldest friends, whom Sarah didn't know, as they walked up the gangplank, and several people turned to watch them. Sarah was a striking figure as she moved just ahead of them, the black hat concealing one eye mysteriously, the other peeking out behind a veil, and her face so serious and young. She almost looked like a Spanish princess. It made people wonder who she was as they stared at her. One woman said she was certain she was a movie star, and was sure she had seen her somewhere. It would have amused Sarah no end if she could have heard them. She paid no attention at all to the people they passed, the elegant clothes, the careful coiffures, the impressive show of jewels, the pretty women and handsome men. She was only interested in finding her cabin. And when she did, Peter and Jane were waiting for them there, with Marjorie and little James, who kept racing around the deck just outside the stateroom. At two and a half, he had become a little terror. Marjorie had taken her first step a few days before and was teetering uncertainly around the cabin. Sarah was happy to see them there, and especially Jane. Her anger at her had evaporated weeks ago, and the two were good friends again, particularly once Sarah had announced that she was going.

They had brought two bottles of champagne with them, and the steward poured yet another bottle liberally as they all stood around Sarah's stateroom and chatted. Her room connected to her parents' suite of rooms through a large living room big enough to accommodate a baby grand

53

piano, which James discovered only moments later, and he began to pound on it happily as his mother begged him not to.

'Do you suppose we should put a sign outside the door to reassure people that James isn't going with you?' his father asked with a dubious grin as he watched him.

'It's good for his musical abilities.' His grandfather smiled indulgently. 'Besides, it'll give us something to remember him by for the next two months, a nice loud send-off.'

Jane noticed how severely her sister was dressed, but she had to admit that she looked beautiful anyway. She had always been the more striking of the two, combining both their parents' looks. Jane had their mother's softer, less defined, gentle blond beauty. It was her father who had the dark Irish looks Sarah had inherited and somehow improved on.

'I hope you have a good time,' Jane said with a quiet smile, relieved that Sarah was actually going. They all wanted her to make new friends, see new things, and then come home and get back in touch with her old friends. Her life had been so lonely for the past year, so bleak, and incredibly empty. Or at least that was how it looked to Jane. She couldn't imagine living as Sarah had done for the past year. But then again, she couldn't even begin to imagine a life without Peter.

They left the ship as its whistle began to blow, and the smoke-stacks roared to life while stewards circulated in the halls, playing chimes and urging people to go ashore if they were going to. There was a flurry of kisses and hugs, and people calling to each other everywhere, last gulps of champagne, last embraces, a sprinkling of tears, and then finally the last of the visitors had gone down the gangplank. The Thompsons stood on the deck and waved to Peter and Jane, as James squirmed in his father's arms, and Marjorie waved as Jane held her. There were tears in

54

Victoria Thompson's eyes as she looked at them. Two months was going to be a long time away from them, but it was a sacrifice she was willing to make if it was going to help Sarah.

'Well,' Edward Thompson said with a satisfied smile. All had gone well as far as he was concerned. They had just left the dock, and they were on their way. They were actually taking Sarah to Europe. 'What shall we do now? A walk around the deck? A visit to the shops?' He was looking forward to the trip and to seeing some of his old friends again. And he was thrilled that they had succeeded in convincing Sarah to go to Europe. It was a good time to go. The political situation there had been increasingly tense recently. Who knew what might happen later. If there was a war in a year or two, this might be their last chance to go to Europe.

'I think I'll unpack,' Sarah said quietly.

'The stewardess will do all of that for you,' her mother explained, but Sarah didn't care.

'I'd rather see to it myself,' she said, looking bleak in spite of the festive surroundings. There were balloons and streamers and confetti everywhere, from the sailing.

'Shall we meet you in the dining room for lunch?'

'I might take a nap.' She tried to smile at them, but she was thinking how difficult the next two months would be, constantly being with them. She had become used to licking her wounds alone, and although most of the wounds seemed to have healed, the scars were still evident, and she preferred keeping them to herself. She couldn't imagine being with them night and day, and enduring their constant efforts to cheer her. She had no desire whatsoever to be cheered. She had come to like her solitary life, and her dark thoughts, and her lonely moments. It was not the way she had been before, but it was who and what she had become, thanks to Freddie Van Deering.

'Wouldn't you rather get some air?' her mother persisted. 'You might get seasick if you spend too much time in your cabin.'

'If I do, I'll come out for a walk then. Don't worry, Mother. I'm fine,' she said, but neither of her parents was convinced as she went back to her cabin.

'What are we going to do with her, Edward?' Her mother looked glum as they took a walk around the deck, glancing at the other passengers, and then out to sea, thinking about Sarah.

'She's not easy. I'll grant you that. I wonder if she's really as unhappy as she seems, or if she just fancies herself a romantic figure.' He wasn't sure he understood her any more, or that he ever had. Sometimes both of his daughters were a mystery to him.

'Sometimes I think being miserable has just become a habit,' Victoria answered him. 'I think at first she was genuinely distraught, and hurt, and disappointed, and she was embarrassed about the scandal Freddie had caused. But you know, in the last six months I've gotten the feeling that she actually enjoys her life like this. I think she likes being alone, and being something of a recluse. I don't know why, but she does. She was always very gregarious when she was young, and much more mischievous than Jane. But it's as though she's forgotten all that and become someone else now.'

'Well, she'd better become the old Sarah again, and damn soon. This reclusive nonsense of hers just isn't healthy.' He completely agreed with his wife. He, too, had the feeling that in the past few months she had come to enjoy it. There was something more peaceful about her than there had been, and she seemed more mature, but she certainly didn't seem happy.

As they went to lunch afterwards, Sarah was sitting quietly in her stateroom, writing a letter to Jane. She never ate lunch any more. She usually went for a long walk on the beach instead, which is why she stayed so thin. But it was no real sacrifice to her, she was very seldom hungry.

Her parents stopped by to see her after lunch, and found her stretched out on her bed, still in the black dress, but with her hat and shoes off. Her eyes were closed, and she didn't move, but her mother suspected that she wasn't really sleeping. They left her alone, and came back to find her again an hour later, and she had changed into a gray sweater and slacks, and she was reading a book in a comfortable chair, oblivious of her surroundings.

'Sarah? A walk on the promenade deck? The shops are fabulous.' Victoria Thompson was determined to be persistent.

'Maybe later.' Sarah never took her eyes off her book, and when she heard the door close, she assumed her mother had left the cabin. She raised her eyes then with a sigh, and gave a start when she found herself looking right at her mother. 'Oh . . . I thought you had gone.'

'I know you did. Sarah, I want you to come outside for a walk with me. I am not going to spend this entire trip begging you to come out of your room. You've decided to come, now try and do it gracefully, or you'll ruin it for everyone, particularly your father.' They were always so worried about each other, it amused Sarah sometimes, but right now it annoyed her.

'Why? Why does my presence every moment of the day make any difference? I like being alone. Why does that upset everyone so much?'

'Because it's not normal. It's not healthy for a girl your age to be alone all the time. You need people and life and excitement.'

'Why? Who decided that for me? Who is it that said that if you are about to turn twenty-two, you need excitement? I *don't* need excitement. I *had* excitement, and I don't ever want it again. Why can't all of you understand that?'

'I do understand, dear. But what you had was not

"excitement", it was disappointment, it was a violation of everything that's decent and good, everything you ever believed in. It was a terrible experience, and we never want you to go through that again. No-one wants that to happen to you. But you *must* go out in the world again. You absolutely have to, or you'll wither and die, spiritually, inside, where it matters.'

'How do you know that?' Sarah looked distressed by what her mother was saying to her.

'Because I see it in your eyes,' Victoria said wisely. 'I see someone dying in there, someone aching and lonely and sad. Someone calling for help, and you won't let her out so she can get it.' As Sarah listened, her eyes filled with tears, and her mother walked to where she sat and hugged her gently. 'I love you very much, Sarah. Please try . . . please try to come out of yourself again. Trust us . . . we won't let anyone hurt you.'

'But you don't know what it was like.' Sarah began to whimper like a child, ashamed of the emotions, and her inability to control them. 'It was so awful . . . and so wrong . . . He was never there, and when he was, it was . . .' She couldn't go on, she just cried as she shook her head, bereft of words to describe the feelings, as her mother stroked her long silky hair and held her.

'I know, darling . . . I know . . . I can only imagine what it was like. I know it must have been awful. But it's over. And you're not. Your life is just beginning. Don't give up before you've given it a chance. Look around, feel the breeze, smell the flowers, let yourself live again. Please . . .'

Sarah clung to her as she listened to her mother's words, and finally told her how she felt, as she continued to cry. 'I can't any more . . . I'm too afraid . . .'

'I'm right here with you.' But they hadn't been able to help her before – until the end, when they'd gotten her out of it. But they couldn't have made Freddie behave, or come home at night, or give up his girlfriends and his prostitutes, and they hadn't been able to save the baby. She had learned the hard way that there were times when no-one else could help you, not even your parents.

'You have to try again, sweetheart. Just in tiny little steps. Father and I will be right here with you.' She pulled away from her then, and looked into her daughter's eyes. 'We love you very, very much, Sarah, and we don't want you hurt again either.'

Sarah closed her eyes and breathed deeply. 'I'll try.' She opened her eyes again then and looked at her mother. 'I really will.' And then she panicked. 'But what if I can't do it?'

'Can't do what?' Her mother smiled at her. 'Can't take a walk with me and Father? Can't have dinner with us? Can't meet a few of our friends? I think you can. We won't ask for too much, and if it really is more than you can do, then you'll tell us.' It was as though she had become an invalid, and in some ways, she had. Freddie had crippled her, and she knew it. The question now was if she could be healed, or helped; if she would recover. Her mother couldn't bear the thought that maybe she couldn't. 'How about a walk?'

'I look awful. My eyes must be swollen. And my nose always gets red when I cry.' She laughed through her tears as her mother made a face at her.

'That's the worst piece of nonsense I've ever heard. Your nose is *not* red.' Sarah hopped out of her chair to look in the mirror and gave a shout of disgust.

'It is too! Look at it, it looks like a red potato!'

'Let me see . . .' Victoria narrowed her eyes and peered at Sarah's nose as she shook her head. 'It must be a very, very small potato. I don't think anyone will notice anything, if you throw a little cold water on your face, and comb your hair, and maybe even put on a spot of lipstick.' She hadn't worn makeup in months, and she didn't seem to care, and up until now, Victoria hadn't pressed it.

'I didn't bring any with me.' Sarah looked deliberately vague. She really didn't know if she wanted to try, but she was touched by what her mother had said, and she didn't want to be completely uncooperative, even if that meant wearing lipstick.

'I'll give you some of mine. You're lucky you look as well as you do without it. I look like a sheet of blank paper without makeup.'

'You do not,' Sarah called after her, as her mother crossed the stateroom to her own rooms, to get her daughter some lipstick. She returned a moment later and held it out to her, as Sarah obediently splashed her face with cold water and combed her hair. In her sweater and slacks, with her hair loose past her shoulders, she looked like a young girl again, and her mother smiled as they left the cabin, arm in arm, to find Sarah's father.

They found him on the promenade deck, comfortably soaking up the sun in a deck chair, while two attractive young men played shuffleboard near him. He had intentionally taken up the deck chair closest to them, the moment he spotted them, hoping that Victoria would eventually appear with Sarah, and he was delighted when he saw them.

'And what have you two been up to? Shopping?'

'Not yet.' Victoria looked pleased, and Sarah smiled, completely oblivious to the two men her father had spotted. 'We thought we'd go for a walk first, and have tea with you, and then ravage the stores and spend all your money.'

'I'll have to throw myself overboard if you two wipe me out.' The two women laughed, and the two young men nearby glanced at Sarah, one of them with considerable interest. But she turned away and began to stroll down the promenade deck with her father. As they talked, Edward Thompson was impressed by how much his daughter knew of world politics. She had apparently spent her time well of late, reading newspapers and magazine articles, and learning everything she could of the situation in Europe. He was reminded of how intelligent she was, how astute, and really was amazed at how much she knew. This was no ordinary girl, and she hadn't just been wasting her time while she was hiding. She talked about the Civil War in Spain, Hitler's annexation of Austria in March, and its implications, as well as his behavior two years before that in the Rhineland.

'How do you know all that?' her father asked, looking vastly impressed. She was wonderful to talk to.

'I read a lot.' She smiled shyly at him. 'I don't have much else to do, you know.' They exchanged a warm smile. 'And I find it fascinating. What do you think will happen, Father? Do you think Hitler will declare war? He certainly seems to be gearing up for it, and I think the bond between Rome and Berlin could be very dangerous. Particularly given what Mussolini is doing.'

'Sarah' – he stopped and stared at her – 'you amaze me.'

'Thank you.' They walked on for a time, talking in depth of the danger of war in Europe, and he hated to stop walking with her an hour later. There was a side to her he had never seen, a side that had clearly been wasted on Van Deering. They continued to talk animatedly over tea, as Edward expounded on his theory that the United States would never be involved in a war over there, and expressing the view that Ambassador Kennedy had already shared with his intimates, that England was in no position to engage in a war in Europe.

'It's a shame we're not going to Germany,' Sarah said, surprising her father. 'I'd love to get a feeling for what's happening there, or maybe even talk to people.' Listening to her made her father very glad they weren't going there. Having Sarah delve into dangerous world politics was not in his plans for her. Being interested in what was happening in the world, being knowledgeable and informed, even to the degree she was, which was certainly rare, especially for a woman, was one thing, but going there and testing the water implied a danger he would never agree to.

'I think it's just as well we're staying in England and France. I'm not even sure we really should go to Rome. I thought we'd decide once we were in Europe.'

'Where's your spirit of adventure, Father?' she teased, but he shook his head, much wiser than she was.

'I'm too old for that, my dear. And you should be wearing beautiful gowns and going to parties.'

'How dull.' She pretended to look bored, and her father laughed.

'You certainly are an unusual girl, Miss Sarah.' No wonder her marriage to Van Deering had been a disaster, and she had gone into hiding on Long Island. She was far too intelligent for him and most of the young men in his circle. And as they came to know each other better on the ship, her father came to understand her better.

By the third day out, Sarah seemed completely at ease walking around the ship. She still kept to herself, and had no particular interest in the young men aboard, but she ate with her parents in the dining room, and on the last night, she dined with them at the captain's table.

'You're not engaged to anyone, Miss Thompson?' Captain Irving asked with a twinkle in his eye, as her mother held her breath as to what she would answer.

'No, I'm not,' Sarah said coolly, with a faint blush on her cheeks, and a hand that trembled as she set down her wineglass.

'How fortunate for the young men in Europe.'

Sarah smiled demurely, but she felt the words like a knife to her heart. No, she wasn't engaged, she was waiting for her divorce to come through in November, one year after the hearing. Divorce. She felt like a ruined woman. But at least no-one here knew, that was a blessing of sorts, and she was grateful for it. And with any luck at all, no-one in Europe would know either.

The captain asked her to dance, and she looked beautiful in his arms, in an ice-blue satin dress her mother had had made for her before her wedding to Freddie. The dress had been part of her trousseau, and she felt a knot in her throat that night as she put it on. And another when a young man she had never met asked her to dance with him, immediately after the captain. She seemed to hesitate for a long time, and then nodded politely.

'Where are you from?' He was very tall, and very blond, and she could hear from his accent that he was English.

'New York.'

'Are you coming to London?' He seemed to be having a very good time, he had been watching Sarah for days, but he had found her to be very elusive and a little daunting. She had offered him no encouragement at all, which he found somewhat dismaying.

Sarah was intentionally vague with him. She had no interest in being pursued by anyone, and in an odd way, he reminded her a little bit of Freddie.

'Where would you be staying?'

'With friends of my parents,' she lied, knowing full well they had reservations at Claridge's, and would be in London for at least two weeks, but she had no desire whatsoever to see him. And mercifully for her, the dance ended quickly. He attempted to hang around after that, but Sarah offered him no encouragement, and a few minutes later, he took the hint and went back to his own table.

'I see young Lord Winthrop is not to your liking,' the captain teased her. He had been the prize catch on the ship, and all the marriageable young ladies seemed determined to pursue him. All except for the extremely aloof Miss Thompson.

63

'Not at all. I simply don't know him,' Sarah said coolly.

'Do you wish to be formally introduced?' the captain offered, but Sarah only smiled as she shook her head.

'No, thank you, Captain.' She danced with her father after that, and the captain commented to Victoria on her daughter's intelligence and beauty.

'She's an unusual girl,' he said, clearly in admiration of her. He had enjoyed talking to her, almost as much as her own father had during the five-day crossing. 'And so pretty. She seems remarkably well behaved for someone so young. I can't imagine you have any problems with her at all.'

'No.' Victoria smiled, proud of her youngest daughter, 'except that she's a little too well behaved.' Victoria smiled in spite of herself, dismayed by Sarah's total indifference to young Lord Winthrop. It didn't bode well for the rest of the young men in Europe. 'She's had a great disappointment in her life,' she confided in him, 'and I'm afraid she's been withdrawn from everyone for some time. We're hoping to bring her out of herself a bit in Europe.'

'I see,' he nodded, understanding better now. It explained her total lack of interest in Phillip Winthrop. 'She won't be an easy young woman to find a man for,' he said honestly. 'She's too intelligent, and too wise, and she doesn't seem to be interested in much in the way of nonsense. Perhaps an older man.' He liked the girl, and he found himself pondering the problem, and then smiled at her mother. 'You've very fortunate. She's a beautiful girl. And I hope she finds a wonderful husband.' Victoria found herself wondering if that was how it looked to all of them, that they were coming to Europe to find a husband for Sarah. Sarah would have a fit if she thought that even for a moment. Victoria thanked the captain, then had one last dance with him, and went to find her daughter and her husband.

'I think we should go to bed at a decent hour, you two.

We have a big day tomorrow.' They were getting off in Cherbourg and going directly to Paris. Sarah had never been there, and they had a heavy sightseeing schedule, with a driver and a car that had been arranged for them by the hotel. They were staying at the Ritz, and after a week there they were moving on to Deauville, and Biarritz, to see friends, and then a week on the Riviera, in Cannes, and a few days in Monte Carlo with an old friend. And after all that, they were going to London.

The ship docked in Cherbourg at eight o'clock the next morning, and the Thompsons boarded the boat train in high spirits. Edward shared a list of places with them that he thought Sarah really should see, among them the Louvre, the Tuileries, Versailles, Malmaison, the Jeu de Paume, the Eiffel Tower, and, of course, Napoleon's tomb. At the end of the recital, Victoria Thompson raised an eyebrow.

'I didn't hear the house of Chanel on that list . . . or Dior . . . or Balenciaga, or Schiaparelli. Did you forget them, dear?' Violet and mauve were 'the' colors in Paris that year, and Victoria was anxious to shop for herself and Sarah.

'I tried to, my love.' He smiled benevolently. 'But I didn't think you'd let me forget for long.' He enjoyed indulging his wife, and was looking forward to indulging his daughter. But he also wanted to show her the more important cultural sights, some of which he began pointing out to her as they rode into Paris.

Their rooms at the Ritz, when they arrived, were absolutely beautiful. This time Sarah had a suite entirely separate from theirs, with a view of the Place Vendôme. She had to admit to herself as she stood in her room that there was something bittersweet about being there alone, and it would have been infinitely more enjoyable if she could have been there with her husband.

She sighed and went to bed alone in the enormous bed,

under the down comforter, and in the morning, they went to the Louvre, and spent hours there. It was a very gratifying day for her parents, as was the rest of the trip. She was no longer resisting them, and in Paris they only had one friend, an old friend of Edward's mother, and she invited them to tea on the rue Jacob. But there were no social events for Sarah to avoid. She could just enjoy the museums and the cathedrals and the shops, and the time she spent there with her parents.

Deauville was a little more strained, because the people they visited there insisted on forcing Sarah to meet their son, and did everything possible to provoke some interest between them. He was very interested in her, but Sarah found him unattractive, uninformed, and incredibly boring. She spent their entire stay there doing everything she could to avoid him. Likewise, the two brothers that were forced on her in Biarritz, and the grandson pressed on her in Cannes, not to mention the two 'charming' young men introduced to her by their friends in Monte Carlo. By the end of their stay on the Riviera, Sarah was in a black mood, and barely speaking to her parents.

'Did you enjoy the Riviera, dear?' Victoria said to her innocently as they packed, preparing to leave the next day for London.

'No, I really didn't,' Sarah said bluntly. 'Not at all.'

'Really?' Her mother looked up in surprise, she thought she had been having a lovely time. They had been on several yachts, had spent a good deal of time on the beach, and had gone to several really splendid parties. 'How disappointing.'

'I want you to know something, Mother.' Sarah looked at her squarely, and put down the white blouse she had been packing. 'I have not come to Europe to find another husband. I might remind you that, until November anyway, I am still married. And after that, I hope never to be

66

married again. I'm sick and tired of everyone you know trying to force their idiot sons on me, or their illiterate grandsons, or their moronic cousins. I haven't met a man here yet whom I can talk to, let alone want to spend as much as an hour with. I don't want another man in my life, and I don't want to be dragged all over Europe, shown off like some sort of backward girl, desperately in need of a husband. Is that clear?' Her mother looked stunned as she nodded. 'And by the way, do any of these people know that I've been married before?'

Victoria shook her head. 'I don't really think so.'

'Well, maybe you should tell them. I'm sure they'd be far less enthusiastic about throwing their little idiot darlings at me if they knew that I was a divorced woman.'

'That's not a crime, Sarah,' her mother said quietly, knowing full well how Sarah viewed it. To Sarah, it was a crime. An unforgivable sin she could not forgive herself, and she didn't expect anyone else to either.

'It's nothing to be proud of. And most people would hardly consider it an asset.'

'I didn't suggest that it was, but it is not an insuperable affliction. There are people you'll meet who will know, and who won't mind. And when the time is right, with people who don't know, you can always tell them, if you feel you have to.'

'Yes, it's rather like a disease. One owes it to people to warn them.'

'Of course not. Only if you want to.'

'Maybe I should just wear a sign. You know, like a leper.' She sounded angry and bitter and sad, but she was sick of being paired off with young boys who held absolutely no interest whatsoever for her, and almost tore her clothes off. 'Do you know what that de Saint Gilles boy did in Deauville? He stole all my clothes while I was changing, and then came in and tried to rip off my towel. He thought he was incredibly amusing.'

'How dreadful!' Her mother looked shocked. 'Why didn't you say something?'

'I did. To him. I told him that if he didn't give me back my clothes at once, I was going straight to his father, and the poor thing was so frightened, he gave me everything back and begged me not to tell anyone. He really was pathetic.' It was something a sixteen-year-old would do, not a man of twenty-seven. And they had all been like that so far, immature, spoiled, arrogant, ignorant, uneducated. She couldn't bear it. 'I just want you and Father to know that I am not here in Europe to look for a husband,' she reminded her mother again, as her mother nodded, and Sarah went back to her packing.

Victoria mentioned the incident to her husband that night, and told him about the young man in Deauville, and he thought the prank was stupid, but certainly harmless.

'The real problem is that she's more mature than all of them. She's been through a lot too. She needs someone older, more mature. These boys have no idea how to handle her. And given how she feels about getting involved with anyone again, they only annoy her. We have to be careful who we introduce her to in London.' The idea was not to turn her away from men completely, but at least to find one or two whose company she might enjoy, to remind her that there was more than solitude in life. But the boys she had met so far only made solitude look more appealing.

They went back to Paris the next day, and crossed the Channel in seven hours by the Golden Arrow train and ferry the following morning. And they arrived at Claridge's in time for dinner. They were met at the desk by the manager, who showed them to their suite of rooms with the utmost formality and decorum. Her parents had a large bedroom with a view over the rooftops toward Big Ben and the Houses of Parliament. They had a sitting room, too, and she had a very pretty room that looked like a boudoir, done in pink satin and rose-covered chintzes. And as she glanced at the desk in her room, she noticed half a dozen invitations, none of which looked like good news to her. She didn't even bother to open them, and her mother mentioned them to her that night at dinner. As they dined in their suite, Victoria explained that they'd been invited to two dinner parties, and a tea given by old friends, a day in the country in Leicester for a picnic, and a luncheon given in their honor by the Kennedys at the embassy in Grosvenor Square. All of which, as far as Sarah was concerned, sounded incredibly boring.

'Do I have to go with you?' There was a whine in her voice that reminded her mother of her teens, but her father looked firm as he answered.

'Now, let's not start that again. We all know why we're here. We're here to see friends, and we're not going to insult them by turning down their invitations.'

'Why do they have to see *me*? They're *your* friends, Father, not mine. They won't miss me.'

'I won't have it.' He planted a fist down firmly on the table. 'And I won't discuss it with you again. You're too old for this nonsense. Be courteous, be pleasant, and be good enough to make an effort. Do you understand me, Sarah Thompson?'

Sarah looked at him icily, but he seemed not to notice, or to care how much she objected. He had brought her to Europe for a reason, and he was not going to be deterred from bringing her back out into the world again. No matter how much she resisted him, he knew instinctively that it was exactly what she needed.

'Very well then.'

They finished their meal in silence. And the next day they went to the Victoria and Albert Museum, and had a wonderful time, followed by a very elegant and very stuffy formal dinner. But Sarah did not complain. She wore a dress her mother had bought for her before the trip, a dark-green taffeta that was almost the color of her eyes and suited her to perfection. She looked very beautiful when they arrived, and totally unexcited to be there. She looked as bored as she was, through most of the evening. Several young people had been invited to meet her, and she tried to make an effort to talk to them, but she found she had nothing in common with them. More than anything, most of them seemed very spoiled and very silly, and surprisingly unaware of the world around them.

Sarah was quiet on the way home, and her parents did not ask her if she'd had a good time. It was clear to everyone that she hadn't. The second formal party was much the same, and the tea party was worse. There, they attempted to force a great-nephew on her, who even her mother had had to admit afterwards, with embarrassment, was foolish and graceless to the point of being childish.

'For God's sake,' Sarah stormed when they went back to Claridge's that night. 'What's wrong with these people? Why are they doing this to me? Why does everyone feel they have to pair me off with their idiot relations? What did you say to them when you told them we were coming?' Sarah asked her father, who refused to look defensive. 'That I was desperate, and they had to help me out?' She couldn't believe the people she was meeting.

'I merely said that we were bringing you. How they interpreted that was up to them. I simply think they're trying to be hospitable by inviting young people for you. If you don't like their relatives or their young friends, then I'm very sorry.'

'Can't you tell them I'm engaged? Or have a contagious disease? Something so they don't feel compelled to match me up with anyone? I really can't bear this. I refuse to keep going to parties and feel like a fool for the entire evening.' She had handled it very well, but her temper was growing short, and it was clear she hadn't enjoyed it.

'I'm sorry, Sarah,' her father said quietly. 'They don't mean any harm. Try not to get so upset.'

'I haven't had an intelligent conversation with anyone but you since we left New York,' she said accusingly, and he smiled. At least she enjoyed his company as much as he enjoyed hers. That was something.

'And who is it you were having such intelligent conversations with while you were hiding on Long Island?'

'At least there, I didn't expect it.' The silence had been peaceful.

'Well, don't expect so much now. Take it for what it is. A visit to a new place, an opportunity to meet new people.'

'Even the women are no fun to talk to.'

'I don't agree with you there,' he said, and his wife raised an eyebrow. He patted her hand apologetically, but she knew he was only teasing.

'All these women are interested in is men, boys,' she said defensively. 'I don't think they've ever even heard of politics. And they all think Hitler is their mother's new cook. How can anyone be so stupid?' Her father laughed outright and shook his head.

'Since when have you been such a political and intellectual snob?'

'Since I've kept my own company. Actually, it's been damn pleasant.'

'Maybe too much so. It's time you remembered that the world is full of a variety of people, intelligent ones, less-intelligent ones, some downright dumb ones, some amusing ones, some very dull ones. But that is what makes a world. You've definitely been on your own for too long, Sarah. I'm happier than ever that you came here.'

'Well, I'm not sure I am,' she growled, but the truth was that she had enjoyed the trip with them. The social aspects had been less than pleasing, but she had enjoyed the trip very much in other ways, and she was happy to be with them. It had brought her closer to her parents again, and in spite of her complaints she seemed happier than she'd been in a long time. And if nothing else, she seemed to have regained her sense of humor.

She balked at going to the country with them the next day, but her father insisted that she had no choice, that the country air would do her good, and he knew the estate where they were going, and said it was well worth seeing. Sarah groaned as she got into the car with them, and complained most of the way down, but she had to admit that the countryside was beautiful, and the weather was unusually hot and sunny for England.

When they arrived, she reluctantly conceded that it was a remarkable place, just as he'd promised. It was a fourteenth-century moated castle, with beautiful grounds and the original farm, which the family had restored completely. The hundred guests they had invited to lunch were welcome to roam everywhere, even to wander down the long baronial halls, where servants waited discreetly to serve them drinks or make them comfortable in one of the many sitting rooms, or outside in the gardens. Sarah thought she had never seen a prettier, or more interesting place, and she was so fascinated by the farm that she stayed forever asking questions, and managed to lose her parents. She stood looking at the thatched roofs of the cottages and huts, with the huge castle looming in the distance. It was an extraordinary sight, and she uttered a small sigh as she looked at it, feeling comfortable and at peace, and completely in the grip of history as she stood there. The people around her seemed almost to disappear; in fact, most of them had by then. They had gone back to the castle for lunch and to stroll through the gardens.

'Impressive, isn't it?' a voice behind her said. She turned around, startled to see a tall man with dark hair and blue eyes just behind her. He seemed to loom there, looking very tall, but he had a warm smile, and they looked almost like brother and sister. 'I always have an extraordinary sense of history when I come here. As though, if you close your eyes for a moment, the serfs and the knights and their ladies will appear in an instant.'

Sarah smiled at what he said, because it was exactly what she'd been feeling. 'I was just thinking that. I couldn't bring myself to go back after I visited the farm, I just wanted to stay and feel exactly what you were just describing.'

'I like it this way. I dread all those awful places that have been manicured to death, and boiled beyond recognition to make them seem modern.' She nodded again, amused by what he said and how he said it, and there was a distinct twinkle in his eye as he spoke to her. He seemed to be amused by everything, and he was pleasant to talk to.

'I'm William Whitfield, captive for the weekend,' he introduced himself. 'Belinda and George are cousins of mine, mad as they are. But they're good people. And you're American, aren't you?'

She nodded, and held out her hand, feeling faintly shy, but not very. 'Yes, I am. I'm Sarah Thompson.'

'Delighted to meet you. From New York? Or somewhere more exciting, like Detroit or San Francisco?'

She laughed at his vision of exciting, and admitted that he'd been right the first time.

'On the Grand Tour?'

'Right again.' She smiled, and he eyed her carefully with piercing blue eyes that held her firmly.

'Let me guess. With your parents?'

'Yes.'

'How awful. And they're boring you to tears going to museums and churches by day, and at night introducing you to all their friends' sons, most of whom drool, and a few of whom can almost speak English. Am I right again?' He was clearly enjoying the portrait he painted.

Sarah laughed openly, unable to deny it. 'You've been

watching us, I assume. Or someone's been telling you what we've been doing.'

'I can't think of anything worse, except perhaps a honeymoon with someone truly dreadful.' But as he said the words, her eyes clouded over, and she almost seemed to take a little distance from him, and he was instantly aware of it as he watched her.

'Sorry, that was tasteless.' He seemed very open and very direct, and she felt incredibly comfortable with him.

'Not really.' She wanted to tell him that she was just sensitive, but, of course, she didn't. 'Do you live in London?' She felt a responsibility to change the subject to put him at ease again, although very little seemed to disturb him.

'I do live in London,' he confessed. 'When I'm not in Gloucestershire, mending old fences. But it's nothing like this, I can promise you. Actually, it never was, and I don't have Belinda and George's imagination. They've spent years bringing this place up to scratch. I've spent years just keeping mine from turning into a pile of rubble. And it has anyway. Dreadful place, if you can imagine it. Full of drafts, and cobwebs, and terrifying sounds. My poor mother still lives there.' He made everything seem amusing as he spoke of it, and they began to move slowly away from the farm as they chatted. 'I suppose we should go back up for lunch, not that anyone will ever notice if we don't. With that mob underfoot, Belinda wouldn't even notice if we went back to London. I imagine your parents would, however. I rather think they'd come after me with a shotgun.'

She laughed at him again, knowing that her parents would have been more likely to use the shotgun to bring him nearer. 'I don't think so.'

'I'm not exactly the image parents are looking for, for their innocent young daughters. Bit old for that, I'm afraid, but in relatively good health for an old man,

74

comparatively speaking.' He was eyeing her carefully, stunned by how beautiful she was, and yet intrigued by something he saw in her eyes as well, something intelligent and sad, and very cautious. 'Would it be terribly rude to ask how old you are?'

She suddenly found herself wanting to say 'thirty', and couldn't imagine why she would lie to him, so she didn't. 'I'll be twenty-two next month.'

He was less impressed than she wanted him to be as he smiled down at her, and helped her over a rock fence with a powerful hand that felt smooth in her own for the instant that she held it. 'A mere baby. I'm thirty-five. I'm afraid your parents would be incredibly depressed if you came home with me as your token European.' He was teasing her, but they were both having fun, and she really liked him. He would have made a good friend, and she liked the fact that she could joke with him, even though she didn't know him.

'The nice thing about you, though, is that you don't drool, I would bet that you can tell time, and you do speak English.'

'I'll admit, my virtues are too many to number. Where do people get those dreadful relatives they bring out for other people's children? I could never understand it. I have met young women in my lifetime, all of them related to seemingly normal people, yet most of whom must be institutionalized by now, poor dears. And everyone I knew was convinced that I was simply aching to meet them. Quite extraordinary, isn't it?'

Sarah could hardly stop laughing as she remembered the boys she had just met all over Europe. She described the one in Deauville to him, and the two in Biarritz . . . the boys in Cannes, and Monte Carlo . . . and they were friends by the time they crossed the moat and reentered the castle.

'Do you suppose they've left any lunch for us at all? I'm

absolutely starving,' he admitted to her. He was a very big man, and it was easy to believe he was hungry.

'We should have taken some of the apples down at the farm, I was dying to, but the farmer didn't offer them, and I was afraid to take them.'

'You should have said something,' Sarah said helpfully. 'I'd have stolen them for you.'

They found the lunch table well laden with roasts and chickens and vegetables and an enormous salad. And they heaped a healthy lunch on to two plates and William led her into a little arbor. She didn't hesitate to follow him for a moment. It seemed entirely natural to be alone with him, and to listen to his stories. Eventually, they began talking politics, and Sarah was fascinated to hear that he had just been to Munich. He said that the tension could be felt acutely there, although not as much as in Berlin, and he hadn't been there since the year before. But all of Germany seemed to be revving up for a major confrontation.

'Do you think it will come soon?'

'It's hard to say. But I think it will come, even though your government doesn't seem to think so.'

'I don't see how it can be avoided.' It intrigued him to find her so aware of world news, and so interested in things seldom followed by women. He asked her about it and she told him that she had spent a lot of time alone for the past year, and it had given her time to learn things that she normally wouldn't.

'Why would you want to be alone?' He looked deep into her eyes, but she looked away from him. He was intrigued by everything about her, and he could see that there was something very painful that she was carrying with her, but determined to keep hidden.

'Sometimes one needs to be alone.' She didn't elaborate further and he didn't want to pry, but he was intrigued, and she talked to him then about the farmhouse she wanted to buy on Long Island.

'That's quite a project for a young girl. What do you suppose your parents will say to all that?'

'They'll have a fit.' She grinned. 'But I don't want to go back to New York any more. Eventually, they'll agree, or I'll buy it myself if I have to.' She was a determined girl, and possibly a very stubborn one. He was amused by the look in her eyes as she said it. This was not a woman one could take lightly.

'I wouldn't think leaving New York is such a bad idea, but going to live alone in a farmhouse at your age is not exactly the height of entertaining either. What about spending summers there, or weekends?'

She shook her head with the same determined look. 'I want to be there all the time. I want to restore it myself.'

'Have you ever done anything like that?' He was amused by her. She was an enchanting creature, and he was amazed at how much he liked her.

'No. But I know that I can.' She sounded a little as though she were practicing to convince her father.

'Do you really think they'll let you do it?'

'They'll have to.' She set her chin, and he gently tweaked it.

'I imagine you must keep them rather busy. No wonder they've brought you to Europe to meet Prince Charming. I'm not sure I blame them. Perhaps you really ought to have one of those sweet young droolers.'

She looked shocked and then took a swipe at him with her napkin, and he laughed as he defended himself and found himself breathlessly close to her, and for a mad instant he wanted to kiss her. But as he looked down at her, he saw something so sad in her eyes that it actually stopped him.

'There's a secret in your life, isn't there? And it's not a happy one, is it?'

She hesitated for a long time before she answered him.

And she did so with caution. 'I don't know if I'd call it that.' But her eyes told their own story.

'You don't have to tell me anything, Sarah. I'm only a stranger. But I like you. You're a great girl, and if something dreadful has happened to you, then I'm truly sorry.'

'Thank you.' She smiled, looking very wise and very beautiful, and more alluring than ever.

'Sometimes the things that hurt us the worst are the ones we forget quickest. They hurt so brutally for a while, and they heal and it's over.' But he could see that this wasn't healed yet, or even over. He imagined she'd been jilted by someone, or perhaps the boy she had loved had died, something sweet and romantic and innocent, and she'd get over it soon enough. Her parents had been right to bring her to Europe. She was a real beauty and a bright girl, and whatever it was, she'd get over it quickly, particularly if she met the right boy in Europe . . . lucky devil!

They chatted for a long time, safely tucked away in their arbor, until at last they ventured out to rejoin the other guests, and within moments they ran smack into their somewhat eccentric hostess, William's cousin, Belinda.

'Good God, there you are! I told everyone you'd gone home. My Lord, William, you're impossible!' She looked amused beyond words as she spotted Sarah with him. 'I was just about to tell you that the Thompsons are convinced their daughter fell into the moat. They haven't seen her since they got here, what on earth have you been up to?'

'I kidnapped her. Told her the story of my life. And she was properly revolted, and asked to be returned to her family at once, so I was just bringing her back to you, with endless remorse, and humblest apologies.' He was grinning from ear to ear, and Sarah was clearly smiling, and entirely at ease beside him.

'You are absolutely dreadful! And what's more, you've never felt remorse in your entire life.' She turned to Sarah with a look of concerned amusement. 'My dear, did he harm you? Should I call the constable?'

'Oh, do!' William encouraged her, 'I haven't seen him in months.'

'Oh, do shut up, you monster.' But Sarah was laughing at them, and Belinda shook her head in mock despair. 'I shall never invite you again, you know. One simply can't. You're far too badly behaved to invite with decent people.'

'It's what everyone says.' He looked mournfully at Sarah, who hadn't been this happy in years. 'Do I dare introduce myself to your parents?'

'I think you'd better,' Belinda growled at him, unaware of the fact that he had every intention of meeting them, and seeing Sarah again, if they'd let him. He had no idea who or what she was, but he knew without a doubt that he wanted to get to know her better. 'I'll take you to them,' Belinda said helpfully, and Sarah and William followed her, giggling and laughing and whispering, like naughty children. But the Thompsons were far from angry at her when they saw her again. They knew that she had to be safe somewhere on the property, among the other guests. And they were very pleased when they saw her with William. He looked pleasant and intelligent, and he was a good-looking man, of reasonable age, and he seemed to be very taken with their daughter.

'I have to apologize,' he explained. 'We got waylaid at the farm, and then we stopped for lunch. And I'm afraid that I detained Sarah far longer than was proper.'

'Don't believe a word of it,' Belinda interjected. 'I'm sure he kept her tied to a tree somewhere, and ate all her lunch while he told her abominable stories.'

'What a good idea,' William said pensively, as the Thompsons laughed at them. 'Sarah, we really ought to try that next time.' He seemed surprisingly comfortable with her, and she with him, and they chatted for a long time, until George appeared, enchanted to find him again, and insisted that he come to the stables to see his new stallion. William was dragged away in spite of himself, and Belinda chatted on with them, raising an admiring eyebrow at Sarah.

'I shouldn't say this, my dear, but you've captured the eye of the most attractive man in England, and possibly the nicest.'

'We had a very pleasant time talking.' But pleasant wasn't exactly the word she would have used, if she'd been talking to her sister. He was really quite terrific.

'He's too smart for his own good. Never married. He's far too choosy.' Belinda shot a warning glance at the Thompsons, as though to tell them he wouldn't be an easy catch, but they seemed not to notice. 'It's remarkable how unassuming he is. One would never know, would one . . .' She turned to Sarah again then. 'I don't suppose he said anything . . . You do know that he's the Duke of Whitfield, don't you?' She opened her eyes wide and Sarah stared at her.

'I . . . uh . . . he just introduced himself as William Whitfield.'

'He does that. Actually, it's one of the things I like most about him. I forget where he is in all that . . . thirteenth or fourteenth in the succession.'

'To the throne?' Sarah asked in a strangled voice.

'Yes, of course. Though it's not likely he'll ever get there. But still, it means something to all of us. We're stupid about things like that here. I suppose it all has to do with tradition. Well, anyway, I'm glad you're all right. I was a bit worried when we couldn't find you.'

'I'm sorry.' Sarah blushed furiously, still staggering mentally from the information about her new friend, William. And then suddenly, she wondered if she had made some really dreadful *faux pas* with him. 'Am I supposed to call him something? . . . I mean . . . some title? Something special?'

Belinda smiled at her. She was so young, and so very pretty. 'Your Grace, but if you do, I suppose he'll shoot us both. I wouldn't say anything about it, unless he does.' Sarah nodded, and William rejoined them just as their hostess left them.

'How was the horse?' Sarah asked in a subdued voice, trying to sound normal, as her parents pretended to ignore them.

'Not nearly as impressive as the price George paid for him, I'm afraid. He's the worst judge of horseflesh I've ever seen. Wouldn't surprise me a bit if the poor beast turned out to be sterile.' And then he looked at her guiltily. 'Sorry, I don't suppose I should have said that.'

'It's all right.' She smiled at him, wondering what he would say if she called him 'Your Grace' now. 'I think I've probably heard worse.'

'I hope not.' And then he grinned. 'Oh . . . the droolers . . . God only knows what they'd say.' She laughed at him and they exchanged a long look, as she wondered to herself what she was doing. He was a duke, in line to the throne, and she was acting as though they were old friends, but that was how she felt after spending the last three hours with him, and she didn't want to go back to London.

'Where are you staying?' She heard him ask her father, as they walked slowly back to the castle again, to the moat where they had entered.

'At Claridge's. Would you join us there sometime? For a drink, or for dinner?' Her father said it very casually, and William looked delighted with the invitation.

'I'd like that. May I call you in the morning?' He addressed the question to Edward, and not to Sarah.

'Certainly. We'll look forward to hearing from you, sir,' Edward said as he shook his hand. Then William turned to

Sarah as her parents walked past her to the waiting car and driver.

'I had a wonderful time today. I really didn't expect that. I almost didn't come . . . you were a lovely surprise, Miss Sarah Thompson.'

'Thank you.' She smiled up at him. 'I had a wonderful time too.' And then she couldn't help saying something to him about what Belinda had told them. 'Why didn't you tell me?'

'About what?'

'Your Grace.' She said it with a shy smile and for a moment she was afraid he'd be angry, but he laughed, after only a moment's hesitation.

'Dear Belinda.' And then, 'Does it matter?' he asked softly.

'No, not at all. Should it?'

'It might. To some. For all the wrong reasons.' But he already knew from talking to her that she wasn't one of those people. And then he looked at her with an expression that was both serious and teasing. 'You know my secret now, Miss Sarah Thompson . . . but be careful!'

'Why?' She looked puzzled, as he moved just a little closer to her.

'If you know my secret, perhaps in time I will ask you to share yours.'

'What makes you think I have one?'

'We both know that, don't we?' he said softly, and she nodded, her eyes very full, as he reached out and touched her hand gently. He didn't want her to be frightened of him. 'Don't worry, little one . . . don't ever tell me anything you don't want to.' He bent and kissed her cheek then, and walked her slowly to the car to return her to her parents. She looked up at him in awe as he stood beside the car, and waved until they were gone. And as they rode back to London, she wondered if he would ever call them.

Chapter 5

The next morning, as Edward was having breakfast with his wife in the living room of their suite at Claridge's, the telephone rang, and a secretary's voice announced a call from the Duke of Whitfield. There was a moment's pause, and William's warm, genial voice came on the line with a friendly greeting.

'I hope I'm not calling you too early, sir. But I was afraid you might get off on your rounds before I could reach you.'

'Not at all.' Edward glanced at his wife with a look of delight, and nodded vehemently as he continued the call, and Victoria immediately understood him. 'We were just having breakfast, except for Sarah, of course. She never eats, I don't know how she does it.'

'We'll have to see about that.' William jotted himself a note to have his secretary send her flowers that morning. 'Are you free this afternoon, all of you, I mean? I thought it might be amusing for the ladies to see the Crown Jewels in the Tower of London. One of the few privileges that comes with rank is that one can have private tours of oddities like that, if one chooses. It might be fun for Sarah and Mrs Thompson to try some of it on. You know . . . that sort of thing . . .' He sounded a little vague this morning, and very British. But Edward liked him a great deal. He was a real man, and it was obvious that he had a considerable interest in Sarah.

'I'm sure they'd love it. And it would keep them out of the stores for an hour or two. I'd be very grateful.' The two men laughed, William said he'd pick them up at two, in front of the hotel, and Edward assured him they'd be waiting. And when Sarah emerged from her room to pour herself a cup of tea, her father mentioned casually that the Duke of Whitfield had called, and was taking them to see the Crown Jewels at two o'clock in the Tower of London. 'I thought you might like that.' He wasn't sure if she was more interested in the jewels or the man, but one look at her face gave him the answer.

'William called?' She looked shocked, as though she hadn't expected to hear from him again. In fact, she had spent most of the night awake, assuring herself that he would never call her. 'Two o'clock *this* afternoon?' She looked as though her father were suggesting something dreadful, which surprised him.

'Do you have something else to do?' He couldn't imagine what, except maybe a shopping trip to Harrods or Hardy Amies.

'It's not that, it's just . . .' She sat down, and completely forgot her cup of tea. 'I just didn't think he'd call me.'

'He didn't call you,' her father teased, 'he called me, and invited me out, but I'm perfectly happy to take you with me.' She gave him a withering glance, and walked across the room to the window. She wanted to tell them to go without her, but she knew how ridiculous that would seem. But what was the point of seeing him again? What could possibly ever happen between them? 'What's the matter now?' her father asked as he watched her face as she stood at the window. She really was an impossible child if she was going to balk at this extraordinary opportunity. He was a wonderful man, and a little flirtation with him wouldn't do her any harm. Her father had absolutely no objection.

She turned slowly to face him. 'I don't see the point,' she said sadly.

'He's a nice man. He likes you. If nothing else, you can be friends. Is that so terrible? Have you no place left in your life for friendship?' She felt foolish when he said it that way, and she nodded. He was right. She was stupid to make so much of it, but he had swept her off her feet at the castle the day before. She had to remember this time not to be so silly and so impulsive.

'You're right. I didn't think of it that way. I just . . . it's different, because he's a duke. Before I knew that, it was . . .' She didn't know what to say to him, but he understood.

'It shouldn't make any difference. He's a nice man. I like him.'

'So do I,' she said quietly as her mother handed her the cup of tea and urged her to eat at least a piece of toast before they went out shopping. 'I just don't want to get into an awkward situation.'

'That's not likely, in a few weeks over here. Don't you think?'

'But I'm getting a divorce,' she said somberly. 'That could be awkward for him.'

'Not unless you marry him, and I think you're being a little premature, don't you?' But he was happy she was at least thinking of him as a man. It would do her good to have a little romance. She smiled at what her father said, and shrugged, and went back to her bedroom to finish dressing. She emerged half an hour later in a beautiful red silk Chanel suit he had just bought her in Paris the week before. And as the British would have said, she looked smashing. She was wearing some of the jewelry Chanel had just designed, some of it simulating pearls, some of it ruby, and she wore two wonderful cuffs that Madame Chanel had worn herself, they were black enamel with multicolored jewels set in them. They weren't real, of course, but they were very chic, and on Sarah they looked very striking.

She wore her dark hair pulled back in a long *queue de cheval*, tied with a black satin bow, and on her ears were the pearl earrings they had given her for her wedding. 'You look pretty in jewels, my dear,' her father commented as they left the hotel, and she smiled at him. 'You should wear them more often.' She didn't have many things, a string of pearls from her grandmother, the pearl earrings she wore, a few small rings. She had given back her engagement ring, and Freddie's grandmother's diamond rivière necklace.

'Maybe I will this afternoon,' she teased back, and Victoria looked knowingly at her husband.

They had lunch at a pub at noon, stopped at Lock's in St James's Street to order a hat for her father, and were back at the hotel promptly at ten minutes to two, and found William already waiting for them in the lobby. He was pacing nervously, and glanced at his watch just as they walked in, and his face lit up when he saw Sarah.

'You look absolutely extraordinary!' He beamed. 'You should always wear red.' She had even agreed to wear her mother's red lipstick, and her parents had just said that she looked beautiful as they walked into the lobby behind her. 'I'm awfully sorry I got here early,' he apologized. 'I always think it's ruder being early than being late, but I didn't want to miss you.'

Sarah smiled quietly as she looked at him. There was something about being with him that just made her feel good. 'I'm happy to see you' – she paused, and her eyes twinkled with mischief – 'Your Grace,' she added in an undertone, and he winced.

'I shall beat Belinda with a stick the next time I see her. If you ever say that to me again, I shall tweak your nose, is that clear, Miss Thompson, or should I call you Your Highness.'

'Actually, that has a nice ring to it. Your Highness . . . Your Opulence . . . Your Vulgarity . . . I really *love* titles!' She put on a strong American drawl and batted her eyes at him, and he pulled at the long tail of shiny dark hair that hung down her back with its black-satin ribbon.

'You are impossible . . . beautiful, but impossible. Do you always behave like this?' he asked blissfully, as her parents inquired for messages at the desk.

'Sometimes I'm worse,' she said proudly, but knowing full well that sometimes she was also very quiet. For almost two years, in fact. There hadn't been much joy in her life since her marriage to Freddie. But now, suddenly, with him, she felt different. He made her want to laugh again. And she sensed that with him, she could create delightful mischief. William sensed that about her, too, and he loved it.

Her parents rejoined them then, and William escorted them outside to his Daimler. He drove them to the Tower of London himself, chatting amiably all the while, and pointing out the sights to the three of them. Her mother had insisted that Sarah sit in the front seat, and her parents sat in the back seat behind them. William cast glances at her from time to time, as though to be sure she was still there, and to admire her. And when they reached the Tower he helped her and her mother out of the car, and offered a hand to Mr Thompson. He handed a card to one of the guards, and they were ushered inside immediately, even though it wasn't visiting hours. And another guard appeared to take them up the small spiral staircase to see the royal treasures.

'It's really quite remarkable, you know. All these extraordinary things just sitting here, some of them incredibly rare, and very old, with histories that are more fascinating than the jewels themselves. I've always loved it.' As a boy, he had been fascinated by his mother's jewels, the way they were made, the stories that went with them, the places they had come from.

And as soon as they reached the rooms where the jewels

were kept, Sarah could see why he thought they were exciting. There were crowns that had been worn by monarchs for the last six hundred years, scepters and swords, and pieces that one wouldn't see any more except at a coronation. The Sceptre with the Cross was particularly breathtaking, with a five-hundred-and-thirty-carat diamond set in it, the largest of the Stars of Africa, presented to Edward VII by South Africa. He insisted that she try several tiaras and at least four crowns, among them Queen Victoria's and Queen Mary's. Sarah was amazed at how heavy they were, and marvelled that anyone could wear them.

'King George wore this one at his coronation.' He pointed out the one, and as he did, she realized that he had been there, and just knowing that seemed remarkable, and reminded her again of who he was. But most of the time, just talking to him, it was so easy to forget it. 'It was a bit of a strain, I must admit, after all of that business with David.' At first, she wondered who he meant, and then she remembered that the Duke of Windsor's Christian name was David. 'Terribly sad, all that. They say he's blissfully happy now, and perhaps he is, but I saw him in Paris a few months ago, and I don't think he looks it. She's a difficult woman, with quite a history behind her.' He was referring to Wallis Simpson, of course, the Duchess of Windsor.

'It all seemed so incredibly selfish of her,' Sarah said quietly. 'And so unfair to him. It's really very sad.' She spoke with real feeling, having felt a terrible bond with her in recent years. But the stigma of divorce seemed to weigh a great deal more heavily on Sarah than it did on Wallis.

'She's not really a bad person. But shrewd. I always thought she knew what she was doing. My cousin . . . the duke' – as though he needed to explain – 'gave her over a million dollars worth of jewels before they were even married. He gave her the Mogul Emerald as an engagement ring. He had Jacques Cartier himself find it for him, and he did, in Baghdad, and they set it for him, or rather, for Wallis. It's the most extraordinary thing I've ever seen, but I've always rather liked emeralds.' It was fascinating hearing him make comments on the jewels they'd seen, rather like a surprisingly intimate tour guide. He didn't tell them gossipy things, but he told them about jewels made for Alexander the Great, and necklaces given to Josephine by Napoleon, and tiaras designed for Queen Victoria. There was even a remarkably pretty diamond-and-turquoise one she had worn as a young girl, which he made Sarah try on, and on her dark hair, it looked lovely. 'You should have one of those,' he said softly.

'I could wear it on my farm.' She smiled up at him and he made a face.

'You're irreverent. Here you are, wearing a tiara Queen Victoria wore as a young girl, and what do you do, you talk about a farmhouse! Dreadful girl!' But it was obvious that he didn't think so.

They stayed with him there until late in the afternoon, and it was a rich lesson in history and the quirks and habits and foibles of the monarchs of England. It was an experience none of them could have had without him, and the elder Thompsons thanked him effusively as they returned to his Daimler.

'It is rather amusing, isn't it? I've always loved going there. My father took me there for the first time. He used to love to buy interesting jewels for my mother. I'm afraid she doesn't wear them any more. She's become a bit frail, and she seldom goes out now. She still looks marvelous in them, but she claims now that she feels foolish.'

'She can't be very old,' Sarah's mother said protectively. She herself was only forty-seven. She had had Jane when she was twenty-three, and she had married Edward at twenty-one, and lost her first baby the year after.

'She's eighty-three,' William said proudly. 'She's

absolutely superb, and she doesn't really look a day over sixty. But she broke her hip, I'm afraid, last year, and it's made her a bit skittish about going out on her own. I try to take her out myself when I can, but it isn't always easy.'

'Are you the youngest of a large family?' Victoria was intrigued by what he'd said, but he shook his head, and said he was an only child.

'My parents had been married for thirty years when I was born, and they had long since given up any hope of having children. My mother always says it was a miracle, a blessing straight from God, if you'll pardon me for being so pompous.' He grinned mischievously at them. 'My father always said that it was a bit of the devil. He died several years ago, and he was a charming man. You would have liked him,' he assured them as he started the Daimler. 'My mother was forty-eight years old when I was born, which really is quite amazing. My father was sixty, and he was eighty-five when he died, which isn't bad. I must admit, I miss him. Anyway, the old girl is quite a character. Perhaps you'll have a chance to meet her before you leave London.' He looked at Sarah hopefully, but she was looking pensively out the window. She was thinking that she was too comfortable with him, that it was all too easy. But the truth was that it wasn't easy at all. They could never be more than passing friends, and she had to keep reminding herself of that, particularly when he looked at her a certain way, or made her laugh, or reached out and took her hand. There was no way they could ever be anything more to each other. Nothing more than friends. She was going to be divorced. And he stood fourteenth in line to the British throne. When they arrived at the hotel, he looked down at her as he helped her from the car, and he saw that she looked worried.

'Is something wrong?' He wondered if he had said something to offend her, but she had seemed to have such a good time, and she had clearly enjoyed trying on the jewels in the Tower. But she was angry at herself, she felt as though she was misleading him, and she owed him an explanation. He had a right to know who and what she was, before he wasted any more kindness on her.

'No, I'm sorry, I just have a headache.'

'It must have been that stupid, heavy crown I made you try on. Sarah, I'm terribly sorry.' He was instantly contrite, which made her feel even worse.

'Don't be silly. I'm just tired.'

'You didn't eat enough lunch.' Her father reproached her, he had seen the look of dismay on the younger man's face and felt sorry for him.

'I was going to invite you all out to dinner.'

'Maybe another time,' Sarah was quick to say, and her mother looked at her with an unspoken question.

'Maybe if you lie down,' she suggested hopefully, and William watched Sarah's face. He knew that there was something more going on, and he wondered if there was a man involved in it. Perhaps she was engaged to someone, and she was embarrassed to tell him. Or her fiancé had died. She had mentioned a year of great sorrow . . . He wanted to know more, but he didn't want to press her.

'Perhaps tomorrow for lunch?' He looked Sarah straight in the eye and she started to speak and then stopped.

'I . . . I had a wonderful time today.' She wanted to reassure him. Her parents thanked him and disappeared upstairs. The two young people had earned the right to be alone, as far as they were concerned, and they sensed that Sarah was having some inner conflicts about him.

'What do you think she's going to say to him?' Victoria asked her husband with a worried frown, as they rode upstairs.

'I'm not sure I want to know. But he'll weather it. He's a good man, Victoria. He's the kind of boy I'd like to see her settle down with.'

'So would I.' But they both knew there was no real hope

of that. He would never be allowed to marry a divorced woman, and they all knew it.

Downstairs, in the lobby, William was looking at Sarah, and she was being vague in answer to his questions.

'Could we go for a walk somewhere? Do you feel up to that?' She did, of course, but what was the point of going anywhere with him, or even seeing him again? What if she fell in love with him? Or he with her? Then what would they do? But on the other hand, it seemed ridiculous to think of falling in love with a man she had just met, and whom she would never see again once she left England.

'I think I'm just being very stupid.' She smiled. 'I haven't been around people in a long time . . . not men, anyway . . . and I think I've forgotten how to behave. I'm really sorry, William.'

'It's all right. Would you like to sit down?' She nodded and they found a quiet spot in the corner of the lobby. 'Have you been in a convent for the past year?' he asked her, only half teasing.

'More or less. Actually, I threatened that for a while. It was more like a convent of my own making. I stayed in my parents' beach home on Long Island.' She said it quietly, he had a right to know, and it didn't seem so unusual now, or as desperate as it had then. Sometimes it was hard to remember just how terrible she had felt when she'd been there.

'And you stayed there for a year without seeing anyone?' She nodded silently in answer, her eyes never leaving his, not sure what she should tell him. 'That's an awfully long time. Did it help?'

'I'm not sure,' she sighed as she spoke honestly to him, 'It seemed to at the time. But it made it very difficult to come back out into the world again. That's why we came here.'

'Europe is a good place to start.' He smiled gently at her, and decided not to ask her any difficult questions. He didn't want to scare her off, or cause her pain. He was falling in love with her, and the last thing he wanted was to lose her. 'I'm glad you came here.'

'So am I,' she said softly, and she meant it.

'Will you have dinner with me tonight?'

'I . . . I'm not sure . . . I think we were going to the theater' – but it was a play she knew she didn't want to see – *The Corn Is Green*, by Emlyn Williams. 'I really should ask my parents.'

'If not, then tomorrow?'

'William . . .' She seemed about to say something important to him, and then she stopped, and looked at him squarely. 'Why do you want to see me?' If the question seemed rude to him, he didn't show it.

'I think you're a very special girl. I've never met anyone like you.'

'But I'll be gone in a few weeks. What's the point of all this, for either of us?' What she really wanted to say to him was that she knew there could be no future for them together. And knowing that, it seemed foolish to pursue their friendship.

'The point is that I like you . . . very much . . . why don't we face your going when we get there?' It was a philosophy of his, live for today, live for now, don't borrow trouble from the future.

'And in the meantime?' She wanted guarantees that no-one would get hurt, but even William couldn't promise her that, no matter how much he liked her. He knew neither her history nor what the future held for them.

'Why don't we just see . . . Will you have dinner with me?'

She hesitated, looking up at him, not because she didn't want to, but because she did, too much so. 'Yes, I will,' she said slowly.

'Thank you.' He looked at her quietly for what seemed like a long time, and then they stood up, and the men at the desk noticed how handsome they were, and how well they looked together. 'I'll pick you up at eight o'clock then.'

'I'll meet you downstairs.' She smiled as he walked her to the elevator.

'I'd rather come up to your rooms. I don't want you waiting alone here.' He was always protective of her, always careful and thoughtful.

'All right.' She smiled at him again, and he kissed her on the cheek again when the elevator came, and took off across the lobby with a long stride and a wave, and Sarah rode upstairs, trying not to feel her heart pound in anticipation.

Chapter 6

The bell to their suite rang at exactly five past eight, and Sarah had no way of knowing that William had been waiting downstairs for the past ten minutes. Her parents hadn't minded her not going to the theater with them, particularly since she was going out with William.

She opened the door to him in a black satin dress, which molded her slim figure like a sheet of black ice that had been poured on her, with a thin edging of rhinestones.

'My God, Sarah! You look amazing.' She had worn her hair swept high on her head, with waves and curls that seemed to cascade loosely as she moved, giving the impression that if you pulled one pin, her mass of dark hair would pour like a waterfall past her shoulders. 'You're extraordinary!' He took a step back to admire her, and she laughed shyly. It was the first time she had been truly alone with him, except in the arbor in the country when they'd met, but even there, there had been other people around them.

'You look very handsome too.' He had worn one of his many dinner jackets, and a beautiful silk vest that had been his father's, and looped across it was a narrow diamond watch chain that had been a gift to his uncle from Czar Nicholas of Russia. As they drove to the restaurant in his car, he explained the story of it to her. Apparently the chain had been sewn into the hem of the gown of a grand duchess and spirited out of Russia. 'You are related to everyone!' she marvelled, intrigued by the story. Thinking

95

of it conjured up images of kings and czars, and fascinating royalty.

'Yes, I am,' he said, looking amused, 'and let me assure you, some of them are really perfectly awful.' He had driven the car himself tonight, because he wanted to be alone with her, and didn't want to be burdened with a driver. He had chosen a quiet restaurant, and they were expecting him. The headwaiter took them to a quiet table in the rear, and addressed him repeatedly as 'Your Grace', bowing slightly to both of them as he left them alone at the table. Champagne appeared instantly, and William had ordered their dinner for them when he made the reservation. They had caviar first, on tiny wedges of toast, with exquisite little wedges of lemon, and salmon after that, in a delicate sauce, followed by pheasant, salad, cheese, soufflé au Grand Marnier, and tiny little buttery French cookies.

'My God, I can't move,' she complained with a smile as she looked at him. It had been a wonderful dinner, and a lovely evening. He had talked about his parents to her, and how much they meant to him, and how distressed his mother had been several years before when he showed no interest in getting married.

'I'm afraid I've been a great disappointment to her,' he said unrepentantly. 'But I refuse to marry the wrong woman, simply to please my relatives, or have children. I think my parents having me so late always gave me the impression that I could do anything I wanted for a very long time, and still make up for it later.'

'You can. You're right not to let yourself make a mistake.' But as she said it, he saw the same mysterious sadness.

'And you, Sarah? Are they pressing you to marry yet?' She had already told him about Peter and Jane, and their babies.

'Not lately. My parents have been very understanding.'

About her mistakes . . . her disasters . . . her disgrace . . .
She looked away from him as she said it. He reached out a
hand to her then, and closed her fingers in his own strong
ones.

'Why is it you never tell me what it is that has been so
painful?' It was difficult for either of them to remember
that they had only known each other for two days. It
already seemed as though they had known each other
forever.

'What makes you think I've been in pain?' She tried to
fob him off, but he would have none of it, and his touch
stayed firm but gentle on her fingers.

'Because I see whatever it is you're hiding from me. I
don't see it clearly. But it lurks there, like a ghost, always
in the shadows, waiting to haunt you. Is it so terrible that
you can't share it with me?' She didn't know what to
answer him, she didn't dare tell him the truth, and her
eyes filled with tears as he asked the question.

'I . . . I'm sorry . . .' She freed her hand from his, to
dab her eyes with her napkin. And their waiter disappeared discreetly. 'It's just . . . it's such an ugly thing
. . . You would never feel the same way about me again. I
haven't met anyone since . . . it happened . . .'

'My God, what *is* it? Did you murder someone? Kill a
relative, a friend? Even at that, it must have been an
accident. Sarah, you must not do this to yourself.' He took
both her hands in his own and held them in his strong
grasp so that she would feel protected. 'I'm sorry, I don't
mean to pry, but it hurts me to see you suffer.'

'How can it?' She smiled unbelievingly, through her
tears. 'You don't even know me.' It was true, and yet they
both knew he did. They knew each other better after two
days than some people after a lifetime.

'I did a terrible thing,' she admitted to him, holding
tightly to his hands, and he didn't flinch, or waver, or
withdraw them.

'I don't believe that. I think *you* think it was terrible. But I would wager that no-one else does.'

'You're wrong,' she said wistfully, and then sighed and looked back at him, but she withdrew her hands as she did so. 'I was married two years ago. I made a huge mistake, and I tried to live by it. I tried everything. I was determined to stay with him, and die trying if I had to.' William seemed unaffected by the news she had expected to rock him so badly.

'And are you still married to him?' he asked quietly, still offering his hands to her, if she wanted to take them, but she didn't. She knew she couldn't now. When he heard all of it, he would no longer want her. But she owed it to him to tell him.

'We have been separated for over a year. In November, the divorce will be final.' She said it like a sentence for murder.

'I'm sorry,' he said seriously. 'Sorry for you, Sarah. I can only imagine how difficult it must have been, and how unhappy you must have been for the past year.' He wondered if her husband had left her for someone else, or what had come between them.

'Did you love him very much?' he asked hesitantly, not wanting to pry, but needing to know it. He needed to know if the pain she felt was longing for him, or simply regret, but she shook her head at him in answer.

'To be honest with you, I'm not sure I ever loved him. I knew him all my life, and it seemed the right thing to do then. I liked him, but I didn't really know him. And the moment we came back from our honeymoon, everything fell apart, and I realized what a mistake I'd made. All he wanted to do was to be out night and day, playing with his friends, chasing other women and drinking.' The tone of sorrow in her voice told him volumes. She didn't tell him about the baby she'd lost, or the prostitutes he'd brought to their anniversary party at her parents'. But he saw in her eyes that she'd suffered far more than she'd told him. She looked away, and William touched her hands again, and waited until she looked at him. Her eyes were full of memories and questions.

'I'm sorry, Sarah,' William said quietly. 'He must be a complete fool.' Sarah smiled and sighed again, feeling relieved, but not redeemed. She knew she would always feel guilty for being divorced, but continuing her life with him would have destroyed her, and she knew it. 'Is this the terrible sin you were hiding from me?' She nodded and he smiled at her. 'How can you be so foolish? This isn't the last century. Other people have become divorced. Would you rather have stayed with him and suffered that torture?'

'No, but I've felt terribly guilty toward my parents. It's been so embarrassing for them. No-one in our family has ever been divorced before. And they've been so incredibly nice about it. I know they must be ashamed, to some extent, but they've never criticized me for it.' Her voice drifted off as he watched her.

'Did they object at first?' he asked bluntly.

'No, not at all.' She shook her head. 'In fact, they encouraged me.' She thought back to the family meeting in Southampton, the morning after her disastrous anniversary party. 'Actually, my father did everything. They were wonderful, but it must have been agonizing for them to face their friends in New York.'

'Did they say that?'

'No. They were too kind to reproach me.'

'And have you faced their friends again, and your own, and been punished for your crime?' She shook her head, and smiled at the way he put it.

'No.' She laughed, suddenly sounding young again, and her heart felt lighter than it had in years. 'I've been hiding on Long Island.'

'Foolish girl. I'm quite sure that if you'd had the

courage to go back to New York, you would have found that everyone applauded your leaving that rotter.'

'I don't know.' She sighed again. 'I haven't seen anyone . . . until now . . . until you . . .'

'How fortunate for me, Miss Sarah Thompson. What a silly, silly girl you've been. I can't believe you've been in mourning for an entire year for a man you don't even think you loved. Sarah, really' – he looked both incensed and amused – 'how *could* you?'

'Divorce is no small thing to me,' she defended herself. 'I kept worrying that people would think that it was like that awful woman who married your cousin.'

'What?' William looked stunned. 'End up like Wallis Simpson? With five million dollars worth of jewels, a house in France, and a husband, however stupid he may have been, who adores her? My God, Sarah, what a ghastly fate, I *hope* not!' It was clear that he was teasing her, but not entirely, and they both laughed.

'I'm serious,' she scolded him, but she was still laughing.

'So am I. Do you really think she ended up so badly?'

'No. But look at what people think of her. I don't want to be like that.' She looked serious again as she said it.

'You couldn't, you goose. She forced a king to give up a throne. You're an honest woman who made a terrible mistake, married a fool, and made it right again. What man, or woman for that matter, could hold that against you? Oh, I'm sure someone will one day, some damn fool who's got nothing better to do than point a finger. Well, to hell with them. I wouldn't give a damn about your divorce, if I were you. When you go back to New York, you ought to shout it from the rooftops. If I were in your shoes, it's marrying him I'd be ashamed of.' She smiled at the way he looked at things, but in some ways, she hoped he was right, and she felt better than she had in a year. Maybe he was right, maybe it wasn't going to be as awful as she had feared.

And then suddenly, she laughed at him. 'If you make me feel better about all this, how am I going to go back to my life as a recluse in my farmhouse?' He poured her another glass of champagne as she smiled at him, and he looked at her seriously for a long moment.

'We'll have to talk about that again sometime. I'm not sure I find that prospect quite as charming as I did when you first told me.'

'Why not?'

'Because you're using it as an escape from life. You might as well go into a convent.' And then he rolled his eyes as he took a sip of champagne again. 'What a revolting waste. God, don't even let me think of it, or I might get really angry.'

'About the convent or the farmhouse?' she teased. He had given her an incredible gift. He was the first person she'd told about the divorce, and he hadn't been shocked, or horrified, or even startled. For her, it was the first step to freedom.

'Both. Let's not talk about it any more. I want to take you dancing.'

'That sounds like a good idea.' Apart from on the boat, she hadn't danced in over a year, and all of a sudden the idea was extremely appealing. 'If I can still dance.'

'I'll remind you,' he offered as he signed the check. And a few minutes later they were on their way to Café de Paris, where his entrance with her made quite a stir, and everyone seemed to go running in a dozen directions to assist him. 'Yes, Your Grace,' 'Absolutely, Your Grace,' 'Good evening, Your Grace.' William began to look extremely bored by it, and Sarah was amused at his expression.

'It can't be as bad as all that. Now, be nice about it,' she said soothingly, as they made their way to the dance floor.

'You have no idea how tedious it becomes. I suppose it's fine if you're ninety years old, but at my age, it's quite awkward. Actually, come to think of it, even my father, at eighty-five, said it bored him.'

'That's life.' She grinned as they began dancing to the strains of 'That Old Feeling', which had been popular since the previous winter. She felt stiff on the dance floor with him at first, but after a little while they moved around the floor as though they had been dancing with each other for years, and she discovered that he was particularly adept at the tango and the rhumba.

'You're very good,' he complimented her. 'Are you sure you've really been in hiding for a year? Or just taking dancing lessons on Long Island?'

'Very funny, William. That was your foot I just stepped on.'

'Nonsense. It was my toe. You're getting much better!'

They laughed and talked and danced until two o'clock in the morning, and as he drove her home she yawned and smiled sleepily at him, then she leaned her head against his shoulder.

'I had such a good time tonight, William. Really, thank you.'

'I had an awful time,' he said, sounding convincing, but only for a moment. 'I had no idea I would be out with a fallen woman. Here I thought you were a nice young girl from New York, and what do I end up with? Used goods. My God, what a blow!' He shook his head mournfully as she swatted him with her handbag.

'Used goods! How dare you call me that!' She was half outraged, half amused, but they were both laughing and smiling.

'All right, then an "old divorcée", if you prefer. Not at all what I thought, in any case . . .' He continued to shake his head, and occasionally grin mischievously at her, and suddenly she began to worry that her status might mean to him that she would be easy prey, and he could use her casually for a few weeks until she left London. The very thought made her grow stiff, and move away from him as he drove her back to Claridge's. Her movement was so abrupt that he was instantly aware that something had happened, and he looked at her, puzzled, as they drew into Brook Street. 'What's wrong?'

'Nothing. I had a kink in my back.'

'You did not.'

'I did.' She looked insistent, but he still didn't believe her.

'I don't think you did. I think something crossed your mind again that upset you.'

'How could you say a thing like that?' How could he know her so well, after so little time? It still amazed her. 'That's absolutely not true.'

'Good. Because you worry more than anyone I've ever met, and it's all stuff and nonsense. If you spent more time thinking about the good things happening now, and less time about the bad things that might, or could, come later, and probably never will, you'll live a much longer, happier life.' He spoke to her almost like a father, and she shook her head as she listened.

'Thank you, Your Grace.'

'You're welcome, Miss Thompson.'

They had reached the hotel by then, and he hopped out of the car and opened the door for her and helped her out, as she wondered what he was going to do next, and if he was going to try to come upstairs. She had already long since decided that she wouldn't let him.

'Do you suppose your parents would let us do this again sometime?' he asked respectfully. 'Perhaps tomorrow night, if I explain to your father that you need some more work on your tango?' She looked at him tenderly. He was much more decent than she gave him credit for, and they had covered so much ground tonight. If nothing else, she knew that they would be friends after this, and she hoped, forever.

'They might. Would you like to come to Westminster Abbey with us tomorrow morning?'

'No' – he grinned honestly – 'but I will, with the greatest pleasure.' He wanted to see her, not the church. But seeing the Abbey was a small price to pay for being with her. 'And perhaps this weekend, we could take a drive out into the country.'

'I'd like that.' She smiled, and as she did, he looked down at her, and moved his lips very close to hers, and slowly kissed her. His arms went around her with surprising strength and he held her close to him, but not so close that she felt threatened in any way, or even frightened. And when he moved away from her at last, they were both breathless.

'I think there's a distinct possibility,' he whispered to her, 'that we're both too old for this . . . but I love it.' He loved the tenderness of it, the promise of what might come later.

He took her to the elevator then, and longed to kiss her again, but thought better of it. He didn't want to draw the desk clerks' attention. 'I'll see you in the morning,' he whispered to her, and she nodded as he leaned slowly toward her. She turned her eyes up to his, wondering what he would say to her, and her heart stopped as she heard the words. They were barely more than a whisper, and it was so soon. But he couldn't stop them. 'I love you, Sarah.'

She wanted to tell him that she loved him, too, but he had already stepped back again, and the elevator doors closed quickly between them.

Chapter 7

They went to Westminster Abbey, as planned, the next day, and the elder Thompsons sensed that something had passed between the two young people. Sarah seemed more subdued than she had been before, and William looked at her differently, in a more possessive way. Victoria Thompson whispered anxiously to her husband as they strolled briefly away.

'Do you suppose something's wrong?' she asked him worriedly in an undertone. 'Sarah seems upset today.'

'I have no idea,' her father said coolly, as William returned to point out some small detail of architecture to them. As he had in the Tower, he regaled them here with private tales of the royals, and interesting details about the various monarchs. He referred to the coronation the year before, and made a couple of benevolent comments about his cousin Bertie. 'Bertie' was now the king, in spite of all his protestations. Having never been prepared for the role, he had been horrified when his brother David abdicated as King Edward.

They walked among the tombs afterwards, and here again, Sarah's mother thought she was being unusually quiet. The older Thompsons went back inside, and left the two young people alone. And as they left, they saw Sarah and William deep in what looked like a serious conversation.

'You're upset, aren't you?' He looked frightened and worried as he took her hands in his own. 'I shouldn't have said what I did, should I?' But he had never felt like this before, with anyone, not as strongly, and certainly never as quickly. He felt like a boy, head over heels in love with her, and he couldn't stop the words as he said them. 'I'm sorry, Sarah . . . I love you . . . I know it sounds quite mad, and you must think I'm crazy. But I do. I love everything you are and think and want . . .' He looked truly worried about her. 'And I don't want to lose you.'

She turned anguished eyes to him, and it was obvious from the way she looked that she loved him, too, but it was equally obvious that she didn't want to. 'How can you say that? About losing me, I mean . . . You can never have me. I'm a divorced woman. And you're in line to the throne. All we'll ever have is this . . . friendship . . . or a casual flirtation.'

He rocked back on his heels for a moment as he looked at her, and there was the hint of a smile on his face as he did so. 'My dear girl, if you call this casual, I would very much like you to explain to me what you consider serious. I have never been this serious about anyone in my life, and we've just met. This, my darling, is not my view of a "casual flirtation".'

'All right, all right.' She smiled in spite of herself, and she looked more beautiful than ever. 'You know what I mean. It can't go anywhere. Why are we torturing ourselves like this? We should just be friends. I'm going back soon, and you have your own life here.'

'And you? What life are you going back to?' He looked abysmally upset at what she was saying. 'Your miserable farmhouse, where you will live out your days like an old woman? Don't be absurd!'

'William, I'm *divorced*! Or I will be. You're a fool even to pursue this as far as you have,' she said in obvious anguish.

'I want you to know that I don't give a damn about your divorce,' he said heatedly. 'It means absolutely nothing to me, almost as little as the damn succession you're so

106

everlastingly worried about. That's what this is all about, isn't it? You've got yourself confused again with that fool who married David.' He meant, of course, the Duchess of Windsor, and they both knew it. And he was right. Sarah did have herself confused with her again, but she was extremely tenacious about her opinions.

'It has to do with tradition and responsibility. You can't just fly in the face of all that. You can't ignore it, or pretend it's not there, and neither can I. It's like driving down a road at full speed and pretending there isn't a brick wall running straight across your path. It's there, William, whether you want to see it or not, it's there, and sooner or later that wall is going to hurt us both very badly, if we don't stop soon, before it's too late.' She didn't want to hurt anyone. Not him or herself. She didn't want to fall head over heels in love with him, and then lose him because she couldn't have him. There was just no point, no matter how much she thought she already loved him, or he her.

'What would you suggest then?' He looked mournfully at her, he didn't like any of what she was saying. 'That we stop now? That we not see each other any more? By God, I won't do that, unless you can look me in the eye and tell me this isn't happening to you, too, and you don't love me.' He pulled at her hands, and looked her in the eyes, until she couldn't face him any longer.

'I can't say that,' she whispered softly, and then she raised her eyes to his again. 'But perhaps we should just be friends. That's all this can ever be. I'd rather have you as my friend forever, William, than lose you. But if we persist in this, rushing headlong into something so dangerous and foolish, sooner or later, everyone you know and love will turn on you, and on me, and it will be disastrous.'

'What faith you have in my family. My mother is half French, you know, and she's always thought the thing about the succession was incredibly stupid. Fourteenth in line to the throne, my darling, is hardly overwhelming. I could give it up in an instant, and never miss it, and neither would anyone else.'

'I would never let you.'

'Oh, please . . . for God's sake, Sarah. I'm a grown man, and you have to believe that I know what I'm doing. And right now, your worries are really premature and absurd.' He tried to make light of it, but they both knew she was right. He would have given the succession up for her in an instant if he thought she would marry him, but he was afraid to ask her. He had too much at stake to want to risk it all too quickly. He had never asked anyone to marry him, and he already knew how much he loved Sarah. 'Good God, it's really quite amazing.' He teased her as they went back into the Abbey to look for her parents. 'Half the girls in England would kill someone to be a duchess, and you won't even speak to me for fear it's a disease you might catch.' He started to laugh then, thinking of how pursued he had always been, and how reluctant and kind this girl was. 'I do love you, you know. I really do love you, Sarah Thompson.' He pulled her firmly into his arms then, for all the world to see, as he kissed her amidst the splendor of Westminster Abbey.

'William . . .' She started to protest and then gave in to him, breathlessly overwhelmed by the sheer power and magnetism of him. And when he pulled away again at last, she looked up at him, and for an instant forgot all her reservations.

'I love you, too . . . but I still think we're both crazy.'

'We are.' He smiled happily, as he put his arm around her shoulders and walked her back toward the main entrance to the Abbey, to find her parents. 'But may it be a madness from which we never recover,' he whispered softly, and Sarah didn't answer.

'Where have you two been?' Edward pretended to be

concerned, but in truth he wasn't. He could see from the look in their eyes that they were closer than ever, and all was going well.

'Talking . . . wandering along . . . your daughter is very distracting.'

'I'll have a word with her later.' Edward smiled at them both, and the two men walked along together for a time, chatting about Edward's bank, and how America viewed the possibility of war. And William told him about his recent trip to Munich.

They had lunch together at Old Cheshire Cheese at Wine Office Court, and had pigeon pie. And after that, William had to leave them.

'I'm afraid I promised my solicitors I would spend the afternoon with them, a dreary necessity from time to time.' He apologized for deserting them, and asked Sarah if she would join him again for dinner and dancing that night. She hesitated, and he looked woebegone. 'Just as friends . . . one more time . . .' he lied, and she laughed at him. She already knew him better than to believe that.

'You're impossible.'

'Perhaps. But you need some serious work on your tango.' They both laughed at that, remembering how many times she had faltered in his arms. 'We'll see to it tonight, shall we?'

'All right.' She agreed grudgingly, wondering to herself how she was ever going to resist him. He was a remarkable man, and she had never been so taken with anyone, certainly not Freddie Van Deering. That had seemed so right at the time, but she had been so stupid and young, and this was wrong, too, in a different way, and yet she had never loved anyone more or felt that she knew anyone better than she had already come to know him.

'He's a charming young man,' her mother said to her, as Edward dropped them off again at Hardy Amies. Sarah couldn't disagree with her. She just didn't want to ruin his life and her own by falling headlong into a romance that could go nowhere. Despite William's willingness to throw caution to the winds, for his sake, she wasn't willing to be as hasty. But she forgot her fears by that afternoon, when her mother bought her a fabulous white satin dress that set off her dark hair and creamy skin and her green eyes to perfection.

When William saw her in it that night, he stared at her, she looked so lovely. 'Good God, you look positively dangerous in that, Sarah. I'm not at all sure you should let me take you out. I must say, your parents are really very trusting.'

'I told them not to be, but you seem to have them completely in your thrall,' she teased as they went outside. This time he had brought his driver and the Bentley.

'You really look remarkable, my dear.' She looked every bit a princess.

'Thank you.' She smiled happily at him.

Once again, they had a wonderful time, and she decided to relax with him. He was fun to be with, she liked his friends that they met, and they were all charming to her. They danced all night, and she finally mastered both the rhumba and the tango, and in the dress she wore, she was quite extraordinary to watch on the dance floor with William.

He took her home at two o'clock again, and the evening seemed to have sped past them like moments. She seemed more relaxed with him, and he was totally at ease with her. And tonight they never mentioned her concerns, or his feelings. It was a pleasant, easy night with him, and when they reached the hotel, she found that she hated to leave him to go upstairs.

'And what monument are you visiting tomorrow, my dear?' She smiled at the way he said it.

'None. We were going to stay here and rest. Father has business to do, and he's having lunch with an old friend, and Mother and I were going to do absolutely nothing.'

'That sounds very appealing.' He looked at her seriously. 'Could I induce you to do nothing with me? Perhaps a little ride in the country for a bit of fresh air?'

She hesitated, and then nodded again. In spite of all her cautions to herself, she knew now that she couldn't resist him. And she had almost decided not to try until they left London.

He picked her up before lunch the next day, in a custom-built Bugatti she had never seen him drive before. And they set off toward Gloucestershire, as he mentioned points of interest to her, and kept her amused as he was driving.

'Where are we going anyway?'

'To one of the oldest country seats in England.' He looked very serious as she listened. 'The main house dates back to the fourteenth century, a bit dreary, I'm afraid, but there are several other houses on the property that are a wee bit more modern. The largest of them was built by Sir Christopher Wren in the eighteenth century, and it's really very lovely. There are extensive stables, a farm, and a sweet hunting box. I think you'll like it.' It sounded very pretty to her, and then she turned to him with a question.

'It sounds wonderful, William. Who lives there?'

He hesitated, and then grinned at her. 'Me. Well, actually, I spend as little time there as possible, but my mother lives there all the time. She lives in the main house. And I prefer the hunting box, it's a bit more rugged. I thought you might like to have lunch with her, as long as you had a bit of spare time.'

'William! You're taking me to have lunch with your mother, and you didn't tell me!' Sarah looked horrified, and suddenly a little frightened by what he had done.

'She's quite nice, I promise you,' he said innocently. 'I really think you'll like her.'

'But what on earth will she think of me? Why does she

think we're coming to lunch?' She was afraid of him again, and of their unbridled feelings, and where they might lead.

'I told her you were desperately hungry. Actually, I rang her yesterday and told her that I'd like her to meet you before you left.'

'Why?' Sarah looked at him accusingly.

'Why?' He looked surprised as he answered her. 'Because you're a friend of mine and I like you.'

'Is that all you said?' she growled at him, and waited for an answer.

'Actually, no, I told her we were getting married on Saturday, and I thought it would be nice if she met the next Duchess of Whitfield before the wedding.'

'William, stop it! I'm serious! I don't want her to think I'm chasing you, or that I'm going to ruin your life.'

'Oh no, I told her about that too. I told her you would come to lunch, but you absolutely refuse to take the title.'

'William!' she screeched, suddenly laughing at him. 'What are you doing to me?'

'Nothing yet, my darling, but how I'd like to!'

'You are impossible! You should have told me we were coming here. I didn't even wear a dress!' She had worn slacks and a silk blouse, and in some circles that was considered pretty racy. Sarah felt sure the dowager Duchess of Whitfield would disapprove when she saw her.

'I told her you were American, that will explain everything.' He teased as he pretended to soothe her, actually he thought she had taken it rather well. He had been a little worried that she would be even more upset than she was when he told her he was taking her to have lunch with his mother, but actually she had been quite a good sport.

'Did you tell her I'm getting divorced, too, since you seem to have told her everything else?'

'Damn, I forgot.' He grinned. 'But do be sure to tell her

over lunch. She'll want to hear all about it.' He smiled at her, more in love with her than ever. And totally indifferent now to her fears and objections.

'You are truly disgusting,' she accused him.

'Thank you, my love. Ever at your service.' He smiled.

They reached the main entrance to the property shortly after that, and Sarah was impressed by how handsome it was. The property was surrounded by tall rock walls that looked as though they had been put there by the Normans. The buildings and the trees looked very old, and everything was impeccably kept up. The scale of it was a little overwhelming. The main house looked more like a fortress than a home, but as they drove past the hunting box where William stayed with his friends, she saw how charming it was. It was larger than their house on Long Island. And the house where his mother lived was beautiful, and filled with lovely French and English antiques, and Sarah was startled to meet the tiny, frail, but still beautiful Duchess of Whitfield.

'I'm happy to meet you, Your Grace,' Sarah said nervously, not sure if she should curtsy or shake her hand, but the older woman took her hand carefully in her own and held it.

'And I you, my dear, William said you are a lovely girl, and I see he's quite right. Do come in.' She led the way inside, walking well but with a cane. The cane had been Queen Victoria's, and had recently been given her by Bertie, as a small gift when he came to visit.

She showed Sarah around the three downstairs sitting rooms, and then they walked outside into the garden. It was a warm, sunny day, in a summer that had been unseasonably warm for England.

'Will you be here for long, my dear?' his mother asked pleasantly, but Sarah shook her head with regret.

'We are leaving for Italy next week. We'll be back in London for a few days at the end of August before we sail, but that's it. My father has to be back in New York at the beginning of September.'

'William tells me that he's a banker. My father was a banker too. And did William tell you that his father was head of the House of Lords? He was a wonderful man . . . he looked a great deal like William.' She looked up at her son with obvious pride, and William smiled at her, and put an arm around her with open affection.

'It's not nice to brag, Mother,' he teased, and it was obvious that she thought the world of him. He had been the delight of her life from the moment he was born, he was the ultimate reward in an extremely long and happy marriage.

'I'm not bragging. I just thought Sarah would like to know about your father. Perhaps one day you will follow in his footsteps.'

'Not likely, Mother. That's too much of a headache by half. I'll fill my seat, but I don't think I'll ever run it.'

'You might surprise yourself one day.' She smiled again at Sarah, and a little while later they went in to lunch. She was a charming woman, amazingly alert for her age, and she clearly doted on William. She didn't seem to cling to him, or complain that he wasn't attentive enough, or that she never saw him. She seemed perfectly content to let him lead his life, and she seemed to take great pleasure in hearing about it from him. She told Sarah about some of his more amusing youthful escapades, and how well he had done when he was at Eton. He had gone to Cambridge after that, and read History and Politics and Economics.

'Yes, and now all I do is go to dinner parties, and do the tango. Fascinating how useful an education is.' But Sarah already knew he did more than that. He ran his estates, the very profitable farm, and was active in the House of Lords; he travelled, he was well-read, and he was still fascinated by politics. He was an interesting man, and

Sarah hated to admit to herself that she liked everything about him. She even liked his mother. And his mother seemed enchanted by Sarah.

The three of them went for a long walk in the gardens in the afternoon, and Annabelle Whitfield told Sarah all about her childhood in Cornwall, as well as her visits to her maternal grandparents in France, and their summers in Deauville. 'Sometimes I really miss it,' she confessed with a nostalgic smile at the two young people.

'We were just there in July. It's still lovely.' Sarah smiled back at her.

'I'm glad to hear that. I haven't been back in fifty years now.' She smiled at her son. 'Once William came, I stayed home. I wanted to be with him every moment, hovering over him, marvelling at his every word and sound. It almost killed me when the poor child went to Eton. I tried to convince George to keep him here with me, with a tutor, but he insisted, and I suppose it was just as well. It would have been too boring for him at home, with his old mother.' She looked at him lovingly and he kissed her cheek.

'It was never boring at home with you, Mother, and you know it. I adored you. And still do.'

'Foolish boy.' She smiled, always happy to hear it.

They left Whitfield late in the afternoon, and the duchess asked Sarah to come back and see her again before she left England. 'Perhaps after your trip to Italy, my dear. I would love to hear all about it when you get back to London.'

'I'd love to come and see you.' Sarah smiled at her. She had had a lovely time, and she and William chatted about it on the way back to London. 'She's wonderful.' Sarah smiled at him, thinking about the things his mother had said. She had been welcoming and warm, and sincerely interested in Sarah.

'She is wonderful, isn't she? She hasn't got a mean bone

in her body. I've never seen her angry at anyone, except perhaps me' – he laughed at the memories – 'or unkind, or speak to anyone in the heat of anger. And she absolutely adored my father, and he her. It's a shame you couldn't meet him, too, but I'm awfully glad you had the time to come and meet my mother.' The look in his eyes said something more to her, but Sarah pretended to ignore it. She didn't dare allow herself to feel any closer to him than she already did.

'I'm glad that you brought me,' Sarah said softly.

'So was she. She really liked you.' He glanced over at her, touched by how frightened she was.

'She would have really loved me if she knew I was divorced, wouldn't she?' Sarah said ruefully as he skillfully handled a sharp turn in the road in his Bugatti.

'I don't think she'd mind at all, you know,' he said honestly.

'Well, I'm glad you decided not to test that.' She smiled again, relieved. But he couldn't resist the opportunity to tease her.

'I thought you were going to tell her at lunch.'

'I forgot. I'll do it next time. I promise,' Sarah teased him back.

'Capital. She'll be excited to hear it.' They laughed and enjoyed each other's company for the rest of the trip home, and he left her at the hotel with regret. That evening she was dining with her parents and their friends. But William had insisted on seeing Sarah the next day, first thing in the morning.

'Don't you have something else to do?' She teased him again as he asked her, while they stood in front of Claridge's, looking like two very happy, windblown young lovers.

'Not this week. I want to spend every moment I can with you, until you leave for Rome. Unless you have an objection.' She thought she should object, for his sake, but she really didn't want to. He was too appealing and his lures were too strong.

'Hyde Park then, tomorrow morning? And then the National Gallery, a short drive to Richmond after that, and a walk in Kew Gardens. And lunch at the Berkeley Hotel.' He had it all planned, and she laughed at him. She didn't care where they went, just so she could be with him. She was getting swept up in being with him constantly, and in spite of all her fears of their getting too involved, she found herself swept along in the excitement of being with him. He was difficult to resist, but they'd be gone soon anyway. And then she would have to force herself to forget him. But what harm was there in a little happiness for a few days? Why not, after all the time she'd spent alone for the past year, and the miserable year she'd spent before that.

For the rest of their time in London, William went almost everywhere with them. He had an occasional business meeting that couldn't be postponed, now and then, but for the most part he was at their disposal. He and Edward had lunch together at White's, William's club, on their last day in town.

'Was it fun?' Sarah asked her father when he returned.

'William was very kind. And it's a marvelous club.' But it wasn't the atmosphere or the food he had liked most about the lunch, it was the man, and what he had said to him. 'He's taking us all out to dinner tonight, and then he's taking you dancing. I imagine Italy will be awfully quiet for you without him, after all this,' he said seriously, anxious to see her expression when she answered.

'Well, I'll get used to that, won't I?' she said firmly. 'This has been fun, and he's awfully kind, but it can't go on forever.' She hugged her father and left the room, and that night they all went to the Savoy Grill for dinner. William was charming company, as usual, and Sarah was in good form too. And after dinner, they dropped off her parents at the hotel, and went on to the Four Hundred Club for the promised dancing.

But she was quiet in his arms tonight, despite all her attempts at gaiety before that. It was easy to see how sad she already was, and finally they went back to their table, and held hands as they talked quietly long into the night.

'Will it be as hard for you next week as it will for me?' he asked her, and she nodded. 'I don't know what I'm going to do without you, Sarah.' They had grown so close to each other in these few short weeks. It still amazed both of them that they had become so close so quickly. William was still trying to absorb it. He'd never known or loved anyone like her.

'You'll find something else to do.' She smiled valiantly. 'Maybe you'll just have to get a job as a guide at the British Museum or the Tower of London.'

'What a good idea!' he teased, and then put an arm around her shoulder and held her close. 'I shall miss you terribly for the next three weeks, and then you'll have such a short time back in London. Barely a week.' The thought of it saddened him. She nodded silently. She wished a great many things, that they had met years before, that she were English, that there had never been a Freddie. But wishing wouldn't change anything, and she had to brace herself to leave now. It was so hard to do, so hard to imagine not seeing him day after day, laughing and teasing, and taking her to new places, or to meet his friends, or even to see the Crown Jewels in the Tower of London, or visit his mother at Whitfield, or simply to sit somewhere quietly and talk.

'Maybe you'll come to New York one day,' she said wistfully, knowing that it wasn't very likely. And even if he did, his visit would be too short.

'I might!' He gave her a brief ray of hope. 'If we don't get ourselves into trouble in Europe. The "supreme leader" in Germany might make transatlantic travel difficult one of these days, you never know.' He was convinced there would be a war eventually, and Edward Thompson didn't disagree with him. 'Perhaps I should plan to come before that.' But Sarah knew that seeing William in New York was a distant dream, one that would probably never come. It was time to say goodbye now, and she knew it. Even if she saw him again when she got back from Italy, by then things would already be different between them. They had to take their distance from each other now, and resume their own lives.

They did a last tango, and executed it perfectly, but even that didn't make Sarah smile. And then they had one more 'last dance', cheek to cheek, both of them lost in their own thoughts, and when they went back to their table, he kissed her for a long, long time.

'I love you so, sweet girl. I really can't bear to leave you.' They had both behaved admirably for the entire two weeks, and there had never been any question of doing anything different. 'What am I going to do for the rest of my life without you?'

'Be happy . . . have a good life . . . get married . . . have ten children . . .' She was only half teasing him. 'Will you write to me?' she asked wistfully.

'On the hour. I promise. Perhaps your parents will hate Italy and come back to London sooner,' he said hopefully.

'I doubt that.' And so did he.

'You know, Mussolini is almost as bad as Hitler, from what everyone tells me.'

'I don't think he's expecting us.' She smiled. 'In fact, I'm not even sure we'll see him while we're there.' She was teasing him again, but she didn't know what more to say to William. Everything they had to say to each other was too painful.

They drove back to her hotel in silence, and tonight he had driven himself. He didn't want his driver intruding on his last moments with Sarah. They sat in his car for a long time, talking quietly about what they'd done, what they would like to do, what they might have done, and what they would do when she came back to London before she sailed.

'I'll spend every minute with you until you sail, and that's a promise.' She smiled as she looked up at him, he was so aristocratic and so handsome. The Duke of Whitfield. Perhaps one day she would tell her grand-children how she had loved him years before. But more than ever she knew she couldn't cost him his succession.

'I'll write to you from Italy,' she promised him, not sure what she'd say. She'd have to confine herself to telling him what they were doing. She couldn't allow herself to tell him all she felt. She was firm in her resolve not to encourage him to do something crazy.

'If I can get through, I'll call you.' And then he took her in his arms and held her. 'My darling . . . how I love you.' She closed her eyes, as tears rolled slowly down her cheeks while they kissed.

'I love you too . . .' she said as their lips parted for the merest moment. She saw that there were tears in his eyes, too, and she gently touched his cheek with her fingertips. 'We have to be good about this, you know. We have no choice. You have responsibilities in your life, William. You can't ignore them.'

'Yes, I can,' he said softly. 'And what if we did have a choice?' It was the closest he'd ever come to promising her a future.

'We don't have a choice.' She put a finger to his lips and then kissed him. 'Don't do this, William. I won't let you.'

'Why not?'

'Because I love you,' she said firmly.

'Then why won't you give us what we both want, and talk about the future.'

'There can't be a future for us, William,' she said sadly.

And when he helped her from the car, they walked

slowly across the lobby, hand in hand. She had worn the white satin dress again, and she looked extravagantly lovely. His eyes seemed to pore over her, as though drinking in every detail so that he would never forget her once she was gone.

'I'll see you soon.' He kissed her again, in plain sight of the men at the desk in the lobby. 'Don't forget how much I love you,' he said softly, and he kissed her once more, as she told him that she loved him. It was agony getting into the elevator without him. The doors closed heavily, and as she rose with it, she felt as though her heart were being torn from her chest.

He stood in the lobby staring at the elevator doors for a long time, and then he turned and went back outside to the waiting Daimler, with an unhappy but determined look. She was stubborn, even if she thought she was doing the right thing for him, but William Whitfield was more so.

Chapter 8

The ride to Rome on the train seemed absolutely endless to Sarah. She was silent and pale, and her parents spoke in hushed tones to each other, but seldom spoke to her. They both knew how unhappy and how uninterested in conversation she was. William had called her just before they left for Victoria Station. The conversation had been brief, but there had been tears on her cheeks as she picked up her handbag and left the room. No matter how much they cared for each other, she knew that this was the beginning of their ultimate separation. She knew better than anyone how hopeless the situation was, and how foolish she had been to let herself fall in love with William. And now she would have to pay the price, suffer for a while, and force herself to forget him in the end. She wasn't sure she wanted to see him again when they went back to London before they sailed. It was possible that seeing him at all would just be too painful.

She stared out the window as they rode on the train, forcing herself to think of Peter and Jane, and little James and Marjorie back home, and even Freddie. But no matter how hard she worked at distracting herself, she always found herself thinking of William . . . or his mother . . . or his friends . . . or the afternoon they'd spent at Whitfield . . . or the times they had kissed . . . or the nights they danced.

'Are you all right, dear?' her mother asked solicitously as they left her to go to the dining car for lunch. Sarah had absolutely insisted she wasn't hungry, and the steward was going to bring her a plate of fruit and a cup of tea, which she said was all she wanted. Her mother suspected she wouldn't even bother to eat that.

'I'm fine, Mother, really.'

But Victoria knew that she wasn't, and she told Edward over lunch how it worried her to see Sarah in so much pain again. She'd been through enough with Freddie without more heartbreak. And perhaps they shouldn't have let her indulge her little romance with the duke.

'Maybe it's important that she learn exactly what she feels about him now,' Edward said quietly.

'Why?' Victoria looked puzzled. 'What difference will that make?'

'One never knows what life will bring, Victoria, does one?' She wondered if William had said something to him, but without asking her husband, she decided that was unlikely. And after lunch, they went back to their compartment and found Sarah reading a book. It was *Brighton Rock* by Graham Greene, which had just come out, and William had given it to her for the long ride on the train. But she couldn't concentrate on it, she couldn't remember anyone's name. In fact, she had absolutely no idea what she was reading, and eventually, she put it away.

They passed through Dover, Calais, and Paris, where they switched to a connecting train, and long after midnight, Sarah lay awake in the dark, listening to the sound of the wheels as they rolled through northern Italy. And with each sound, each mile, each turn of the wheel, all she could think of was William and her moments with him. It was far worse than anything she had ever felt after Freddie, and the difference with William was that she really loved him, and she knew he loved her in return. It was just that the price of a future together would cost him too dearly, she knew, and she refused to let him pay it.

She awoke tired and pale, after only a few hours'

troubled sleep, as they rolled into the Stazione di Termini, overlooking the Piazza dei Cinquecento.

The Excelsior Hotel had sent a car to meet them there, and Sarah made her way indifferently toward the driver. She carried a small makeup case, her handbag, and she wore a large hat to shield herself from the Roman sun, but she was oblivious to everything around her. The driver pointed out various sights to them on the way to the hotel, the Baths of Diocletian and the Palazzo Barberini, and then the Borghese Gardens, as they approached the hotel. But in truth, she was sorry they had come, and she was dreading three weeks of sightseeing with her parents in Rome, Florence, and Venice, feeling the way she did after William.

When they reached the hotel, Sarah was relieved to be alone in her room for a while. She closed the door, and lay down on the bed with her eyes closed. But the moment she did, all she could think of was William again. It was almost like being haunted. She got up, splashed cold water on her face, combed her hair, took a bath, which felt heavenly after the long ride on the train, dressed again in a fresh cotton dress, and an hour later went to find her parents. They had bathed and changed, too, and everyone seemed to feel revived in spite of the crushing heat of Rome in August.

Her father had planned an outing to the Colosseum that afternoon, and the sun was blazing as they explored each minute detail. It was late in the afternoon when they got back to the hotel, and Sarah and her mother were feeling seriously wilted by the heat. Her father suggested they stop for something to drink before they went upstairs, and even that didn't really revive them. Sarah drank two lemonades, and she felt a hundred years old as she left the table to go back to her own room alone. She left them chatting there, over two glasses of wine, and she walked slowly back into the lobby, carrying the large straw hat she had been wearing since that morning, feeling vague, and thinking of nothing for once, which was a relief.

'Signorina Thompson?' One of the managers asked her discreetly as she passed the desk.

'Yes?' She was distracted as she glanced their way, wondering why they had called her.

'There is a message for you.' He extended an envelope to her, addressed in a strong, familiar hand, and she glanced at it, wondering absentmindedly how it had reached her so quickly. She opened it while still standing there, and all it said was 'I will love you forever, William.' She smiled as she read the words, and slowly folded the letter and put it back in the envelope, realizing that he must have mailed it to the hotel before she even left London. As she began to walk slowly up the stairs to the second floor, her heart was full of him. Visions of him were flooding into her head, as someone brushed past her.

'Sorry,' she murmured without looking up, and then suddenly she was literally swept off her feet and into someone's arms, and he was there, in Rome, in the hotel, and he was kissing her as though he would never let her go again. She couldn't believe what had just happened. 'What . . . I . . . you . . . *William*, where are you? . . . I mean . . . Oh my God, what are you doing?' She was breathless and totally shocked by what he'd done. But she was also very, very pleased, and he was delighted.

'I'm coming to spend three weeks in Italy with you, if you must know, you silly girl. You walked right by me in the lobby.' He had been pleased by how forlorn she looked. It was precisely how he had felt when he had left her at Claridge's in London. It had taken him less than an hour after that to decide to throw all caution to the wind and meet her in Rome. And seeing her now made him doubly glad he'd done it. 'I'm afraid I've got bad news for you, my dear.' He looked serious as he gently touched her cheek, and for an instant she was worried about his mother.

'What is it?'

'I don't think I can live without you.' He grinned broadly and she smiled in answer. They were still standing on the stairs, as people below them smiled, watching them talk and kiss. They were two very attractive young people in love, and it warmed people's hearts just to see them.

'Shouldn't we at least try to resist?' Sarah asked nobly, but she was too happy he had come to discourage him now.

'I couldn't bear it. It will be bad enough when you go to New York. Let's take the month and enjoy it.' He put his arms around her and kissed her again, just as her parents started up the stairs, and stopped to look at them in amazement. At first they couldn't see who he was, all they could see was their daughter in a man's embrace, but Edward knew instantly who it was, and he smiled at them with pleasure. They walked slowly up the stairs, and a moment later the four of them stood together. Sarah was flushed with happiness, and she was still holding William's hand as her parents reached them.

'You've come to guide us around Italy, I see,' Edward said to him with amusement. 'Very considerate of you, Your Grace. Thank you very much indeed for coming.'

'I felt it my duty,' William said, looking happy and a little sheepish.

'We've very happy to see you.' He spoke for them all, and clearly Sarah, who was beaming. 'It should be a much happier trip now. I'm afraid Sarah didn't think much of the Colosseum.' Sarah laughed, in fact, she had hated every moment without William.

'I'll try to do better tomorrow, Father.'

'I'm sure you will.' And then he turned to William. 'You have a room, I assume, Your Grace?' They were becoming good friends, and the elder Thompson liked him.

'I do, sir, an entire suite of them, I might add. Very handsome. My secretary made the accommodation, and God only knows what he told them. Second in line to the crown at the very least, judging by what they've done.' The four of them laughed and walked up the stairs, chattering amiably about where they should go for dinner. And as they walked, William gently squeezed her hand, thinking of the future.

Chapter 9

The time in Rome flew by on wings, visiting cathedrals, museums, Palatine Hill, and visiting some of William's friends in some very lovely villas. They went to the beach at Ostia, and dined in elegant restaurants, with an occasional foray into some quaint trattorias.

And at the end of the week they moved on to Florence, for more of the same. Until at last, in their third week, they went to Venice. And by then, William and Sarah were closer than ever and more in love. They seemed to think and move as one. To people who watched them and didn't know who they were, it would have been difficult to believe that they weren't married.

'It's been such fun,' Sarah said, as they sat by the swimming pool at the Royal Danieli late one afternoon. 'I love Venice,' she said. The entire trip had been like a honeymoon, except that her parents were there, and she and William had not done anything they shouldn't have, which hadn't been entirely easy for either of them. But at the outset, they had promised each other they'd behave.

'I love you desperately,' he said happily, soaking up the sun. He had never been happier in his life, and he knew for sure now that he would never leave her. 'I don't think you should go back to New York with your parents,' he said half jokingly, but he opened one eye to see her reaction to what he was saying.

'And what do you suggest I do instead? Move in with your mother at Whitfield?'

'That's a nice idea. But frankly, I'd prefer to have you

with me in London in the house there.' She smiled at him. She would have liked nothing more, but it was a dream that would never come to fruition.

'I wish I could, William,' she said softly, as he rolled over on his stomach and got up on his elbows to discuss the matter with her further.

'And just why is it that you can't? Remind me.' She had a long list of objections that he always pooh-poohed, the first of which was her divorce, and the second his succession to the throne.

'You know why.' But he didn't want to. And finally she kissed him and urged him to be grateful for what they had. 'It's more than some people have in a lifetime.' She had come to be infinitely grateful for him, and for each moment they shared. She knew only too well how precious it all was, and how rare, and how unlikely that it would ever happen again in her lifetime.

He sat up next to her then, as they watched the boats and the gondolas in the distance, as the spires of St Mark's Cathedral rose toward the sky. 'Sarah . . .' He took her hand in his. 'I'm not playing at this.'

'I know that.'

He leaned over and kissed her gently on the lips, and said something he had never said to her quite that openly before. 'I want to marry you.' He kissed her again then in a way that told her he meant it, but eventually she pulled away from him and shook her head with anguish.

'You know we can't,' she whispered to him as he kissed her.

'We can. I am not going to let my place in the succession or your divorce stop us now. That's absolutely absurd. No-one, but no-one, in England gives a damn what I do. The only one I care about is my mother, and she adores you. I told her before you ever met her that I wanted to marry you, and after she met you she said she thought it a very sensible plan. She's completely for it.'

'You told her *before* you took me to lunch at Whitfield?' Sarah looked horrified and he grinned at her wickedly.

'I thought she ought to know that you were important to me. I've never told her that about anyone before, and she said she was just grateful that she'd lived long enough to see me fall in love with such a nice girl.'

'If I'd known that when you took me there, I'd have gotten out of the car and walked back to London. How could you do that to her? Does she know about the divorce?'

'She does now,' he said seriously. 'I told her afterwards. We had a very serious talk before you left London, and she agrees with me completely. She said that feelings like this only come once in a lifetime. And that certainly must be true for me. I'm almost thirty-six years old, and I've never felt anything for anyone except occasional desire and frequent boredom.' She laughed at what he said and shook her head in amazement, thinking how totally unpredictable life was, how wonderful, and amazing.

'What if you become an outcast because of me?' She felt as though she had a responsibility to him, but she was greatly relieved by his mother's reaction.

'Then we'll come here, and live in Venice. Actually, that might be rather nice.' He looked nonplussed by all her objections. They didn't worry him at all.

'William, your father was the head of the House of Lords. Think of the disgrace you'll bring to your family and your ancestors.'

'Don't be absurd. And they won't take my seat away. Dear girl, the only thing I cannot be is king. And let me assure you now, there was never the remotest chance of it, thank God. I can't think of anything I'd hate more. If I thought there was a chance, I'd have given it up myself years ago. Fourteenth in line is purely a matter of prestige, my dear, and barely that, I assure you. It's nothing I can't very happily live without.' But she still didn't want their love for each other to cost him something that could have been important to him, or his family.

'Won't it embarrass you when people whisper that your wife was married before?'

'Frankly, no. I don't give a damn. But I also don't know how everyone would know, unless you tell them. You are not, thank heaven, Wallis Simpson, despite what you seem to think. Does that answer all your ridiculous objections, my love?'

'I . . . you . . .' She was stumbling over her own words as she tried to force herself to listen to reason, but the truth was that she loved him to distraction. 'I love you so much.' She kissed him hard then, and he held her for ages, and then pulled away from her only slightly to threaten her this time.

'I will not let you go until you agree to be the next Duchess of Whitfield,' he whispered to her. 'And if you don't agree, I shall tell everyone at this swimming pool that you are really Wallis Simpson . . . I beg your pardon, the Duchess of Windsor.' Her title stuck in his throat still, and he was very glad they had not accorded her the right to be called Her Royal Highness, which had infuriated David. 'Will you agree?' he whispered fiercely, kissing her . . . 'Sarah, will you?' But he didn't have to ask her again, she nodded, as tears filled her eyes and he kissed her even more longingly than before. It was a long time before he let her go again, and he smiled as he turned away from her and wrapped himself quickly in a towel when he stood up. 'It's settled then,' he said calmly as he held out a hand to her. 'When is the wedding?' It stunned her to hear him talk that way. She couldn't believe that they were really getting married. How was it possible? How did they dare? What would the King say? And her parents? And Jane? And all their friends . . .

'You're really serious, aren't you?' She looked at him, still stunned by it all, but incredibly happy.

'I'm afraid so, my dear. You're in for a lifetime of it.' A lifetime of love with him. 'All I want from you is the date of the wedding.'

Her eyes clouded for a moment as she looked at him, and she lowered her voice slightly when she answered at last. 'My divorce will be final on November nineteenth. It could be any time after that.'

'Are you free on the twentieth?' he asked more than half seriously. And she laughed, giddy with the thrill of what he was saying.

'I think that might be Thanksgiving.'

'Very well. What is it you eat for that? Turkey? We'll have turkey at the wedding.'

She thought about the preparations they'd have to make, and the work for her mother, right after Thanksgiving, and smiled shyly up at him. 'How about December first? That way we could have Thanksgiving with my family, and you'd have a little time to meet people before the wedding.' But they both knew it would be a small gathering this time. Particularly after the horror of her anniversary party, she had no desire for an enormous party.

'December first it is.' He pulled her close to him again, against the splendid backdrop of Venice. 'I believe, Miss Thompson, we are engaged then. When do we tell your parents?' He looked like a happy schoolboy, as she answered with a giddy grin.

'How about tonight at dinner?'

'Excellent.' After he left her at her room, he called the desk and sent a telegram to his mother at Whitfield. 'Happiest moment of my life. Wanted to share it with you at once. Sarah and I are to be married in New York on December first. Hope you will feel up to the journey. God bless. Devotedly, William.'

And that evening in the hotel's dining room, he ordered the finest champagne, and had it served before they even began dinner, although they usually preferred their champagne at dessert.

'We're off to quite a start this evening, aren't we?' Edward commented as he sipped the champagne. It was an exquisite vintage.

'Sarah and I have something to share with you,' William said quietly, but he looked happier than Sarah had ever seen him. 'With your permission, and with your blessing, we hope, we would like to get married in New York, in December.'

Victoria Thompson's eyes flew open wide as she looked at her daughter in amazed delight, and for a fleeting instant, which neither woman saw, a bond of understanding passed between the two men. William had spoken to him before they had ever left London. And Edward had told him that if it was what Sarah wanted, he would gladly give the union his blessing. And now he was genuinely thrilled to hear it.

'You have our blessing, of course,' Edward assured him officially as Victoria nodded her consent. 'When did this all come about?'

'This afternoon at the swimming pool,' Sarah answered.

'Excellent sport.' Her father commented wryly, and they all laughed. 'We're very happy for you. Good Lord' – it finally dawned on him then – 'Sarah is going to be a duchess.' He looked pleased, and impressed, but most of all he was pleased with William, and the kind of man he was.

'I apologize for that, of course, but I'll try to make up for it for her. I would like you to meet Mother when we go back. I hope she'll be strong enough to come to New York for the wedding.' He doubted it, but at the very least they would ask her, and try to talk her into coming. But William knew that it was a very long trip for a woman her age.

Sarah's mother broke into the conversation then,

wanting to know what kind of wedding they had in mind, what dates they had talked about, where the reception should be, where they were going to honeymoon, all the details that gave mothers gray hair when it came to weddings. Sarah explained quickly that they had decided on December first, but that William would come over for Thanksgiving.

'Or sooner,' he added. 'I couldn't bear a day without her when you came here. I'm not at all sure how I'll last when she leaves for New York.'

'You'll be welcome anytime,' her father assured him, and the foursome spent a delightful evening celebrating William and Sarah's engagement. The Thompsons left them eventually, and the young couple spent a long time on the terrace, dancing to the romantic strains of the orchestra, and talking about their plans in the moonlit darkness. Sarah still couldn't believe this was happening to her. It was all like a dream, so different from the nightmare she had experienced with Freddie. William gave her faith in life again. He gave her love and happiness, and more than she had ever dreamed.

'I want to make you happy always,' William said to her quietly, as they held hands in the dark and sipped more champagne. 'I always want to be there for you when you need me. That's how my parents were. They were never apart, and so seldom angry with each other.' And then he smiled. 'I hope we don't have to wait as long as they did to have children. I'm almost an old man now.' He was soon to be thirty-six, and Sarah had just spent her twenty-second birthday with him in Florence.

'You'll never be an old man.' Sarah smiled at him. 'I love you so,' she whispered as they kissed again. And she could feel now, as they kissed, increasing waves of desire and passion that would be even harder to deny now, knowing they could indulge them so soon. 'I wish we could run away for a few days,' she said brazenly, and he smiled, his teeth white and shining in the darkness. He had a wonderful smile. In truth, she loved everything about him.

'I thought about suggesting it once or twice, but my conscience got the best of me. And your parents have helped to keep me honest while we've been abroad at least. But I can't vouch for how I'll behave when we go back to London.'

She laughed at his rueful tone, and nodded. 'I know. I think, for grown people, we've been extremely well behaved.'

'Please don't count on that in the future. My good behaviour, as you call it, is not a sign of indifference, let me reassure you, only of extremely good manners and restraint.' She laughed at his look of pain, and he kissed her hard on the mouth to prove it. 'I think we should take an extremely long honeymoon somewhere very far away . . . Tahiti perhaps? On a deserted beach, alone with a few idle natives.'

'That sounds wonderful.' But she knew he was only teasing. That evening they talked about France, which appealed to them both, even in December. She didn't mind the bleak weather there. In fact, she thought it would be cozy, and she rather liked it.

He talked to her seriously then about something they had never discussed before, but she had opened the door now. 'I didn't want you to think that I would ever take advantage of the fact that you were divorced. I wanted things to be the way they would have been if you had never been married. I wouldn't have taken advantage of you then, and I haven't now. I hope you understand.' She did, and she was grateful to him. It would have complicated matters still further if she had had a brief affair with him, and then they had ended it when she left Europe to return to New York. Now they had nothing to regret, only a lifetime of shared joy to look forward to, and she could hardly wait to begin their marriage.

They talked long into the night that night, and when he walked her to her room, it was harder than ever to leave her there alone. But they forced themselves to stop kissing after a while, and he watched wistfully as she closed the door of her suite behind her.

Everyone enjoyed the last few days in Venice together and the four of them rode the train back to London in triumph. There was a telegram from Peter and Jane waiting for them at Claridge's, congratulating Sarah on her engagement, and William had already received one from his mother in Venice saying much the same thing to him. Although she had also told him that she felt it would be impossible for her to go to New York to be with him at the wedding, she would be with him in spirit, she assured them both.

The next few days were a whirlwind for them, seeing friends, making plans, and making announcements. William and Edward wrote a formal announcement, which appeared in *The Times*, causing disappointment among the debutantes and dowagers of London who had been chasing William for fifteen years, and now were being told the chase was off forever. His friends were extremely pleased for him, and his secretary couldn't keep up with the calls and telegrams and letters that poured in as people heard of his engagement. Everyone wanted to give parties for him, and, of course, they all wanted to meet Sarah, and he had to explain again and again that she was an American and she was leaving for New York in a few days, and they would have to wait to meet her until after the wedding.

He also managed to have a long audience with his cousin Bertie, King George VI, before she left, and explained to him that he would give up his right to the succession to the throne. The King was not pleased, particularly after what his brother had done, but this was assuredly far less dramatic, and he agreed to it, although with some regret, merely from the standpoint of tradition, and the deep affection they shared. William asked him if he might introduce Sarah to him before he left, and the King said that he would be pleased to meet her. Dressed in formal striped trousers, his morning coat, and his homburg, William brought Sarah back to Buckingham Palace for a private audience the following afternoon. She wore a simple black dress, no makeup, and pearls on her ears and at her throat, and she looked dignified and lovely. She curtsied low to His Majesty, and tried to make herself forget that William always referred to him as Bertie, although he didn't do so now. He addressed him as 'Your Majesty', and her introduction to the King was extremely formal. It was only after a few moments that the King seemed to unbend, and chatted amiably with her about their plans and their wedding, and told her he hoped to see them at Balmoral when they returned. He liked it there because it was more informal, and Sarah was both impressed and very touched by the invitation.

'You'll be coming back to England to live, of course, won't you?' he asked her with a worried frown.

'Of course, Your Majesty.' He seemed relieved then, and he kissed her hand before he left. 'You'll make a beautiful bride . . . and a lovely wife, my dear. May your life together be long and happy, and blessed with many children.' Her eyes filled with tears as he spoke to her, and she curtsied deeply to him again as he and William shook hands, and then the King left to attend to more important business.

William smiled at her openly with pride as they stood alone in the room once the King had left it. He was so proud of her and so happy, and it was a relief of sorts to know that their marriage would have the royal blessing, in spite of his giving up his right to the succession. 'You'll make a beautiful duchess,' he said softly to her, and then he lowered his voice further. 'Actually, you'd make a damn fine queen too!' They both laughed nervously then and were ushered out by a chamberlain who had appeared to assist them. Sarah was overwhelmed by how nervous she had been. This was definitely not an everyday experience. She tried to explain it to Jane later, in a letter, just so she wouldn't forget it, and even to her it sounded absurd and incredibly pretentious as she explained . . . 'and then King George kissed my hand, looking a little nervous himself, and said . . .' It was truly impossible to believe it. And she herself wasn't at all sure she did.

They arranged to go to Whitfield again so that her parents could meet his mother. The dowager duchess gave a beautiful dinner for them. She seated Sarah's father on her right, and spent the entire evening praising the beautiful girl who was to marry William. 'You know,' she said nostalgically, 'I never expected to have children, not after a certain point in my life . . . and then William came along, and he was the most extraordinary blessing. He's never been a disappointment to me for a moment. He's remained a blessing all his life. And now he's found Sarah, and the blessing has been doubled.' It was such a sweet thing to say that it brought tears to Edward's eyes, and they all felt like old friends by the end of the evening. He tried to urge her to come to New York with her son, but she insisted that she was too old, and too frail, and the long voyage would be too exhausting. 'I haven't even been to London in four years. I'm afraid that New York would really be too much. And it would be a nuisance for all of you to have an old woman to take care of, at such a busy time. I shall wait and see them when they come back here. I want to see to some improvements here in William's house. I'm afraid my son has absolutely no idea what they'll need, or what might make Sarah comfortable and happy. I want to make a few changes in his rustic little house, to make it more comfortable for her. And I think they should have a tennis court, don't you? I hear they're all the rage, and poor William is so old-fashioned.' As they went home that night, Edward marvelled at how lucky his daughter would be, to have a husband whom she loved so much, and who clearly adored her so passionately, and even a mother-in-law who cared so much about her happiness and comfort.

'Thank God,' he said gratefully to his wife that night as they undressed.

'She's a very lucky girl,' Victoria agreed, but she felt lucky, too, and she kissed her husband tenderly, thinking of their own wedding, and their honeymoon, and how happy they had always been. She was happy knowing that Sarah would know some of that joy too. She had had such a dreadful time with Freddie, and the poor child really didn't deserve it. But the Fates had more than made it up to her now. William was larger than life, and a blessing for a lifetime.

On their last day in London, Sarah was a nervous wreck. She had a thousand things to do, and William wanted her to take a serious look at his house in London. He had bought it when he was eighteen, and it was a delightful accommodation for a bachelor, but he couldn't imagine her being happy in it for very long. And he wanted to know now if she wanted him to look for something larger, or wait until they got back from their honeymoon in France, after Christmas.

'Darling, I love it!' she exclaimed as she examined the well designed and extremely tidy quarters. It wasn't large, but it was, in all, no smaller than the apartment she had shared with Freddie. 'I think it's perfect. For now anyway.' She couldn't imagine their needing more room until they had a baby. There was a large, sunny living room downstairs, a small library filled to the brim with beautifully bound old books William had brought from Whitfield years before, there was a cozy kitchen, a tidy dining room large enough for any dinner party she could manage, and upstairs there was one large, very handsome, and somewhat masculine bedroom. There were two baths, one which he used, and another for guests downstairs. As far as Sarah was concerned, it was perfect.

'What about cupboards?' He was trying to think of everything and this was all new to him, but more than anything he wanted her to be happy. 'I'll give you half of mine. I can move most of what I have down to Whitfield.' He was amazingly accommodating for a man who had always lived alone, and never been married.

'I just won't bring any clothes.'

'I have a better idea. We'll stay naked.' He was getting friskier knowing that soon she would be his wife.

But in any case, she loved his house, and she assured him that he didn't need to find her another. 'You're very easy to please.'

'Wait,' she said mischievously at him. 'Maybe I'll turn into a shrew once we're married.'

'If you do, I shall beat you, and it won't be a problem.'

'That sounds exotic.' She raised an eyebrow and he laughed. He could hardly wait to take off her clothes and make love to her for days on end. It was a good thing she was sailing the following morning.

They had dinner alone that night, and William brought her back to the hotel reluctantly. He would much rather have taken her home with him for their last night, but he was determined to behave like a man of honor, no matter what it cost him. And it was costing him dearly as they stood outside her hotel.

'This isn't easy, you know,' he complained, 'this respectable nonsense. I may appear in New York next week, and have to kidnap you somewhere. Waiting until December is beginning to seem inhuman.'

'It is, isn't it,' she mused, but they both thought they should wait, although she was no longer quite sure why it had once seemed so important to both of them. And it was odd, as sad as it still made her to think about it, she was more philosophical about her miscarriage. If she hadn't had that, she would have Freddie's child, or maybe even still be married to Freddie. And now she was free to start a new life, with a clean slate, and she fervently hoped that she and William would have many, many children. They talked about five or six, or at least four, and the prospect obviously pleased him. Everything about his life with her excited him, and they could hardly wait, as he took her upstairs and stood outside her suite.

'Do you want to come in for a minute?' she suggested, and he nodded. Her parents had long since gone to bed, and he wanted to be with her for every possible moment they could share before she sailed in the morning.

He followed her in, and she dropped her wrap and her evening bag on a chair and offered him a brandy, but he declined it. There was something he had been waiting all evening to give her.

'Come and sit down with me, Miss Sarah.'

'Will you behave?' She looked at him teasingly and he laughed.

'Not if you look like that, and probably not anyway, but come and sit down for a minute. I can be trusted for that long, if not longer.'

He sat down on the chintz settee, and she sat down beside him, as he reached for something in his coat pocket. 'Close your eyes,' he told her with a smile.

'What are you going to do to me?' She was laughing, but she closed her eyes anyway.

'Paint a mustache on you, you goose . . . What do you think I'm going to do?' But before she could answer, he kissed her. And as he did, he took her left hand in his, and slipped a ring on her finger. She felt the chill of cool metal as it went on, and after he kissed her, she looked down at her hand nervously, and gasped at what she saw there. Even in the dimly lit room, she could see that it was an exquisite stone, and an old cut, which she greatly preferred to modern. There was a perfectly round, twenty carat, absolutely flawless diamond on her left hand.

'My father had it made for my mother at Garrard's when they got engaged. It's a very, very fine stone, and an old one. And she wanted you to have it.'

'This is your mother's engagement ring?' She looked at him with tear-filled eyes.

'It is. She wants you to have it. We talked about it for a long time, and I was going to buy you a new one, but she wanted you to have this one. She can't wear it any more anyway, since she's had arthritis.'

'Oh, William . . .' It was the most beautiful thing she'd ever seen, and she held out her hand and flashed it in the dim light. It was an absolutely fabulous engagement ring, and Sarah had never been so happy in her entire life.

'That's just to remind you who you belong to, when you get on that bloody ship tomorrow, and go so damn far away I can't bear to think about it at all. I'm going to be calling you every hour in New York until I get there.'

'Why don't you come over early?' She was looking at the ring as she said it, and he smiled. He was pleased that she obviously loved it, and he knew his mother would be pleased too. It had been an incredibly generous gesture on her part.

'Actually, I might. I was thinking about October, but I've got so damn much to do here. I'll have to see what's happening with the farm by then.' There had been some problems he still had to work out, and he had to make an appearance at the House of Lords before he left London. 'In any case, I'll be there by the first of November without fail. I'm sure you'll be half mad by then with plans for the wedding. And I'll get in everyone's hair, but I don't give a damn. I can't wait to see you any longer than that.' He kissed her longingly then, and the two of them almost forgot themselves as they lay on the couch, and he ran long, hungry fingers along her exquisite body. 'Oh, Sarah . . . God . . .' She could feel him throbbing for her, but she wanted to wait until their wedding. She wanted this to be like the first time, as though there had been no other wedding, and no Freddie. If William had been the first man in her life, they would have waited, and so she wanted to now, except that there were moments like this one when she almost forgot that. Her legs moved aside, gently welcoming him, and he moved toward her powerfully, and then he forced himself to pull away from her and stood up with a groan of regret, but he wanted to wait, too, out of respect for her and their marriage. 'Maybe it's a good thing you're leaving,' he said huskily as he walked around the room trying to calm his senses, and she stood up looking dishevelled and passionate as she nodded at him. And then suddenly, she laughed at him. They both looked like overheated children.

'Aren't we awful?'

'Not really.' He laughed. 'I can hardly wait.'

'Neither can I,' she confessed.

And then he asked her something he knew he shouldn't. 'Was it . . . was it ever like this . . . with him?' His voice was deep and sexual as he asked her, but he had wanted to know that for a long time. She had said she hadn't loved him, but he always wondered a little about the rest.

Sarah shook her head slowly and sadly. 'No, it wasn't. It was empty . . . and without feeling . . . Darling, he never loved me, and I know now that I never loved him. There has never been a love in my life like ours . . . I have never loved, or lived, or even existed until you found me. And from now until I die, you will be my only love.' There were tears in his eyes this time when he kissed her. But this time, he didn't let it go too far, and feeling happier than he had in his entire life, he left her until the next morning.

She lay awake for most of that night, thinking of him,

and admiring her engagement ring in the dark. And the next morning, she called the Duchess of Whitfield to tell her how much the ring meant to her, how grateful she was to have it, and how much she loved William.

'That's all that matters, dear. But jewels are always such fun, aren't they? Have a safe trip . . . and a beautiful wedding.'

Sarah thanked her and finished her packing, and William met them an hour later in the lobby. She was wearing a white wool Chanel suit, made especially for her in Paris by Coco Chanel, and her smashing new engagement ring, and William almost devoured her when he kissed her. He hadn't forgotten the desire she had aroused in him as they lay on the couch in her suite the night before, and he wished he were going with them on the *Queen Mary*. 'I imagine your father is glad I'm not.'

'I think he's been very impressed by your exemplary behavior.'

'Well, he wouldn't be for long,' William groaned privately. 'I think I've about reached my limit.' She grinned and they held hands as they followed her parents into his Bentley. He had volunteered to drive them to Southampton, and their luggage was going on ahead. But the two-hour drive went much too quickly. Sarah saw the familiar shape of the *Queen Mary* again, remembering how different things had been when they sailed from New York only two months before.

'You never know what life has in store for you.' Edward smiled benevolently at them, and offered to show William around the ship. But William was far more interested in staying close to Sarah, and he politely declined the invitation. Instead, he went to their staterooms with them, and then they went out on the deck. He stood there with an arm around her and a woebegone face until the last gong sounded and the last smoke-stack had roared to life, and he suddenly found himself terrified that they would meet some disaster. A cousin of his had been on the *Titanic* twenty-six years before, and he couldn't bear thinking of anything happening to Sarah.

'Please God . . . take care of yourself . . . I couldn't live without you . . .' He clung to her like a life raft for their last moments.

'I'll be fine, I promise. Just come to New York as soon as you can.'

'I will. Possibly by next Tuesday,' he said sadly, and she smiled again, and tears filled her eyes as he kissed her again.

'I'm going to miss you so awfully,' she said softly.

'Me too.' He clung to her, and at last one of the officers approached them with awe.

'Your Grace, I apologize for the intrusion, but I'm afraid . . . we will be sailing very shortly. You must go ashore now.'

'Right. Sorry.' He smiled apologetically. 'Please take good care of my wife and her family, won't you? My future wife, that is . . .' He beamed down at her, and the large, round diamond on her left hand glinted powerfully in the September sunshine.

'Of course, sir.' The officer looked impressed, and made a mental note to mention it to the captain. The future Duchess of Whitfield was travelling with them to New York, and there was no doubt that she would get every possible courtesy and service.

'Take care, darling.' He kissed her one last time, shook hands with his future father-in-law, kissed Victoria warmly on the cheek and gave her a hug, and then he was down the gangplank. Sarah was crying in spite of herself, and even Victoria dabbed at her eyes with her hankie, it was so sweet to see them. He waved frantically from the shore until they could see him no more, and Sarah stood on the deck for two hours after they sailed, staring out to sea, as though if she tried hard enough she could still see him.

'Come downstairs now, Sarah,' her mother said gently. But there was nothing to mourn now. Only cause for celebration. And by the time Sarah got downstairs, there was a cable from William, and a bouquet of roses so large it barely fit through the door of her stateroom. 'I can't bear waiting another moment. I love you, William', the card said, and her mother smiled, glancing at the beautiful engagement ring again. It was amazing to think what had happened to them in two short months. She could hardly believe it.

'You're a very lucky girl, Sarah Thompson,' her mother said, and Sarah could only agree with her, while mentally trying out her new name . . . Sarah Whitfield . . . She liked the way it sounded . . . it had a wonderful ring to it . . . The Duchess of Whitfield, she whispered grandly, and then laughed to herself as she went to smell the huge bouquet of red roses on the table beside her bed.

The crossing on the *Queen Mary* seemed to drag by this time. All she wanted to do was get home and start planning for her wedding. She was pampered by everyone on the ship, once they realized that she was the future Duchess of Whitfield. They were invited to the captain's table several times, and this time Sarah felt an obligation to be more obliging. Now she had a responsibility to William to be more outgoing, and her parents were pleased to see the change in her. William had done wonderful things for their daughter.

And when they arrived in New York, Peter and Jane were waiting for them, and this time they hadn't brought the children. Jane was beside herself at all the news, and squealed with delight, unable to believe how beautiful Sarah's ring was. They showed photographs of William to her in the car, and Peter and Edward chatted endlessly about the news from Europe.

In fact, it was a week to the day after their return that normal radio broadcasts were interrupted to bring

146

Americans Hitler's speech to his Nazi Congress at Nuremberg. It was an awesome, frightening speech, and his threats to Czechoslovakia were clear to all who heard them. He declared that Germany would no longer tolerate the oppression of the Sudeten Germans by the Czechs, and he revealed that close to three hundred thousand Germans were working to reinforce the German border along the Siegfried Line. The dangers were obvious, but the question remained as to what Hitler would actually do about it, and how the world would react when he did it. The venom and fury and hatred that had emanated from him as he spoke had shaken Americans to the core, as they listened to him, broadcast live to them over the airwaves, and for the first time the threat of war in Europe seemed real. It was obvious that, if nothing else, the Czechs were going to be devoured by the Germans. And no-one who listened thought that was good news.

For the next week people spoke of nothing else. The newspapers announced that the armies of Europe were being mobilized, the fleets were at the ready, and Europe was waiting for Hitler's next move.

And on September twenty-first, at eight-fifteen New York time, events in Prague finally reached a climax. The French and British ministers there announced that they would not mobilize on behalf of the Czechs, and risk Hitler's fury. They offered Czechoslovakia no choice but to capitulate, and give itself over to the Nazi forces of Adolf Hitler. By 11 a.m. in New York, 5 p.m. in Prague, the government had come to the conclusion that it had no choice. Prague capitulated to the German forces, as their supporters around the world heard the news and cried.

And by then it was raining in New York, as though God were crying for the Czechs, as Sarah did as she listened to the broadcast. The broadcast had come to New York in an oddly roundabout way, due to 'difficult' weather on the Atlantic, and in order to circumvent the problem, the broadcast had gone from Prague to Cape Town to Buenos Aires to New York. And could then be clearly heard. But by noon there was nothing left to hear. It was six o'clock in Czechoslovakia by then, and for them the fight was over. Sarah snapped off her radio, as did everyone else, and never heard the storm warnings that were issued at 1 p.m., announcing that a storm that had been hovering over the Atlantic might hit Long Island. The wind had picked up by then, and Sarah had been talking to her mother about going out to Southampton to start getting organized for the wedding. She had a thousand things to plan and do, and the house on Long Island was a peaceful place to do them.

'You don't really want to go out there in this awful weather, dear,' her mother replied. But the truth was, she really didn't mind. She liked the beach in the rain. There was always something peaceful and soothing about it. But she knew her mother worried about her driving in bad weather, so she stayed home to help her mother in town. Her father had already called the man who owned the farm she had put the deposit on, and had explained to him that his daughter was getting married and moving to England instead. He had been extremely nice, and given Sarah her money back, although her father had still scolded her for doing something so foolish, and he assured her that he would never have let her live alone in a fallen-down farmhouse on Long Island. She had taken the money back from him apologetically, and put it in the bank. It was the thousand dollars she had gotten for selling the wedding ring she had gotten from Freddie, a useless item she had never missed.

But she wasn't thinking of the farm, or even the wedding, that afternoon, as the rain grew worse in New York. She was thinking about Prague and the terrifying situation there, when she suddenly heard a ferocious rattling of her bedroom windows. It was two o'clock by then, and when she looked at the window it was so dark it almost looked like midnight. The trees outside her parents' apartment were bent low in the wind, and she thought she'd never seen such a fierce storm in New York, and at that exact moment her father came home early.

'Is something wrong?' Victoria asked him worriedly.

'Have you seen that storm?' he asked her. 'I could barely make it out of the car and into the building. I had to hold on to the awning poles and two men on the street had to help me.' He turned to his daughter then with a worried frown. 'Have you been listening to the news?' He knew how well-informed she was, and that she often listened to the news bulletins in the afternoon, if she was at home with her mother.

'Only about Czechoslovakia.' She told him the latest about that then, and he shook his head.

'This is no ordinary storm,' he said ominously, and went to his bedroom to change. He came back out in rough gear five minutes later.

'What are you doing?' Victoria asked nervously. He had a habit of doing things beyond his skills or his years, as though to prove that he could still do them, even if he never had before. He was a strong, able man, but he was clearly no longer as young as he had been.

'I want to drive out to Southampton and make sure everything's all right there. I called Charles an hour ago, and the phone didn't answer.' Sarah looked at her father's eyes only for an instant, and then spoke firmly.

'I'll come with you.'

'No, you won't,' he argued with her, and Victoria began to look really angry at both of them.

'You're both ridiculous. It's just a storm, and if something is wrong out there, there's nothing either of you can do about it.' An old man and a young girl were not going to be able to fight the forces of nature. But neither of them shared that opinion with her. As her father put his overcoat on, Sarah emerged from her room in some of the old clothes she had worn during her year of solitude on Long Island. She had on heavy rubber boots, khaki pants, a fisherman's sweater, and a slicker.

'I'm coming with you,' she announced again, and he hesitated, and then shrugged. He was too worried to argue.

'All right. Let's go. Victoria, don't worry, we'll call you.' She was still furious with both of them when they left. She put the radio on as they went downstairs, got in the car, and set off toward the Sunrise Highway en route to Southampton. Sarah had offered to drive, but her father had laughed at her.

'I may be old and feeble in your eyes, but I'm not crazy.' She laughed and reminded him that she was a very competent driver. But they said little to each other after that. The force of the winds made it almost impossible for him to keep the car on the road, and more than once, the wind pushed the heavy Buick a dozen feet sideways.

'Are you all right?' she asked him once or twice, and he only nodded grimly, his lips a tight line across his face, his eyes narrowed to see through the driving rain.

They were still driving along the Sunrise Highway when they both saw a strange, high bank of fog roll across the sea and settle itself against the coastline. And it was only shortly after that they realized that what they were seeing was not fog, but a giant wave. A forty-foot wall of water was pounding relentlessly against the eastern seaboard, and as they watched in horror, houses disappeared in its jaws, and two feet of water eddied and swirled across the highway around their car.

It was another four hours of relentlessly driving through the pounding rain before they reached Southampton. And as they approached the estate they loved so dearly, they both were silent, and then Sarah realized that the landscape had brutally changed. Houses that she had known all her life had disappeared, entire estates, most of Westhampton seemed to have vanished. And some of the houses there had been enormous. They only learned later that Edward's lifelong friend, J. P. Morgan, had lost his entire estate in Glen Cove. But for the moment, all they could see was the endless desolation around them. Trees uprooted everywhere, houses reduced to kindling if they were there at all. In some cases, an entire segment of land, and dozens of houses built on it for hundreds of years, had vanished. There were cars overturned everywhere, and Sarah suddenly realized the extraordinary skill her father had used to get them there. In fact, as they looked around them as they continued driving, Westhampton seemed literally to have disappeared from the face of the Long Island coast. They learned later that a hundred and fifty-three of the hundred and seventy-nine houses there had vanished entirely, and the land they sat on was gone too. And of those that were left, they were too battered to rebuild or live in.

Sarah felt her heart sink as they drove slowly toward Southampton, and when they reached their own house, their gates were gone. They had been picked up out of the ground and uprooted, along with the stone posts that held them, and all of it had been turned to rubble and tossed hundreds of yards away. It looked like a child's model railroad, but the tragedy was that the damage was real, the losses too great to fathom.

All of their beautiful old trees were down, but the house still stood in the distance. From where they were, it looked as though it had been untouched. But as they drove past the caretaker's cottage, they saw that it literally stood on end, and all of its contents had been spilled across the ground like so much garbage.

Her father parked the old Buick as close to the main house as he could. Half a dozen huge trees lay across the road, barring him from going any further. They left the car and walked through the driving rain, battered by the winds, with sharp needles of rain lashing at their faces. Sarah tried to turn her face away from the wind, but it was virtually useless, and as they walked around the house they saw that the entire eastern side, facing the beach, had been torn off and part of the roof with it. You could see some of the contents still within, her parents' bed, her own, the piano in the parlor. But the entire face of the building had been ripped off by the relentless wall of water that had come and washed it away. It brought tears to her eyes, which mingled with the rain, but when she turned to her father, she could see that he was crying as hard as she was. He loved this place, and he had built it years before, carefully planning everything. Her mother had designed the house when the children were small, and together they had chosen each tree, each beam, and everything in it. And the huge trees that had been there had been there for hundreds of years before they came, and now they were gone forever. It all seemed impossible to believe or understand. This had been her joy through her childhood, and her refuge for an entire year, and now it was so desperately damaged. And one look at her father's face told her he feared worse.

'Oh, Papa . . .' Sarah moaned as she clung to him, the two of them tossed together intermittently by the wind as though they floated on waves. It was a sight that defied the imagination. He pulled her close to him and shouted above the shrieking of the wind that he wanted to go back to the gatehouse.

'I want to find Charles.' He was a kind man, and during the year she had hidden out there, Charles had taken care of her like a father.

But he was nowhere in the little house, and everywhere on the grass around them were his belongings, his clothes, his food, his furniture smashed to bits, even his radio lay yards from the house, but he was nowhere to be found, and Edward was seriously worried about him. They went back to the main house then, and when they did, Sarah realized that the little bathhouse was gone, as was the boathouse, and the trees around them. The trees stood on end, or lay broken on the narrow lip of beaten sand that had been a broad white beach only at noontime that day. And as she looked at the trees in dismay, suddenly she saw him. There were ropes in his hands, as though he'd been trying to tie things down, and he was wearing his old yellow slicker. He had been pinned to the ground by a tree that had previously stood on the front lawn, and had flown at least two hundred yards to kill him. The sand might have cushioned his fall, but the tree was so enormous, it must have broken his neck or his back as it felled him. She mourned silently as she ran to him, and knelt beside him, brushing the sand from his bruised face as she touched him. Her father saw her then, and he cried pitifully as he worked to help her free him, and together they carried him to the shelter of the other side of the house and laid him gently down in what had been the kitchen. He had worked for Edward's family for over forty years, and they had known and liked each other as young men. He was ten years older than Edward, and Edward couldn't believe he was gone now. He was like a boyhood friend, faithful to the end, killed in the storm no-one had warned them of, as all eyes turned to Prague and everyone forgot Long Island. It was the largest storm of its kind ever to hit the eastern seaboard. Entire towns were gone, and it lashed its way with equal force across Connecticut, Massachusetts, and New Hampshire after that, taking seven hundred lives, injuring close to two thousand, and destroying everything it touched before it was finally gone.

The house in Southampton was not irreparably destroyed, but the death of Charles affected all the Thompsons. Peter and Jane and Victoria came out for the funeral, and for a week the elder Thompsons and Sarah stayed in the house to try to assess the damage and bring some kind of order back to the estate. Only two rooms were even usable, there was no heat, no electricity, and they used candles, and ate in the only restaurant still functioning in Southampton. It would take months to repair the house, years perhaps, and Sarah was sad to be leaving them when this had happened.

Sarah managed to get a call through to William from the little restaurant where they ate, fearing that he might have heard of the storm in the papers and been worried. Even in Europe the destruction of Long Island had caused quite a flutter.

'My God, are you all right?' William's voice had crackled across the line.

'I'm fine,' she said, relieved to hear his calm, strong voice. 'But we've pretty much lost our house. It's going to take my parents forever to rebuild it, but we didn't lose the land. Most people lost everything.' She told him about Charles losing his life, and he told her he was very sorry.

'I'll be awfully happy when you're back here. I almost died when I heard about this blasted storm. I somehow imagined you might have been out there for the weekend.'

'I almost was,' she admitted to him.

'Thank God, you weren't. Please tell your parents how sorry I am, and I'll be over as soon as I can, darling. I promise.'

'I love you!' she shouted across the crackling wires.

'I love you too! Try to stay out of trouble till I get there!'

They went back to the city shortly after that, and eight days after the storm, the Munich Pact was signed, giving everyone in Europe the delusion that any threat from Hitler was over. Neville Chamberlain called it 'peace with honor' when he returned from Munich. But William wrote and told her that he still didn't trust the little bastard in Berlin.

William was planning to come in early November, and Sarah was busy with plans for the wedding, while her parents tried to organize both that and the extensive repairs to the house on Long Island.

William arrived on November fourth, on the *Aquitania*, with full fanfare. Sarah was waiting for him at the pier, with her parents, her sister, her brother-in-law, and their children. And the next day her parents gave a huge dinner party for him, and it seemed as though everyone she'd ever known in New York wanted to send them invitations to parties. It was a social whirl without end.

Six days later, they were having breakfast together in the dining room, as Sarah frowned and looked up at him from the morning paper.

'What does all this mean?' She looked at him accusingly, it seemed, and he looked blank. He had only just arrived from his hotel and hadn't yet read the paper.

'What does what mean?' He came to read the paper over her shoulder, and frowned as he read the accounts of *Kristallnacht*, while trying to assess the implications. 'Sounds like an ugly business, that.'

'But why? Why would they do that?' The Nazis had smashed the windows of every Jewish shop and home, looted, killed, and destroyed synagogues, and generally terrorized people. And it said that some thirty thousand Jews had been taken off to labor camps. 'My God, William, how can they do that?'

'The Nazis don't like Jews. That's no secret, Sarah.'

'But this? This?' There were tears in her eyes as she read it, and finally handed the paper to him so he could read it too. When Sarah's father came in to breakfast, they told him everything and spent an hour discussing the continuing dangers in Europe, and then her father thought of something as he looked at them both. 'I want you both to promise me, if war breaks out over there, that you'll come back to the States until it's over.'

'I can't promise that for myself,' William told him honestly, 'but I promise you, I'll send you Sarah.'

'You'll do no such thing.' She looked angrily at her fiancé for the first time. 'You can't just dispose of me like a suitcase, or mail me home like a letter.'

William smiled at her. 'I'm sorry, Sarah. I didn't mean to be disrespectful. But I think your father's right. If something happens there, I think you should come home. I remember the last war, when I was a boy, and it's not pleasant living with the threat of invasion.'

'And you? Where would you go?'

'I'd probably have to go back to active duty. I don't think it looks quite right if the peers all disappear and take a long vacation abroad.'

'Aren't you too old to go?' She suddenly looked frankly worried.

'Not really. And darling, I'd really have to.'

The three of them earnestly hoped there wouldn't be a war, but none of them were hopeful as they finished their breakfast.

The following week, Sarah went to court with her father and was given her final papers. Her divorce decree was handed to her, and in spite of everything, in spite of the future waiting for her, she felt a crushing wave of humiliation. She had been such a fool to marry Freddie, and he had turned out to be such a louse. He was still engaged to marry Emily Astor in Palm Beach at Christmas. And she didn't really care now, but Sarah was sorry she had ever married him at all.

It was only two weeks until their wedding by then, and all William cared about was being near her. They went out constantly, and it was a relief when they settled down to a quiet family meal on Thanksgiving at the apartment in New York. It was a new experience for William and he liked it, and found it very touching to be there with them all.

'I hope you'll do that for us every year,' he told Sarah afterwards, as they sat in the living room, and her sister

156

played the piano. The children had already been taken upstairs, and it was a nice quiet time among them. Peter and William seemed to get on well, and Jane was enormously impressed with William. She had told literally everyone she knew that Sarah was going to be a duchess. But it wasn't that which impressed Sarah about him, it was William's gentleness she loved, his wit, his sharp mind, his kindness. Oddly enough, the title seemed to mean nothing to her.

The last week was exhausting for her. There were last-minute details to attend to for the wedding, as well as packing the small things. Her trunks with her clothes had been sent ahead. And she wanted to see a few old friends, but the truth was that she was ready to leave now. She spent the day before the wedding with him, and they went for a long quiet walk on Sutton Place, next to the East River.

'Will you be sad to leave, my love?' He liked her family a lot, and imagined it would be hard for her to leave them, but her answer surprised him.

'Not really. In a way, I left all this last year, even before that. In my heart of hearts, I never planned to come back here once I settled on Long Island.'

'I know,' he smiled. 'Your farmhouse . . .' But now, even that was gone. All of its buildings and its land had vanished in the storm that hit Long Island in September. She would have lost everything, maybe even her life, as Charles had. And William was deeply glad she had not.

She smiled up at him then. 'I'm anxious for our life now.' She wanted a life with him, wanted to know him better, his heart, his life, his friends, his likes and dislikes, his soul . . . his body. She wanted to have children with him, to have a home with him, to be his, to be always there to help him.

'So am I,' he confessed. 'It has seemed a long wait, hasn't it?' And there had been so many people around them to distract them. But that was almost over. Tomorrow, at this same time, they'd be husband and wife, the Duke and Duchess of Whitfield.

They stood looking at the river for a moment then, and he pulled her close to him with a serious air. 'May our life always run smoothly . . . and when it doesn't, may we be brave, for each other and ourselves.' He turned to look at her then with immeasurable love, which was more important to her than any title. 'May I never disappoint you.'

'Or I you,' she whispered softly, as they watched the river drift by.

Chapter 10

There were ninety-three friends in her parents' home that afternoon, and Sarah came down the stairs on her father's arm looking beautiful and demure. She wore her long, dark hair in a full chignon, and above it a beautiful beige lace-and-satin hat, with a small veil that just seemed to add a touch of mystery when she wore it. Her dress was beige satin and lace, and she carried an armful of small beige orchids. Her shoes were beige satin, too, and she looked tall and elegant as she stood in the flower-filled dining room beside the duke. The dining room had been turned into a chapel of sorts for the occasion. Jane wore navy-blue silk organza and Victoria wore a brilliant-green satin suit, designed for her by Elsa Schiaparelli in Paris. The guests were a group of the most distinguished names in New York, and understandably, none of the Van Deerings were among them.

After the ceremony, where William discreetly kissed the bride and she beamed up at him, knowing that her life had just changed forever, the guests were seated for dinner at tables in the drawing room, and the dining room became a ballroom. It was a perfect evening for all of them, subtle, discreet, beautiful, and everyone thought it was a lovely wedding, especially the bride and groom. They danced almost until the end, and then Sarah had a last dance with her father, while William danced with his new mother-in-law, and told her how much he had enjoyed the wedding.

'Thank you, Papa, for everything,' Sarah whispered to her father as they danced to the strains of 'The Way You

Look Tonight'. 'It was perfect.' They were always so good to her, so kind, and if they hadn't insisted on taking her to Europe the summer before, she wouldn't have met William. She tried to say all that to him in the course of one dance, but her voice was too full of tears, and he was afraid he'd cry, too, and he didn't want to in front of all their friends.

'It's all right, Sarah.' He squeezed her lovingly for an instant, and then smiled down on his younger daughter, thinking how much he loved her. 'We love you. Come and see us when you can, and we'll visit you!'

'You'd better!' She sniffed delicately, and they danced on as she clung to him for a last time. It was her second chance to be his baby, just for one last moment. And then William gently cut in on them, and looked down at her, and saw not the child, but the woman.

'Are you ready to leave, Your Grace?' he asked her politely, and she giggled.

'Are people really going to call me that for the rest of my life?'

'I'm afraid so, darling. I told you . . . it's an awesome burden at times.' What he said was only half in jest. 'Her Grace, the Duchess of Whitfield . . . I must say, it suits you.' She looked extremely aristocratic as he looked at her when they stopped dancing, and she was wearing the magnificent pear-shaped diamond earrings he had given her as a wedding present, with a necklace of matching diamond drops.

They said their goodbyes quickly then, and she threw her bouquet from the stairs before she left. She kissed her parents, and thanked them, knowing she'd be seeing them again at the ship the next day when they sailed. She kissed Peter and Jane, and ran out to the kitchen for a last time to thank the servants. And then suddenly, in a hail of rice and flowers, they were gone, in a borrowed Bentley, to stay at the Waldorf-Astoria for the night. There were tears in Sarah's eyes for a moment as she left them. Her life was going to be so different now. It was all very different this time. She loved William so much more, but they were going to be living so far away, in England. And for an instant, she already felt homesick at the thought of leaving all of them. She was quiet in the car, on the way to the hotel, overwhelmed by her own emotions.

'My poor love.' It was as though he read her mind most of the time. 'I'm taking you away from all these people who love you. But I love you, too, I promise you. And I promise that I will always do my best to make you happy wherever we are.' He pulled her tight into his arms and she felt safe there as she whispered to her husband:

'So will I.'

They rode the rest of the way to the hotel holding each other close, and feeling tired and at peace. It had been a wonderful day, but it had also been exhausting.

As they arrived at the Waldorf-Astoria on Park Avenue, the manager of the hotel was waiting for them, bowing and scraping, and assuring them of his abject devotion. Sarah found herself amused by the whole thing. It was so ridiculous, and by the time they got to their enormous suite in the Towers, she was laughing and her spirits had revived.

'Shame on you,' William scolded her, but he didn't really mean it. 'You're supposed to take that sort of thing very seriously! Poor man, he would have kissed your feet if you'd let him. And you probably should have,' William teased. He was used to that sort of performance, but he knew she wasn't.

'He was so silly. I couldn't keep a straight face.'

'Well, you'd better get used to it, my love. This is only the beginning. And it will all go on for a long, long time. Longer than we will, I'm afraid.'

It was the beginning of many things, and William had thought of everything to start their life off happily and well. Her luggage had been brought there that morning, her white lace nightgown and dressing gown had been laid out with her white lace slippers. He had ordered champagne, which was already waiting in the room for them. And shortly after they arrived, while they were still chatting about the wedding, and sipping champagne in the suite's little room, two waiters delivered a midnight supper. He had ordered caviar and smoked salmon, some scrambled eggs, in case she'd been too nervous to eat before, which she had, and she hadn't wanted to admit to him now that she was starving. And there was a tiny wedding cake, complete with a marzipan bride and groom, courtesy of the manager of the hotel and their master baker.

'You really do think of everything!' she exclaimed, looking like a tall, graceful child as she clapped her hands, looking at the cake and the caviar. The waiters instantly disappeared. William took a step closer to her and kissed her.

'I thought you might be hungry.'

'You know me too well.' She laughed as she dove into the caviar, and he joined her. And at midnight, they were still chatting, although they had finished their supper by then. There seemed to be an endless source of common interests, and fascinating subjects to discuss, and tonight most of all. But he had other things in mind, and at last he yawned and stretched, trying to give her the hint discreetly.

'Am I boring you?' She looked suddenly worried and he laughed. In some ways, she was still very young and he loved that.

'No, my love, but this old man is tired to the bone. Could I induce you to continue this fascinating conversation in the morning?' They had been discussing Russian literature, as compared to Russian music, a subject that was hardly pressing on that very special night.

'I'm sorry.' She was tired, too, but she was so happy

being with him that she didn't mind if they stayed up all night talking. And she was very young. In some ways, at twenty-two, she was still barely more than a child.

The suite had two bathrooms, and he disappeared into his own a few moments later. Sarah went to hers, humming to herself, with her lace nightgown and her slippers, and her little makeup case in her hand. It seemed hours before she emerged again, and he waited for her discreetly with the lights off, beneath the sheets. But in the soft light from the bathroom he could see how stunning she looked in the lace nightgown as she emerged.

She tiptoed hesitantly toward the bed, her long, dark hair hanging alluringly over one shoulder, and even at a short distance he could smell the magic of the perfume she wore. She always wore Chanel No. 5, and just the scent of it reminded him of her whenever he smelled it. He lay quietly there for a moment, in the dim light from across the room, watching her, and she looked like a young doe as she hesitated and then moved slowly toward him.

'William . . .' she whispered softly. 'Are you asleep . . . ?' And as he looked at her hungrily, he could only laugh. He had waited five months for this, and she actually thought he had gone to sleep on their wedding night before she got there. He loved her innocence sometimes, and her absurd sense of humor. She was wonderful, but tonight, he loved her even more.

'No, I'm not sleeping, my love,' he whispered in the darkness with a smile. He was anything but asleep as he reached out gently for her and she came toward him. She sat down on the bed next to him, a little bit afraid now that there were no longer any barriers between them any more. He sensed that easily, and he was infinitely gentle and patient with her as he kissed her. He wanted her to want him as much as he did now. He wanted everything to be easy and perfect and right. But it only took an instant to kindle her flame for him, and as his hands began to drift toward places they had never been, she found a passion awakening in herself that had never before been there. What she had known of love before was limited, and brief, and almost entirely devoid of tenderness or feeling. But William was a very different man than any she had ever known, and certainly a lifetime away from Freddie Van Deering.

William was aching for her as he gently fondled her breasts, and then moved his hands down over her slim hips to where her legs joined. His fingers were gentle and deft, and she was moaning as he pulled the nightgown over her head finally and tossed it somewhere on the floor. He rolled gently over on her then, and entered her with all the restraint he could muster. But he didn't have to restrain himself for long. He was surprised and pleased to find her an eager and energetic partner. And trying to fulfill the desire they had both felt for so long, they made love until the dawn, until they both lay back, entwined in each other's limbs, sated to the soul, and totally exhausted.

'My God . . . if I'd had any idea that's how it would have been, I'd have thrown you to the ground and attacked you right there, that first afternoon at George and Belinda's.' Sarah smiled sleepily as she looked at him. She was happy that she had satisfied him, and he had done things to her that she had never even dreamed of.

'I didn't know it could be like that,' she said softly.

'Neither did I.' He smiled and rolled over to look at her. She was even more beautiful to him now that he had possessed her. 'You're a remarkable woman.' She blushed faintly as he said the words, and a few minutes later, they drifted off to sleep, holding each other tightly, like two happy children.

They were both startled two hours later, when the phone rang at eight o'clock. It was the front desk, with their wake-up call. They had to be on board the ship at ten o'clock that morning.

'Oh, God . . .' He groaned, blinking as he groped for the light and the phone at the same time, and then he thanked them politely for calling. He wasn't sure if he was feeling their love or the champagne, but he felt as though someone had drained him of every drop of life force he had ever had. 'I suddenly know what Samson must have felt like after he met Delilah.' He tugged at a long wisp of dark hair curled loosely over one firm breast, and he bent to kiss her nipple and felt himself rise again, unable to believe it. 'I think maybe I've died and gone to heaven.' They made love again before they got up, and then they had to hurry to dress for the sailing. They didn't even have time to eat, just to swallow a quick cup of tea before they left, and they were laughing and teasing as they closed their bags and hurried to the waiting limousine, while Sarah tried to look dignified, and suitably like a duchess.

'I had no idea duchesses did things like that,' she whispered to him in the car after they had put up the window between themselves and the driver.

'They don't. You're quite remarkable, my darling, believe me.' But he looked as though he had found the Hope Diamond in his shoe as they boarded the *Normandie* at Pier 88 on West 50th Street. He felt faintly disloyal taking a French ship, but they were so much more fun, and he had heard that the *Normandie* offered a marvelous crossing.

They were greeted as royalty, and put in the Deauville suite, on the Sun Deck. Its twin suite, the Trouville, was occupied at the time by the maharaja of Karpurthala, who had occupied it several times since his trip on the maiden voyage.

William was very pleased as he looked around their stateroom. 'I hate to say it, but the French Line has poor Cunard beaten sadly when it comes to creature comforts.' He had never seen such luxury on a ship, in all his travels around the world. It was a glorious ship, and what they had seen of her as they boarded promised a truly extraordinary crossing.

Their stateroom was filled with champagne and flowers and baskets of fruit, and Sarah noticed that one of the prettiest bouquets came from her parents, and there was another from Peter and Jane. A moment later they arrived, and as Jane whispered a question to her sister the two of them giggled like young girls. But before they sailed Sarah and William both thanked the Thompsons again for the lovely wedding.

'We had a marvelous time,' William assured Edward again. 'It was perfect in every way.'

'The two of you must have been exhausted.'

'We were.' William tried to look vague, and hoped that he succeeded. 'We had a little champagne when we got to the hotel, and then just collapsed.' But as he said it, Sarah caught his eye, and William hoped that he wasn't blushing. He pinched her bottom discreetly as he went by, and Victoria was telling Sarah how well her new dress looked on her. They had bought it at Bonwit Teller for her trousseau. It was a white cashmere dress with a wonderful drape on one hip, and over it she had worn the new mink coat her parents had just given her as a present. They told her it would keep her warm during the long English winters. And it looked very stylish on her with a rakish hat trimmed with two enormous black feathers that were attached at the back.

'You look lovely, dear,' her mother said, and for the flash of a moment, Jane felt a pang of jealousy for her sister. She was going to have such a glamorous life, and William was such a dashing man. She loved her own husband dearly but their life was certainly not exciting. But poor Sarah had had such a difficult time before. It was hard to believe that the sad tale had ended so happily for her. It really was a storybook ending. But the story wasn't over yet either, and she hoped that Sarah would be happy in England with the duke. It was hard to think otherwise, he was so kind, and so handsome. Jane sighed as she looked at them, standing hand in hand, looking blissfully happy.

'Your Grace . . .' The chief ship's officer came to the door of their stateroom and discreetly announced that all guests had to be ashore in the next few minutes. The announcement brought tears to Victoria and Jane's eyes, and Sarah had to fight back tears as she kissed them, and her father, and Jane's babies. She clung to all of them, and then hugged her father close for a last time.

'Write to me, please . . . don't forget . . . we'll be back in London just after Christmas.' They were going to spend the holiday on the Continent alone. William's mother insisted that she had so many things to do at Whitfield that she would scarcely miss them. And William loved the idea of spending Christmas alone with Sarah in Paris.

She put her fur coat back on, and they all went out on the deck where they kissed her again, and shook hands with William, and then Edward shepherded his little tribe down the gangplank. There were tears in his eyes, too, and as his eyes met Sarah's from the dock, the tears began to slide unrestrained down his cheeks and he didn't even try to hide them.

'I love you,' she mouthed, waving frantically with one hand, and clinging to William with the other. She blew kisses to all of them as they left the dock in a hail of confetti and streamers, and somewhere on another deck a band played the 'Marseillaise', and as she watched them drift away from her, she knew she would never forget how much they all meant to her at that moment.

William held tightly to her hand until the huge ship began slowly to turn into the Hudson River, and then they could no longer see anyone on the dock. There were tears running down her cheeks, and a sob caught in her throat as he pulled her into his arms again. 'It's all right, darling,

I'm here . . . We'll come back to see them soon. I promise.' And he meant it.

'I'm sorry . . . it seems so ungrateful of me . . . It's just . . . I love them all so much . . . and I love you . . .' So much had happened in the past few days, she was still a little overwhelmed by all her emotions. He led her back to their cabin again, and offered her some more champagne, but she admitted with a tired smile that what she really longed for was a cup of coffee.

He rang for the steward then and ordered coffee for her, and jasmine tea for himself, and a plate of cinnamon toast in lieu of breakfast. And they sat munching and drinking and chatting and soon her grief had ebbed, and she was feeling better. He liked that about her though, that she cared so much, and she was so open about her feelings.

'What would you like to do today?' he asked as he glanced over the menus and the brochures, showing them all the sports and diversions that were offered on the enormous ship. 'Want to swim in the pool before lunch? Or have a game of shuffleboard? We can go to the cinema right after tea. Let's see, they've got Marcel Pagnol's *The Baker's Wife* playing, if you haven't seen it.' In truth, she had, and she had loved Pagnol's *Harvest* the year before, but she didn't care. It was so much fun doing things with him, and she moved closer to look at the brochure with him. She was amazed at how much the French Line offered their passengers, and as she read, she felt him touch her neck, and then his hand slid slowly to her breast, and then suddenly he was kissing her, and the next thing she knew they were on the bed, and all other forms of diversion were forgotten. It was lunchtime by the time they came to their senses again, and she laughed huskily as she munched on a piece of the cinnamon toast that still sat on a plate near the bed.

'I guess we're not going to be doing much in the way of sports this trip, eh?'

'I'm not entirely sure we're ever going to get out of the cabin.' And as though to prove that to him, she teased him again and he took her up on it rather more quickly than she had expected.

They made it all the way to the bathtub after that, and made love again there, and by the time they ventured out again, it was late afternoon, and they were both looking a little embarrassed at the hours they'd kept.

'We're going to get a hell of a reputation on this ship,' William whispered to her. 'It's a good thing we've come over on the French Line.'

'Do you suppose they know?' Sarah looked a little nervous. 'After all, it is our honeymoon . . .'

'Oh God, that's right. How could I forget. You know, I think I forgot my wallet on the desk. Do you mind if we go back for it?'

'Not at all,' she agreed amenably, but unable to imagine why he needed it here. But he was quite insistent. So she went back to the stateroom with him, and followed him inside. He shut the door as she walked in, and as soon as the door was closed behind them, he grabbed her.

'William!' she squealed, as he laughed, and she began to giggle. 'You're a sex fiend!'

'I'm not . . . I assure you, normally I'm quite respectable. It's all your fault!' he said as he devoured her neck and her arms and her breasts and her thighs and even more appealing places.

'My fault? What have I done?' But she was loving every minute of it, as they collapsed to the floor of the sitting room and he began to make love to her again.

'You're far, far too appealing,' he said as he closed his eyes and entered her while they still had half their clothes on, and lay on the stateroom floor.

'So are you,' she muttered, and then gave a small cry, and it was a long time before they got up again and made it all the way to the bedroom, leaving a trail of clothes in their wake.

They didn't even bother to go to dinner that night, and when their room steward called them on the phone, offering dinner in their rooms, William declined, announcing mournfully that they were both seasick. He offered crackers and soup instead, but William insisted that they were both sleeping, and after he hung up, the little Frenchman grinned at the maid.

'*Mal de mer*?' she asked knowingly, wondering if they were seasick, but the little steward winked. He had gotten a good look at them, and knew better.

'*Mon oeil. Lune de miel.*' Honeymoon, he explained, and she laughed as he pinched her bottom.

William and Sarah emerged on to the deck the next morning looking healthy and rested, and William seemed unable to stop smiling at her. Sarah laughed at him as they walked around the deck and settled into two deck chairs.

'You know, people really will know what we've been up to if you don't stop grinning.'

'I can't help it. I've never been so happy in my life. When can we go back to the cabin? I swear, it's becoming an addiction.'

'I'm going to call the captain if you lay a hand on me again. I'm not going to be able to walk by the time we get to Paris.'

'I'll carry you.' He grinned as he leaned over and kissed her again. But she didn't look the least bit dismayed by what had happened. She was loving it, too, and loving him. But that day they made an effort to discover the ship, and managed to stay out of bed until teatime. Then they allowed themselves a brief reward, and forced themselves to get their clothes on again in time for dinner.

Sarah loved going to thé dining room on the *Normandie*. It was a fairyland of elegance, with ceilings three decks high, and the room itself was slightly longer than the Hall of Mirrors at Versailles, and no less impressive. The ceiling was gilt, and on the walls there were columns of soft lighting twenty feet high. They descended an endless, blue-carpeted staircase when they arrived, and William was wearing white tie, as were all the other men.

'Does the fact that we're eating in the dining room tonight,' she whispered to him, 'mean that the honeymoon is over?'

'I was a little bit afraid of that myself,' he confided to her as he devoured his soufflé. 'I think we ought to go back to the room as soon as we finish.' She giggled at him, and they managed to stop in the Grand Salon above the dining room and dance for a while, before they took a last walk on the deck and kissed beneath the stars. Then at last they went back to their stateroom. It was the perfect honeymoon, and they had a wonderful time, swimming and walking and dancing and eating, and making love. It was like being suspended between two worlds, their old one and their new one. They tried to stay away from everyone, although most people in first class were aware of who they were, and more than once she heard people whisper as they walked by, 'The Duke and Duchess of Whitfield . . .' 'Windsor?' one dowager asked. 'She's much younger than I thought . . . and better looking . . .' Sarah had been unable to repress a smile, and William had subtly pinched her and called her Wallis after that.

'Don't ever call me that, or I shall start calling you David!'

Sarah hadn't met them yet, but William had told her they would probably have to pay a visit to them in Paris. 'You might like her better than you expect. She's not my cup of tea, but she's really very charming. And he's happier than he used to be, claims he can sleep now. I suppose I know why.' William grinned. He was sleeping remarkably well himself, in between orgies with his bride.

They dined at the captain's table on the last night, and

attended the Gala. They'd actually gone to the Fancy Dress Ball the night before, dressed as a maharaja and maharani, in costumes loaned to them by the purser, and jewels Sarah had brought along herself. The roles suited them well. William looked very handsome and Sarah looked extremely exotic. But her expertise with her makeup and naked belly had only won her an early return to their stateroom. The stewards were making bets now as to how long they could stay out of bed. And so far, four hours seemed to have been their limit.

'Maybe we should just stay on the ship,' Sarah suggested as she lay in bed, on their last night, dozing sporadically after they'd made love after the captain's dinner. 'I'm not at all sure I want to go to Paris at all.' William had reserved an apartment for them at the Ritz, and they were going to stay there for a month, while taking driving tours around the châteaux outside Paris. They wanted to go to Bordeaux, and the Loire, and Tours . . . and the Faubourg-St. Honoré, she had said with a grin . . . to Chanel and Dior and Mainbocher . . . and Balenciaga.

'You're a wicked girl,' William accused her, as he got back into bed beside her, suddenly wondering if after all this lovemaking for the past week, they might have made a baby. He wanted to ask her about it, but he still felt a little awkward, and finally, later that night, he got up his courage. 'You . . . uh . . . you never got pregnant, did you, when you were married before, I mean?' He was just curious, and he had never asked her. But her answer surprised him.

'Yes, I did, as a matter of fact.' She said it very softly, and she didn't look at him as she said it.

'What happened?' It was obvious she didn't have a child, and he couldn't help but wonder why. He hoped she hadn't had an abortion, it would have been so traumatic for her, and might have left her unable to have more children. He had never asked her about that before their marriage.

'I lost it,' she said quietly, the memory of that loss still pained her, even though she knew it was for the best now.

'Do you know why? Did something happen?' And then he realized what a stupid question he had asked her. With a marriage like hers, anything might have happened. 'Never mind. It won't happen again.' He kissed her gently and she drifted off to sleep a little while later, dreaming of babies and William.

The next morning, they left the ship at Le Havre, and took the boat train into Paris, and they laughed and chatted all the while, and as soon as they arrived they went straight to the hotel, and back out again to go shopping.

'Aha! I've found something you enjoy doing as much as making love. Sarah, I'm bitterly disappointed.' But they had a wonderful time going to Hermès, and Chanel, and Boucheron, and a handful of small jewelers. He bought her a wonderful wide sapphire bracelet, set with a diamond clasp, and a ruby necklace and earrings that were really stunning. And a huge ruby brooch at Van Cleef in the shape of a rose.

'My God, William . . . I feel so guilty.' She knew he had spent an absolute fortune, but he didn't seem to mind it. And the jewelry he had bought her was fabulous and she loved it.

'Don't be silly!' He brushed it off as an ordinary event. 'Just promise me we won't leave the room again for two days. That is the tax I will demand of you each time we go shopping.'

'Don't you like to shop?' She looked briefly disappointed, he had seemed such a good sport about it the summer before.

'I love it. But I'd rather make love to my wife.'

'Oh that . . .' She laughed, and addressed his needs the moment they went back to their room at the Ritz. They

173

went shopping repeatedly after that. He bought her beautiful clothes at Jean Patou, and a fabulous leopard coat at Dior, and an enormous string of pearls at Mouboussin, which she wore every hour of every day after that. They even managed to go to the Louvre, and on their second week there, they went to tea with the Duke and Duchess of Windsor. And Sarah had to admit that William was right. Although she'd been predisposed to dislike her, she actually found the duchess extremely charming. And he was a lovely man. Shy, cautious, reserved, but extremely kind when you got to know him. And very witty when he relaxed with people he knew well. It had been an awkward meeting with them at first, and much to Sarah's chagrin, Wallis had tried to draw an unfortunate comparison between them. But William was quick to discourage any such comparison, and Sarah was faintly embarrassed by how cool he was to the duchess. There was no question about how he felt about her, and yet he had the utmost affection and respect for his cousin.

'Damn shame he ever married her,' he said on their way back to the hotel. 'It's incredible to think that, if it weren't for her, he could still be the King of England.'

'I don't get the feeling he ever really enjoyed it. But I could be mistaken.'

'You're not. He didn't. It didn't suit him. But it was his duty anyway. I must say though, Bertie is doing a bang-up job of it. He's an awfully good sport. And he absolutely hates that woman.'

'I can see why people are so taken with her though. She has a way of winding you around her little finger.'

'She is one of the truly great connivers. Did you see the jewelry he's given her? That diamond-and-sapphire bracelet must have cost him an absolute fortune. Van Cleef made it for him when they got married.' And she had an entire parure to go with it by then, necklace, earrings, brooch, and two rings.

'I like the bracelet she was wearing on her other hand better,' Sarah said softly. 'The little diamond chain with the little crosses.' It was far more discreet, and William made a mental note of it for a present for her later on. She'd also shown them a wonderful bracelet from Cartier that she'd just gotten, all made up of flowers and leaves in sapphires, rubies, and emeralds. And she'd called it her 'fruit salad'.

'Anyway, we've done our duty, my dear. It would have been rude if we hadn't called them. And now I can tell Mother we did. She was always so fond of David, I thought it would kill her when he gave up the throne.'

'And yet she said she didn't mind when you did,' Sarah said sadly, still feeling guilty for what she'd cost him. She knew it would bother her for a lifetime, but it never seemed to bother William at all.

'That's hardly the same thing,' William said gently. 'He had the throne, darling. I never would have. Mother feels very strongly about these things. But she's not ridiculous, she didn't expect me to be king.'

'I suppose not.'

They got out of the car a few blocks before the hotel, and walked slowly back, talking again about the Duke and Duchess of Windsor. They had invited them to come back again, but William had explained that they were going to begin their driving trip the following morning.

They had already planned to visit the Loire, and he wanted to stop and see Chartres on the way. He had never been there.

And when they left the next morning, in a small hired Renault, which he drove, they were both in high spirits. They had taken a picnic lunch with them, in case they couldn't find a restaurant along the way, and an hour outside Paris, everything was wonderfully rural and still green here and there. There were horses and cows and farms, and after another hour, sheep wandering across the road, and a goat stopped to stare at them as they ate their lunch in a field by the roadside. They had brought blankets and warm coats, but it wasn't cold, and the weather was surprisingly sunny. They had expected rain, but so far, the weather had been perfect.

They had reservations at small hotels along the way, and they were planning to be away from Paris for eight or ten days. But on the third day, they were still only a hundred miles from Paris, in Montbazon, and loving the inn where they were staying too much to leave it.

The owner of the inn had told them several places to go, and they had gone to tiny churches, and a wonderful old farm, and two terrific antiques shops. And the local restaurant was the best they'd ever been to.

'I love this place,' Sarah said happily, devouring everything on her plate. She had been eating a lot better since they'd been in Paris, and she wasn't quite as thin, which suited her very well. Sometimes William worried that being quite that thin wasn't healthy.

'We really ought to move on tomorrow.'

They were both sorry to go when they left, and an hour later, much to William's annoyance, their car stalled on the road. A local peasant helped them to get it started again, and gave them some more gas to get on their way, and half an hour later, they stopped for lunch near an ancient stone gate, with an elaborate iron grille that stood open, leading to an overgrown old road.

'It looks like the gate to heaven,' she teased.

'Or hell. Depending on what we deserve.' He smiled back. But he already knew his fate. He had been in heaven ever since he married Sarah.

'Want to go exploring?' She was always adventuresome and young and he enjoyed that about her.

'I suppose we could. But what if we get shot by some angry landlord?'

'Don't worry. I'll protect you. Besides, it looks like the

place has been deserted for years,' she encouraged him.

'The whole country looks like that, you goose. This isn't England.'

'Oh, you snob!' she hooted at him, and they began to walk down the lane that drifted away from the gates. They decided to leave their car near the road, so as not to draw more attention to their adventure.

And for a long time, it appeared to be nothing more than an old country road, until at last there was a long *allée*, bordered by huge trees, and overgrown with bushes. Had it been tidier, it might even have looked a little like the entrance to Whitfield, or the Southampton estate.

'It's pretty here.' They could hear birds singing in the trees, and she hummed as they wandered through the tall grass and the bushes.

'I don't think there's much here,' William finally said, when they were almost at the end of the double border of tall trees, and just as he said it, he saw an enormous stone building in the distance. 'Good Lord, what is that?' It looked like Versailles, sitting there, except as they approached they could see that it was in desperate need of repair. The entire place was ramshackle and deserted, and some of the outbuildings seemed almost ready to collapse. There was a small cottage at the foot of the hill that must have been a caretaker's cottage years before, but now it was barely still a building.

There were stables off to the right, and huge barns for carriages as well. William was fascinated and glanced inside as they walked past them. There were two ancient carriages still sitting there, with the crest of the family carefully gilded on the panels.

'What an amazing place.' He smiled at her, glad that she had urged him to explore it.

'What do you suppose it is?' Sarah looked around her, at the carriages, the halters, the old blacksmith tools, with fascination.

'It's an old château, and those were the stables. The whole place looks as though it's been deserted for two hundred years.'

'Maybe it has been.' She smiled excitedly. 'Maybe there's a ghost!' He began to make ghostly noises then, and pretended to lunge at her as they went back to the road, and headed up the hill to what looked like a castle in a fairy story, or a dream. It was clearly not as old as Whitfield was, or as Belinda and George's castle where they had met, but William estimated that this one was easily two hundred and fifty or three hundred years old, and as they approached it, they saw that the architecture was very fine. There had obviously been a park, and gardens, and perhaps even a maze, most of which was overgrown now, and the entrance to the house was truly regal as they stood before it. William tried the windows and the doors, but they were all locked. But a look into the shuttered rooms, through rotting slats, showed lovely floors, delicately carved moldings, and high ceilings. It was hard to see more, but it was clearly an incredible place. Being there was like taking a huge step back in time, and reaching out to the time of Louis XIV or XV or XVI. One expected a carriage full of men in wigs with satin breeches to come around the corner at full tilt at any moment, and to ask them why they were there.

'Whose do you suppose it was?' she asked, greatly intrigued by the surroundings.

'The locals ought to know. It can't be much of a secret. It's an enormous place.'

'Do you suppose anyone still owns it?' It looked as though it had been abandoned years ago, but someone had to own it.

'Someone must. But obviously not anyone who wants it, or can afford to keep it up.' It was in a terrible state, even the marble front steps were badly broken. It all looked as though it had been deserted for decades.

But Sarah's eyes had lit up as she looked around her. 'Wouldn't you love to take a place like this, tear it apart, and put it back together again, the way it once was . . . you know, restore it perfectly to everything it used to be.' Her eyes danced just thinking of it, and he rolled his eyes in feigned horror and exhaustion.

'Do you have any idea how much work that would be? Can you even imagine it . . . not to mention the cost. It would take an army of workers just to bring this place around, and the entire Bank of England.'

'But think of how beautiful it would be in the end. It really would be worth it.'

'To whom?' He laughed, looking at her in amusement. He had never seen her so excited about anything since they'd met. 'How can you get so worked up over a place like this? It's an absolute disaster.' But the truth was, it excited him too. But the enormity of the work that needed to be done was more than a little daunting. 'We'll ask about it when we get back to the road again. I'm sure they'll tell us ten people were murdered here, and it's a terrible place.' He teased her about it all the way back to the car, but she didn't want to hear it. She thought it was the most beautiful thing she'd ever seen, and if she could have, she would have bought it then and there, she said, and William readily believed she would have.

As it turned out, they met an old farmer just near the main road, and William asked him in French about the crumbling château they had just seen, and he had a great deal to tell them. Sarah struggled to understand as much as she could, and she got most of it. But afterwards, William filled her in on the rest of the details. The place they had seen was called Le Château de la Meuze, and it had been deserted for some eighty years, since the late 1850s. It had been inhabited before that by the same family for more than two hundred years, but the last of them had died out, having no children. It was passed on through generations of cousins and distant relatives after that, and the old man was no longer sure who owned it. He said there had still been people there when he was a boy, an old woman who couldn't take care of the place, La Comtesse de la Meuze, who was a cousin of the French kings. But she died when he was a child, and the place had been shuttered up ever since then.

'How sad. Why hasn't anyone ever tried to fix it up, I wonder.'

'It would take too much money probably. The French have had some hard times. And places like this aren't easy to run once you restore them.' He knew only too well how much money and attention it took to run Whitfield, and this would be far more costly.

'I think it's a shame.' She looked sad as she thought of the old house, thinking of what it might have been, or had been once. She would have loved to roll up her sleeves and help William restore it.

They got back in the car and he looked at her curiously. 'Are you serious, Sarah? Do you really love this place? Would you really like doing something like this?'

'I'd love it.' Her eyes lit up.

'It's a hell of a lot of work. And it doesn't really work unless you do some of it yourself. You have to hammer and bang and work and sweat along with the men who help you do it. You know, I saw Belinda and George restore their place, and you have no idea how much work that was.' But he also knew how much they loved it, and how dear to them it had become in the process.

'Yes, but that place is much more complicated than this, and it's a lot older,' Sarah explained, wishing she could wave a magic wand and take possession of the Château de la Meuze.

'This wouldn't be easy either,' William said intelligently. 'Absolutely everything needs to be restored, even the caretaker's cottage and the barns and stables.'

'I don't care,' she said stubbornly. 'I'd love to do something like this' – she looked up at him – 'if you'd help me.'

'I thought I was beyond taking on a project like this. It's taken me fifteen years to get Whitfield running right, but I don't know, you make it sound very exciting.' He smiled at her, feeling lucky and happy again, as he had since they'd met.

'It could be so wonderful . . .' Her eyes glowed at him, and he smiled. He was putty in her hands, and he would have done almost anything she wanted.

'But in France? What about England?' She tried to be polite about it, but the truth was that she had fallen in love with the place, but she didn't want to be pushy with him. Perhaps it was far too expensive, or maybe just too much work.

'I'd love to live here. But maybe we could find something like it in England.' But there didn't seem to be much point. He already had Whitfield, and thanks to him, it was in excellent repair. But here it was different. It could have been someplace of their own that they could put back together with their own hands, something they could create and rebuild side by side. She had never been as excited about anything in her whole life, and she knew it was really crazy. The last thing they needed was a ramshackle château in France. She tried to forget about it as they drove away, but for the rest of the trip, all she could think of was the lonely château she had come to love. All it needed, she thought, was people to love it. It almost seemed to have a soul of its own, like a lost child, or a very sad old man. But whatever it was, it was not destined to be hers, she knew, and she never mentioned it again once they went back to Paris. She didn't want him to feel she was pressing him, and she knew how impossible her fascination with it was.

It was Christmas week by then, and Paris looked beautiful. They went to dinner once at the Windsors', at their house on the Boulevard Suchet, which had been decorated by Boudin. And the rest of the time they spent alone, enjoying their first Christmas. William called his mother several times to make sure that she wasn't lonely. But she was constantly out at neighboring estates, dining with relatives, and on Christmas Eve she was at Sandringham with the royal family for their traditional Christmas dinner. Bertie had sent a car, two footmen, and a lady-in-waiting especially for her.

Sarah called her parents in New York when she knew Peter and Jane would be there on Christmas Eve, and for a moment, she felt a little homesick. But William was so good to her, and she was so happy with him. On Christmas Day he gave her an extraordinary emerald-cut sapphire ring from Van Cleef, set with diamonds around it, and a beautiful bracelet from Cartier, made of diamonds and cabochon emeralds and sapphires and rubies, all in a flower design. She had seen one like it on the arm of the Duchess of Windsor and admired it. It was a very unusual piece, and when William gave it to her she was stunned.

'Darling, how you spoil me!' She was in awe of everything he'd given her, and there were bags and scarves, and books he knew she'd like, from vendors along the Seine, and little trinkets that made her laugh, like a doll that was just like one she'd told him she'd had as a little girl. He knew her so well, and he was so incredibly generous and thoughtful.

She gave him a brilliant blue enamel and gold cigarette case by Carl Fabergé, with an inscription from the Czarina Alexandra to the Czar in 1916, and some wonderful riding gear from Hermès that he had admired, and a very stylish new watch from Cartier. And on the back of it she had engraved, 'First Christmas, First Love, with all my heart, Sarah.' He was so touched when he read it, there were tears in his eyes, and then he took her back to bed, and made love to her again. They spent most of Christmas Day in bed, enchanted that they hadn't gone back to London for all the pomp and ceremony and endless traditions.

And when they woke up again late that afternoon, he smiled down at her as she slowly opened her eyes. He kissed her neck, and told her again how much he loved her. 'I have something else for you,' he confessed. But he wasn't sure if she would hate it or love it. It was the craziest thing he had ever done, the maddest moment in his life, and yet he had a feeling that she might truly love it. And if she did, it was worth all the trouble it had cost. He took a small box out of a drawer. It was wrapped in gold paper, and tied with a thin gold ribbon.

'What is it?' She looked at him with the curiosity of a child, while he quaked inside.

'Open it.'

She did, slowly, carefully, wondering if it was a piece of jewelry. It was small enough to be. But when she took the paper off, there was another smaller box inside, and in it was a tiny wooden house made of a matchbox. She wasn't quite sure what it was, and she looked at him with her eyes filled with questions. 'What is it, sweetheart?'

'Open it,' he said, sounding choked and terrified.

She opened the matchbox, and inside was a tiny slip of paper, which said only, 'Le Château de la Meuze. Merry Christmas 1938. From William with all my love.'

Sarah looked at him in astonishment, as she read the words and suddenly understood what he'd done, and she gave a shout of amazement, unable to believe he'd done anything so wonderfully crazy. She had never, ever wanted anything as much.

'You bought it?' she asked wondrously, as she threw her arms around his neck, and tossed herself naked into his lap with excitement. '*Did* you?'

'It's yours. I'm not sure if we're crazy, or brilliant. If you don't want it, we can just sell the land, and let it rot, or forget it.' It hadn't cost him very much. It had just been a lot of trouble to put the deal together. But the amount he had paid for it had been pathetically small. It had cost him more to remodel his hunting lodge in England than to buy the Château de la Meuze with all its land and buildings.

She was so excited, she was beside herself, and he was thrilled that she was so pleased with his present. It had been more complicated than he thought. There were four heirs, two of whom were in France, one of whom was in New York, and the other was in the wilds of England. But his solicitors had helped him with all that. And Sarah's father had contacted the woman in New York through the bank. They were distant cousins of the countess who had died eighty years before, just as the farmer had said. In fact, the people he had bought the château from were several generations removed from her, but no-one had ever known what to do with the property or how to divide it, so they had abandoned it to its fate, until Sarah found it and fell in love with it.

And then she looked worriedly at William. 'Did it cost you a fortune?' She would have felt terribly guilty if it had, even though in her heart of hearts, she thought it was worth it. But the truth was that he had bought it for nothing at all. All four heirs were vastly relieved to be free of it, and none of them had been particularly greedy.

'The fortune will come when we try to restore it.'

'I promise you, I'll do all the work myself . . . everything! When can we come back and start?' She was jumping up and down on him like a child as he groaned with mixed delight and anguish.

'We have to go back to England first, and I have to get a few things settled there. I don't know . . . February perhaps . . . March?'

'Can't we come sooner?' She looked like a happy little girl on Christmas morning as he smiled.

'We'll try . . .' He was immensely pleased that she really liked it. He was excited about it now, too, and doing the work with her might actually be fun, if it didn't kill them both. 'I'm happy that you like it. I had a bad moment or two, thinking that you had forgotten all about it, and didn't really want it. And I promise you, your father thinks I'm quite mad. I'll have to show you some of the cables sometime. He said this sounded almost as bad as that farm you tried to buy on Long Island, and it's now completely obvious to him that we're both mad and obviously well suited.' She giggled with glee, as she thought of the house again, and then she looked at William with a mischievous look of her own, which he was quick to notice.

'I have something for you too . . . I think . . . I didn't want to say anything until we got back to England, and I was sure . . . but I think it's possible . . . we might be having a baby . . .' She looked sheepish and pleased all at the same time, and he looked at her in wonder and amazement.

'So soon? Sarah, are you serious?' He couldn't believe it.

'I think I am. It must have happened on our wedding night. I'll be sure in a few more weeks.' But she had already recognized the early signs. This time she had recognized them herself.

'Sarah, my darling, you are truly amazing!' In one night they had acquired a family and a château in France, except the child had barely been conceived, and the château had been falling to rack and ruin for the better part of a century, but nevertheless they were both pleased.

They stayed in Paris, walking by the Seine, and making love, and having quiet dinners in little bistros until just after the new year, and then they returned to London to be the Duke and Duchess of Whitfield.

Chapter 11

William insisted that Sarah go to his doctor on Harley Street, the moment they returned to London. And he confirmed what she had guessed weeks before. By then she was five weeks pregnant, and he told her that the child would be born in late August or early September. And he urged her to be cautious for the first few months because of the miscarriage she'd had. But he found her in excellent health, and congratulated William on his heir, when he came to fetch her. William was clearly very pleased with himself, and with her, and they told his mother when they went to Whitfield that weekend.

'My dear children, that is marvelous!' she raved, acting as though they had accomplished something no-one else had since Mary with Jesus. 'I might remind you that it took you thirty days what it took your father and me thirty years to accomplish. You are to be congratulated on your speed, and your good fortune! What clever children you are!' She toasted them and they laughed. But she was enormously pleased for them, and she told Sarah again that having William had been the happiest moment in her life, and had remained thus in all the years since then. But as the doctor had done, she urged her not to be foolish and overdo, lest it hurt the baby or herself.

'Really, I'm fine.' She felt surprisingly well, and the doctor had said they could make love, 'reasonably', he had suggested they not hang off the chandelier or try to set any Olympic records, which Sarah had passed on to William. But he was desperately afraid that making love at all would hurt her or the baby. 'I promise you, it won't do anything. He said so.'

'How does he know?'

'He's a doctor,' she reassured him.

'Maybe he's no good. Maybe we should see someone else.'

'William, he was your mother's doctor before you were born.'

'Precisely. He's too old. We'll see someone younger.'

He actually went so far as to find a specialist for her, and just to humor him, she saw him, and he told her all the same things as kindly old Lord Allthorpe, who Sarah much preferred. And by then she was two months pregnant, and had had no problems.

'What I want to know is when are we going back to France,' she said after they'd been in London for a month. She was dying to get started on their new home.

'Are you serious?' William looked horrified. 'You want to go now? Don't you want to wait until after the baby?'

'Of course not. Why wait all these months when we could be working on it now? I'm not sick, for heaven's sake, darling, I'm pregnant.'

'I know. But what if something happens?' He looked frantic and wished she weren't so determined. But even old Lord Allthorpe agreed that there was no real reason for her to stay at home, and as long as she didn't wear herself out completely, or carry anything too heavy, he thought the project in France would be fine.

'Keeping busy will be the best thing for her,' he assured them, and then suggested they wait till March, so she would be fully three months pregnant before they left. It was the only compromise Sarah was willing to make. She would wait until March to go back to France, but not a moment longer. She was dying to get to work on the château.

William tried to drag out his projects at Whitfield as best he could, and his mother kept urging him to tell Sarah to take it easy.

'Mother, I try, but she doesn't listen,' he finally said in a moment of exasperation.

'She's just a child herself. She doesn't realize one has to be careful. She wouldn't want to lose this baby.' But Sarah had already learned that lesson the hard way long before. And she was more careful than William thought, taking naps, and getting off her feet, and resting when she was tired. She had no intention of losing this baby. Nor did she intend to sit around. And she pressed him until finally he was ready to go back to France, and couldn't stall her any longer. By then it was mid-March, and she was threatening to leave without him.

They went to Paris on the royal yacht, when Lord Mountbatten was on his way to see the Duke of Windsor, and he agreed to take the young couple over as a favor. 'Dickie', as William and his contemporaries called him, was a very handsome man, and Sarah amused him during the entire crossing, telling him about the château and the work they were going to do there.

'William, old man, sounds like you have your work cut out for you.' But he thought it would be good for them too. It was obvious that they were very much in love, and very excited about their project.

William had had the concierge at the Ritz hire a car for them, and they had managed to find a small hotel two and a half hours outside Paris, not far from their crumbling château. They rented the top floor of the hotel, and planned to live there until they had made the château habitable again, which they both knew could be a long time.

'It might be years, you know,' William grumbled as they saw it again. And he spent the next two weeks lining up workmen. Eventually, he had hired a sizeable crew, and they began by prying off the boards and shutters to see what lay within. There were surprises everywhere as they worked, and some of them were happy ones, and some of them were not. The main living room was a splendid room, and eventually they found three salons, with beautiful *boiseries*, and fading gilt on some of the moldings; there were marble fireplaces and beautiful floors. But in some places the wood had been destroyed by mold and years of dampness, and animals who had ventured in through the boards and gnawed at the lovely moldings here and there.

There was a huge, handsome dining room, a series of smaller salons, still on the main floor, an extraordinary wood-panelled library, and a baronial hall worthy of any English castle, and a kitchen so antiquated it reminded Sarah of some of the museums she'd visited with her parents the year before. There were tools there that surely no-one had used for two hundred years, and she collected them carefully with the intent to save them. And they carefully stored the two carriages they had found in the barn.

William ventured cautiously upstairs after their initial investigations on the main floor of the château. But he absolutely refused to let Sarah join him, for fear that the floors might cave in, but he found them all surprisingly solid, and eventually he let Sarah come up to see what he'd found. There were at least a dozen large sunny rooms, again with lovely *boiseries*, and beautifully shaped windows, and there was a handsome sitting room with a marble fireplace, which looked out over the main entrance and what had once been the park and the gardens of the château. But suddenly Sarah realized as she walked from room to room, that there were no bathrooms. Of course, she laughed to herself, there wouldn't have been. They took baths in tubs in their dressing rooms, and they had chamber pots instead of toilets.

There was a lot of work to do, but it was clearly well worth doing. And even William looked excited now. He made drawings for the men, and drew up work schedules and spent every day from dawn to dusk giving directions, while Sarah worked beside him, sanding down old wood, refinishing floors, cleaning *boiseries*, repairing gilt, and polishing brass and bronze until it shone, and eventually she spent most of every day painting. And while they worked on the main house, William had assigned a crew of young boys to repair the caretaker's cottage so that eventually they could move there from the hotel, and be right on the site of their enormous project.

The caretaker's cottage was small. It had a tiny living room, a smaller bedroom beside it, and a large cozy kitchen, and upstairs there were two slightly larger sunny bedrooms. But it was certainly adequate for them, and possibly even a serving girl downstairs, if eventually Sarah felt she needed one. They had a bedroom for themselves, and even one for their baby when it arrived.

She could feel the baby moving inside her now, and each time she felt it, she smiled, convinced that it would be a boy and look just like William. She told him that from time to time, and he insisted that he didn't care if it was a girl, they wanted more anyway. 'And it's not as though we're supplying an heir to the throne,' he teased her, but there was still his title, and the matter of inheriting Whitfield and its lands.

But they both had more than Whitfield, or even their château, on their minds these days. In March, Hitler had raised his ugly head, and had 'absorbed' Czechoslovakia, claiming that in effect, it no longer existed as a separate entity any more. He had, in effect, swallowed ten million persons who were not Germans. And he had no sooner devoured them, than he turned his sights on Poland, and began threatening them about issues that had been a problem for some time, in Danzig, and elsewhere.

A week after all that, the Spanish Civil War came to an end, having taken well over a million lives, as the well-being of Spain lay in ruins.

But April was worse. Imitating his German friend, Mussolini took over Albania, and the British and French governments began to growl, and offered Greece and Romania their help if they felt it was needed. They had offered the same thing weeks before to Poland, promising this time to stand by if Hitler came any closer.

By May, Mussolini and Hitler had signed an alliance, each promising to follow the other into war, and similar discussions between France, England, and Russia stopped and started, and went nowhere. It was a dismal spring for world politics, and the Whitfields were deeply concerned, yet at the same time they were moving ahead with their enormous work at the Château de la Meuze, and Sarah was deeply engrossed in her baby. She was six months pregnant by then, and although he didn't say so to her, William thought she was enormous. But they were both tall, and it was reasonable to think that their child might be large. He would feel it moving inside her at night as they lay in bed, and once in a while when he moved close to her, he'd feel the baby kick him.

'Doesn't that hurt?' He was fascinated by it, by the life he felt inside her, her growing shape, and the baby that would soon come from the love they had shared. The miracle of it all still overwhelmed him. He still made love to her from time to time, but he was more and more afraid to hurt her, and she seemed less interested now. She was hard at work on the château, and by the time they fell into bed at night they were both exhausted. And in the morning the workmen arrived at six o'clock and began hammering and banging.

They were able to move into the caretaker's house in late June, and give up their rooms at the hotel, which pleased them. They were living on their own turf now and the grounds had begun to look civilized. He had brought a fleet of gardeners from Paris to cut and chop and plant, and turn a jungle back into a garden. The park took more time, but by August there was hope for that, too, and by then it was amazing, the progress they had made with the whole house. William was beginning to think they would move in at the end of the month, just in time to have their baby. He was working particularly hard on their suite of rooms so that Sarah would be comfortable there, and they could go on working on the house after they moved in. It would take years for all the minute details to be finished, but they had already accomplished an astonishing amount of work in a remarkably short time.

In fact, George and Belinda had come by in July, and they had been vastly impressed by how much William and Sarah had done by then. Jane and Peter also came to visit, and it was all too short a visit for the sisters. Jane was crazy about William, and thrilled for Sarah about the baby. And she promised to come again after it was born, so she could see it, although she was expecting again, too, and it would be a while before she could come back to Europe. Sarah's parents had wanted to come, too, but her father hadn't been feeling well, though Jane assured her it wasn't serious. And they were frantically busy rebuilding Southampton. But her mother had every intention of coming to visit in the fall, after Sarah had the baby.

After Peter and Jane left, Sarah felt lonely for several days, and absorbed herself in the house again to boost her spirits. She worked frantically to finish her own room, and especially the lovely room next to it that she had set aside for the baby.

'How's it coming in there?' William called out to her one afternoon, as he brought her a loaf of bread and some cheese and a steaming cup of coffee. He had been so kind to her family, just as he was to everyone, and to her. And more than ever, Sarah loved him deeply.

'I'm getting there,' she said proudly. She had been carefully gilding some *boiserie*, and it looked better than what they had seen at Versailles.

'You're good.' He admired her work with a gentle smile. 'I'd hire you myself,' he said as he bent down to kiss her. 'Are you feeling all right?'

'I'm fine.' Her back was killing her, but she wouldn't have told him for anything in the world. She loved what she did there every day, and she wouldn't be pregnant for much longer. Only for another three or four weeks, and they had found a small, clean hospital in Chaumont where she could have the baby. There was a very sensible doctor there, and she had gone to see him every few weeks. He thought everything was going well, although he warned her that she might have a very large baby.

'What does that mean?' she had asked, trying to sound casual. Lately, she had been getting a little nervous about the birth, but she hadn't wanted to frighten William with her concerns, they seemed so silly.

'It could mean a cesarean,' the doctor confessed to her. 'It can be disagreeable, but mother and child are sometimes safer that way if the baby is too large, and yours could be.'

'Would I be able to have more children, if I had one?' He hesitated and then shook his head, feeling he owed her the truth.

'No, you wouldn't.'

'Then I don't want one.'

'Then walk a great deal, move around, get exercise, swim if there is a river near your house. It will all help you with the birth, Madame la Duchesse.' He always bowed politely when she left, and although she didn't like his threat of a cesarean, she liked him. And she said nothing at all to William about the baby being large, or the possibility of a cesarean section at the birth. There was one thing she was sure of, and that was that she wanted more children.

And she was going to do everything she could not to jeopardize that.

The baby was still a week or two away when Germany and Russia signed a pact of nonaggression, leaving only France and Britain as potential allies, since Hitler had already signed a pact with Mussolini, and Spain was virtually destroyed and could help no-one.

'It's getting serious, isn't it?' Sarah asked him quietly one night. They had just moved into their room in the château, and with all the little details still to be done, she thought she had never seen anything as beautiful, which was exactly how William felt when he looked at Sarah.

'It's not good. I should probably go back to England at some point, just to see what they think at Number Ten, Downing Street.' But he hadn't wanted to worry her with it. 'Maybe we'll both go back for a few days, after the baby comes.' They wanted to show it to his mother anyway, so Sarah made no objection to the plan.

'It's hard to believe we'd go to war, England, I mean.' She was beginning to think of herself as one of them, even though she had kept her American citizenship when she married William, and he saw no particular reason for her to change it. All she wanted was for the world to settle down long enough for her to have her baby. She didn't want to have to worry about a war, when she wanted to find a quiet home for their child. 'You won't leave if something happens, William, will you?' She looked at him in sudden panic, running all the possibilities over in her mind.

'I won't leave before the baby comes. I promise you that.'

'But afterwards?' Her eyes were wide with terror.

'Only if there's a war. Now stop worrying about all that. It's not healthy for you right now. I'm not going anywhere, except to the hospital with you, so don't be silly.'

She had mild pains as she lay in their new room with him that night, but by morning they were gone and she felt better. It was silly to worry about war now, she was just nervous about the baby, she told herself the next morning when she got up.

But on September first, as she hammered on a cabinet upstairs, on the floor of small bedrooms above theirs, which would make wonderful children's bedrooms one day, she heard someone shout something unintelligible below her, and then she heard running downstairs, and thought someone might be hurt, so she went all the way down to the main kitchen to help. But they were listening to the wireless there.

Germany had just attacked Poland, with ground troops and by air. William was standing there, listening to the broadcast, and with him every man in the place. Afterwards they all argued about whether or not France would attempt to rescue Poland. A few of them thought they should, many of them didn't care. They had their own troubles at home, their families, their problems, some of them thought Hitler should be stopped before it was too late for all of them, and Sarah stood there, in terror, staring at William and the others.

'What does this mean?'

'Nothing good,' he said honestly. 'We'll have to wait and see.' They had just finished the roof on the house, the windows were sealed, the floors were done, the bathrooms had been put in, but the details remained to be attacked. Nonetheless, the lion's share of the work had been done, her home was complete and safe from the elements and the world, in time for her to have her baby. But the world itself was no longer safe, and there was no easy way to change that. 'I want you to forget about it right now,' he urged. He had noticed for the past two days that she had been sleeping fitfully, and he suspected that her time was coming closer. And he wanted her free of fear and concerns and worries when their baby came. It was a real possibility that Hitler wouldn't stop with Poland. Sooner or later, Britain had to step forward and stop him. William knew that, but he didn't say it to Sarah.

They ate a quiet dinner in the kitchen that night. As always, Sarah's mind turned to serious things, but William tried to distract her. He wouldn't let her talk about the news, he wanted her to think about something pleasant. He tried to keep her mind off world events by talking about the house, but it wasn't easy.

'Tell me what you want to do with the dining room. Do you want to restore the original panelling, or use some of the *boiseries* we found in the stables?'

'I don't know.' She looked vague as she tried to focus on his question. 'What do you think?'

'I think the *boiserie* has a brighter look. The panelling in the library is enough.'

'I think so too.' She was playing with her food, and he could see she wasn't hungry. He wondered if she was feeling ill, but he didn't want to press her. She looked tired tonight, and worried. They all were.

'And what about the kitchen?' They had exposed all the original brick from four hundred years before, and William loved it. 'I like it like this, but maybe you want something a little more polished.'

'I don't really care.' She looked at him desolately suddenly. 'I just feel sick every time I think of those poor people in Poland.'

'You can't think about that now, Sarah,' he said gently.

'Why not?'

'Because it's not good for you or the baby,' he said firmly, but she started to cry as she left the table and began to pace the kitchen. Everything seemed to upset her more, now that she was so close to having their baby.

'What about the women in Poland who are as pregnant as I am? They can't just change the subject.'

'It's a horrifying thought,' he admitted to her, 'but right now, right this minute, we can't change that.'

'Why not, dammit? Why? Why is that maniac doing that to them?' she ranted, and then sat down again, breathless and obviously in pain.

'Sarah, stop it. Don't upset yourself.' He made her go upstairs and insisted that she lie down on the bed, but she was still crying when she did. 'You can't carry the weight of the world on your shoulders.'

'Those aren't my shoulders, and that's not the world, it's your son.' She smiled through her tears, thinking again how much she loved William. He was so unfailingly good to her, so tireless, he had been so incredible restoring the château, he had worked endlessly only because she loved it. Except that he had come to love it, too, by then, and knowing that touched her as well.

'Do you suppose this little monster is ever going to come out?' she asked, sounding tired as he rubbed her back. He still had to go downstairs and put away the dinner things, but he didn't want to leave her until she'd relaxed, and it was obvious to him that she hadn't, and probably wouldn't for a while.

'I think he will eventually. He's right on schedule for the moment. What did Lord Allthorpe say? September first? That's today, so he's only late as of tomorrow.'

'He's so big.' She was worried about being able to get the baby out. In the past few weeks she had grown even more enormous. And she still remembered what the local doctor had said about the baby being large.

'He'll come out. When he's ready.' William bent over her and kissed her tenderly on the lips. 'You just rest for a little while. I'll bring you a cup of tea.' But when he returned with what the French called an 'infusion' of mint, she was sound asleep, on their bed, in her clothes, and he didn't disturb her. She slept beside him that way until morning, and she was startled when she woke up, she had a sharp pain, but she had had them before, and they always came and went and eventually subsided. Actually, she felt stronger than she had in a long time, and there was a long list of things she wanted to finish in the nursery before she had the baby. She hammered and banged there all day, forgetting her worries, and she refused even to come down for lunch when he called her. William had to bring her lunch upstairs, and he scolded her for working too hard, as she turned to face him and laughed. She looked better and happier than she had in weeks, and he smiled, feeling relieved.

'Well, at least we know I'm not going to lose the baby.' She patted her huge belly, and the baby kicked her soundly, as she took a bite of baguette, and another of apple, and went back to work. Even the baby's clothes and diapers were waiting in the drawers. By the end of the day, she had done everything she had set out to do, and the room looked lovely. She had done everything in white lace, with white satin ribbons. There was an antique bassinet, a beautiful little armoire, a commode that had been in the house, which she had bleached and sanded herself, and the floors were a pale honey color, and there was a tiny Aubusson on the floor. The room was filled with love and warmth, and the only thing missing was the baby.

She went downstairs to the kitchen at dinnertime, and put together some pasta and cold chicken and a salad for them both. She warmed some soup, and bread, and then she called upstairs for William. She poured him a glass of wine, but said she didn't want any. She couldn't drink any more, it gave her terrible heartburn.

'You did a good job.' He had just been upstairs to see, and he was impressed by how much energy she had, she hadn't been that lively in weeks, and after dinner she suggested they go for a walk in the garden.

'Don't you think you should rest?' He looked faintly worried, she was overdoing it. No matter that she was twenty-three years old, she was about to go through an ordeal that he had always heard wasn't easy, and he wanted her to rest.

'What for? The baby may not come for weeks. I'm beginning to feel like I could go on like this forever.'

'You certainly act like it. Are you all right?' He eyed her intently, but she looked well. Her eyes were sparkling and clear, her cheeks pink, and she was teasing him as she laughed.

'I'm fine, William, I promise.' Her conversation tonight was about her parents, and Jane, and his mother, and the house on Long Island. Her parents had done extensive work there, too, and her father said everything would be back to normal again by the following summer. That was a long time, but there had been a lot of damage from the storm. They still missed Charles, and there was a new caretaker now. A Japanese man, and his wife.

She seemed very nostalgic as they walked along through the gardens. Tiny bushes were beginning to grow here and there, and the garden seemed filled with hope and promise, just as she did.

They went back to the house finally, and she seemed content to lie down and rest. She read a book for a while, and then she got up and stretched and went to look out the window at the moonlight. Their new home was beautiful, and she loved everything about it. It was the dream of her life.

'Thank you for all this,' she said gently from where she stood, and he looked at her from the bed, touched by how sweet she looked. She looked so young and so enormous. And then as she started back toward the bed, she looked around, at the floor, and then up at the ceiling above. 'Damn, we've got a terrible leak from someplace, one of the pipes must have burst.' She couldn't see it above her or on the wall, but the entire floor was covered with a pool of water.

He stood up with a frown, and looked at the ceiling as she had. 'I don't see anything. Are you sure?' But she pointed to the floor, and he looked around her, and then at her back again. He had understood before she did. 'I think you're the one with the leaky pipes, my love,' he said gently, not sure what he should do to help her, as he smiled.

'I beg your pardon!' She looked highly insulted as he brought out a pile of towels from the bathroom they had fashioned from the room next to their own, and suddenly understanding began to dawn in her eyes. It had never even occurred to her. Her water had broken.

'Do you think it's that?' She looked around, as he soaked it up with the towels, and she realized then that her nightgown was damp. He was right. It was her water.

'I'll call the doctor,' he said as he stood up.

'I don't think we have to. He said it could be an entire day before anything happens after that.'

'I'd still feel better if we called him.' But he felt a great deal worse after he called the hospital in Chaumont. Le Professeur Vinocour, as they referred to doctors in France, had left with three colleagues for Warsaw. They were going to offer their services to help there, and do whatever they could, and in addition there had been a terrible fire in the next village that night. All the nurses were helping there, and there were literally no doctors. They were desperately shorthanded and the last thing they needed to concern themselves with was an ordinary accouchement, even for Madame la Duchesse. For once, absolutely no-one was impressed with his title. 'A baby is no great thing to deliver,' they told him. They suggested he call one of the women from a neighboring farm, or someone at the hotel, but they couldn't help him. He wasn't even sure what to say to Sarah as he walked back upstairs, feeling sick, knowing that he should have taken her back to London, or at the very least Paris. And now it was too late. He had delivered puppies once, but he certainly had no idea how to deliver a baby, and neither did Sarah. She was even more ignorant than he was, except for her miscarriage, and they had given her a general anesthetic for that. He didn't even have anything to help her with the pain, or to use to help the baby, if there was a problem. And suddenly, he remembered what she had said, that sometimes there was a lapse of an entire day before the pains began. He would drive her to Paris. They were only two and a half hours away, it was the perfect solution, he decided as he ran up the stairs to their bedroom. And then he saw her face with dismay, when he walked back into the room. The contractions had started out of nowhere with a vengeance.

'Sarah.' He ran to the bed, where she seemed to be struggling for air, as she wrestled with the pain that overwhelmed her. 'The doctor isn't there. Do you feel strong enough for me to drive you to Paris?' But she looked at him with horror at the suggestion.

'I can't . . . I don't know what happened . . . I can't move . . . they just keep coming . . . and they're so awful . . .'

'I'll be right back.' He patted her arm and dashed back downstairs, deciding to take the woman's advice. He called the hotel and asked if anyone could help him there, but the girl who answered was the owner's daughter, and she was only seventeen and very shy, and he knew she would be of no use. She said everyone else had gone to the fire, including her parents.

'All right, if someone comes back, anyone, any woman who thinks she could help, send her up to the château. My wife is having a baby.' He hung up on her then and ran back upstairs to Sarah, who was lying on their bed, bathed in sweat, rasping as she breathed, and moaning by the time he reached her.

'It's all right, darling. We're going to do this together.'

He went to wash his hands and came back with another huge stack of towels, and surrounded her with them. He used a cool cloth on her head, and she started to thank him, but the pain was too great for her to speak. For no reason, he glanced at his watch, it was almost midnight. 'Well, we're going to have a baby tonight.' He tried to sound cheerful as he held her hand and she thrashed with the pain while he watched her. He had no idea what to do to help, and she begged him to do something each time one of the vicious pains ripped through her. 'Try to go with it. Try to think of it as something that will bring you our baby.'

'It's too awful . . . William . . . William . . . Make it stop . . . *Do something!* . . .' she wailed, and he sat helplessly beside her, wanting to help, but not knowing how. He wasn't sure anyone could, and she was over-whelmed by how awful the pain was. The miscarriage had been terrible, but this was infinitely worse. This was worse than her worst fears of what the birth would be like. 'Oh, God . . . oh, William . . . oh . . . I feel it coming!' He was relieved that it was so soon, if it was going to be ghastly for such a short time, then she would survive it. He prayed that it would be quick now.

'May I look?' he asked hesitantly, and she nodded and moved her legs further apart as though to make room for the baby, and when he looked he could see the head, but just a bit of it, covered with blood and fair hair. The space he could see was about two inches across, and it seemed to him that it would be only moments before the baby was born, as he called to her in his excitement. 'I can see it, darling, it's coming. Push it out. Go ahead . . . push out our baby . . .' He kept encouraging her, and he could see the result of her pushing briefly. For an instant, the baby seemed to come closer, and then it would move back. It was a slow dance, and for a long time, there was no progress. And then the portion of the baby's head that he could see seemed to grow a fraction larger at last. He braced her legs against his chest so she could push harder, but the baby wouldn't move, and Sarah looked desperate as she screamed with each pain, remembering what the doctor had said, that the baby might be too big to be born that way.

'Sarah, can you push any harder?' he begged her. The baby seemed to be stuck. And they had been at it for hours. It was after four o'clock, and she had been trying to push it out since just after midnight. There was no respite between the pains, she got only a few seconds each time to catch her breath and push again, and he could see that she was panicking and losing control. He gripped her legs again and spoke to her firmly. 'Push again now . . . now . . . come on . . . that's it . . . more! Sarah! Push *harder*!' He was shouting at her, and he was sorry for it, but there was no other way. The baby wasn't even far enough out for him to try to maneuver it or pull it. And as he shouted at her, he could see the head come a little farther forward again. They were getting there, but it was after six o'clock, and the sun was coming up, and they weren't there yet.

She kept pushing and trying, and by eight o'clock she was losing a lot of blood. She looked deathly pale, and the baby hadn't moved in hours, and then he heard a stirring downstairs and he called out to anyone who might hear him. Sarah was barely conscious and her pushing had grown weaker. She just couldn't any more. He heard rapid footsteps on the stairs, and a moment later, he saw Emanuelle, the young girl from the hotel, with wide eyes, in a blue gingham dress and an apron.

'I came to see if I could help Madame la Duchesse with the baby.' But only William suspected that Madame la Duchesse was dying and there would be no baby. She was hemorrhaging, though not uncontrollably, but the baby wasn't moving, and she no longer had the strength to push when the pains came. She just lay there and moaned between screams, and if they didn't do something soon, he was going to lose them both. By then, she had been in hard labor for nine hours and gotten nowhere.

'Come quickly and help me,' he said to the girl urgently, and she stepped forward and came to the bedside without hesitation. 'Have you ever delivered a baby?' He spoke to her without taking his eyes off Sarah. She was a gray color now, and her lips were slightly blue. Her eyes were rolling back in her head, and he was still talking to her and making her hear him. 'Sarah, listen to me, you *have* to push, you have to, as hard as you can. Listen to me, Sarah. *Push! Now!*' He had learned to feel for the contractions by keeping a hand on her stomach. And then he spoke to the girl from the hotel again. 'Do you know what to do?'

'No,' she said honestly. 'I have only seen animals,' she said with a heavy French accent, but she spoke good English. 'I think we must push it out for her now, or . . . or . . .' She didn't want to tell him his wife might die, but they both knew it.

'I know. I want you to push down as hard as you can, to push the baby toward me. When I tell you to . . .' He was feeling for the next pain and it was already coming, as he gave a sign to the girl, and began shouting at Sarah again, and this time the baby moved more than it had in hours. Emanuelle was pushing down as hard as she could, and she was afraid that she might kill the duchess herself, but she knew they had no choice. She just kept pushing and pushing and pushing, trying to squeeze the baby out, and bring it into life, before they lost both mother and child.

'Is it coming?' she asked, and she saw Sarah open her eyes as he nodded. She seemed to be aware of them, but only for an instant, and then she sank back into her sea of pain.

'Come on, darling. Push again. Try to help us this time,' he said quietly, fighting back his own tears as she cried. Emanuelle bore down on her with her full weight and all the force she could exert this time, as William watched and prayed, and slowly . . . slowly . . . the head pushed slowly out of Sarah, and before they had freed the baby, it gave a long wail. Sarah stirred when she heard it, and looked around as though she didn't understand what had happened.

'What's that?' she asked groggily, staring at William.

'That's our baby.' There were tears running down his cheeks, and Sarah began to panic as the pains started again, and she had to push some more. They still had to free the shoulders, but now William was helping, trying to get them free, as mother and child cried, and William felt his sweat mix with tears. Sarah just couldn't help them. She was too weak, and the baby was much too large. The doctor in Chaumont had been right. She should never have tried to give birth to this child, but it was too late now. It was half born, and they had to free it from its mother at last. 'Sarah! Push again!' William shouted at her this time, and Emanuelle continued to press on her abdomen until it looked like she would go right through her. But the baby inched forward again, and William got one arm out, but he couldn't get the other. And then suddenly he remembered the puppies he had delivered so long ago. There had been one like that, and it had been terrible for the mother, but he had saved them both. The pup has been unusually large, as he could see his own child was.

And this time when the pains ripped through Sarah and she screamed, William reached inside her and gently tried to turn the baby to a different angle, while feeling gently around the shoulder, and Sarah jumped in anguish and fought him as hard as she could. 'Hold her down!' he told the girl. 'Don't let her move!' Or she might kill the child. But Emanuelle held her firmly, while William forced her legs down and tried to free the baby, and then suddenly with an odd little sound, the other arm popped out, the shoulders were free, and a moment later, William delivered the rest of him. He was a boy, and he was beautiful, and absolutely enormous.

Willian held him aloft in the morning sun, to look at him in all his beauty, and now he knew what his mother meant when she spoke of a miracle, for truly this was one.

He carefully cut the cord, and handed the baby to the girl, while he tenderly bathed Sarah's face with damp cloths, and tried to stop the bleeding with towels.

But this time Emanuelle knew what to do. She gently set the baby down in a little nest of blankets on the floor and came to show William. 'We must press down very hard on her stomach . . . like so . . . so she will stop bleeding. I have heard my mother say this about women who have had many children.' And with that she pressed down on Sarah's lower abdomen even harder than she had before, and kneaded it like bread as Sarah screamed weakly and begged them to stop, but he saw that the girl was right, the bleeding slowed and eventually all but stopped, except for what seemed normal to both of them.

It was noon by then, and William couldn't believe that it had taken twelve hours to deliver their son. Twelve hours that Sarah and the baby had barely survived. She was still deathly pale, but her lips were no longer blue, and he brought the baby to her and held the baby for her so she could see him. She smiled, but she was too weak to hold him herself, and she looked up at William gratefully, instinctively knowing that he had saved them. 'Thank you,' she whispered as tears rolled down her cheeks and he kissed her. He gave the baby back to Emanuelle then, and she took him downstairs to wash him and then bring him back to his mother later on. William bathed Sarah and changed the bed, and wrapped her in clean blankets and towels. She was too weak to move herself, or even to speak to him, but she watched him gratefully, and finally lay back against the pillows and drifted off to sleep. It was the worst thing William had ever seen, and at the same time the most beautiful, and he felt overwhelmed by his own emotions, as he went downstairs to make her a cup of tea and lace it with brandy. As he made it, he couldn't resist taking a quick swallow himself.

'He's a beautiful boy,' Emanuelle said to him as she watched him. 'And he weighs five kilos. More than ten pounds!' she announced in amazement, which explained all of Sarah's agony.

William smiled in amazement, and tried to express his thanks to the girl. She had been very brave, and incredibly helpful and he knew that without her, he could never have saved the baby or Sarah.

'Thank you.' He looked at her gratefully. 'I couldn't have saved them without you.' She smiled, and they went back upstairs to see Sarah. She took a sip of the tea, and smiled again when she saw the baby. She was still in pain, and very weak, but she knew the brandy would help her. And even in her weakened state, she was thrilled about the baby.

William told her he weighed ten pounds, and he wanted to apologize to her for what he had put her through, but he didn't have the chance to say anything. She fell sound asleep before she had turned her head on the pillow. And she slept that way for hours, as William sat quietly in a chair at her bedside and watched her. But when she woke again at dusk, she looked more like herself, and asked him to help her to the bathroom. He did and then brought her back to bed, and marvelled at the endurance of her sex.

'I was so worried about you,' he confessed as she lay in their bed again. 'I had no idea the baby was so large. Ten pounds is enormous.'

'The doctor thought he might be,' she said, but she didn't tell him that she hadn't wanted a cesarean, for fear that they couldn't have had any other children. She knew that if she had told William there was even a question of it, he would have forced her to go back to London. But she was glad she hadn't, she was glad she had been brave, even if she had been a little foolish. There would be more babies now . . . and her beautiful son . . . They were going to name him Phillip Edward, after William's grandfather and her father. And she had never seen anyone as beautiful, she thought, as she held her son for the first time.

Emanuelle finally left them at dusk to go back to the hotel, and when he walked her downstairs, he saw some of the men who worked for them waving at him from the distance. He waved back with a smile, thinking they were congratulating him on the arrival of the baby, but as he looked at them, he realized that they were calling something to him, something he didn't understand at first, and then he heard a word that made his blood run cold and he began to run toward them.

'C'est la guerre, Monsieur le Duc . . . C'est la guerre . . .' It was war, they were telling him. Britain and France had declared war on Germany that afternoon . . . His baby had just arrived, and his wife had almost died . . . and now he would have to leave them. He stood listening to them for a long moment, knowing he would have to go back to England as soon as he could. If he was able to, he'd have to send a message to England now. And what would he tell Sarah? Nothing yet. She was too weak to hear it. But she'd have to know soon enough. He couldn't stay much longer with them.

And as he hurried back to their room to check on her and the sleeping child, there were tears rolling down his cheeks. It was so unfair . . . why now? She looked at him as though she knew, as though she sensed something.

'What was all that noise outside?' she asked weakly.

208

'Some of the men came to congratulate you for bringing such a handsome boy into the world.'

'That's sweet.' She smiled sleepily, and drifted back to sleep again, as he lay beside her and watched her, fearing what would happen.

Chapter 12

The next morning dawned sunny and warm, and the baby woke them just after dawn with muffled cries for his mother. William went to bring him to her, and put him to her breast as he watched them. The hearty boy seemed to know exactly what to do, as Sarah smiled at him weakly. She could still hardly move, but she was better than she'd been the night before, and then suddenly she remembered the noise outside, and the look on William's face, and she knew something had happened, but William still hadn't told her what it was yet.

'What was all that last night?' she asked softly, as the baby nursed hungrily from his mother, and William wondered if it was still too soon to tell her the truth. And yet, he knew he had to. He had called the Duke of Windsor in Paris the night before, and they had both agreed, they would have to go back to England very quickly. Wallis was going with him, of course, but William knew there was no way he could move Sarah so soon. Certainly not now, and perhaps not for weeks, or even months. It all depended on how quickly she would recover, and that was impossible for anyone to predict now. And in the meantime, William knew he had to go back to London and report to the War Office. She would be safe in France, but he hated to leave her alone. And as she watched him, Sarah saw all his anguish and worries. For William, it had been an agonizing two days. 'What's wrong?' Sarah asked as she reached out to touch him.

'We're at war,' he said sadly, no longer able to hide it

from her, and praying she was strong enough to take the news, and all its implications for them. 'England and France against Germany. It happened yesterday, while you were busy bringing Phillip into the world.' It had been quite a task, they both knew, and understandably they'd all been distracted. But now there was no running away from the truth.

Tears filled her eyes the moment she heard it, as she looked at William in fear. 'What does that mean for you? Will you have to go soon?'

'I have to.' He nodded mournfully, devastated to leave her now, but there was clearly no choice. 'I'll try to send a cable today and tell them that I'll come in a few days. I don't want to leave until you're a bit stronger.' He gently touched her hand, remembering all that she'd been through. Watching them seemed like a double miracle to him now, and he hated to have to leave them. 'I'll ask Emanuelle to stay here with you when I go. She's a good girl.' She had certainly proved that, and more, the day before, while he had delivered the baby.

Emanuelle came back that morning, just after nine, looking spotlessly clean in another blue dress and a freshly starched apron. Her dark red hair was pulled neatly back in a thick braid that fell down her back and was tied with a blue ribbon. She was seventeen, and her younger brother was twelve. They had lived all their lives in La Marolle. Her parents were simple and hard-working, and intelligent, as were their children.

And when she was there, William went to the post office to send a cable to the War Office. But just after he got back to the château, Emanuelle's brother, Henri, arrived from the hotel. 'Your phone is out of order, Monsieur le Duc,' he announced. And the Duke of Windsor had called and left a message at the hotel to tell him that the HMS *Kelly*, would come to pick them up the next morning in Le Havre, and he had to come to Paris at once.

The boy was still breathless as he told William what he had said, and William thanked him and gave him ten francs, and then he went back upstairs to tell Sarah.

'I just got a message from David,' he started vaguely, walking slowly around the room, trying to see everything so he could take the memories with him. 'He . . . uh . . . Bertie's sending a boat for us tomorrow.'

'Here?' She looked confused. She had been dozing while he went out to send the cable.

'Hardly.' He smiled as he sat down beside her on the bed. They were a hundred and fifty miles from the shore, here in La Marolle. 'To Le Havre. He wants me to meet him in Paris by eight o'clock tomorrow morning. I suppose Wallis will be going with us.' And then he looked at his wife again, with a worried frown. 'I don't suppose you feel strong enough to come with us.' He knew she didn't, but at least he had to ask her, for his own peace of mind, although he knew that she could start hemorrhaging again if they moved her too soon. And she had already lost so much blood when she had the baby. She was still very pale, and very weak. It would be a month before she was strong enough to go anywhere, let alone drive to Paris or take a boat trip to England. She shook her head in answer to his question. 'I don't like leaving you here.'

'France is our ally. No harm will come to us here.' She smiled gently at him. She didn't want him to leave, but she didn't mind staying. This was their home now. 'We'll be fine. Will you be able to come back soon?'

'I don't know. I'll get a message to you as soon as I can. I have to report to the War Office in London, and then find out what they want to do with me. I'll try to get back here as quickly as I can. And when you feel well enough, you should come home,' he said almost sternly.

'This is home,' she whispered as she looked at him. 'I don't want to leave. Phillip and I will be safe here.'

'I know. But I'd feel better about it if you were at

Whitfield.' The prospect of that depressed her. She was fond of his mother, and it was a pretty place, but the Château de la Meuze had become home to them, and they had worked so hard to make it what they wanted that now she didn't want to leave it. There was still a lot of work to do, but she could do some of it herself when she felt strong again, while they waited for him to come from England. 'We'll see,' he said vaguely, and went to pack a bag to take with him the next morning.

Neither of them slept that night, and even the baby cried more than he had the day before. Her milk wasn't plentiful enough yet for the enormous child, and she was nervous and worried. She saw William get up at five, when he thought she was finally asleep, and she spoke softly in the darkened room as she watched him.

'I don't want you to go,' she said sadly, and he came to stand beside her and touched her hand and her face, wishing he didn't have to.

'I don't want to go either. Hopefully, it'll all be over soon, and we can get on with our life again.' She nodded, hoping he was right, and trying not to think of the poor people in Poland.

He was shaved and dressed half an hour later, and stood beside the bed again, and this time she stood up beside him. Her head reeled for a moment as she did, and he put a strong arm around her. 'I don't want you to come downstairs, you might hurt yourself trying to get back up.' She was still very wobbly and she might faint and hit her head, but she was too weak to even try and she knew it.

'I love you . . . Please take care of yourself . . . William . . . be careful . . . I love you . . .' There were tears in her eyes and in his, too, as he smiled and helped her back into bed.

'I promise . . . you be careful too . . . and take good care of Lord Phillip.'

She smiled at her son. He was such a beautiful little boy.

He had big blue eyes and blond curls, and William said that he looked just like photographs of his father.

He kissed her as hard as he dared, and then he tucked her tightly into bed and kissed her again, as he touched the long silky hair cascading over her shoulders. 'Get strong again . . . I'll be back soon . . . I love you . . . so much . . .' He was grateful again that she was alive, and then he strode across the room, and looked at her one last time from the doorway. 'I love you,' he said softly, as she cried, and then he was gone.

'I love you . . .' She called out to him, as she could hear him on the stairs. 'William! . . . I love you! . . .'

'. . . I love you too! . . .' The echo came back to her, and then she heard the enormous front door bang. And a moment later she heard his car start. She got out of bed again just in time to see his car disappear around the bend toward the entrance to the château, as tears fell down her cheeks on to her nightgown. She lay in bed crying, thinking of him for a long time, and then Phillip wanted to be nursed and finally Emanuelle came again. But now, she was going to move in with them. She was going to stay and help Madame la Duchesse with the baby. It was a wonderful opportunity for her, and she was already filled with admiration for Sarah, and crazy about the baby she had helped deliver. But she was never overly familiar. She was unusually poised for a girl her age, and an invaluable help to Sarah.

The days seemed endless to Sarah after William left, and it was weeks before she even began to get her strength back. By October, when Phillip was a month old, she got a call from the Duchess of Windsor to tell her that they were back in Paris. They had seen William just before they left London, and he looked fine. He was attached to the RAF, and he was stationed north of London. The Duke of Windsor had been sent back to Paris as a major general, with the Military Mission to the French Command. But mostly it meant they were doing a lot of entertaining, which suited them both to perfection. She congratulated Sarah again on the birth of her son, and told her to come up to Paris and visit them when she felt a little stronger. William had told them what a hard time she'd had, and Wallis urged her not to overdo it.

But Sarah was already moving around the house again, keeping an eye on things, and making small repairs. She had gotten a woman from the hotel to help her clean, and Emanuelle was helping her take care of the baby. He seemed huge to her and he had gained three more pounds in four weeks. He was absolutely enormous.

Emanuelle's brother, Henri, was helping Sarah by doing errands, but most of the men and boys who had worked for them had already disappeared and gone into the army. There was no-one left to work on the château, except old men and very young boys. Even the sixteen and seventeen years olds had tried to lie their way into the army, and were gone. Suddenly, it seemed like a nation of women and children.

Sarah had heard from William several times by then. His letters had gotten through, and he had called once. He said nothing much had happened yet, and he hoped to get a little time to visit her in November.

She had also heard from her parents, and they were desperate for her to come home, and bring the baby. The *Aquitania* had made a crossing to New York just after war was declared, despite everyone else's fears, but she had still been too weak to move then, so they hadn't suggested it to her. But three more ships came over to England from New York after that, the *Manhattan*, the *Washington*, and *The President Roosevelt*, to take Americans home to safety. But just as she insisted to William that she was safe where she was, she wrote the same thing in letters to her parents, but she still hadn't convinced them.

They were terrified of her remaining in France for the

war, but she knew how absurd that was. Life around the Château de la Meuze was quieter than it had ever been before, and the region was completely peaceful.

By November, she felt like her old self again. She went for long walks, and often carried Phillip with her. She worked in the garden, and on her beloved *boiseries*, and she even did some heavier work down at the stables whenever Henri had time to help her. His parents had lost all their male employees at the hotel and he helped out there as well. He was a nice little boy, very engaging, and very willing to help her. And he loved living at the château, as did Emanuelle. Sarah no longer needed Emanuelle's help at night, but she moved into the cottage and came up to the château to work in the morning.

It was late November, one afternoon, as she walked home from the woods, singing to Phillip as she carried him in a sling Emanuelle had made her. He was almost asleep as she reached the front door of the château with a sigh, and stepped inside, and then she screamed as she saw him. It was William, standing there in his uniform, looking more handsome than ever. She rushed into his arms, and he held her, trying not to squash the baby. She quickly took off the sling and set him down gently. He had been startled by her scream and he was beginning to cry, but all she could think of now was William as he held her.

'I've missed you so . . .' Her words were muffled by his chest, and he held her so tightly, he almost hurt her.

'God, I've missed you too.' He pulled away from her then to see her. 'You look wonderful again.' Thinner, but strong and well, and very healthy. 'How beautiful you are,' he said, looking as though he wanted to devour her, and she laughed as she kissed him.

Emanuelle had heard them talking. She'd seen the duke when he arrived, and now she came to take the baby. He would want feeding soon, but at least she could free them from him for a little while, so Sarah could spend some time with her husband. They went upstairs hand in hand, talking and laughing, as she asked him a thousand questions about where he was going, where he had been, and where they would send him after advanced training. He had flown in the RAF before and had only needed an update on the new equipment. He was careful not to tell her what he knew. That they were sending him to Bomber Command, to fly Blenheim bombers. He didn't want to worry her, and he made light of all of it. But he did tell her how seriously people were taking the war in England.

'They're taking it seriously here too,' she explained. 'There's no-one left except Henri and his friends and a bunch of old men, who are too weak to work. I've been doing everything myself, with Emanuelle and Henri. But I've almost finished the stables. Wait till you see them!' He had wanted half of them set up for the horses they would buy, and a few he wanted to bring over from England, and the rest of it was set up in small rooms for their staff, and bunks for some of the hands they might hire on a temporary basis. It was an excellent system, and the way they'd done it there was room for about forty or fifty men, and at least as many horses.

'It sounds like you don't need me here at all.' He pretended to sound miffed. 'Perhaps I should stay in England.'

'Don't you dare!' She reached up and kissed him again, and as they entered their bedroom, he spun her around and kissed her so hard that she knew exactly how much he'd missed her.

He locked the door behind them and looked at her adoringly, as she began unbuttoning the jacket of his uniform, and he pulled off her heavy sweater. It was one of his own, and he tossed it halfway across the room as he looked at the full breasts and the waist that was so small again. It was difficult to believe she had ever had a baby.

'Sarah . . . you're so beautiful . . .' He was almost speechless, and almost out of control. He had never wanted her as much, even on their first night together. They almost didn't make it to the bed, but as they lay together there, they found each other quickly and well, and their longings exploded almost instantly as they gave in to their hunger.

'I've missed you so much . . .' she confessed. It had been so lonely without him.

'Not half as much as I've missed you,' he confided.

'How long can you stay?'

He hesitated, it seemed so little to him now, and at first it had seemed such a gift. 'Three days. It's not much, but it'll have to do. I'm hoping to get back again around Christmas.' That was only a month away, and at least it would give her something to look forward to when he left. But right now, she couldn't bear to think of him leaving.

They lay together on the bed for a long time, and then they heard Emanuelle with the baby outside their room, and Sarah put on a dressing gown and went to get him.

She brought Phillip back into the room, loudly demanding his dinner. And William smiled at him as he watched him eat hungrily, choking on the milk he was so anxious for, and making all kinds of funny little noises.

'His table manners are appalling, aren't they?' William grinned.

'We'll have to work on that,' Sarah said, switching him to the other breast. 'He's a terrible little pig. He wants to eat all the time.'

'It looks to me like he does. He's three times the size he was when he was born, and I thought he was enormous then.'

'So did I,' Sarah said ruefully, and then William thought of something he had never thought of before, and he looked at her gently.

'Do you want me to be careful?' She shook her head as she smiled at him. She wanted to have lots more of his babies.

218

'Of course not, but I don't think we need to worry about that yet anyway. I don't think I can get pregnant while I'm nursing.'

'Then all the more fun,' he teased. They spent the next three days as they had their honeymoon, in bed most of the time. And in between times, she took him around the property to show him what she'd done in his absence. She had worked on a number of things, and he was very impressed when he saw the stables.

'You really are quite remarkable!' he praised. 'I couldn't have done this myself, certainly not without help from anyone. I don't know how you did it!' She had spent many, many nights, hammering and sawing and pounding nails well after midnight, with little Phillip in a cradle next to her, bundled up in his blankets.

'I had nothing else to do.' She smiled. 'With you gone, there isn't much to do here.'

William glanced at his son with a rueful smile. 'Wait till he starts getting into things. I have a feeling you'll be kept extremely busy.'

'And what about you?' she asked sadly, as they walked back toward the château. Their three days had already passed, and he was leaving her in the morning. 'When will you be home again? How does it look out in the big, bad world?'

'Pretty ugly.' He told her what they knew, or some of it, of what had happened in Warsaw. The ghetto, the pogroms, the mountains of bodies, even those of children who had fought and lost. It made her cry when he told her. There were tales from Germany that were pretty ugly too. There were fears that Hitler might make a move on the Low Countries, too, but he hadn't so far, and they were keeping him at bay as best they could, but it wasn't easy. 'I'd like to think it'll be over soon, but I just don't know. Perhaps if we scare the little bastard enough, he'll back off. But he seems pretty gutsy.'

'I don't want anything to happen to you,' she said, looking anguished.

'Darling, nothing will, it would be such a dreadful embarrassment to them if anything happened to me. Believe me, the War Office will keep me wrapped up in cotton wool. It just gives the men a bit of heart to see someone like me dressed up in a uniform and playing the same games they are.' He was thirty-seven years old, and they were hardly going to use him in the front lines at this point.

'I hope you're right.'

'I am. And I'll be back over to see you before Christmas.' He was beginning to like the idea of her staying in France. Things seemed so frenzied and so frightening in England. And here, everything seemed so peaceful by comparison. It almost looked as though nothing had happened at all, except that there were no men visible anywhere, or at least no young ones, only children.

They spent their last night together in bed, and eventually Sarah slept in his arms. And William had to wake her when the baby cried for her. She had been in a deep, happy sleep. And after she fed the baby, they made love again. And William had to drag himself out of bed in the morning.

'I'll be back soon, my love,' he promised as he left, and this time his leaving didn't seem quite so desperate. He was well and safe, and he didn't seem to be in any real danger.

And true to his word, he came back to see her a month later, two days before Christmas. He spent Christmas Day quietly with her, and he noticed something he'd seen before, but couldn't quite fathom this time.

'You've gained weight,' he commented. She wasn't sure if it was a compliment or a complaint. She had gained it around her waist, and her hips, and her breasts seemed fuller. It was only a month since he'd been gone, but her body had changed, and it made him wonder. 'Could you be pregnant again?'

'I don't know.' She looked a little vague, she had wondered the same thing once or twice. She was feeling vaguely nauseated from time to time, and all she wanted to do was sleep. 'I didn't think so.'

'I think you are.' He smiled, and then suddenly he began to worry. He didn't like leaving her alone here again, particularly if she was pregnant. He said something about it that night, and asked if she would be willing to go to Whitfield.

'That's silly, William. We don't even know if I am.' She didn't want to leave France, pregnant or not. She wanted to be here, at their château, hammering and banging away until it was fully restored, and taking care of her child.

'You think you are, too, don't you?'

'I think I might be.'

'Oh, you wicked girl!' But all it did was excite him again, and after they made love, he gave her the only Christmas present he'd been able to bring, a beautiful emerald bracelet of his mother's. It was made of large cabochon stones surrounded by very old diamonds, and had been commissioned years before at Garrard's by a maharaja. It was hardly something she could wear every day, but when he came home, and they went out again, it would be splendid. 'You're not disappointed I don't have more for you?' He felt guilty not to have brought her anything else, but he really couldn't. He had grabbed that out of the safe at Whitfield, with his mother's blessing, the last time he'd seen her.

'This is awful,' she teased. 'What I really wanted was a set of plumber's tools. I've been trying to fix some of these damn toilets they started to install last summer.'

'I love you.' He laughed. She gave him a beautiful painting they had found hidden in the barn, and an old, well-worn watch that she loved, that had been her father's.

She had brought it to Europe with her, as a souvenir of him, and now she gave it to William to carry with him. And he genuinely seemed to love it.

The Duke and the Duchess of Windsor spent their Christmas in Paris, busy with social events, while the Whitfields worked side by side, reinforcing beams in their barn, and cleaning out the stables.

'Hell of a way to spend Boxing Day, my dear,' William said as they stood side by side, covered in dirt and dried manure, holding their hammers and shovels.

'I know,' she said, grinning, 'but think how great this place will look when we're finished.' He had given up trying to talk her into going to Whitfield. She loved this place too much, and she was at home here.

He left her again on New Year's Eve, and Sarah saw the New Year in alone, in their bed at the château, as she held their baby. She hoped that it would be a better year, and the men would all soon be home again. And she crooned 'Auld Lang Syne' to Phillip as she held him.

By January, she was certain that she was pregnant again. And she managed to find an ancient doctor in Chambord, who confirmed it. He told her that the old wives' tale that you couldn't get pregnant while you were nursing was sometimes true, but not always. But she was very happy about it. Phillip's baby brother or sister was due to arrive in August. Emanuelle was still helping her, and she was excited about the baby too. She promised to do everything she could to help the duchess with the new baby. But Sarah also hoped that William would be home again by then. She wasn't afraid. She was pleased. She wrote William and told him the news, and he wrote back and urged her to take care of herself, and said he'd try to come over as soon as he could, but instead they sent him to Watton in Norfolk with the 82 Squadron Bomber Command, and he wrote her again that there would be no hope of his coming to France for several months now. He did mention that he wanted her in Paris by July, and she could stay with the Windsors if she had to. But he didn't want her having the baby at the château again, particularly if he wasn't there, which he hoped he would be.

In March, she received another letter from Jane, who had another little baby girl, and they named this one Helen. But Sarah felt strangely distant from her family now, as though they were no longer intimately a part of her life, as they once had been. She tried to stay abreast of their news, but letters came so late, and so many of the names they referred to were unfamiliar. For the past year and a half, her life had been totally removed from them. They all seemed so far away now. She was totally involved in her own life with her son, restoring the château and listening to the news in Europe.

She listened to every broadcast she could hear, read every newspaper, listened to every bit of gossip. But the news was never very good, or very hopeful. Only in his letters, William kept promising that he would be home soon. Hitler seemed to be stalling for time in the spring of 1940, and William and some of his friends began to wonder if he wasn't going to back off. In the States, they were calling it the Phony War, but to the people in the countries Hitler had occupied, it was very real and far from phony.

The Windsors invited her to a dinner party in Paris at the end of April, but she didn't go. She didn't want to leave Phillip at the château, even though she trusted Emanuelle. Also she was five months pregnant, and she didn't think it proper to go out without William. She sent them a polite note instead, and in early May she caught a terrible cold, and she was in bed on the fifteenth, when the Germans invaded the Low Countries. Emanuelle came rushing upstairs to tell her. Hitler was on the move again, and Sarah came downstairs to the kitchen to listen to the radio, and see if she could pick up a broadcast.

She listened to what news she could find all afternoon, and the next day she tried to call Wallis and David, but she was told by the servants there that they had left for Biarritz the previous morning. The duke had taken the duchess to the South for her safety.

Sarah went back to bed, and a week later she had a raging case of bronchitis. And then the baby caught it from her, and she was so busy taking care of him that she scarcely understood what it meant when she heard the broadcast about the evacuation of Dunkirk. What had happened to them? How had they been driven back?

When Italy entered the war against France and England, Sarah began to panic. The news was terrible, and the Germans were attacking France, and everyone in the country was terrified, but no-one knew where to go or what to do. Sarah knew they would never give in to the Germans, but what if they bombed France? She knew William and her parents must be frantic about her, and there was no way for her to reach them. They had been cut off from the world. She hadn't been able to call England or the States. It had been absolutely impossible to get a connection. And on the fourteenth of June, she and every-one else sat in stunned silence as they heard the news. The French government had declared Paris an open city. They had literally handed it to the Germans, and they had marched in, in waves, by nightfall. France had fallen to the Germans. And as she listened, Sarah couldn't believe it. She sat staring at Emanuelle, as they listened to the news, and the younger girl started to cry when she heard it.

'*Ils vont nous tuer . . .*' she wailed. 'They will kill us. We will all be dead.'

'Don't be silly,' Sarah said, trying to sound stern, and hoping the girl wouldn't see how badly her own hands were shaking. 'They're not going to do anything to us. We're women. And they probably won't come here.

Emanuelle, be sensible . . . calm down . . .' But she didn't believe her own words as she said them. William had been right. She should have left France, but now it was too late. She had been so busy taking care of Phillip that she hadn't see the warning signs, and she could hardly make a dash for the South now, as the Windsors clearly had. She wouldn't have gotten far with her baby in her arms, and she was seven months pregnant.

'Madame, what will we do?' Emanuelle asked, still feeling that she owed it to her to protect her. She had promised William.

'Absolutely nothing,' Sarah said quietly. 'If they come here, we have nothing to hide, nothing to give them. All we have is what we've grown in the garden. We have no silver, no jewels.' She suddenly remembered the emerald bracelet William had give her for Christmas, and the few things she'd brought with her, like her engagement ring and the first Christmas gifts William had brought her in Paris. But she could hide those things, there weren't many, and if she had to, she would give them up to save their lives. 'We have nothing they want, Emanuelle. We are two women alone here, with a baby.' But nonetheless, she took one of William's guns to bed with her that night, and slept with the baby in the bed next to her, and the gun under her pillow. She hid the jewelry under the floorboards in the baby's room, and then nailed them down again expertly, and spread the Aubusson rug on top carefully.

Nothing happened for the next four days. She had just decided that they were as safe as they had been before, when a convoy of jeeps appeared, coming down the *grande allée*, and a flock of German soldiers in uniform jumped out of the jeeps and ran toward her. Two of the soldiers pointed guns at her and signalled to her to put her hands up, but she couldn't because she was holding Phillip. She knew that Emanuelle was clearing away the breakfast things in the kitchen, and she prayed that she wouldn't panic when she saw them.

They shouted at her to move, and she stood where they wanted her to, but she tried to appear unruffled as she clung to Phillip with shaking hands, and spoke to them in English.

'What can I do to help you?' she asked quietly and with great dignity, trying to give her best imitation of William's aristocratic and commanding demeanor.

They rattled at her in German for a little while, and then another soldier of obviously superior rank spoke to her. He had angry eyes, and a nasty little mouth, but Sarah tried to force herself not to notice.

'You are English?'

'American.' That seemed to stump him for a while, and he rattled on with the others in German, before speaking to her again.

'Who owns this house? This land? The farm?'

'I do.' She spoke firmly for all to hear. 'I am the Duchess of Whitfield.'

More chattering, more German, more consultation. He waved her aside with the gun again. 'We will go inside now.'

She nodded her agreement, and they went into the house, and as they did, she heard a scream from the kitchen. They had obviously startled Emanuelle, and two of the soldiers brought her out at gunpoint. She was crying as she ran toward Sarah, and Sarah put an arm around her and held her. They were both shaking as they stood, but nothing on Sarah's face would have told them she was frightened. She was the portrait of a duchess.

A group of soldiers stood guarding them, as the others reconnoitered inside. And then they returned as a fresh line of jeeps came up the driveway. The first soldier in command came back to her then and asked her where her husband was. She told him he was away, and he showed her that he had found the gun she had concealed under her pillow. Sarah looked unimpressed and continued to watch them. And as she stood, a tall, thin officer emerged from one of the recently arrived jeeps and walked toward them. The man currently in charge spoke to him, showed him the gun, and waved at the women as he made his explanations, and then waved toward the house, obviously explaining what he had found there. She also heard him say the word 'Amerikaner'.

'You are American?' The new officer asked, in very clipped British tones, with only the faintest hint of German. He clearly spoke excellent English, and he looked very distinguished.

'I am. I am the Duchess of Whitfield.'

'Your husband is British?' he asked quietly, his eyes looking deep into hers. In another place, another time, she would have thought him handsome. And they probably would have met at a party. But this was not. It was war, and they both kept their distance.

'Yes, my husband is British' was all she answered.

'I see.' There was a long pause as he looked at her, and he was not indifferent to what he saw of her belly. 'I regret to inform you, Your Grace,' he addressed her very politely, 'that we must requisition your home. We will be bringing troops here.'

She felt a wave of shock and anger rip through her, but nothing showed as she nodded.

'I . . . I see . . .' Tears filled her eyes. She didn't know what to say to him. They were taking her home, the house she had worked so hard on. And what if they never got it back again? If she lost it, or they destroyed it? 'I . . .' She stumbled over the words, and he looked around him for a moment.

'Is there . . . a smaller house? A cottage? Somewhere where you and your family could reside, while we stay here?' She thought of the stables, but they were too large, and he would want them as barracks for his men as well, and then she thought of the caretaker's cottage where Emanuelle lived and she had first stayed with William. It was certainly adequate for her, Emanuelle, Phillip, and the new baby.

'Yes, there is,' she said bleakly.

'May I invite you to stay there?' He bowed with Prussian dignity, and his eyes were gentle and apologetic. 'I am very sorry to . . . to ask you to move now –' he glanced at the child that was to be born in August – 'but I am afraid we are bringing a great many troops here.'

'I understand.' She tried to sound dignified, like a duchess, but suddenly she felt like a twenty-three-year-old girl, and she was very frightened.

'Do you feel that you would be able to move the necessary things by this evening?' he asked politely, and she nodded. She didn't have that much there, mostly work clothes, and a few suits and dresses, and William didn't have much there either. They had worked so hard, they hadn't brought all their things over yet from England.

She couldn't believe what she was doing as she packed their clothes, and a few other personal things as well. She didn't have time to rescue her jewelry from under the floorboards, but she knew it was safe there. She put her clothes and William's and the baby's into valises, and Emanuelle helped her pack up all the kitchen things, and some food, and soap, and all their sheets and towels. It was more work than she thought, and the baby cried all day, as though he sensed that something terrible had happened. It was almost six o'clock when Emanuelle took the last load of things to the cottage, her own things were already there, and Sarah stood in her bedroom for the last time, the room where Phillip had been born, and their second child had been conceived, the room she had shared with William. It seemed a sacrilege to give it to them now, but she had no choice, and as she stood in the room, looking around hopelessly, one of the soldiers arrived, one she hadn't seen, and urged her out of the room at gunpoint.

'*Schnell!*' he told her. Quickly! She went down the stairs with as much dignity as she could, but there were tears rolling down her cheeks, and at the bottom of the stairs, the soldier poked her belly with the point of his rifle, and there was a sudden roar, the voice of a man who could strike fear in a moment. The soldier jumped a mile and stepped backwards like lightning, as the commandant approached them. It was the same man who had spoken to her in excellent English that morning. And now he raged at his soldier in a voice that was so icy and so controlled that the man visibly trembled, and then he turned and bowed apologetically to Sarah before running from the building. The commandant looked at her unhappily, deeply upset by what had just happened. And in spite of her efforts to appear nonplussed, he could see that she was shaking.

'My apologies for the incredibly bad manners of my sergeant, Your Grace. It won't happen again. May I drive you to your home?' I am in my home, she wanted to tell him, but she was grateful to him, too, for controlling the sergeant. He could easily have shot her in the stomach for the fun of it, and the thought of that made her dizzy.

'Thank you,' she said coolly. It was a long walk, and she was exhausted. The baby had been kicking all day, obviously sensing her anger and her terror. She had cried as she packed her things, and she felt completely drained as they got into the jeep, and he started the engine as a few of the men watched him. He wanted to set a tone for them that they would follow to the letter. And he had already explained that. They were not to touch the local girls, shoot anyone's pet for fun, or venture into the town while drunk. They were to control themselves at all times, or face his fury, and possibly a trip back to Berlin to be shipped elsewhere. And the men had promised him they'd obey him.

'I am Commandant Joachim von Mannheim,' he said quietly. 'And we are very grateful for the use of your home. I am very sorry for the imposition, and the unhappiness it must cause you.' They drove down the *grande allée*, and he glanced at her. 'War is a very difficult thing.' His own family had lost a great deal in the first one. And then he surprised her by asking about the baby. 'When is your child expected?' he asked quietly. He seemed oddly human, despite the uniform he wore, but she wouldn't let herself forget who he was, or who he fought for. She reminded herself again that she was the Duchess of Whitfield and owed it to them to be polite, but nothing more.

'Not for another two months,' she answered brusquely, wondering why he had asked her. Maybe they were going to send her somewhere. That was a truly terrifying thought, and more than ever she wished she had gone to Whitfield. But who would ever have thought that France would fall, that they would give themselves to the Germans?

'We should have doctors here by then,' he reassured her. 'We are going to use your home for wounded soldiers. A hospital of sorts. And your stables will do very well for my men. The food at the farm is plentiful. I'm afraid' – he smiled apologetically at her as they reached the cottage, where Emanuelle was waiting for her with Phillip in her arms – 'for us, it's an ideal situation.'

'How fortunate for you,' Sarah said tartly. It was hardly ideal for them. Losing their home to the Germans.

'It is, indeed.' He watched her get out of the car and take Phillip from Emanuelle. 'Good evening, Your Grace.'

'Good evening, Commandant,' she said, but she did not thank him for the ride, and she didn't say another word as she walked into the cottage that was her home now.

Chapter 13

The occupation of France depressed everyone, and the occupation of the Château de la Meuze was incredibly painful for Sarah. Within days, there were German soldiers everywhere, the stables were full of them, three and four to a room, and even in the horse stalls. There were close to two hundred men there, although she and William had only planned it for forty or fifty of their own people. The conditions there were rugged for them as well. But they took over the farm, too, and housed more men there, while making the farmer's wife sleep in a shed. She was an old woman, but she was taking it well. The farmer and their two sons were in the army.

And just as the commandant had said, the château itself became a hospital for wounded men, a kind of convalescent home, with wards in each room, and a few of the smaller rooms reserved for high-ranking officers who had been wounded. The commandant lived at the château, in one of the smaller rooms. Sarah had seen a few female nurses there, but most of the attendants seemed to be orderlies and male nurses, and she had heard that there were two doctors, but she had never seen them.

She had very little to do with any of them. She kept to herself, and stayed with Emanuelle and the baby at the cottage. She chafed to get back to her own work again, and worried at the damage they would do during their occupation. But there was nothing she could do now. She went for long walks with Emanuelle, and chatted with the farmer's wife whenever she could get to the farm, to make sure that she was well. She seemed in good spirits, and said they had been decent to her. They took everything she grew, but they hadn't touched her. So far, they seemed to be behaving. But it was Emanuelle who worried Sarah. She was a pretty girl, and she was young, she had just turned eighteen that spring, and it was dangerous for her to be living in such close proximity to three hundred German soldiers. More than once, Sarah had told her to go back to the hotel, but Emanuelle always insisted that she didn't want to leave her. In some ways, they had become good friends, and yet there was always a chasm of respect between them. And Emanuelle had taken to heart her promise to William, not to leave the duchess or Lord Phillip.

Sarah was out walking one day, on her way back from the farm, a month after they had come, when she saw a cluster of soldiers shouting and hooting on an old dirt path near the stables. She wondered what was going on, but knew enough never to go near them. They were all potentially dangerous men, and in spite of her neutral American citizenship, she was the enemy to them, and they were the forces of the Occupation. She could see them laughing at something, and she was about to continue on her route home, when she saw a basket full of berries overturned by the roadside. The basket was one of hers, and the berries were the ones Emanuelle always picked for Phillip because he loved them. And then she knew. They were like cats with a small mouse, a tiny prey they were taunting and torturing in the bushes. And without thinking, she hurried to where they stood, her old faded yellow dress making her look even larger in the bright sunlight. She was wearing her hair in a long braid, and as she approached the group, she tossed it back over her shoulder, and then gasped as she saw her. Emanuelle was standing there, her blouse torn off, her breasts bare, her skirt torn and sliding down on her hips as they taunted and jeered and teased her. Two men held her arms, and another teased her nipples as he kissed her.

'Stop that!' she shouted at all of them, outraged by what he was doing. She was a child, a girl, and Sarah knew from their conversations in the past month that she was still a virgin. 'Stop that immediately!' she shouted at them and they laughed at her, as she grabbed at one man's gun and he pushed her roughly away, shouting at her in German.

Sarah walked immediately to where Emanuelle stood, her face streaked with tears, humiliated and ashamed and frightened. She picked up the shreds of Emanuelle's blouse and tried to cover her with it, and as she did, one of the men reached out and pulled Sarah close to him, grinding himself into her buttocks. She tried to turn on him, but he held her there, fondling her breast with one hand, while holding her vast belly painfully tight with the other. She fought to free herself from him, as he ground suggestively against her, and she could feel him become aroused and wondered in horror if he would rape her. Her eyes found Emanuelle's, and the look in Sarah's eyes tried to reassure the younger girl, but it was obvious that the child was desperately frightened. Even more now for her employer, as one of the men held Sarah's arms, and another put a hand between her legs as Emanuelle screamed at what she thought was about to happen, but as she did, within seconds, there was an explosion of gunshot. Emanuelle jumped, and Sarah used the moment to pull free of the men, tearing herself away from them, as one of them held to her old yellow dress and tore it. Her long shapely legs were visible, and her enormous pregnant stomach. But she went quickly to Emanuelle, and walked her away from them, and it was only then that she realized the commandant was standing there, his eyes blazing, his shouted orders an avalanche of fury in German. He still held the gun aloft in his hand and shot it off again so that they knew he meant it. He then lowered it at each of them, took aim, and said something more in German, before he lowered his hand, put the gun back in its holster and dismissed them. He ordered each of them to be put in the jail they had fashioned in the back of the stables for the next week. As soon as they left, he moved quickly toward Emanuelle and Sarah. His eyes were filled with pain, and he spoke in hurried German to an orderly standing near, who reappeared instantly with two blankets. Sarah covered Emanuelle first, and then wrapped the other blanket around her middle. She saw that it was one of hers, one of the few she had forgotten when they moved to the cottage.

'I promise you, this will never happen again. These men are pigs. They have grown up in barnyards, most of them, and they have absolutely no idea how to behave. The next time I see one of them do something like that, I will shoot him.' He was white with rage as he spoke, and Emanuelle was still shaking. Sarah felt nothing except fury for what had happened, and she turned to him with her eyes blazing just before they reached the cottage, where Henri was in the garden, playing with the baby. They had warned him to stay away for fear that the soldiers might go after him, but he had come anyway, to see his sister, and she had asked him to stay with the baby, while she went to pick berries.

'Do you realize what they could have done?' Sarah waved Emanuelle away, back to the house. She faced the commandant alone and addressed him. 'They could have killed my unborn child,' she screamed at him, and his eyes didn't waver.

'I realize very well, and I sincerely beg your pardon.' He looked as though he meant it, but his good manners did nothing to mollify her. As far as Sarah was concerned they should never have been there.

'And she's a young girl! How dare they do a thing like

234

that to her!' She was suddenly shaking from head to foot and she wanted to beat him with her fists, but she had the good sense not to.

The commandant felt bad about Emanuelle, but he was most upset by what they had almost done to Sarah. 'I apologize, Your Grace, from the bottom of my heart. I realize only too well what could have happened.' She was right. They might very well have killed her baby. 'We will keep a tighter watch on the men. I give you my word as an officer and a gentleman. I assure you, it won't happen again.'

'Then see that it doesn't.' She stormed at him, and then marched into the cottage, somehow managing to look both beautiful and regal in her blanket as he watched her. She was an extraordinary woman, and he had wondered more than once how she had come to be the Duchess of Whitfield. He had found photographs of her in William's study, which was his room now, and of both of them, and they looked remarkably handsome and happy. He envied them. He had been divorced since before the war, and he scarcely saw his children. They were two boys, seven and twelve, and his wife had remarried and moved to the Rhineland. He knew her husband had been killed in Poznan in the first days of the war, but he hadn't seen her again, and the truth was that he didn't really want to. The divorce had been extremely painful. They had married when they were very young, and they had always been very different. It had taken him two years to recover from the blow, and then the war had come, and now he had his hands full. He had been pleased with the assignment to France. He had always liked it there. He had studied for a year at the Sorbonne, and he had finished his studies at Oxford. And through all of it, in all of his travels, in all his forty years, he had never met anyone like Sarah. She was so beautiful, so strong, so decent. He wished they had met in other circumstances, at another time. Perhaps then things might have been different.

The administration of his convalescent hospital kept him busy enough, but in the evenings, he liked to go for long walks. He had come to know the property well, even the far reaches of it, and he was coming back one evening at dusk from a little river he had found in the forest, when he saw her. She was walking slowly, by herself, awkwardly now, and she seemed very pensive. He didn't want to frighten her, but he thought he should say something to her, lest his unexpected presence surprise her. She turned her face toward him then, as though she sensed someone near her. She stopped walking and looked at him, not sure if his presence was a threat, but he was quick to reassure her.

'May I assist you, Your Grace?' She was climbing bravely over logs, and little stone walls, and she could easily have fallen, but she knew the terrain well. She and William had come here often.

'I'm fine,' she said quietly, every inch the duchess. And yet she looked so young and so lovely. She seemed less angry than she usually was when she saw him. She was still upset over what had happened to Emanuelle the week before, but she had heard that the men were truly jailed to punish them for it, and she was impressed by his sense of justice.

'Are you well?' he asked, walking along with her. She looked pretty, in a white embroidered dress made by the locals.

'I'm all right,' she said, looking at him as though for the first time. He was a handsome man, tall, fair, and his face was lined, she could see that he was a little older than William. She wished he weren't there, but she had to admit, he had always been extremely polite to her, and twice now, very helpful.

'You must get easily tired now,' he said gently, and she shrugged, looking sad for a moment, thinking of William.

'Sometimes.' Then she glanced back at Joachim. Her news of the war was limited these days, and she had had no word of William since the Occupation. There was no way his letters could reach her. And she knew he must be frantic for news of her and Phillip.

'Your husband's name is William, isn't it?' he asked, and she looked at him, wondering why he asked. But she only nodded.

'He's younger than I. But I think I might have met him once when I was at Oxford. I believe he went to Cambridge.'

'That's right,' she said hesitantly, 'he did.' It was odd to think that the two men had met. Life did strange things sometimes. 'Why did you go to Oxford?'

'I always wanted to. I was very fond of all things English then.' He wanted to tell her that he still was, but he couldn't. 'It was a wonderful opportunity, and I thoroughly enjoyed it.'

She smiled wistfully. 'I think that's the way William felt about Cambridge.'

'He was on the soccer team, and I played against him once.' He smiled. 'He beat me.' She wanted to cheer, but she only smiled, suddenly wondering about this man. In any other context, she knew she would have liked him.

'I wish you weren't here,' she said honestly, sounding very young, and he laughed.

'So do I, Your Grace. So do I. But better here than in battle somewhere. I think they knew in Berlin that I am better suited to repairing men than destroying them. It was a great gift to be sent here.' He had a point there, but she wished that none of them had come. And then he looked at her with curiosity.

'Where is your husband?' But she wasn't sure if she should tell him. If she told him that William was in Intelligence, it might put all of them in greater danger.

'He's attached to the RAF.'

'Does he fly?' The commandant seemed surprised.

'Not really,' Sarah said vaguely, and he nodded.

'Most of the pilots are younger than we are.' He was right of course, but she only nodded. 'It's a terrible thing, war. No-one wins. Everyone loses.'

'Your Führer doesn't seem to think that.'

Joachim was silent for a long moment, and then answered her, but there was something in his voice that caught her attention, something that told her he hated this war as much as she did. 'You're right. Perhaps in time,' he said bravely, 'he will come to his senses, before too much is lost, and too many are killed.' And then he touched her by what he said next, 'I hope that your husband stays safe, Your Grace.'

'So do I,' she whispered as they reached the cottage. 'So do I.' He bowed, and saluted her then, and she left him and went back to the cottage, musing at what an interesting contradiction he was. A German who hated the war, and yet, he was the commandant of the German Forces in the Loire Valley region. But when she walked back into the cottage that night, thinking of her husband, she forgot all about Joachim.

She ran into him again a few days later, in the same place, and then again, and eventually it was as though they expected to meet there. She liked to go and sit in the forest at the end of the day, by the riverbank, and think, with her feet dangling in the cool water. Her ankles got swollen sometimes, and it was so peaceful here. All she could hear were the birds and the sounds of the forest.

'Hello,' he said quietly, one afternoon, after he had followed her there. She didn't know that he had guessed her routine, and watched for her now, from his window, as she left the cottage. 'It's hot today, isn't it?' He wished he could give her a cool drink, or feel the long silky hair, or even touch her cheek. She was beginning to fill his dreams at night, and his thoughts in the daytime. He even kept

238

one of William's photographs of her locked in his desk, where he could see it whenever he wanted. 'How are you feeling?'

She smiled at him; they were not yet friends, but at least they were neutral. It was something. And he was someone to talk to, other than Emanuelle and Henri and Phillip. She missed her long, intelligent conversations with William. She missed other things about him as well. She missed everything. But at least this man, with his worldly views and his gentle eyes, was someone to talk to. She never forgot who he was, or why he was there. She was the duchess, and he was the commandant. But it was a relief of sorts, talking to him, even for a few moments.

'I'm feeling fat,' she admitted to him with a small smile. 'Enormous.' And then she turned to him with curiosity. She knew nothing about him. 'Do you have children?'

He nodded, sitting on a large rock, just near her, and ran a hand through the cool water. 'Two sons. Hans and Andi – Andreas.' But he looked sad as he said it.

'How old are they?'

'Seven and twelve. They live with their mother. We're divorced.'

'I'm sorry,' she said, and she meant it. Children were a separate thing from war. And whatever nationality they were, she couldn't bring herself to hate them.

'Divorce is a terrible thing,' he said, and she nodded.

'I know.'

'Do you?' He raised an eyebrow, wanting to ask her how, but he didn't. It was obvious that she couldn't know. She was clearly happy with her husband. 'I scarcely saw my sons once she left. She remarried . . . and then the war came . . . It's all very difficult at best.'

'You'll see them again when the war ends.'

He nodded, wondering when that would be, when the Führer would let them go home, and if his ex-wife would really let him see them, or if she would say it had been too long, and they no longer wanted to see him anyway. She had played a lot of games with him, and he was still very hurt and very angry. 'And your baby?' He changed the subject again. 'You said it would be here in August. That's very soon.' He wondered how shocked everyone would be if he let her have it at the château, with their doctor's help, or if that would cause too much talk. It might just be easier to send one of the doctors down to the cottage. 'Was it easy with your son?'

It was odd to be discussing this with him, and yet here they were in the woods, alone, captor and prisoner, and what difference did it make what she told him? Who would ever know? Who would even know if they became friends, as long as no-one was hurt, and nothing was damaged? 'No, it wasn't easy,' she admitted to him. 'Phillip weighed ten pounds. It was very hard. My husband saved us both.'

'There was no doctor?' He looked shocked. Surely the duchess had had her baby in a private clinic in Paris, but she surprised him.

'I wanted to have him here. He was born on the day war was declared. The doctor had gone to Warsaw, and there was no-one else. Just William . . . my husband. I think it frightened him even more than it did me. I didn't really know what was happening after a certain point. It took a long time, and . . .' She spared him the details, but she smiled shyly at him. 'It doesn't matter. He's a lovely boy.' He was touched by her, by her innocence and her honesty, and her beauty.

'You're not afraid this time?'

She hesitated, for some reason wanting to be honest with him, though she didn't know why. But she knew she liked him, in spite of who he was, and where he lived, and how they had met. He had only been kind to her, and decent. And he had intervened to protect her twice now.

'A little,' she admitted. 'But not very.' She hoped it

would be quicker and that this baby would be smaller.

'Women always seem so brave to me. My wife had both of our boys at home. It was beautiful, but for her it was very easy.'

'She's lucky.' Sarah smiled.

'Perhaps we can help you this time with some German expertise.' He laughed gently and she looked serious.

'They wanted to do a cesarean last time, but I didn't want one.'

'Why not?'

'I wanted to have more children.'

'Admirable of you. And brave . . . just as I said, women are so much more courageous. If men had to have babies, there would be no more children.' She laughed, and they talked about England then, and he asked her about Whitfield. She was intentionally vague with him. She didn't want to give away any secrets, but it was the spirit of it that interested him, the stories, the traditions. He really did seem to love all things English.

'I should have gone back,' she said wistfully. 'William wanted me to, but I thought we'd be safe here. I never thought France would surrender to the Germans.'

'No-one did. I think it even surprised us how quickly it went,' he confessed to her, and then he told her something he knew he shouldn't. But he trusted her, and there was no way she could betray him. 'I think you did the right thing staying here. You, and your children, will be safer.'

'Than at Whitfield?' She looked surprised and it seemed an odd thing to say to her, as she looked at him with a puzzled frown, wondering what he meant.

'Not necessarily Whitfield, but England. Sooner or later, the Luftwaffe will turn its full force on Britain. It will be better for you to be here then.' She wondered if he was right, and as they walked back to the cottage afterwards she wondered if he had told her anything he shouldn't. She assumed that the British knew all about the

Luftwaffe's plans, and maybe he was right, maybe it was safer here. But whether or not it was, she had no choice now. She was his prisoner.

She didn't see him again for a few days, and at the very end of July, she ran into him again in the forest. He seemed distracted and tired, but he cheered up when she thanked him for the food that had begun appearing outside the cottage. First, berries for the child, and then a basket of fruit for all of them, loaves of fresh bread that their bakers were making at the château, and carefully wrapped in newspaper and well hidden from prying eyes, a kilo of real coffee.

'Thank you,' she said cautiously. 'You don't have to do that.' He didn't owe them anything. They were the forces of the Occupation.

'I'm not going to eat, while you starve.' His cook had made a wonderful Sacher torte for him the night before, and he was planning to take the rest of it to her himself that night, but he didn't mention it as they walked slowly back to the cottage. She seemed to be slowing down, and he noticed that in the past week, she had gotten considerably larger. 'Is there anything else you need, Your Grace?'

She smiled at him. He always addressed her by her title. 'You know, I suppose you really could call me Sarah.' He already knew that was her name. He had seen it when he had taken her passport. And he knew that she was about to turn twenty-four years old in a few more weeks. He knew her parents' names, and their addresses in New York, and how she felt about some things, but he knew very little else about her. And his curiosity about her knew no bounds. He thought about her more than he would have admitted. But she sensed none of that, as she walked with him. She sensed only that he was a caring man, and as best he could, given his position here, he wanted to help her.

'Very well then, Sarah,' he said it carefully, like a great honor, as he smiled at her, and she noticed for the first time that he was actually very handsome. Usually, he looked so serious that one didn't notice. But as they came out into a sunny part of the woods, for just a moment, he had looked years younger. 'You shall be Sarah and I shall be Joachim, but only when we are alone.' They both understood why and she nodded. And then he turned to her again. 'Is there anything you need from me?' He was sincere, but she shook her head anyway. She would never have taken anything from him, except the extra food he left her for Phillip. But she was touched that he had asked, and she smiled.

'You could give me a ticket home,' she teased. 'How about that? Straight to New York, or maybe to England.' It was the first time she had joked with anyone since they'd arrived, and he laughed.

'I wish I could.' His eyes grew serious then. 'I imagine your parents must be very worried about you,' he said sympathetically, wishing that he could help her. 'And your husband.' He would have been frantic if Sarah had been his wife, and she was behind enemy lines, but she seemed to take it very coolly. She shrugged philosophically, as he longed to reach out and touch her, but he knew that he couldn't do that either.

'You'll stay safe, if I have anything to do with it,' he reassured her.

'Thank you.' She smiled up at him, and then suddenly stumbled on a tree root that crossed her path. She almost fell, but Joachim quickly reached out and caught her. He held her in his powerful hands, and then she steadied herself and thanked him. But for just that instant he had felt how warm she was, how smooth the ivory skin on her arms, and the dark hair had brushed his face like silk. She smelled of soap, and the perfume her husband loved. Everything about her made Joachim feel as though he would melt when he was near her, and it was an increasing agony not to let her know that.

He walked her back to the cottage then, and left her near the gate, and went back to work at his desk for the rest of the evening.

She did not see him after that for a full week. He had to go to Paris to see the ambassador, Otto Abetz, to arrange for shipments of medical supplies, and when he came back, he was so busy he had no time for walks or air, or pleasant things. And four days after his return there was a terrible explosion at a supply depot in Blois. They brought more than a hundred wounded in, and even the staff they had was inadequate to help them. There were wounded men everywhere, and their two doctors were running from one critical case to another. They had mounted a small operating theater in the dining room, but some of the men were so badly burned that no-one could help them. Limbs had been blown off, faces torn away. It was a hideous scene of carnage, as Joachim and his staff surveyed the crowded rooms and one of the doctors came to demand more help. He wanted them to bring in the locals to help him.

'There must be some people with medical skills here,' he insisted, but the local hospital was closed, the doctors were gone, and the nurses had gone to military hospitals months before, or fled just before the Occupation. There were only the people from the farms, most of whom were too ignorant to help them. 'What about the châtelaine? Would she come?' He was referring, of course, to Sarah, and Joachim thought she might, if he asked her. She was very human, but she was also very pregnant, this would hardly be good for her, and Joachim felt very protective of her.

'I'm not sure. She's expecting a baby at any moment.'

'Tell her to come. We need her anyway. Does she have a maid?'

'There's a local girl with her.'

'Get them both,' the doctor ordered him curtly,

although Joachim outranked him. And a few moments later, Joachim sent a handful of his men out to the countryside to speak to the women at the farms, to see if anyone would come to help them, or order them to if they had to. And then he got in a jeep himself, and drove down to the cottage. He knocked firmly on the door, the lights went on, and a few minutes later, Sarah appeared, looking very stern at the door in her nightgown. She had heard the ambulance and the trucks coming all night long, and didn't know why, and now she was afraid that the soldiers had come to taunt them. But when she saw Joachim, she opened the door a fraction wider, and her face eased a little.

'I'm sorry to disturb you,' he apologized. He was wearing his shirt, and had taken off his tie, his hair looked rumpled and his face looked worn, and he had left his jacket in his office. 'We need your help, Sarah, if you'll come. There's been an explosion at a munitions depot, and we have an incredible number of wounded. We can't manage. Can you help us?' She hesitated for an instant, looking into his eyes, and then she nodded. He asked her if she would bring Emanuelle, too, but when she went upstairs to ask her, the girl insisted that she wanted to stay at the cottage with the baby. And Sarah met Joachim downstairs alone, five minutes later.

'Where's the girl?'

'She's not well,' Sarah covered for her. 'And I need her to stay here with my son.' He didn't question her, and she followed him to the jeep in an old, faded blue dress and flat shoes, with her hair neatly braided. She had scrubbed her hands and face and arms, and had covered her hair with a clean white scarf, which made her look even younger.

'Thank you for coming,' he said as they drove back, and he glanced at her with a look of gratitude in his eyes, and new respect. 'You know, you didn't have to.'

'I know that. But dying boys are just that, whether they're English or German.' It was how she seemed to feel about the war. She hated the Germans for what they'd done, yet she couldn't hate the ones who'd been hurt, or even Joachim, who was always so decent to her. It didn't make her sympathetic to his cause, only to those whose need was greater than her own, and she nodded as he helped her from the car, and hurried inside to help the boys she'd been called for.

She worked for hours in the operating room that night, holding bowls filled with blood, and towels soaked with anesthetic. She held instruments, and assisted both of the doctors. She worked tirelessly until dawn, and then they asked her if she would go upstairs with them, and for the first time, as she entered her own bedroom, filled with wounded men, she was suddenly aware of where she was, and how odd it was to be here. There were cots and mattresses on the floor, at least forty wounded men were lying there beside each other, shoulder to shoulder, and the orderlies were barely able to step over them to get to the next one.

She did whatever she could, applying bandages, cleaning wounds, and it was bright daylight again by the time she made her way back downstairs to what had once been her kitchen. There were half a dozen orderlies eating there, some soldiers and two women who looked at her as she walked in, and said something to each other in German. Her dress and hands, and even her face, were covered in young men's blood, her hair hung in wisps around her face, but she seemed not to notice. And then one of the orderlies said something to her. She couldn't understand what they said, but it was impossible to mistake the tone of respect, as he seemed to thank her. She nodded, and smiled at them as they handed her a cup of coffee. One of the women pointed to the baby then, and seemed to ask if she was all right, and she nodded and sat down gratefully with the steaming coffee. It was only then that she began to feel her own exhaustion. She hadn't thought of herself in hours, or her baby.

Joachim came in a moment after that, and asked her to come into his office. She followed him down the hall, and as she walked in, she felt strange here too. Even the desk and the curtains were the same. This was William's favorite room, and the only thing that had changed was the man who lived there.

Joachim invited her to sit down in the chair she knew so well, and she had to resist the urge to curl up, as she always had when she and her husband had long, cozy conversations. Instead, she sat politely on the edge of the chair, and sipped at her coffee, reminding herself that in this room, she was now a stranger.

'Thank you for all you did last night. I was afraid it might have been too much for you.' He looked at her with worried eyes. He had passed her frequently in the night, working doggedly to save someone's life, or just closing some boy's eyes they had lost, with tears in her own eyes. 'You must be exhausted.'

'I'm tired.' She smiled honestly, her eyes still sad. They had lost so many boys. And for what? She had cradled one like a child, and he had held her just as Phillip did, but this boy had died in her arms, from a wound in his stomach. She could do nothing to save him.

'Thank you, Sarah. I'll take you home now. I think the worst is over.'

'Is it?' she said with a look of surprise, in a tone that startled him with its sharp edge. 'Is the war over?'

'I meant for now,' he said quietly. His views were no different than her own, although he couldn't allow himself to express them.

'What difference does it make?' she asked, setting down her coffee cup on William's desk. She noticed that they were also using her china. 'It'll all just happen again somewhere else today, or tomorrow, or next week. Won't it?' There were tears in her eyes. She couldn't forget the boys who had died, even if they were Germans.

'Yes, it will,' he said sadly, 'until all this is over.'

'It's so senseless,' she said, walking to the window and looking out at the familiar scene. Everything seemed so deceptively peaceful. And Joachim walked up slowly behind her until he stood very near her.

'It is senseless . . . and stupid . . . and wrong . . . but right now, there is nothing you and I can do to change it. You are bringing life into the world. We are bringing death and destruction. It's a terrible contradiction, Sarah, but I am helpless to change it.' She didn't know why then, but she felt sorry for him. He was a man who didn't believe in what he was doing. At least William had the comfort of knowing that he was doing the right thing, but Joachim didn't. She wanted to reach out and touch him as she turned to face him, and tell him that it would be all right, that one day he would be forgiven.

'I'm sorry,' she said softly, and walked past him toward the door. 'It was a long night. I shouldn't have said what I did. It's not your fault.' She stood and looked at him for a long moment, as he longed to be near her again. But he was touched by what she had said.

'That's not much comfort sometimes,' he said softly, still looking at her. She looked so tired now, and she needed rest, or the baby might come early. He still felt guilty for asking her to come and help, but she had done a splendid job and the doctors were very grateful to her.

He took her home after that, and Emanuelle had just come downstairs with Phillip. She looked at Sarah as Joachim left, and saw how tired she was and she felt guilty for not going to help her.

'I'm sorry,' she whispered to her, as Sarah sat down heavily in an old chair. 'I just couldn't . . . they're Germans.'

'I understand,' Sarah said, wondering why it hadn't made more difference to her, but it hadn't. They were boys, and a few men . . . just people . . . But she understood more when Henri came to the cottage a little while later. He looked at his sister, and something Sarah didn't understand passed between them. He nodded, and then she saw his hand, wrapped in bandages, and she wondered.

'Henri, what happened to your hand?' she asked calmly.

'Nothing, Madame. I hurt myself helping my father saw wood.'

'Why were you sawing wood?' she asked wisely. It was far too warm for anyone to need a fire, but the boy knew that.

'Oh, we were just building a house for our dog,' he said, but Sarah also knew they didn't have one, and then she understood all too clearly. The explosion at the munitions dump had been no accident, and somehow, for some reason she didn't even want to know, Henri had been there.

That night as they were getting ready to go to bed, she looked at Emanuelle as the two women stood in the kitchen. 'You don't have to say anything . . . but I just want to tell you to tell Henri to be very careful. He's only a child. But if they catch him, they'll kill him.'

'I know, Madame,' Emanuelle said, with terror in her eyes for her little brother. 'I told him that. My parents don't know anything. There is a group in Romorantin—' But Sarah stopped her.

'Don't tell me, Emanuelle. I don't want to know. I don't want to accidentally put anyone in danger. Just tell him to be careful.'

Emanuelle nodded, and they both went to their rooms, to bed, but Sarah lay awake for a long time that night, thinking of the boy and the carnage he'd done . . . all those boys with lost limbs, and faces, and lives that ended so quickly. And little Henri with his burned hand. She wondered if he understood what he and his friends had done, or if he would be proud of it. Officially, what he'd done was considered patriotic, but Sarah knew better. Whatever side you were on, in her eyes, it was still murder. But as she lay there, she only hoped that the Germans didn't catch Henri, or hurt him.

Joachim was right. It was an ugly war. An ugly time. As she thought of it, her hand drifted across her belly, and the baby kicked her. It reminded her that there was still hope in the world, and life, and something decent to look forward to . . . and somewhere, out there, there was William.

Chapter 14

Sarah saw Joachim almost every day after that, not by any prearranged plan. He just knew her walking schedule now, and seemingly by accident, he always joined her. They walked a little more slowly each day now, and sometimes they went to the river, and sometimes to the farm. And little by little, he was getting to know her. He tried to get to know Phillip, too, but the boy was reticent and shy, as his own son had been at the same age. But Joachim was incredibly kind to him, much to Emanuelle's displeasure. She didn't approve of anyone or anything German.

But Sarah knew he was a decent man. She was more sophisticated than Emanuelle, although she was no more fond of the Germans. But there were times when he made her laugh, and times when she was quiet, and he knew she was thinking of her husband.

He knew it was a difficult time for her. Her birthday came and went. She had no word from William or her parents. She was cut off from everyone she loved, her parents, her sister, her husband. All she had was her son, and the baby about to be born that William had left her.

But on her birthday Joachim brought her a book that had meant a great deal to him when he was at Oxford, and was one of the few personal things he had brought with him.

It was a dog-eared copy of a book of poems by Rupert Brooke, and she loved it. But it wasn't a happy birthday for her. Her heart was full of the news of the war, and the heartache of the bombing of Britain. On the fifteenth of August, the blitz on London had begun, and it tore at her heart to think of the people she knew there, their friends, William's relatives . . . the children . . . Joachim had warned her this would come, but she hadn't expected it so soon, or fully understood how destructive it would be when it happened. London was being ravaged.

'I told you,' he said quietly, 'you are safer here. Especially now, Sarah.' His voice was kind as he said it, and he gently helped her over a rough spot on the road, and after a while they sat down on a large rock. He knew it was better not to talk about the war, but about other things that wouldn't upset her.

He told her about his childhood trips to Switzerland, and his brother's pranks when they were children. Oddly enough, it had struck him early on how much his brother had looked like her baby. Phillip was just walking now, with golden curls and big blue eyes, and when he was with his mother or Emanuelle, he was full of mischief.

'Why haven't you married again?' Sarah asked him one afternoon, as they sat and rested. The baby was so low she could barely move, but she liked her walks with him and she didn't want to stop them. It was a relief to talk to him, and without realizing it, she had come to count on his presence.

'I never fell in love with anyone,' he said honestly, smiling at her, wanting to say, 'Until now.' But he didn't. 'It's an awful thing to say, but I'm not even sure I was in love with my first wife. We were young, and we had been together since we were children. I think it was just . . . expected of us,' he explained, and Sarah smiled. She felt so comfortable with him, she felt no need to keep her secrets.

'I didn't love my first husband either,' she admitted to him, and he looked surprised. There were things about her that always amazed him, like the constant realization of how strong she was, how fair, how just, and how devoted to her husband.

'You were married before?' He looked genuinely surprised.

'For a year. To someone I'd known all my life, just like you and your wife. It was awful. We should never have gotten married. When we got divorced, I was so ashamed I went into hiding for a year. My parents took me to Europe after that, and that's where I met William.' It all sounded so simple now, she thought, but it hadn't been then. It had all been so painful. 'It was pretty grim for a while. But with William' – her eyes lit up as she said his name – 'but with William, everything is so different . . .'

'He must be a wonderful man,' Joachim said sadly.

'He is. I'm a very lucky woman.'

'And he's a lucky man.' He helped her up again, and they continued to the farm and then back. But the next day, she couldn't make it, and he sat quietly in the park with her. She seemed quieter than usual, more nostalgic, and more pensive. But the day after, she seemed more herself again, and she insisted on going all the way to the river.

'You know, you worry me sometimes,' he said as they walked along. There was more of a spring in her step today, and she seemed to have regained her sense of humor.

'Why?' She looked intrigued, it was odd to think of the head of the German Occupation Forces in the area worrying about her, and yet she sensed that they were friends now. He was serious, intense, and he was clearly a kind, decent man, and she liked him.

'You do too much. You take too much on your shoulders.' He had learned by then how much of the château she had restored herself, and it still amazed him. She had given him a tour of some of the rooms herself one day, and he couldn't believe the precision and the thoroughness of some of the work she'd done, and then she had shown him all that she had done in the stables.

'I don't think I'd have let you do it if you were my wife,' he said firmly and she laughed.

'Then I guess it's a good thing I married William.'

He smiled at her, envious of William again, but nonetheless grateful to know her. They lingered at her gate that day for a long time. It was as though she didn't want to let him go this afternoon, and for the first time, as she left him, she reached out and touched his hand and thanked him.

The gesture startled him, and warmed him to the core, but he pretended not to notice. 'What for?'

'Taking the time to walk with me . . . and talk to me.' It had come to mean a lot to her, having him to talk to.

'I look forward to seeing you . . . perhaps more than you know,' he said softly, and she looked away, not sure what to answer. 'Perhaps we are each fortunate that the other is here,' he said gently. 'A kind of kismet . . . a higher destiny. This war would be even worse for me, if you weren't here with me, Sarah.' In truth, he hadn't been this happy in years, and the only thing that frightened him was that he knew he loved her, and he would have to leave one day, and she would go back to William, never knowing what he had felt, or all that she had meant to him. 'Thank *you*,' he said, wishing he could reach out and touch her face, her hair, her arms . . . but he was not as brave or as foolish as his soldiers.

'I'll see you tomorrow then,' she said softly.

But the next afternoon he watched for her, and worried when she didn't come. He wondered if she wasn't well, and he waited until nightfall before strolling toward the cottage. All the lights were burning there, and he could see Emanuelle in the kitchen windows. He knocked on one of them and she came to the door with a frown, with Phillip in her arms and he looked fretful.

'Is Her Grace ill?' he asked her in French, and she shook her head. She hesitated, and then decided to tell him. She knew that no matter what she thought of him and his kind, Sarah liked him. She didn't like him too much. Emanuelle never questioned that. But there was an odd mutual respect between them.

'She's having the baby.' But there was something more in her eyes, a faint line of fear that he sensed more than saw, and he remembered what she had said of her previous delivery.

'Is it going well?' he asked, searching the girl's eyes. Emanuelle hesitated and then nodded and he was relieved, because all of their nurses and both doctors were gone to a conference in Paris. As they had no terribly ill soldiers in residence at the time, there were only orderlies in attendance. 'You're sure she's all right?' he pressed her.

'Yes, I am,' she snapped. 'I was there the last time.' He told her to give Sarah his best, and left a moment later, thinking of her, and her pain, and the baby that would come, wishing it were his and not someone else's.

He went back to William's study then, and sat there for a long time. He took out the photograph of her he'd found. She was laughing at something someone had said, and she was standing beside William at Whitfield. They made a handsome pair, and he put the photograph away again and poured himself a shot of brandy. He had just tossed it down, when one of the men on duty came to get him.

'There's someone here to see you, sir.' It was eleven o'clock and he was ready to go up to bed, but he came out and was surprised to see Emanuelle standing in the hallway.

'Is something wrong?' he asked, instantly worried about Sarah, and Emanuelle started wringing her hands and speaking quickly.

'It's not going well again. The baby just won't come.

Last time . . . Monsieur le Duc did everything . . . he shouted at her . . . it took hours . . . I pushed on her . . . and finally he had to turn it . . .' Why hadn't he kept the doctors there, he berated himself. He knew she had had a difficult birth the last time, and he had never thought of it when they left for Paris. He grabbed his jacket and followed Emanuelle outside. He had never delivered a baby, but there was absolutely no-one else to help them. And he knew there were no doctors left in town. There hadn't been in months. There was no-one he could send to help her.

When they reached the cottage, all the lights were still lit, and as he ran up the stairs two at a time, he saw that little Phillip was sound asleep in his bed in the room next to hers. When Joachim saw her, he saw instantly what Emanuelle meant. She was thrashing terribly and in dreadful pain, and the little French girl said she had been in labor since that morning. It had been sixteen hours since it started.

'Sarah,' he said gently as he sat down next to her in the room's only chair, 'it's Joachim. I'm sorry to be the one to come, but there's no-one else,' he apologized politely, and she nodded, aware that he was there, and she didn't seem to mind it. She reached out and clung to his hand, and as the pain began again and continued endlessly, she started crying.

'Terrible . . . worse than last time . . . I can't . . . William . . .'

'Yes, you can. I'm here to help you.' He sounded remarkably calm, and Emanuelle left the room to bring more towels. 'Has the baby started to come at all?' he asked her as he watched her.

'I don't think so . . . I . . .' She clutched at both of his hands then. 'Oh, God . . . oh, I'm . . . sorry . . . Joachim! Don't leave me!' It was the first time she had said his name, although he had often said hers, and he wanted to take her in his arms and tell her how much he loved her.

'Sarah, please . . . you have to help me . . . it's going to be all right.' He told Emanuelle how to brace her legs, and held her shoulders for her as the pains came, so she could push the baby out more easily. She fought him terribly at first, but his voice was quiet and strong, and he seemed to know what he was doing. After an hour or so, the baby's head started to come, and she wasn't bleeding nearly as badly as she had the last time. It was just obviously another large child, and it was going to take a long time to push it out, but Joachim was determined to stay there and help her for as long as he had to. It was almost morning when she finally pushed the head out, and a small wrinkled face poked out, but unlike Phillip, this baby didn't take a breath, and the room was filled with silence. Emanuelle looked at him worriedly, wondering what it meant, as he watched the child, and then quickly turned to Sarah.

'Sarah, you have to push the baby out!' he said urgently, looking again and again at the blue-tinged face of the baby. 'Come now . . . Now, Sarah, push!' he commanded, sounding more like a soldier than a doctor, or even a husband. He was commanding her to do it, and this time he did what Emanuelle had once done, pressing down hard on her stomach to help her. And little by little the baby came out, until it lay lifelessly between her legs on the bed, and she looked down and cried in sorrow.

'It's dead! My God, the baby's dead!' she cried, and he took it in his hands, still attached to its mother. It was a little girl, but there was no life in her as he held her and massaged her back, and patted her. He slapped the soles of her feet, and then he shook her, holding her upside down, and suddenly as he did, a huge plug of mucus flew out of her mouth, and she gave a gasp and then a cry, and wailed louder than any child he had ever heard as he held her. He was covered with blood, and he was crying as hard as

Sarah and Emanuelle, with relief, and the beauty of life. And then he cut the cord and handed her to Sarah, with a tender smile. He couldn't have loved Sarah more if he'd been the child's father.

'Your daughter,' he said, as he laid her gently beside Sarah, wrapped in a clean blanket. And then he went to wash his hands, and do what he could to repair his shirt, and he returned a moment later to Sarah's bedside. She held out a hand to him, and she was still crying as she took his hand in her own and kissed it.

'Joachim, you saved her.' Their eyes met and held for a long time, and he felt the power of having shared the gift of life with her in these last hours.

'No, I didn't,' he denied what he had done. 'I did what I could. But God made the decision. He always does.' And then he looked down at the peaceful child, so pink and round and perfect. She was a beautiful little girl, and except for her blond fluff of hair, she looked just like Sarah. 'She's beautiful.'

'She is, isn't she?'

'What are you going to call her?'

'Elizabeth Annabelle Whitfield.' She and William had decided that long before, and she thought it suited the peacefully sleeping baby.

He left her after that, and came back again late that afternoon to see how they were doing. Phillip was watching the baby in fascination, but snuggling close to his mother.

Joachim brought flowers, and a big piece of chocolate cake, a pound of sugar, and another precious kilo of coffee. And she was sitting up in bed, looking surprisingly well considering all she'd been through. But this time had been easier than the first, and the baby weighed 'only' nine pounds, Emanuelle announced as they all laughed. The near tragedy had ended well, thanks to Joachim. Even Emanuelle treated him kindly. And as Sarah looked at

258

him, after Emanuelle left the room again, she knew that no matter what happened in their lives, she would always be grateful to him, and she would never forget that he had saved her baby.

'I'll never forget what you did,' she whispered to Joachim as he held her hand. That morning, an undeniable bond had formed between them.

'I told you. It was God's hand that touched her.'

'But you were there . . . I was so frightened . . .' Tears filled her eyes as she remembered. She couldn't have borne it if the baby had died. But he had saved her.

'I was frightened too,' he confessed to her. 'We were very lucky.' He smiled at her then. 'Funnily enough, she looks a little like my sister.'

'Mine too,' Sarah laughed softly. They each had a cup of tea, and he had smuggled over a bottle of champagne, and he toasted her and the long life of Lady Elizabeth Annabelle Whitfield.

Eventually, he stood up to leave. 'You should sleep now.' Without saying a word he stooped to kiss the top of her head. His lips brushed her hair, and he closed his eyes just for an instant. 'Sleep, my darling,' he whispered, as she drifted off to sleep before he even left the room. She had heard what he said in the distance, but she was already dreaming of William.

Chapter 15

By the summer of the following year, London had almost been destroyed by the constant bombing, but not the British spirit. She had had only two letters from William by then, smuggled in to her through circuitous routes in the Resistance. He insisted that he was well, and reproached himself repeatedly for not getting her out of France when he should have. And in the second letter, he rejoiced over the arrival of Elizabeth, after he had gotten Sarah's letter. But he hated knowing that they were in France, and that there was no way for him to reach them. He didn't tell her that he had explored numerous possibilities of being smuggled into France, at least for a visit, but the War Office had objected. And there was no way of getting Sarah out of France, either, for the moment. They just had to sit tight, he said, and he assured her that the war would soon be over. But it was a third letter from him in the fall that brought Sarah the news which almost killed her. But he hadn't dared not to tell her, lest she heard the news some other way. Her sister Jane had written to him, since she knew she could not contact Sarah. Their parents had been killed in a boating accident off Southampton. They had been on a friend's yacht when a huge storm had come up. The yacht had sunk, and all of the passengers onboard had drowned before the Coast Guard could reach them.

Sarah was consumed with grief when she heard the news, and for an entire week she didn't speak to Joachim. By then he had learned that his sister had been killed in the bombing of Mannheim. Their losses were not small, for any of them. But the loss of her parents came as a crushing blow to Sarah.

The news only seemed to go from bad to worse after that. The entire world was stunned when they learned of the attack on Pearl Harbor.

'My God, Joachim, what does that mean?' It was he who had come to tell her. They were close friends by then, regardless of their nationalities, and the fact that he had saved Elizabeth's life weighed heavily with her. He continued to bring them food and small things, and he seemed always to be there for them when she needed him. He had gotten some medicine for her when Phillip got another bout of bronchitis. But now, this news seemed to change everything. Not for them. But for the entire world. By the end of the day, America had declared war on the Japanese, and hence the Germans. Directly, it changed nothing for her. She was already his prisoner, technically. But it was a frightening thought to realize that America had been attacked. What if New York was next? She thought of Peter and Jane and their children. It was so terrible not to be with them, so they could grieve for their parents together.

'This could change many things,' he said to her quietly, as he sat in her kitchen. Some of his men knew that he came to see her sometimes, but no-one seemed to think much of it. She was a pretty woman, but she behaved with dignity as the châtelaine of the château, but to Joachim she was far more than that. She was someone he cherished. 'I imagine it will have serious implications for us very shortly,' he said somberly. And he was right, of course. Every possible aspect of the war stepped up, and the bombing of London continued.

It wasn't until two months later that Sarah learned that her brother-in-law was in the Pacific, and Jane was staying at the house on Long Island with the children. It was odd to think that the house belonged to them now, that it was hers and Jane's, as well as the house in New York. And that Jane was there with her children. She felt so far away from all of them, and so sad to realize her children would never know her parents.

But she was in no way prepared for the news that reached her in the spring. Phillip was eighteen months old by then, and Elizabeth, their miracle baby, as Joachim called her, was seven months old, had four teeth, and was constantly happy. All she did was coo and laugh and sing, and every time she saw Sarah she squealed with delight, and threw her arms around her neck and squeezed her. And Phillip loved her too. He always kissed her and tried to hold her, and called her 'his' baby.

Sarah was holding her on her lap when Emanuelle came in with a letter for her, from the hotel, with a postmark from the Caribbean.

'How did you get this?' Sarah asked and then stopped herself. She had realized long since that there was a lot about Emanuelle and Henri's lives that she didn't want to know, and possibly even those of their parents. She had heard echoes about people being hidden at the hotel, and she had even let them use an old shed near the farm once, to hide someone for a week. But she'd tried not to know enough to harm them. Henri had had minor injuries more than once. Even more worrisome was the realization that Emanuelle had become romantically involved with the mayor's son, who was intimately involved with the Germans. And Sarah sensed correctly that her involvement with him was more political than romantic. It was a sad way to begin one's love life. She had tried to talk to Emanuelle about it once, but the girl was very closed and very firm. She didn't want to involve Sarah in anything she did, with or for the Resistance, unless she had to. But she brought her the letter now, and Sarah saw from the crest on the back of it that it was from the Duke of

Windsor. She couldn't imagine why they were writing to her. They never had before, although she had heard, on the radio Emanuelle's parents kept hidden at the hotel, that he was now the governor of the Bahamas. The government was afraid he might become a pawn for the Germans if he was captured, so they were keeping him well out of harm's way. And before he left, his German sympathies had been no particular secret in England.

The letter began with a warm greeting to her, in which he assured her Wallis joined him, and then went on to tell her that he had the greatest regret in being the one to inform her that William was missing in action. There was a distinct possibility that he had been taken prisoner, but it was not a certainty, he was sad to tell her. In fact, the letter told her as she read it with glazed eyes, the only thing certain was that William was missing. He described in detail how it had occurred, and assured her that he had every conviction that his cousin had acted with wisdom and courage. He might well have been killed going down, or he might have survived. But he had been parachuted into Germany on an intelligence mission that William himself had volunteered for, despite the objections of everyone at the War Office, for precisely these reasons.

'He was a very stubborn young man, and it has cost us all dearly, I'm afraid . . .' He went on, 'You most of all, my dear. You must be very brave, as he would want you to be, and have every faith that if God wants it thus, he will indeed be safe, or he may well be already in the hands of our Maker. I trust that you are well, and we send our deepest condolences and our deepest love to you and the children.' She stared at the letter in her hand, and read it again, as sobs welled up in her throat and began to choke her. Emanuelle had been watching her face and could see it was not good news. She had sensed that when she brought it to her from the hotel, and she took Elizabeth from her quickly and left the room, not knowing what to

say. She came back a few moments later, and found Sarah
sobbing at the kitchen table.

'Oh, Madame . . .' She put the baby on the floor and
put her arms around her bereft employer. 'Is it Monsieur
le Duc?' she asked in a strangled voice, and Sarah slowly
nodded, and then lifted tear-filled eyes to hers.

'He's missing . . . and they think he might have been
taken prisoner . . . or he might be dead . . . they don't
know . . . The letter was from his cousin.'

'Oh, *pauvre* Madame . . . he cannot be dead . . . Don't
believe that!'

She nodded, unsure of what she believed. She only
knew that she couldn't survive a world without William.
And yet he would want her to, for their children, for him,
but she just couldn't bear it. She cried where she sat for a
long time, and then she left the house and went for a long
walk alone in the forest. Joachim didn't see her this time.
She knew that it was late for him, and he would already
be at dinner. She wanted to be alone anyway. She needed
to be. And finally, she sat on a log in the darkness and
cried, wiping her tears on the arms of her sweater. How
could she bear living without him? How could life be so
cruel? And why had they let him do a dangerous mission
that involved dropping him into Germany? They had
sent David to the Bahamas. Why couldn't they have sent
William somewhere safe too? She just couldn't bear
the thought of what might have happened. She sat in the
forest in the dark for hours, trying to hear her own
thoughts, and pray, and feel some messages from William.
But she felt nothing. She felt numb until late that night,
when she lay in the bed they had shared when they first
came to the château and she was first pregnant with
Phillip. And suddenly as she lay there she felt certain that
he was alive. She didn't know how or where or when she
would see him again, but she knew she would, one day. It
felt almost like a sign from God, it was so powerful that

she couldn't deny it, and it reassured her. She fell asleep after that, and in the morning, she woke refreshed, and more certain than ever that William was alive, and had not been killed by the Germans.

She told Joachim about it later that day, and he listened quietly, but he was not totally swayed by her religious belief.

'I'm serious, Joachim . . . I felt this power . . . this absolute certainty that he's alive somewhere. I know it.' She spoke with the conviction of the deeply religious, and he didn't want to tell her how skeptical he was, or how few of those captured actually survived it.

'Perhaps you're right,' he said quietly, 'but you must also prepare yourself for the possibility that you could be wrong, Sarah.' He tried to say it as gently as he could. She had to accept the fact that he was missing, and perhaps dead. There was more than just a vague possibility that at that very moment she was already a widow. He didn't want to force her to face that fact yet, but eventually, no matter what she had felt that night, or what she wanted to feel or believe, she would have to.

As time went on, with no reassuring news of him, and no reports of his capture or survival, it was obvious to Joachim that he was dead, but not to Sarah. Sarah always acted now as though she'd seen him the previous afternoon, as though she'd heard from him in a dream. She was more at peace and more determined and more sure than at the beginning of the war, when she still got occasional letters. Now there was nothing, there was silence. He was gone. Presumably forever. And sooner or later, she would have to face it. Joachim was waiting for that time, but he knew that until she accepted William's death, the time was wrong for them, and he didn't want to press her. But he was there for her, when she needed him, when she wanted to talk, when she was sad, or lonely, or afraid. It was difficult to believe sometimes that they were on opposite sides of the war. To him, all they were were a man and a woman who had been together for two years now, and he loved her with all his heart, all his soul, everything he had to give her. He didn't know how they would sort it out after the war or where they would live or what they would do. But none of it was important to him. The only thing that mattered to him was Sarah. He lived and breathed and existed for her, but she still didn't know it. She knew how devoted he was to her, and sensed that he was very fond of her and the children, and especially close to Elizabeth, after he saved her life when she was born, but Sarah never truly understood how much he loved her.

That year, on her birthday, he tried to give her a magnificent pair of diamond earrings that he had bought for her in Paris, but she absolutely refused to take them.

'Joachim, I can't. They're incredible. But it's impossible. I'm married.' He didn't argue the point with her, although he no longer believed that. He felt certain that she was a widow now, and with all due respect to William, he had been gone for six months, and she was free now. 'And I'm your prisoner, for heaven's sake,' she laughed. 'What would people think if I accepted a pair of diamond earrings?'

'I'm not entirely sure we have to explain that to them.' He was disappointed, but he understood. He settled for giving her a new watch, which she did accept, and a very pretty sweater, which he knew she desperately needed. They were very modest gifts, and it was very much like her not to accept anything more expensive. He respected that about her too. In fact, in two years, he had never discovered anything about her that he didn't like, except for the fact that she continued to insist she was still married to William. But he even liked that about her too. She was loyal to the end, kind and loving, and devoted. He used to envy William for all that, but he no longer envied him, he pitied him. The poor man was gone. And sooner or later, Sarah would have to face that.

But by the following year, even Sarah's staunch hopes were starting to dim, although she didn't admit it to anyone, not even Joachim. But William had been gone for so long by then, over a year, and none of the intelligence sources had turned up anything about him. Even Joachim had tried to make discreet inquiries without causing any trouble for either of them. But the general consensus on both sides of the Channel seemed to be that William had been killed in March of 1942, when he was parachuted into the Rhineland. She still couldn't believe it, and yet when she thought of him now, sometimes even their most precious memories seemed dim, and it frightened her to feel that. She hadn't seen him in almost four years. It was a terribly long time, even for a love so great as theirs, to hold up in the face of so little hope and so much anguish.

She spent Christmas quietly with Joachim that year. He was incredibly sweet and loving to them. It was particularly nice for Phillip, who was growing up without a father, and had no memories whatsoever of William, because he hadn't been old enough to remember. In his mind, Joachim was a special friend, and in a pure, simple way, he really liked him, just as Sarah liked him. She still hated everything the Germans represented to her, and yet she never hated him. He was such a decent man, and he worked hard with the wounded men who came to the château to recover. Some of them had no hope, no limbs, no future, and no home to return to. And somehow he managed to spend time with everyone, to talk to them for hours on end, to give them hope, to make them want to continue, just as sometimes, he did with Sarah.

'You're an amazing man,' she said to him quietly, as they sat in her cottage kitchen. Emanuelle was with her family and Henri had been away for the past few weeks, in the Ardennes somewhere, Emanuelle said, and Sarah

267

had learned not to ask any questions. He was sixteen by then, and he led a life filled with passion and danger. Emanuelle's own life had grown increasingly difficult. The mayor's son had grown suspicious of her, and eventually there'd been a huge row when she left him. Now she was involved with one of the German officers, and Sarah never said anything, but she suspected that she was getting information from him, too, and feeding it to the Resistance. But Sarah stayed clear of all of it. She did what she could to continue to restore the château in small ways, helped with medical emergencies when she was either demanded or desperately needed, and the rest of the time she took care of her children. Phillip was four and a half, and Elizabeth was a year younger. And they were lovely children. Phillip was turning out to be as hugely tall as he had started out to be, and Elizabeth had surprised her by being delicate, and much more small featured than her mother. She was frail in some ways, just as she was when she was born, and yet she was always full of spunk and mischief. And it was obvious to everyone who saw him with them that Joachim adored them. He had brought beautifully made German toys for them the night before on Christmas Eve, and helped them to decorate a tree, and he had somehow managed to find a doll for Lizzie, who had immediately pounced on her, clutched her in her arms and cradled her 'baby'.

But it was Phillip who climbed on to Joachim's lap and put his arms around his neck, as he snuggled close to him, and Sarah pretended not to see it.

'You won't leave us, like my papa did, will you?' he asked worriedly, and Sarah felt tears sting her eyes as she heard him. But Joachim was quick to answer.

'Your papa didn't want to leave you, you know. If he could, I'm sure he'd be right here with you.'

'Then why did he go?'

'He had to. He's a soldier.'

'But you didn't go.' The child said logically, not realizing that Joachim had had to leave his own children, his own home, to come here. And then he threw his arms around Joachim's neck again, and stayed there until Joachim took him up to bed, as Sarah carried the baby. Phillip still had an absolute passion for her, which always delighted Sarah.

'Do you suppose it'll all finally end this year?' Sarah asked sadly as they each sipped some brandy after the children were in bed. He had brought her the finest Courvoisier, and it was powerful, but pleasant.

'I hope so.' The war seemed as if it would never end. 'It seems endless sometimes. When I see those boys they send to us, day after day, week after week, year after year, I wonder if anyone realizes how senseless it is, and that it's simply not worth it.'

'I think that's why you're here and not at the front.' Sarah smiled at him. He hated the war almost as much as she did.

'I'm glad I've been here,' he said gently. He hoped he had made it easier for her, and he had in many ways. He reached across the table and touched her hand cautiously then. He had known her for three and a half years, and in some ways it seemed a lifetime. 'You're very important to me,' he said quietly, and then, with the brandy and the sentiments of the day, he could no longer hide his emotions. 'Sarah' – his voice was husky and at the same time gentle – 'I want you to know how much I love you.' She looked away from him, trying to hide her own feelings from him, and from herself. She knew that no matter what she felt for this man, out of respect for William, she couldn't.

'Joachim, don't . . . please . . .' She looked up at him imploringly and he took her hand in his own and held it.

'Tell me that you don't love me, that you never could, and I will never say those words again . . . but I do love

269

you, Sarah, and I think you love me too. What are we doing? Why are we hiding? Why are we merely friends, when we could be so much more?' He wanted more from her now. He had waited for years, and he wanted her so badly.

'I do love you,' she whispered across the table at him, terrified by what she was saying, almost as much as by what she was feeling. But she had felt it for a long time, and she had resisted it . . . for William. 'But we can't do this.'

'Why not? We're grown people. The world is coming to an end. Aren't we allowed some happiness? Some joy? Some sunshine . . . before it's over?' They had both seen so much death, so much pain, and they were both so tired.

She smiled at what he said. She loved him too, loved the man he was, loved what he did for her children, and for her. 'We have each other's friendship . . . and our love . . . we don't have a right to more, as long as William is alive.'

'And if he isn't?' He forced her to face the possibility, and she turned away as she always did. It was still too painful.

'I don't know. I don't know what I'd feel then. But I know that right now I'm still his wife, and I probably will be for a long time. Maybe forever.'

'And I?' he said, demanding something from her for the first time. 'And I, Sarah? What am I to do now?'

'I don't know.' She looked at him unhappily and he stood up and walked slowly toward her. He sat down next to her, and looked into her eyes at the sorrow and longing he saw there, and then he gently touched her face with his fingers.

'I will always be here for you. I want you to know that. And when you accept the fact that William is gone, I will still be here. We have time, Sarah . . . we have a lifetime.' He kissed her gently then, on the lips, with everything he

270

had wanted to tell her for so long, and she didn't stop him. She couldn't stop him. She wanted this just as badly as he did. It had been more than four years since she'd seen her husband, and she had lived three and a half years with this man, side by side, day by day, growing to love and respect him. And yet she knew they had no right to what they both thought they wanted. To her, there was more to life than that. There was a vow that she had made, and a man that she had loved more than any other.

'I love you,' Joachim whispered to her, as they kissed again.

'I love you too,' she said. But she still loved William, too, and they both knew it.

He left her a little while after that, and went back to the château, respectful of who she was and what she wanted of him. The next day he came back and played with the children and their life continued as before, as if their conversation never took place.

And in the spring, things were not going well with the war for the Germans, and he would come and talk to Sarah about what he thought and what he feared might happen. By April he was sure that they would be pulled back closer to Germany, and he feared he might have to leave Sarah and the children. He promised to come back once the war was won or lost, and he almost didn't care, as long as they both survived it. He had remained careful with her, and although they kissed now and then, neither of them had allowed it to go any further. It was better that way, and he knew they would have no regrets, and that she needed to move slowly. She still wanted to believe that William was alive, and might return. But he knew that even if he did, it would be painful for her now to give up Joachim. She had come to rely on him, and to need him as much as she respected him. They were more than friends now, no matter how much she still loved William.

But while he was concerned with the news from Berlin,

for once Sarah was paying no attention. She was busy with Lizzie, who had had a ferocious cough since March, and was still weak and ill at Easter.

'I don't know what it is,' Sarah complained to him, one night in her kitchen.

'Some kind of influenza. They had it in the village all winter.' She had taken her up to the doctor at the château, who assured her it wasn't pneumonia, but the medicine he'd given her had done nothing for her either.

'Do you think it's tuberculosis?' she asked Joachim worriedly, but he didn't think so. He had asked the doctor to get more medicine for her, but they hadn't been able to get anything lately. All their supplies had been cut off, and one of their doctors had already left for the front, the other was leaving in May. But long before that, Lizzie lay in bed again, with a blazing fever. She had lost weight and her eyes were glazed, and she had that terrible look that children get when they're being beaten by a fever. And little Phillip sat at the foot of her bed day after day, singing to her, and telling her stories.

Emanuelle kept Phillip busy during the day, but he was frantic now about Lizzie. She was still 'his' baby and it frightened him to see her so ill, and his mother so worried. He kept asking if she'd be all right, and Sarah promised she would be. Joachim came to sit with them every night. He bathed Lizzie's head, and tried to make her drink, and when she coughed too hard he rubbed her back, just as he had when she was born to help her breathe and bring her to life. But this time he couldn't seem to help her. She grew worse day by day, and on the first of May, she lay blazing with fever. Both of their doctors had left, and all of their medical supplies had been sorely depleted. He had no medicine to bring, no suggestions to make, all he could do was sit with the two of them day after day, praying that she would get better.

He thought of taking her to Paris to the doctors there,

but she was too sick to make the trip, and things weren't going well there either. The Americans were advancing on France, and the Germans were beginning to panic. Paris was being stripped, and most of the military personnel were either being sent to the front, or back to Berlin. It was a dismal time for the Reich, but Joachim was far more upset about Lizzie.

In early May, he came back to the cottage one afternoon, and found Sarah sitting beside her, as she had for weeks, holding her hand, and bathing her head, but this time Lizzie wasn't moving. He sat with her for several hours, but eventually he had to go back to his office. There was too much going on there now for him to be absent without explanation. But he came back again late that night, and Sarah was lying on the child's bed, holding her in her arms, as she dozed there. He looked down at them, and as he did, Sarah looked up at him, and he saw real agony there, as he sat down gently beside her.

'Any change?' he whispered, and Sarah shook her head. She hadn't woken up since that morning. But as he stood watching them, Lizzie stirred, and for the first time in days, she opened her eyes, and smiled up at her mother. She looked like a little angel, with curls of blond hair and huge, green eyes like Sarah's. She was three and a half years old, but now that she was so sick, she looked older, as though the weight of the world had been on her shoulders.

'I love you, Mommy,' she whispered, and closed her eyes as Sarah held her, and suddenly Sarah knew. It was as though she could feel her begin to slip away. She wanted to hold her or pull her back. She wanted to do something desperately, but there was nothing she could do. They had no doctor, no medicine, no nurse, no hospital to give her . . . only love, and prayers, and then, as Sarah watched her, she sighed again, and Sarah touched the fine curls and whispered to her baby that she loved so desperately.

'I love you, sweet baby . . . I love you so much . . . Mommy loves you . . . and God loves you too . . . You're safe now . . .' she whispered over and over as she and Joachim cried, and with a sweet smile, Lizzie looked up at them for the last time, and then drifted away, her little spirit lifted up to heaven.

Sarah felt it when she'd gone, and it took Joachim a moment to understand. He sat down on the bed next to them and sobbed, holding them both in his arms as he rocked them. He remembered how he had brought her to life, and now she was gone . . . taken so swiftly and so sweetly. Sarah looked up at him with broken eyes, and she held little Lizzie for a long time, and finally, she set her gently down, and Joachim led her downstairs, and went back up to the château with her, to speak to someone about making arrangements for the funeral.

But in the end, Joachim did it all himself. He drove into town to get a tiny coffin for her, and together, crying softly, they put her in it. Sarah had combed her hair, and put on her prettiest dress, and put her favorite doll in with her. It was the most terrible thing that had ever happened to her, and it almost killed her when they lowered her into the ground. All she could do was cling to Joachim and cry, as poor Phillip stood by, clinging to her hand, unable to believe what had happened.

Phillip looked angry and afraid, and as they began shovelling earth into her grave, he leapt forward and tried to stop them. And as Joachim gently held him, he cried, looking furiously at his mother.

'You lied to me! You lied,' he screamed, trembling and sobbing. 'You let her die . . . my baby . . . my baby . . .' He was inconsolable as he clung to Joachim and suddenly wouldn't let Sarah near him. He had loved Lizzie so much, and now he couldn't bear to lose her.

'Phillip, please . . .' Sarah could barely gasp the words, as she caught the flailing arms in her own, and held him as he hit her. She took him from Joachim then and carried him gently home, as they both cried. And she held him long into the night as he sobbed agonizingly for 'his baby'.

It was unbelievable for all of them, Phillip, Emanuelle, Joachim . . . Sarah . . . One moment she had been there . . . and the next gone. Sarah felt as though she were in a trance for days, as did Phillip. They just kept ambling around, waiting for her to come home, to go upstairs and see her there, to find out that it had been a cruel joke and she was up to some mischief. Sarah was so blind with pain that Joachim didn't even dare tell her what was going on, and it was four weeks later when he had to tell her that they were leaving.

'What?' She sat staring at him, still wearing the same old black dress she had worn for weeks now. She felt a hundred years old and the dress hung on her like a scarecrow. 'You're what?' She seemed truly not to understand him.

'We're leaving,' he said gently. 'We got our orders this morning. We're pulling out tomorrow.'

'So soon?' She looked sick when he told her. It was one more loss, one more sorrow.

'It's been four years.' He smiled sadly at her. 'That's rather a long time to have houseguests, don't you think?'

She smiled sadly at him too. She couldn't believe that he was leaving. 'What does this mean, Joachim?'

'The Americans are in Saint-Lô. They'll be here soon, and then they'll move on to Paris. You'll be safe with them. They'll take good care of you.' At least that relieved him.

'And you?' she asked with a worried frown. 'Will you be in danger?'

'I'm being recalled to Berlin, and then we're moving the hospital to Bonn. Apparently someone is pleased with what I've being doing.' What they didn't know was how little his heart was in it. 'I think they'll keep me there till it's over. God knows how long that will be. But I'll come back as soon as I can afterwards.' It was amazing to think that after four years he was leaving, and she knew how much she would truly miss him. He had meant so much to her, and she knew that he always would, but she also knew that she could not promise him the future he wanted. In her heart, her life still belonged to William. Perhaps even more now after Lizzie's death, it was like losing a part of him, and more than ever, it made her long for William. They had buried her at the back of the property, near the forest where she had always walked with Joachim, and she knew that nothing that ever happened in her life would be as terrible or as painful as losing Lizzie. 'I won't be able to write to you,' he explained, and she nodded her understanding.

'I should be used to that by now. I've had five letters in the last four years.' One from Jane, two from William, one from the Duke of Windsor, and another from William's mother, and none of them had ever brought good news. 'I'll listen for the news.'

'I'll contact you as soon as I can.' He came closer to her then and held her close to him. 'Good God, how I'm going to miss you.' As he said it, she realized how much she would miss him, too, how much lonelier she would be than she was even now. And she looked up at him sadly.

'I will miss you too,' she said truthfully. She let him kiss her then, as Phillip stood watching them from the distance with a strange look of anger.

'Will you let me take a photograph of you before I go?' he asked, and she groaned.

'Like this? Good Lord, Joachim, I look awful.' He was going to take the other one with him anyway. The one of her with her husband at Whitfield, when they were all carefree and young, and life hadn't taken such a toll on them. She was not quite twenty-eight now, but at the moment, she looked somewhat older.

He gave her a small photograph of himself, too, and they spent all of that night talking. He would have liked to spend the night in bed with her, but he never asked, and he knew she wouldn't. She was that rare breed, a woman of integrity, a human being of extraordinary merit, and a great lady.

She and Phillip stood watching them leave the next day. Phillip clung to him as though to a life raft, but Joachim explained to him that he had to leave them. And Sarah kept wondering if Phillip felt he was losing another link to Lizzie. It was difficult for all of them, and painful and confusing. Only Emanuelle looked pleased as he prepared to leave. The soldiers went first, the trucks half full of their few remaining medical supplies, the supplies that hadn't been plentiful enough to save Lizzie. And then the ambulances with the patients.

Joachim had gone to her grave with Sarah before he left. He had knelt for a moment, and left a small bunch of yellow flowers, and they had both cried, and he had held Sarah for the last time, far from the eyes of his men, who knew anyway. They knew how much he loved her, but they knew, too, as soldiers do in close quarters, that nothing had ever happened between them. And they respected her for it too. She was the spirit of hope and love, and decency, to them. She was always polite and kind, no matter what she thought of their war, or what side they fought on. And they hoped, in their heart of hearts, that their own wives were being as strong as she was. Most of the men who had come to know her would have died to protect her, as would Joachim.

He stood looking down at her, as the last jeep waited for him, and his driver turned the other way discreetly. Joachim pulled Sarah close to him. 'I have loved you more than anyone or anything in my life,' he said, lest by the hand of Fate he never saw her again, he wanted her to know that, 'more even than my children.' He kissed her gently then, and she clung to him for an instant, wanting to tell him everything she had felt for him, but it was too late now. She couldn't do it.

She looked into his eyes, and he saw it all there anyway. 'Godspeed . . .' she whispered. 'Take care . . . I do love you . . .' She choked on the words, and then he stooped to Phillip, still holding tightly to Sarah's hand, wanting to say something to him. They all had been through so much together.

'Goodbye, little man.' Joachim choked on the words. 'Take good care of your mother.' He kissed the top of his head, and then ruffled his hair, as Phillip held him and then finally let go. And Joachim stood up and looked at Sarah for a long moment. Then he let go of her hand, and got into the jeep, and he stood and waved until they reached the front gate. She saw him as he left in a swirl of dust on the road, and then he was gone, as she stood there sobbing.

'Why did you let him go?' Phillip looked up at her angrily as she cried.

'We had no choice, Phillip.' The politics of the situation were far too complicated to explain to a child his age. 'He's a fine man, even if he is a German, and he has to go home now.'

'Do you love him?'

She hesitated, but only for a moment. 'Yes, I do. He's been a good friend to us, Phillip.'

'Do you love him better than my daddy?'

This time she did not hesitate, even for an instant. 'Of course not.'

'I do.'

'No, you do not,' she said firmly. 'You don't remember your daddy any more, but he's a wonderful man.' Her voice drifted off then as she thought of William.

'Is he dead?'

'I don't think he is,' she said carefully, not wanting to

278

mislead him, but wanting to share her own faith with him that one day they might find William. 'If we're very lucky, he'll come home to us one day.

'Will Joachim?' he asked sadly.

'I don't know,' she said honestly, as they walked back to the house, hand in hand, in silence.

Chapter 16

When the Americans arrived on August seventeenth, Sarah and Phillip and Emanuelle were watching when they came. They had heard news of their coming for weeks, and Sarah was eager to see them. They drove up the road to the château in a convoy of jeeps, just as the Germans had four years before. It was a crazy sense of déjà vu, but they didn't point guns at her, and she understood everything they said, and they gave a cheer when they discovered she was American. She still thought of Joachim every day, but she could only assume that he had reached Berlin safely. And Phillip still talked about him constantly. Only Emanuelle never mentioned the Germans.

The commanding officer of the American troops was Colonel Foxworth, from Texas, and he was very pleasant, and apologized profusely for putting his men in her stables. But the rest of them pitched tents, and used the caretaker's cottage she had so recently vacated, and even the local hotel. They didn't put her out of her house again, so soon after she'd moved back into it with Emanuelle and Phillip.

'We're used to it by now.' She smiled about the men in their stables. And he assured her that they would do as little damage as possible. He had good control of his men, and they were friendly, but they kept their distance. They flirted a little with Emanuelle, but she had no great interest in them, and they always brought candy to Phillip.

They all heard the church bells toll when the Americans liberated Paris in August. It was August twenty-fifth, and

France was free at last. The Germans had been driven out of France, and her day of shame had ended.

'Is it all over now?' Sarah asked Colonel Foxworth incredulously.

'Almost. As soon as we get to Berlin, it will be. But it's over here at least. You can go back to England now if you want to.' She wasn't sure what to do, but she thought she should at least go to Whitfield and see William's mother. Sarah hadn't left France since war had been declared five years before. It was amazing.

The day before Phillip's birthday, Sarah and Phillip left for England, leaving Emanuelle at the château to watch over it. She was a responsible girl and she had paid her price for the war too. Her brother Henri had been killed in the Ardennes the previous winter. But he had been a hero in the Resistance.

Colonel Foxworth and his counterpart in Paris had made arrangements for Sarah and Phillip on a military flight going to London, and there had been a great deal of hush-hush talk, telling the air force to expect the Duchess of Whitfield and her son, Lord Phillip.

The Americans provided a jeep to Paris for her, and they circumvented the town as they headed for the airport. They arrived with only moments to spare, and she swept Phillip into her arms, running for the plane, carrying their one small suitcase with the other. And as she reached the plane, a soldier stepped forward and stopped her.

'I'm sorry, madam. You can't get on this plane. This is a military flight . . . *militaire* . . .' he said in French, thinking she didn't understand him. '*Non . . . non . . .*' He wagged a finger at her and she shouted at him above the din from the engines.

'They're expecting me! We are *expected*!'

'This flight is only for military personnel,' he shouted back, 'And some old—' And then he realized who she was, and blushed to the roots of his hair, as he reached out to take Phillip from her. 'I thought . . . I'm really sorry, ma'am . . . Your, er . . . Majesty . . .' It had dawned on him too late that she was the promised duchess.

'Never mind.' She smiled, and stepped into the plane behind him. He had been expecting some old crone, and it had never dawned on him that the Duchess of Whitfield would be a young woman with a little boy. He was still apologizing when he left them.

The flight to London didn't take very long, it took them less than an hour to cross the Channel. And on the way over, several soldiers spoke to her admiringly for having weathered the Occupation. It seemed odd to Sarah as she listened to them, and remembered how relatively peaceful her life had been, during her four years in the cottage, protected by Joachim. When they arrived in London, an enormous Rolls-Royce was waiting for them. She was to go directly to the Air Ministry for a meeting with Sir Arthur Harris, the commander in chief of Bomber Command, and the King's private secretary, Sir Alan Lascelles, who was there by order of the King, and also to represent the secret intelligence service. They had flags and little insignia to give to Phillip, and all the secretaries kept calling him Your Lordship. It was a good deal more ceremony and respect than he was used to, but Sarah noticed with a smile that Phillip definitely seemed to like it.

'Why don't people at home call me that?' he whispered to his mother.

'Like whom?' She was amused by the question.

'Oh . . . Emanuelle . . . the soldiers . . .'

'I'll be sure to remind them,' she teased, but he didn't hear the humor in her voice and he was pleased that she agreed with him.

Several of the secretaries and two aides kept Phillip busy for her. When she went into the meeting, she found herself with Sir Arthur and Sir Alan. They were extremely kind to her, and what they wanted to tell her was what she already knew, that for two and a half years there had been no word of William.

She hesitated, trying to compose herself, and to get up the courage to ask a question. She took a deep breath and then looked at them. 'Do you think it's possible he's still alive?' she asked softly.

'Possible,' Sir Arthur said deliberately. 'But not likely,' he added sadly. 'By now we would have heard something from someone. Someone would have seen him in one of the prisoner-of-war camps. And if they know who he is at all, they'd be parading him all over. I think it's most unlikely they don't know who he is if they have him.'

'I see,' she said quietly. They talked to her for a little while longer, and then finally they all stood up, congratulating her again on her courage in France, and the fact that she and her son had come through it. 'We lost a little girl,' she said in a small voice, 'in May of this year . . . William had never seen her.'

'We're terribly sorry, Your Grace. We didn't know . . .'

They ushered her back outside eventually, and restored Phillip to her, and then drove her ceremoniously to Whitfield. The dowager duchess was waiting for them there, and Sarah was amazed by how well she looked. She was thinner and very frail, but she was eighty-nine now. She was really quite remarkable, and she had even done whatever she could for the war effort around Whitfield.

'It's so good to see you,' she said as she embraced Sarah, and then stood back a step, leaning on her cane to look at Phillip. She was wearing a bright-blue dress, the color of her eyes, and Sarah felt a wave of emotion wash over her, thinking of William. 'What a beautiful young man. He looks a great deal like my husband.' She smiled. It was exactly what William had said when Phillip was born, that he looked so much like his father.

She took them both inside then, and fed Phillip a cup of tea and homemade shortbread cookies. He watched her in awe, but he seemed surprisingly at home with her. And afterwards, one of the servants took him outside to show him the horses and the stables while the dowager duchess chatted with Sarah. She knew she'd been to the Air Ministry that day and she was anxious to know what they'd said to her, but she wasn't surprised that the news was disappointing. In fact, she was a great deal more philosophical about it than Sarah was, which surprised her.

'I don't think we'll really know what happened to him until after Germany falls, and I hope it does soon. I think there must be someone who knows, but for whatever reason they're not talking.' On the other hand, he could have died hanging from a tree when he parachuted in, or been shot by a soldier who never knew who he was, and left him there to be buried by a farmer. There were a lot of ways he could have been killed, and fewer explanations for him being alive, Sarah realized now. She was beginning to realize that it was less than likely that her husband was still alive, and still she clung to some small shred of hope, particularly now that she was back in England. And much to her chagrin, she had just learned, when she called Jane, that Peter, her brother-in-law, had been killed at Kiska, in the Aleutians, and Jane sounded as devastated as Sarah was without William.

At Whitfield, William seemed so much a part of her life. Everything here reminded her of him. It touched her particularly the next day when her mother-in-law gave Phillip a pony for his birthday. He was so excited, and so happy. Sarah hadn't really seen him smile like that since Lizzie died, and Joachim left. And here, Phillip was so much a part of his father's world, and the life he had been born to. The child thrived just being there. And he told her adamantly that he wanted to stay, when she finally announced that they were going back to France in October.

'Can I take my pony back to France with us, Mama?' he asked, and Sarah shook her head. They were going back to France on another military flight, and there was no way she could transport a horse with them. And some of the Americans were still at the château, there was too much turmoil in their lives even to think about taking back a pony. And behind the turmoil, Sarah was beginning to feel real grief now over the loss of William. Coming back to Whitfield had made his absence more real, and she missed him more than ever.

'We'll be back soon, sweetheart, and Grandmother will keep the pony for you here.' He was sad not to be bringing it back to France. It was amazing, though, to realize that all of this was going to be his one day. But it cut her to the quick when the servants began calling him Your Grace by the end of the trip. In their minds, William was gone, and Phillip was the duke now.

'I still believe we may hear something from him,' William's mother said the night before Sarah left. 'Don't completely give up all hope of him,' she urged. 'I shan't.' And Sarah promised that she wouldn't either, but in her heart of hearts, she was beginning to mourn now.

They went back to France the next day, and the War Office had arranged for transportation for her once she got there. Things seemed more orderly than when they'd left six weeks before, and everything was in order when they got back to the château. Emanuelle was in residence, and the colonel had kept his men in good control, and most of them had left now. Some of the men who used to work for her returned to do some gardening, and after their return, she began working on some of the *boiseries* again, and making repairs after years of neglect by the Germans. But thanks to Joachim's vigilance they had actually done surprisingly little damage.

She thought of him frequently, but she had no way of knowing where or how he was. She worried about him at times. And she always prayed for him and William.

By Christmas that year, things were quiet at the château, and very lonely for Sarah. Everything was seemingly back to normal, but what wasn't normal, of course, was the fact that the world was still at war. But the Allied forces were winning, and people thought now that it was almost over.

In the spring, the Allies marched on Berlin, and in May, at last, the fight in Europe was over. Hitler had committed suicide, many of his officers had fled. Chaos reigned in Germany, terrible tales were coming out about atrocities committed in concentration camps, and still Sarah had no news of William or Joachim. She had no idea what had happened to either of them, or if they were still alive. She just went on living day by day, at the château, until the War Office called her.

'We have news for you, Your Grace,' the voice crackled across the line, and she found herself crying before they even told her what it was. Phillip stood in the château kitchen watching her, wondering why his mother was crying. 'We believe we may have found our man . . . or . . . er . . . rather, your man. We liberated one of the prisoner-of-war camps only yesterday, and there were four unidentified soldiers in . . . er . . . rather poor condition . . . I'm afraid he's one of them, if it's him . . . but he had no identification on him. But the officer in charge attended Sandhurst with him, and swears it's him. We're not sure yet, but we're flying him back tonight. We'd like to fly you to London, if you can come.' If she could come? After no word of him for three years? Were they joking?

'I'll be there. Can you arrange transport for me? I'll come at once.'

'I don't think we can get you out till tomorrow, Your Grace,' he said politely. 'Things are a bit chaotic everywhere, what with the frightful mess in Berlin, and the Italians, and all that.' All of Europe was in chaos at the moment, but she was ready to swim the English Channel if she had to.

The War Office contacted the Americans in France again, and this time a jeep from the Allied Forces office in Paris came for her at the château, and she and Phillip were impatiently waiting. She hadn't told him why they were going to London yet, she didn't want to disappoint him if William wasn't the man they'd found, but he was enchanted to be going to visit his grandmother anyway, and to see his horses. She was going to send him directly down to Whitfield to stay with her, and the War Office had a car and driver to take her to the hospital where the men they flew out of Germany would be staying. They had told her that all four men were desperately ill and some of them were severely wounded, but they hadn't told her in what way, or what was wrong with William. She didn't really care as long as he was alive, and he could be saved. And if he was alive at all, she vowed that she would do anything she could to save him.

The flight to the London airport went very smoothly, and the car to take Phillip to Whitfield was there waiting for them when they arrived, and they saluted Phillip decorously with full military honors and he loved it. And then they whisked Sarah off to Chelsea Royal Hospital, to see the men they had just flown in from Germany the night before, at midnight. She prayed that one of them was indeed William.

There was only one man who was even a remote possibility. He was approximately William's height, but they said he had weighed approximately one hundred and thirty or forty pounds, his hair was white, and he seemed a great deal older than the Duke of Whitfield. Sarah said nothing as they described it all to her on the way to the hospital, and she was frighteningly silent as they took her upstairs, past wards of critically ill men, and busy doctors and nurses. With what had just happened in Germany, they had their hands full. Men were being flown in as fast as they could bring them in, and doctors were being called in from all over England.

They had put the man they thought was William in a small room by himself. And an orderly was standing in the room with him, to monitor his breathing. There was a tube going up his nose, and a respirator, and there was a multitude of machines and devices hovering over him, including an oxygen tent, which concealed him.

The orderly pulled back the flap a little bit so she could see him better to identify him, and the men from the War Office stood back at a discreet distance. The hospital was still waiting for dental charts from Bomber Command so that they could make a positive identification. But Sarah didn't need dental charts to identify this man. He was barely recognizable, he was so thin, and he looked like his own father, but as she stepped closer to the bed, she reached out and touched his cheek. He had returned to her from the dead, and he didn't stir now, but there was not a shred of doubt in her mind. It was William. She turned and looked at them then, and the look on her face told them everything, as the tears poured down her cheeks and theirs too.

'Thank God . . .' Sir Alan whispered, echoing Sarah's feelings. She stood rooted to the spot, unable to take her eyes from his as she touched his face, and his hands, and lifted his fingers to her lips and kissed them. His hands had a waxy look to them, as did his face, and she could see that he was hovering near death, but she knew that they would do everything to save him. The orderly dropped the flap on the oxygen tent again, and a moment later two doctors and three sisters came in, and began doing assorted things, and then the doctors asked her to leave the room, which she did, with a last look at him. It was a miracle. She had lost Lizzie . . . but now they had found William. Perhaps God wasn't as unkind as she had feared for a while. And she asked the men from the War Office before they left if they would arrange for her to call William's mother at Whitfield. They organized it at once from the office of the head of the hospital, and the dowager duchess gave a gasp of relief at the other end of the phone, and then gave in to tears, as did Sarah.

'Thank God . . . the poor boy . . . how is he?'

'Not very well, Mother, I'm afraid. But he'll be better soon.' She hoped she wasn't lying to her, because she wanted to believe it. But he hadn't survived this long in order to die now. She just simply wouldn't let him.

The men from the War Office left then, and the head of the hospital came to speak to her about William's condition. He didn't waste any words and went straight to the point with a serious expression.

'We don't know if your husband will live, Your Grace. He has gangrene in both legs, extensive internal wounds, and he's been ill for a long time. Years possibly. He had compound fractures of both legs that never healed. He's probably had infections in both legs since he fell. We can't save his legs, and we may not be able to save his life. You have to know that.' She knew it, but she refused to accept it. Now that he was back, she absolutely refused to lose him.

'You *have* to save his legs. He didn't come this far in order for you to lose them.'

'We have no choice, or very little in any case. His legs will be of no use to him now anyway, the muscles and nerves are far too damaged, he'll have to be in a wheelchair.'

'Fine, but let him have his legs in that wheelchair.'

'Your Grace, I'm not sure you understand . . . it's a delicate balance . . . the gangrene . . .' She assured him that she understood perfectly, but begged him to at least try to save William's legs, and looking exasperated, he promised her that they would do what they could, but she had to be realistic.

There were four operations in the next two weeks, and William barely survived each of them, but he did, although he had never regained consciousness once since he was flown to London. The first two operations were on his legs, the third to his spine, and the last one to make internal repairs to injuries that eventually might have killed him. And none of the specialists who worked on him could understand how he had made it. He was wracked with infection and disease, malnourished in the extreme, bones had been broken and never healed, and there were visible signs of torture. He had suffered everything and he had lived . . . but barely.

By the third week they had done all they could, and now all they could do was wait, to see if he regained consciousness, or remained in a coma, or simply died. No-one could say now, and Sarah sat with him day after day, holding his hand, talking to him, willing him back to life, until she almost looked worse than he did. She was desperately thin and pale, and her eyes were almost glazed as she sat beside him and nursed him. One of the sisters came in and saw her one day, and shook her head quietly, and then said to her, 'He can't hear you, Your Grace. Don't exhaust yourself.' She had brought Sarah a cup of tea, and Sarah had accepted it gratefully, but she still insisted that William could hear her.

They tried one last surgery on his spleen at the end of July, and then once again they waited, and Sarah nursed and talked and encouraged and kissed his fingers, and watched him, never leaving his bedside for a moment. They had put a cot in his room for her, and she had borrowed some of the sisters' uniforms, and she sat there day after day, without giving up hope for an instant. The only time she ever left William's side at all was when the dowager duchess brought Phillip to the hospital, to see his mother in the waiting room. He wasn't allowed to go upstairs to see William, and in truth he would have been afraid to. He had been told how very ill he was, and the fact was that to Phillip, William was a stranger. In the years he might have remembered him, the child had never seen him. But Sarah was happy to see the child, she missed him terribly, and he missed her, but she didn't feel she could leave William.

It was the first of August when the head surgeon told her that she needed to get away, that they had become convinced that His Grace was never going to wake from his coma. He simply wasn't going to wake up again. He might exist that way for years, or days, but if he had been going to wake, by then he would have, and she had to face it.

'How do you know he won't suddenly come to, this afternoon?' she asked, sounding faintly hysterical to him. But all she knew was that they had managed to save his legs for him, and now they were going to give up and throw him away like so much garbage. She hadn't had a decent night's sleep in five weeks, and she was not giving up on him now, no matter what they said, but the doctor insisted that they knew better.

'I've been a surgeon for nearly forty years,' he told her firmly, 'and sometimes you have to know when to fight and when to give up. We fought . . . and we lost . . . you have to let him give up now.'

'He was a prisoner of war for three and a half years, is that what you call giving up?' she screamed. But she didn't care who heard her. 'He didn't give up then, and I won't give up now. Do you hear me?'

'Of course, Your Grace. I understand completely.' He left the room quietly and asked the matron if she might suggest a mild sedative to the Duchess of Whitfield, but she only rolled her eyes at him. The woman was possessed.

She was obsessed with the idea of saving her husband.

'The poor man is almost gone. She ought to let him go in peace,' she said to the sister working beside her, and the other woman shook her head, too, but she had seen stranger things. They had had a man on one of the wards who'd revived recently, after nearly six months in a coma from a head wound he'd gotten in an air raid.

'You never know,' she said, and went back to check on Sarah and William. Sarah was sitting in the chair, speaking softly to him about Phillip, and his mother, and Whitfield, and the château, and she even vaguely mentioned Lizzie. She would have said anything if she'd thought it would work, but so far nothing had, and although she wouldn't admit it to anyone, she was nearing the end of her rope. The sister put a gentle hand on her shoulder as she watched them, and then for an instant she thought she saw him stir, but she didn't say anything. But Sarah had seen it, too, she sat very still, and then began talking to him again, asking if he would open his eyes to look at her just once . . . just one teeny tiny time . . . just to see if he liked the way her hair looked. She hadn't seen herself in a mirror in over a month, and she could just imagine what she looked like, but she went on and on, kissing his hands and talking to him as the sister watched in fascination, and then slowly, his eyes fluttered open and he looked at her and smiled, and then closed them again as he nodded and she began to sob silently. They had done it . . . he had opened his eyes . . . The sister was crying too, and she squeezed Sarah's hand as she spoke to her patient.

'It's very nice to see you awake, Your Grace, it's about time too.' But he didn't stir again for a little while, and then ever so slowly, he turned his head and looked straight at Sarah.

'It looks very nice,' he whispered hoarsely.

'What does?' She had no idea what he was talking

about, but she had never been so happy in her life. She wanted to scream with relief and joy as she bent to kiss him.

'Your hair . . . wasn't that what you asked me?' The nurse and Sarah laughed at him, and by the next day they had him sitting up and sipping soup and weak tea, and by the end of the week he was talking to all of them and slowly regaining his strength, although he looked like a ghost of his former self. But he was back. He was alive. That was all Sarah cared about. It was all she had lived for.

The War Office and the Home Office came to see him eventually, too, and when he was strong enough, he told them what had happened to him. It took several visits, and it defied belief. It made them all sick to hear what the Germans had done, and William wouldn't let Sarah stay in the room when he told them. They had broken his legs again and again, left him in filth till they festered, tortured him with hot irons and electric prods. They had done everything short of killing him. But they had never figured out who he was, and he had never told them. He had been carrying a false passport, and false military papers when they dropped him in, and that was all they ever knew till the end. And he had never revealed his aborted mission.

He received the Distinguished Flying Cross for his heroism, but it was small consolation for losing the use of his legs. It depressed him at first to realize that he would never walk again, but Sarah had been right to fight for them, he was glad he still had them. He would have hated it if they'd amputated his legs.

They had both lost so much, and one afternoon, before he left the hospital, she told him about Lizzie, and they had both cried copiously as he listened.

'Oh, my darling . . . and I wasn't there with you . . .'

'There was nothing you could have done. We didn't have the medicines or the doctors . . . We had nothing by then. The Americans were on their way, and the Germans were getting ready to leave, they had nothing left by then, and she wasn't strong enough to survive. The commandant at the château was very good to us, he gave us everything he had . . . but she didn't have the stamina . . .' She sobbed, and then looked up at her husband. 'She was so sweet . . . she was such a lovely little girl . . .' Sarah could hardly speak as he held her. 'I wish you could have known her . . .'

'I will one day,' he said through his own tears. 'When we are all together again, in another place.' And in some ways, for both of them, it made Phillip doubly precious. But she still missed Lizzie terribly sometimes, especially when she saw a little girl who looked anything like her. She knew that there were other mothers who had lost their children during the war, but it was a pain that almost couldn't be borne. She was grateful that now William was there to share it.

She thought about Joachim sometimes now, too, but he was part of the distant past. In the loneliness, and the pain, and the terror, and loss of the war, he had been her only friend, except for Emanuelle. But the memories of him were slowly fading.

Sarah turned twenty-nine years of age while William was still in the hospital. The war in Japan had ended days before, and the whole world was rejoicing. William went home to Whitfield the day the Japanese officially surrendered on the battleship *Missouri*, on the eve of Phillip's sixth birthday. It was the first time William saw his son since he was only a few months old, and the meeting was emotional for him, and a little strange for Phillip. Phillip stood and stared at him for a long time before finally approaching him, and putting his arms around his father, at his mother's urging. Even in his wheelchair William was such a big man that Phillip was in awe of him. And more than ever, his father regretted the years he'd lost in getting to know him.

The time they spent at Whitfield was good for all of them. William learned to get around more easily in his wheelchair, and Sarah got a much-needed rest for the first time in a long time. Phillip adored being there, and it gave him the time he needed to get to know his father.

He talked to him about Lizzie once, and it was obvious that talking about her at all was painful to him.

'She was very beautiful,' he said softly, looking into the distance. 'And when she got sick, Mommy couldn't get any medicine for her, so she died.' There was the merest hint of reproach in his voice, which William noticed, but didn't understand. Was it possible that he blamed her for the child's death? But that seemed so unlikely that he didn't dare broach the subject to him. Surely he knew that his mother would have done everything she could for her . . . or did he know that? William wondered.

Phillip talked about Joachim sometimes too. He didn't say much, but it was easy to sense that the child had liked him. And whatever his nationality, William was grateful for the man's kindness to his children. Sarah never spoke of him, but when William asked her, she said he was a kind man and a decent person. They celebrated William's mother's ninetieth birthday that year. She was remarkable, and especially now, with William back, she was better than ever.

They were all better than they had been. But there was no denying, they had suffered enormous losses . . . of time . . . of hope . . . of people they loved . . . sweet Lizzie lost to all of them. William gone for so long and almost lost forever . . . Joachim come and gone from their lives . . . The losses and the sorrows had taken their toll, and they were recovering now. But at times, Sarah wondered if the hardest hit of all had been Phillip. He had lost a father he'd never known for the first six years of his life, and now he had to get to know him and build a relationship with him, which wasn't easy for him. He had lost a friend in

Joachim when he left . . . and a sister he would never forget, and still mourned for.

'You miss her, don't you?' she asked him softly when they were walking in the woods, and he nodded, lifting his eyes to hers painfully as he always did when they talked about his sister. 'I do, too, sweetheart.' She held tightly to his hand as they walked on, and Phillip looked away from her and said nothing. But his eyes said something William had already understood, and Sarah hadn't. He blamed his mother for his sister's death. It was her fault Lizzie had died for lack of medicine . . . just as it was her fault Joachim had gone . . . He wasn't quite sure what she'd done to make these calamities fall into his life, but he knew she'd done something . . . or at least she hadn't stopped them. But he was happy at Whitfield anyway. He rode, he walked in the woods, he enjoyed his grandmother, and little by little, he began to know William.

Chapter 17

They didn't go back to France until the spring, and by then William was in full control of their lives again. He seemed to have made his peace with losing the use of his legs by then, and he was back to his normal weight. Only the white hair he suddenly had made him look different. He was only forty-two, but his experience in the prisoner-of-war camp had aged him by years. Even Sarah looked more serious than she had been before the war. They had all paid a high price for what had happened, including Phillip. He was a serious little boy and he was very unhappy when they left Whitfield. He said he wanted to stay there, with his grandmother and his pony, but, of course, his parents overruled him.

William cried when they got back to the château. It looked so exactly the way he'd remembered it, the way he dreamed it would be if he ever came home again, that all he could do was hold Sarah and sob like a child. Everything looked beautiful when they arrived. Emanuelle and her mother had everything ready. Sarah had left Emanuelle in charge for almost a year, and she had run the place to perfection. There were no longer signs of armies of any kind, not in the château, or on the grounds, or even in the stables. Emanuelle had employed scores of men to clean everything up and get it ready for the Whitfields.

'It looks beautiful,' Sarah complimented her when they returned, and Emanuelle was pleased. She was very mature for a girl of her years. She was only twenty-three, but she ran things well, and she had an eye for detail and precision.

Sarah took William to Lizzie's grave the afternoon they arrived, and he cried when he saw the small grave, they both did. And on their way back to the house, he asked Sarah again about the Germans.

'They were here for an awfully long time,' he said casually. 'It's amazing they didn't do more damage.'

'The commandant was very good. He was a nice man, and he kept his men under control. He didn't like the war any better than we did.' William raised an eyebrow as she said it.

'Did he ever say that to you?'

'Several times,' she answered quietly, not sure why he was asking these questions, but there was something in his voice that told her he was worried.

'Were you good friends with him?' he asked off-handedly, knowing how often Phillip had mentioned him. There were times when he worried that his son preferred the German officer to his own father. It was a blow to him, of course, but he understood it. And as Sarah looked at him now, she understood his questions. She turned so that she could see William in his wheelchair.

'We were only friends, William. Nothing more. He lived here for a long time, and a lot of things happened to us . . . Elizabeth was born.' She decided to be honest with him, she had to be, she always had been. 'He delivered her, he saved her life, she would have died at birth if he hadn't saved her.' But she had died anyway, so maybe it no longer mattered. 'We survived for four years here through all that. It's hard to ignore that. But if you're asking me what I think you are . . . no, nothing ever happened.'

He startled her then with his next words, and a little shiver of shock ran through her.

'Phillip says you kissed him when he left.' It was wrong

of him to tell his father, or in just that way, but maybe he didn't understand what he was doing, or perhaps he did. Sometimes she wasn't sure she understood him. He had been so angry at her ever since Lizzie died . . . and Joachim left . . . and William came home . . . and now he often seemed withdrawn. He had a lot to absorb and understand. They all did.

'He's right. I did,' Sarah said quietly. She had nothing to hide from William, and she wanted him to know that. 'He became my friend. Joachim hated what Hitler was doing as much as we did. And he helped keep us safe. When Joachim left, I knew I'd never see him again. I don't know if he lived or died after that, but I wish him well. I kissed him goodbye, but I did not betray you.' There were tears rolling slowly down her cheeks as she said it. And what she said was true, she had been faithful to him, and it had been wrong of Phillip to make him jealous. She had known at the time that he was angry at her for kissing Joachim, and also for letting him go. He was angry about a lot of things, but she had never expected him to do anything about it. She was only glad now that she could tell William honestly, she hadn't betrayed him. It was the only thing that made all those lonely nights worth it.

'I'm sorry I asked,' he said guiltily, but she knelt next to him and took his face in her hands.

'Don't be. There's nothing you can't ask me. I love you. I always did. I never gave up on you. Never, I never stopped loving you. And I always believed you'd come home.' It was true, and he could see it in her eyes – that, and how much she loved him.

He sighed then, relieved by what she had said, and he believed her. He had been terrified when Phillip told him. But he also knew that in his own way Phillip was also punishing him for having left them. 'I never thought I'd come back. I kept telling myself I would, just so I could survive another hour, another night, another day . . . but I never thought I'd make it. So many didn't.' He had seen so many men die, tortured to death by the Germans.

'They're a nation of monsters,' he told her as they went back to the house, but she didn't dare tell him again that Joachim was different. As he had said, war was an ugly thing. But thank God, it was over.

They had been back at the château for a mere three weeks when Emanuelle and Sarah were making bread in the kitchen. They talked about many things and then Emanuelle began to ask questions.

'You must be very glad to have Monsieur le Duc back,' she began, which was certainly obvious to anyone who saw them. Sarah hadn't been this happy in years, and they were slowly making new discoveries about their sex life. Some of the alterations were unfortunate, but very little seemed to have changed, much to William's delight now that he had a chance to try it.

'It's wonderful.' Sarah smiled happily, kneading the bread as Emanuelle watched her.

'Has he brought a great deal of money back from England with him?' It was an odd question, and Sarah looked up, astonished.

'Why, no. Of course not. Why would he?'

'I just wondered.' She looked embarrassed, but not very, and she seemed to have something on her mind, but Sarah couldn't figure out what. She had never asked anything like it before.

'Why would you ask something like that, Emanuelle?' She knew she had had strange involvements before, with the Resistance through her brother, during the war, and with the black market afterwards, but now she had no idea what she was up to.

'There are people . . . sometimes . . . who are in need of money. I wondered if you and Monsieur le Duc would lend it to them?'

'You mean, just give them money? Just like that?' Sarah looked a little surprised, and Emanuelle looked pensive.

'Perhaps not. What if they had something to sell?'

'You mean food?' Sarah still didn't understand what she was after. She finished making the bread and wiped her hands, looking long and hard at the young woman, wondering more than ever what she was up to. She had never been suspicious of her before, but she was now. And Sarah didn't like the feeling. 'Are you talking about food or farm equipment, Emanuelle?'

She shook her head and lowered her voice again when she spoke. 'No . . . I mean like jewels . . . There are people . . . *dans les alentours* . . . in the region, who need money to rebuild their homes, their lives . . . They have hidden things . . . sometimes gold . . . or silver . . . or jewelry . . . and now they need to sell it.' Emanuelle had been thinking for some time of how to make some serious money for herself now that the war was over. She didn't want to clean houses forever, even for them, although she loved them. And she'd come up with this idea. She knew several people who were anxious to sell important things, jewels, silver, Fabergé cigarette cases, expensive objects they'd been hiding. She particularly knew of a woman in Chambord who had a fantastic string of pearls she was desperate to sell for any amount. The Germans had destroyed her house and she needed the money to rebuild it.

It was a kind of matchmaking of sorts, and Emanuelle knew people with beautiful objects and acute needs, and the Whitfields had the money to help them. She had wanted to approach them for a while, but she wasn't sure how. But more and more people were contacting her, knowing how close to them she was, and begging her to help them. The woman with the pearls had already come to see her twice, and so had many others.

There were Jews coming out of hiding too. And women

who had accepted expensive gifts from Nazis and were afraid to keep them. There were jewels that had been traded for lives or information in the Resistance. And Emanuelle wanted to help people sell them. She would make a profit, too, but a small one. She didn't want to take advantage of them. She wanted to help them, but herself too. But Sarah was still looking at her in confusion.

'But what would I do with jewelry?' Only that morning they had taken hers out from under the floorboards of Phillip's bedroom.

'Wear it.' She smiled. She would have liked to herself, but she couldn't afford to buy anything yet. Perhaps one day. 'You could sell it again. There are many possibilities, Madame.'

'One day' – Sarah smiled at her – 'you will be a great woman.' They were only six years apart, but Emanuelle had an incredible sense of enterprise and survival, in clever ways that Sarah knew that she didn't. What she had was inner strength and endurance, which was different from what Emanuelle had. Emanuelle Bourgois had cunning.

'Will you ask Monsieur le Duc,' she begged as Sarah left the kitchen with his lunch tray. There was something very anxious in Emanuelle's voice, which Sarah heard.

'I will,' she promised, 'but I guarantee you, he'll think I'm crazy.'

The funny thing was that he didn't think she was crazy at all, when she told him. He was amused. 'What an intriguing idea. That girl is quite extraordinary, isn't she? It's actually a very nice, clean way of helping people, and lending them money. I really rather like it. I'd been thinking recently about what we could do to help the locals. I wasn't thinking of anything quite so exotic.' He grinned. 'But it's possible. Why don't you just tell Emanuelle that I will entertain the possibility, and see what happens.'

What happened was that three days later, the bell on the front door of the château rang at nine o'clock in the morning. And when Sarah went downstairs, she found a woman standing there, in a shiny black dress that looked as though it might have been expensive, and worn shoes, and an Hermès bag Sarah recognized at once. But she did not recognize the woman.

'*Oui . . . ?* Yes . . . ? May I help you?'

'*En effet . . . je m'excuse . . .* I . . .' She looked frightened, and she kept looking over her shoulder as though she expected someone to grab her. And as Sarah looked at her more closely, she suspected she might be Jewish. 'I must apologize . . . a friend of mine suggested . . . I have a terrible problem, Your Grace, my family . . .' Her eyes filled with tears as she started to explain, and Sarah gently invited her into the kitchen, and gave her a cup of tea. She explained that her family had all been deported to concentration camps during the war. To the best of her knowledge, she was the only one left. She had been hidden for four years in a cellar by her neighbors. Her husband had been a doctor, the head of an important hospital in Paris. But he had been deported by the Nazis, as had her parents, her two sisters, even her son . . . She began to cry again as Sarah fought back tears of her own as she listened to the story. The woman said that she needed money to find them. She wanted to go to Germany and Poland, to the camps there, to see if she could find any record of them among the survivors.

'I think the Red Cross would help you, Madame. There are organizations to do this for people all over Europe.' She knew William had already donated quite a lot of money to them in England.

'I want to go myself. And some of the private organizations are very costly. And after I find them, or . . .' She couldn't bring herself to say the words. 'I want to go to Israel.' She said it as though it were truly the promised land, and Sarah's heart went out to her, as the woman drew two large boxes from her handbag. 'I have something to sell . . . Emanuelle said you might . . . she said that you are very kind.' And that her husband was very rich, but Mrs Wertheim was polite enough not to say that. What she brought out of her purse were two boxes from Van Cleef, one with an enormous emerald-and-diamond necklace, the other with the matching bracelet. The pieces looked like lace. They were beautifully articulated, quite astonishing, and most impressive.

'I . . . good Lord . . . ! They're really beautiful! I don't know what to say . . .' She couldn't imagine wearing anything even remotely like them. They were both important pieces, and certainly worth whatever she wanted, but how did one begin to put a price on something like that? And yet, looking at them, for reasons she couldn't explain, Sarah had to admit she found the idea of buying them exciting. She had never owned anything like them. And the poor woman was shaking in her shoes, praying they would buy them. 'May I show them to my husband? I'll only be a moment.' She ran up the stairs then with both boxes in her hands, and burst into their bedroom. 'You'll never believe this.' She was breathless as she told him. 'There's a woman downstairs . . .' She opened the boxes and tossed the contents into his lap. 'And she wants to sell us these . . .' She shook the magnificent emeralds at him and he whistled.

'Very pretty, darling. They'd look lovely on you in the garden. Go wonderfully with green . . .'

'Be serious.' She told him the woman's story then, and he felt sorry for her too.

'Can't we just give her a check? I feel like a scoundrel taking these away from her. Even though I must say they'd look very pretty on you.'

'Thank you, my love. But what are we going to do about her?'

'I'll come down and talk to her myself.' He had already shaved, and was wearing trousers and his shirt and his dressing gown. He was getting very good at dressing himself in spite of his limitations. He followed Sarah out of the room, and worked his way downstairs on the ramp they had had made for him.

Mrs Wertheim was still waiting nervously for them in the kitchen. She was so frightened, she was almost tempted to flee without her jewels, for fear they would do something terrible to her, but Emanuelle had insisted they were nice people. Emanuelle knew the people who had hidden Mrs Wertheim in the cellar, she had met them in the Resistance.

'Good morning.' William greeted her with a smile, and she tried to look relaxed as she waited to hear about her emeralds. 'I'm afraid we've never done anything like this before, and it's a bit of a novel idea to us.' He decided to put the woman out of her misery and go right to the point. He had already decided he wanted to help her. 'How much do you want?'

'I don't know. Ten? Fifteen?'

'That's ridiculous.'

She quaked, and spoke in a whisper. 'I'm sorry, Your Grace . . . five?' She would have sold them for next to nothing, she was so desperate for money.

'I was thinking more like thirty. Does that seem reasonable? That is, thirty thousand dollars.'

'I . . . oh, my God . . .' She started to cry, unable to control herself any longer. 'God bless you . . . God bless you, Your Grace.' She dabbed at her eyes with an old lace hankie, and kissed them both when she left with his check in her handbag. Even Sarah had tears in her eyes when she left.

'The poor woman.'

'I know.' He looked somber for a moment, and then put the necklace and bracelet on Sarah. 'Enjoy them, my

305

darling.' But they both felt good about the charitable deed they had done.

And before the end of the week, they had the chance to do another.

Sarah was helping Emanuelle clean up after dinner, and William was in his study, which still vaguely reminded Sarah of Joachim, when a woman appeared at the kitchen door. She was young and looked even more frightened than Mrs Wertheim. She wore her hair short, but not as short as she had just after the Occupation. Sarah thought she had seen her with one of the German officers who had lived in the château and worked with Joachim. She was a beautiful girl, and before the war she had been a model for Jean Patou in Paris.

Emanuelle almost growled when she saw her, but she had told her to come. This time though, she promised herself, she would take a bigger commission. From Mrs Wertheim she had taken almost nothing at all, but the old woman had insisted on at least something.

The girl glanced nervously at Emanuelle and then at Sarah. And it began again. 'May I speak to you, Your Grace?' She had a diamond bracelet to sell. It was from Boucheron and it was very pretty. It was a gift, she told Sarah. But the German who had given it to her gave her more than that. He had left her with a baby. 'He's sick all the time . . . I can't buy him food . . . or medicine. I'm afraid he'll get TB . . .' The words went straight to Sarah's heart as she thought of Lizzie. She glanced at Emanuelle and asked her if it was true, and she nodded.

'She has a German bastard . . . he's two years old, and always sickly.'

'Will you promise to buy him food and medicine and warm clothes if we give you some money?' Sarah asked her sternly, and the girl swore she would.

And with that, Sarah went to see William, and he returned to look at the girl and the bracelet. He was impressed by both, and after talking to her for a while, he decided she was honest. He didn't want to find himself buying stolen jewels, but there seemed to be no question of that here.

They bought the bracelet from her for a fair price, probably what the German had paid for it, and she left them, thanking them profusely. And then Sarah looked at Emanuelle and laughed, as she sat down in her kitchen.

'Just exactly what are we doing?'

Emanuelle grinned broadly. 'Maybe I'm going to get rich and you're going to get a lot of very nice jewelry.' Sarah couldn't help smiling at her. It was all a little mad, but fun and touching at the same time. And the next day they bought the extraordinary pearls from the woman in Chambord so she could rebuild her house. The pearls were fabulous, and William insisted that she wear them.

By the end of the summer, Sarah had ten emerald bracelets, three necklaces to match, four ruby suites, a cascade of beautiful sapphires, and several diamond rings, not to mention a very lovely turquoise tiara. They had all come to them from people who had lost fortunes or houses or children, and needed money to find lost relatives, or rebuild their lives, or simply put food on their table. It was philanthropy neither could have described to their friends without feeling foolish, and yet it helped the people they bought from, and Emanuelle was indeed growing rich from her commissions. She had begun to look very sleek. She was getting her hair done in town, and buying her clothes in Paris, which was more than Sarah had done since before the war. And next to Emanuelle, she was beginning to feel positively dowdy.

'William, what are we going to do with all this stuff?' she asked one day, as she upset the balance of half a dozen Van Cleef and Cartier boxes in her closet, and all of them fell on her head, and he only laughed at her.

'I have absolutely no idea. Maybe we ought to hold an auction.'

'I'm serious.'

'Why don't we open a shop?' William asked good-naturedly, but Sarah thought the idea absurd. But within a year, they seemed to have more inventory than Garrard's.

'Maybe we really ought to sell it,' Sarah suggested this time, but now William wasn't as sure. He was involved in planting extensive vineyards around the château, and didn't have time to worry about the jewelry. Yet it kept coming to them. They were too well known now for their generosity and kindness. In the fall of 1947, William and Sarah decided to go to Paris to be alone and leave Phillip with Emanuelle for a few days. They'd been home from England for a year and a half and hadn't left the château, they'd been so busy.

Paris was even more wonderful than Sarah had expected. They stayed at the Ritz and spent almost as much time in bed as they had on their honeymoon. But they found lots of time for shopping, too, and they went to dinner at the Windsors' on the Boulevard Sachet, in yet another lovely house decorated by Boudin. Sarah wore a very chic new black dress she got at Dior, her spectacular pearls, and a fabulous diamond bracelet they'd bought months before from a woman who'd lost everything at the hands of the Germans.

And everyone at dinner wanted to know where she got the bracelet. But Wallis was wise enough to spot the pearls, and told Sarah kindly she'd never, ever seen any like them. She was intrigued by the bracelet, too, and when she asked where it was from, the Whitfields said 'Cartier,' without further explanation. It even made Wallis's jewels look a little pallid by comparison.

And much to her surprise, for most of their trip to Paris, Sarah found herself fascinated by the jewelers. They had some lovely things, but so did they at the château; in fact, they had a lot more, and some of what she had was even better. In fact, most of it was.

'You know, maybe we really ought to do something with it sometime,' she said vaguely as they drove home, in the special Bentley that had been built for William after they left England.

But it was another six months before they thought of it. She was busy with Phillip, and wanted to enjoy him before he left for Eton the following year. Sarah really wanted to keep him in France with her, but in spite of having been born there, and having lived at the château all his life, he had a passion for all things English, and he was absolutely begging to go to Eton.

William was too busy with his wine and his vineyards to think much about the jewelry. It was the summer of 1948 before Sarah absolutely insisted they do something with the mountain of jewelry they'd collected. It was no longer even a good investment. It just sat there, except for the few pieces she wore, and they were lovely, but not many.

'After Phillip leaves, we'll go up to Paris and sell it all off. I promise,' William said, distractedly.

'They'll think we robbed a bank in Monte Carlo.'

'It does look a bit like that.' He grinned. 'Doesn't it?' But when they went back to Paris in the fall, they suddenly realized that there was clearly too much to take with them. They took a few pieces, but they left the rest at the château. Sarah was feeling bored, and a little lonely, with Phillip recently gone. And once they'd been in Paris for two days, William looked at her and announced that he'd found a solution.

'To what?' She was looking at some new suits at Chanel with him when he told her.

'The jewelry dilemma. We'll start a shop of our own, and sell it.'

'Are you crazy?' She stared at him, still looking very handsome in his wheelchair. 'What would we do with a shop? The château is two hours from Paris.'

'We'll let Emanuelle run it. She has nothing to do now

with Phillip gone away, and she's gotten a little fancy to do housework.' She'd been buying her clothes at Jean Patou and Madame Grès, and she was looking very elegant.

'Are you serious?' She had never even thought of it, and she wasn't sure if she liked the idea. But in some ways it might be fun, and they both liked jewelry. And then she began to worry. 'You don't think your mother will think it's vulgar?'

'To own a shop? It is vulgar.' He laughed. 'But such fun. Why not? And she's such a good sport, I daresay she'll love it.' At over ninety, she seemed to get more and more open-minded with the years, rather than less so. And she was enchanted with the prospect of having Phillip stay with her for holidays and weekends. 'Who knows, one day we can call ourselves Jewelers to the Crown. We'll have to sell something to the Queen to do that. And I daresay Wallis will go mad, and want a discount.' It was a totally insane idea, but they talked about it all the way back to the château, and Sarah had to admit that she loved it.

'What'll we call it?' she asked excitedly, as they lay in bed and talked about it the night they went back to the château.

'"Whitfield's", of course.' He looked at her proudly. 'What else would you call it, my dear?'

'Sorry.' She rolled over in bed and kissed him. 'I should have thought of that.'

'You certainly should have.' It was almost like having a new baby. It was a wonderful new project.

They wrote down all their ideas, inventoried the jewelry they had, and got it appraised by Van Cleef, who were staggered by what they'd collected. They spoke to attorneys, and went back to Paris before Christmas and rented a small but extremely elegant shop on the Faubourg-St Honoré, and set architects and workmen to work, and even found Emanuelle an apartment. She was beside herself with excitement.

'Are we totally mad?' Sarah asked him, as they lay in bed at the Ritz on New Year's Eve. Now and then she still got a little worried.

'No, my darling, we're not. We've done an awful lot of people an awful lot of good with the things we bought from them, and now we're having a little fun with it. There's no harm in that. And who knows, it might turn out to be a very successful business.'

They had explained it all to Phillip, and William's mother, when they'd flown over to England to spend Christmas at Whitfield with them. William's mother thought it was a fine idea, and promised to buy their first piece of jewelry, if they'd let her. And Phillip announced that one day he'd open a branch in London.

'Wouldn't you want to run the one in Paris?' Sarah asked, surprised at his reaction. For a child who had grown up abroad, and was only half English anyway, he was amazingly British.

'I don't want to live in France ever again,' he announced, 'except for vacations. I want to live at Whitfield.'

'My, my,' William said, more amused than distressed. 'I'm glad someone does.' He could never imagine living there again. And like his cousin, the Duke of Windsor, he was happier in France, and so was Sarah.

'You'll have to tell me all about the opening,' the dowager duchess had made them promise when they left. 'When is it?'

'In June,' Sarah said tremulously, looking at William with excitement. It *was* like having a new baby, and since that had never happened to them again, Sarah threw herself into it with all her energy for the next six months, and the night before the opening, everything looked smashing.

Chapter 18

The opening of the shop was a huge success. The interior had been exquisitely done by Elsie de Wolfe, an American who conveniently was living in Paris. The entire shop was done in pale-grey velvet. It looked like the interior of a jeweler's box, and all the chairs were Louis XVI. William had brought a few small Degases and some Renoir sketches from Whitfield. There was a lovely Mary Cassatt that Sarah loved, but it wasn't the art one looked at as one sat there. The jewelry was absolutely staggering. They had weeded out some of the less exciting pieces, but they themselves were amazed by how remarkable most of it really was. Each piece stood out on its own merits, fabulous diamond collars, and enormous pearls, remarkable diamond drop earrings, and a ruby choker that had belonged to the czarina. The jeweler's marks were clearly discernible on everything they sold, even those of Van Cleef on the turquoise tiara. They had pieces of Boucheron, Mauboussin, Chaumet, Van Cleef, Cartier, and Tiffany in New York, Fabergé, and Asprey. Their inventory was truly staggering, and so was their reception by the Parisians. There had been a little discreet press that the Duchess of Whitfield was opening a shop called 'Whitfield's' on the Faubourg-St Honoré, offering remarkable jewels to extraordinary women.

The Duchess of Windsor came to the opening, as did most of her friends, and suddenly *le tout Paris* was there, all of Paris society, and even a few curious acquaintances from London.

They sold four pieces the night of the party they gave, a lovely pearl-and-diamond bracelet by Fabergé with little blue-enamel birds, and a pearl necklace that was one of the first things Emanuelle had brought them. They sold Mrs Wertheim's emerald set, too, and it brought a handsome price, as did a huge cabochon ruby ring made by Van Cleef for a maharaja.

Sarah stood looking in wonder at all of it, unable to believe what had happened, as William looked on, with obvious pleasure. He was so proud of her, and so amused by what they'd done. They had bought all of it with kind hearts and the hope that they'd helped someone. And suddenly it had turned into this most extraordinary business.

'You've done a beautiful job, my love,' he praised her warmly as waiters poured more champagne. There had been cases of Cristal for the opening, and endless tins of caviar.

'I just can't believe it! Can you?' She looked like a girl again, she was having such fun, and Emanuelle looked like a grande dame as she made her way among the elite, looking very beautiful in a black Schiaparelli.

'Of course I can believe it. You have exquisite taste, and these are beautiful things,' he said calmly, taking a sip of his champagne.

'We're a hit, aren't we?' She giggled.

'No, my darling, *you* are. You're the dearest thing in life to me,' he whispered. His years as a prisoner had taught him more than ever what he held dear, his wife, and his children, and his freedom. His health hadn't been as strong as it had once been, since he'd been home again. But Sarah took good care of him and he was getting stronger. At times he seemed as vital as he once had been, at others he looked tired and worn and she knew that his legs pained him. The wounds had finally healed, but the damage to his system never would. But at least he was alive and well and they were together. And now they had this remarkable business. It really was fun for her, and she thoroughly enjoyed it.

'Do you believe this?' she whispered to Emanuelle a few minutes later. Emanuelle had been looking very cool showing a handsome man a very expensive sapphire necklace.

'I think' – Emanuelle smiled mysteriously at her *patronne* – 'we are going to have a great deal of pleasure here.' Sarah could see that she was, and she was doing a great deal of very subtle flirting with some very important men, and it seemed to mean nothing at all to her if they were married.

In the end, David bought Wallis a very pretty little diamond ring with a Cartier leopard on it, to match those she was already wearing, and that made their fifth sale of the evening. And at last, everyone went home, and they locked their doors at midnight.

'Oh, darling, it was wonderful!' Sarah clapped her hands again, and William pulled her down on his lap in the wheelchair, as the guards locked up, and Emanuelle told the waiters where to leave the remaining caviar. She was going to take it home and share it with some friends the next day. Sarah had said she could. She was having a little cocktail party the next day in her apartment on the rue de la Faisanderie, to celebrate her new position as manager of Whitfield's. It was a long way from La Marolle for her, from her days in the Resistance, and sleeping with German soldiers to get information about what munitions depot to blow up, and selling eggs and cream and cigarettes on the black market. It had been a long road for all of them, a long war, but it was a good time now, in Paris.

William took Sarah back to their suite at the Ritz shortly after that. They had been talking about finding a small apartment, where they could stay when they were in Paris. It was only two hours and a little bit to the château, but it was still a long way to drive all the time. And she wasn't going to be at the shop constantly, as Emanuelle and the other girl were. But she wanted to look for new pieces whenever she could, now that people weren't coming to them any more for help, and she wanted to design some new things. They were going to Paris a lot more than they used to. But for the moment the Ritz was convenient, and Sarah yawned as she walked in behind William's wheel-chair. And she was in bed beside him a few minutes later.

As she slipped into bed, he turned over, and pulled a box out of the drawer in the nightstand. 'How silly of me.' He sounded vague, but she knew him well enough to know he was up to some mischief. 'I forgot this . . .' He handed her a big, square, flat box. 'Just a little trinket to celebrate the opening of Whitfield's,' he said with a smile, as she grinned, wondering what was inside it.

'William, you are so naughty!' She always felt like a child with him. He spoiled her so much, and he was so good to her in all the ways that were more important. 'What is it?' She rattled it once she had the paper off. She could see it was a jeweler's box by then, and the box bore an Italian name. Buccellati.

She opened it carefully, with a gleam of excitement in her eye, and then gasped when she saw it. It was an exquisite, beautifully made, and very important diamond necklace.

'Oh, my God!' She closed her eyes and instantly snapped the box shut. He had given her some lovely things, but this was incredible, and she had never seen anything like it. It looked like a lace collar, all intricately woven in platinum, hung with huge drops of diamonds that seemed just to lie on the skin like enormous dew-drops. 'Oh, William . . .' She opened her eyes again, and threw her arms around him. 'I don't deserve this!'

'Of course you do,' he scolded her, 'don't say things like that. Besides, as the owner of Whitfield's, people are going to be watching to see what you wear now. We'll have to buy you some really interesting jewelry, some really fabulous things,' he said with a grin, amused by the prospect. He loved spoiling her, and as his father had before him, he had always liked buying jewelry.

She put the necklace on, and lay back in bed with it, as he admired it, and her, and they both laughed. It had been a perfect evening.

'Darling, you should always wear diamonds to bed,' he said as he kissed her on the lips, and then let his mouth wander to the necklace and then past it.

'Do you suppose it'll be a big success?' she murmured softly as she put her arms around him.

'It already is,' he said huskily, and then they both forgot the shop until the morning.

The next day, the papers were full of it, stories about the people who'd been there, about the jewels, about how beautiful they were, and how elegant Sarah and William had been, the fact that the Duke and Duchess of Windsor had been there. It was perfect.

'We're a hit!' She grinned at him over breakfast, wearing nothing but her diamond necklace. She was almost thirty-three years old, and her figure was better than it had ever been, as she sat back in her chair, with her legs crossed and her hair piled high on her head, as the diamonds sparkled in the morning sun. William smiled with pleasure as he watched her.

'You know, you're more beautiful than that bit of flashy stuff around your neck, my dear.'

'Thank you, my love.' She leaned toward him and they kissed, and eventually they finished their breakfast.

They went back to the shop that afternoon, and things seemed to be going well. Emanuelle said they had sold six more things, and some of them were quite expensive. The curious came to ogle, too, to see the people who were there, the jewels, and the excitement. Two very notable men had come shopping, too, one for his mistress, and one for his wife. And Emanuelle had a dinner date with the last one. He was a government official, well known for his affairs, incredibly handsome, and Emanuelle thought it might be amusing to go out with him at least once. There would be no harm done. He was a grown man, and she was certainly not a virgin.

William and Sarah stayed for a little while to see what was happening, and that evening they drove back to the château, still excited about the success of the opening of Whitfield's. And that night, Sarah sat in bed, and made sketches of things she wanted to have made. They couldn't always count on finding fabulous existing pieces. She wanted to go to some of the auctions in New York, and at Christie's in London. And she knew Italy was a marvelous place to have jewelry made. Suddenly she had a thousand things to do. And she always asked William's advice. He had such good taste and excellent judgment.

By fall, their efforts had come to fruition. The shop was doing extremely well, some of her designs had been made up, and Emanuelle said people were crazy about them. She had a great eye, and William knew stones. They bought carefully, and she insisted on the finest workmanship. The things flew out of the store, and in October she was designing more, hoping to have them in time for Christmas.

Emanuelle was deeply involved with Jean-Charles de Martin, her government friend, by then, but the press hadn't discovered them yet. They had been extremely discreet, because of his involvement in the government. They always met at her apartment.

Sarah couldn't believe how busy she was. They were coming to Paris all the time, still staying at the Ritz, she hadn't had a minute to look for an apartment. And by Christmas she was absolutely exhausted. They had made an absolute fortune at the store, and William had given her the most fabulous ruby ring that had belonged to Mary

Pickford. They'd gone to Whitfield for Christmas again and they wanted to bring Phillip back to Paris with them, but he disappointed them no end when he begged to stay at Whitfield.

'What are we going to do with him?' Sarah asked sadly as they flew home again. 'It's incredible to think he was born in France and grew up here, and all he wants to do is stay in England.' He was her only child now, and it pained her unbearably to lose him. No matter how busy she was here, she always had time for him, but he seemed to have very little interest in them. And the only thing France meant to him were memories of the Germans, and the lonely years without his father.

'Whitfield must be in his bones,' William tried to comfort her. 'He'll grow out of it. He's ten years old, he wants to be with his friends. In a few years, he'll be happy back here. He can go to the Sorbonne and live in Paris.' But he was already talking about going to Cambridge, like his father, and in some ways Sarah felt as though they had already lost him. She was still depressed about it over the New Year when they went back to the château, and she caught a dreadful cold. She'd had another one the month before, and she was incredibly tired and rundown after all the dashing about they'd done just before Christmas.

'You look terrible,' William said to her cheerfully, as she came downstairs on New Year's morning. He was already in the kitchen, making coffee.

'Thank you,' she said gloomily, and then asked him if he thought Phillip would be happier there if they bought more horses.

'Stop worrying about him, Sarah. Children have their own lives to lead, independent of their parents.'

'He's only a little boy,' she said, as tears filled her eyes unexpectedly. 'And he's the only little boy I have.' She started to really cry then, thinking of the little girl she had lost during the war, the sweet baby girl she had loved so much, and this boy who no longer seemed to need her. She felt as though her heart would break sometimes when she thought about it. It seemed so awful to have him so far away, and not have any more children, but she had never gotten pregnant again since William had come back from Germany. The doctors said it was possible, but it just hadn't happened.

'My poor darling,' William soothed as he held her. 'He's a naughty boy for being so independent.' He himself had never gotten close to him, although he'd tried. But it had been awfully difficult coming back from the war, meeting a six-year-old child, and striking up a relationship with him at that point. In some ways, William knew that they would never be close now. And he also sensed that Phillip would never forgive him. It was as though he blamed William for going off to war and not being there for him, just as he blamed Sarah for the death of his sister. He never said exactly those words after his outburst at the funeral, but William always sensed that those were his feelings, and he never mentioned it to Sarah.

William made her go back to bed with some hot soup and hot tea that day, and she stayed in bed and cried over Phillip, and made drawings, and eventually dozed, while he came upstairs to check on her. He knew what was wrong with her, she was absolutely exhausted. But when the cold went to her chest, he telephoned the doctor to come and see her. He was always worried about her. He couldn't bear it when she was ill, it was as though he was always afraid to lose her.

'That's ridiculous. I'm fine.' She argued with him, coughing horribly, once he told her he had called the doctor.

'I want him to give you something for that cough, before you wind up with pneumonia,' William said sternly.

'You know I hate medicine,' she said querulously. But the doctor came anyway, a sweet old man from another village. He had retired there after the war, and he was very nice, but she was still annoyed that he had come, and she repeated to him that she didn't need a doctor.

'*Bien sur, Madame* . . . but Monsieur le Duc . . . it is not good for him to worry,' he told her diplomatically, and she relented as William left the room to get another cup of tea for her, and when he came back Sarah looked very subdued, and a little startled.

'Well, will she live?' William asked the doctor jovially, and the old man smiled and patted Sarah's knee as he stood up to leave them.

'Most definitely, and for a very long time, I hope.' He smiled down at her and pretended to grow stern. 'You will stay in bed, though, until you feel better, *n'est-ce pas*?'

'Yes, sir,' she said obediently, and William wondered what he had done to make her so docile. All the fight had suddenly gone out of her and she looked very calm and very quiet.

The doctor hadn't given her any medicine, for all the reasons he'd explained to her while William was out of the room, but he urged her to drink hot soup, and hot tea, and continue just what she was doing. And after he left, William wondered if he was too old and didn't know his business. There were a lot of medications one could take these days so one didn't wind up with pneumonia, or TB, and he wasn't sure soup was enough. It almost made him wonder if he should take her to Paris.

She was lying in bed, looking out the window pensively as he came back upstairs, and he moved his wheelchair close to her, and touched her cheek. But the fever was gone, all she had was that ghastly cough, and he was still worried.

'I want to take you to Paris tomorrow if you're not better by then,' he said quietly. She was too important to him, to ever risk losing her.

'I'm fine,' she said quietly, an odd look in her eyes as

320

she smiled at him. 'I'm perfectly fine . . . only very stupid.' She hadn't figured it out herself. For the past month she had been so busy, all she could think of was Christmas and Whitfield's and jewels, and nothing else. And now . . .

'What does that mean?' He frowned as he looked at her, and she rolled over on her back with a grin.

She sat up in bed and leaned close to him, kissing him gently in spite of the cold, but she had never loved him as much as at this moment. 'I'm pregnant.'

Nothing registered on his face for an instant, and then he stared at her in amazement. 'You're what? Now?'

'Yup.' She beamed at him, and then lay back against her pillows again. 'I think it's about two months, I've been so completely absorbed by the shop that I forgot everything.'

'Good Lord.' He slumped back into his wheelchair with a grin, and took her fingers in his own, and then leaned forward again to kiss them. 'You are amazing!'

'I didn't do this by myself, you know. You must have given it a bit of help sometime too.'

'Oh, darling . . .' He leaned close to her again, knowing full well how much she had wanted another baby. And so had he. But they had both given up after the last three years when nothing happened. 'I hope it's a girl,' he said softly, and he knew she did, too, not to take Lizzie's place, but to be a balance to Phillip. And William had never even seen his little girl, never known her before she died, and he longed to have one. Sarah secretly hoped, too, that in some way, the birth of the baby might heal Phillip. He had loved Lizzie so much, and been so different, and so angry, and so distant once they lost her.

William pulled himself out of his wheelchair, and laid down beside Sarah. 'Oh, darling, how I love you.'

'I love you too,' she whispered, holding tightly to him, and they lay there together for a long time, thinking how blessed they were, and looking forward to the future.

Chapter 19

'I'm not sure.' Sarah frowned as she looked at the new pieces with Emanuelle. They had just been delivered from the same workshop Chaumet used, and Sarah wasn't sure if she liked them. 'What do you think?'

Emanuelle picked up one of the heavy bracelets in her hands. They were pink-gold bangles encrusted with diamonds and rubies. 'I think they're very chic, and very well made,' she pronounced finally. She was looking very stylish herself these days, with her red hair in a chignon, and a black Chanel suit that made her look very dignified, as they sat in Sarah's office.

'They're also going to be very expensive,' Sarah said honestly. It bothered her to charge too much for things, and yet good workmanship commanded incredible prices. She refused to cut corners, and use poor workmanship or bad stones. At Whitfield's one bought only the best, it was her credo.

'I don't think anyone will care,' Emanuelle said, smiling at Sarah as she lumbered across the room to look at one of the bracelets in the mirror. 'People like paying for what they get here. They like the quality, the design. They like the old pieces, but they like yours, too, Madame.' She still called her that, even after all these years. They had known each other well for eleven years now, ever since Emanuelle had come to help deliver Phillip.

'Maybe you're right,' Sarah decided finally. 'They're beautiful pieces. I'll tell him we'll take them.'

'Good.' Emanuelle was pleased. They had spent the

whole morning going over things. This was Sarah's final trip to Paris, to have the baby. It was the end of June, and the baby was expected to arrive two weeks later. But William was taking absolutely no chances this time. He had told his wife months before that he had given his last performance as a midwife, and she was not doing that to him again, particularly after what he'd heard of her second difficult delivery when he was gone.

'But I want the baby to be born here,' she had said again before they left the château, and William absolutely wouldn't hear of it.

They had come to Paris to stay at the apartment they'd finally bought that spring. It had three lovely bedrooms and two servants' rooms, a handsome salon, a lovely study, a boudoir off their bedroom, and a very pretty dining room and kitchen. Sarah had somehow managed to find the time to decorate it herself, and they had a lovely view of the Jardin des Tuileries, with the Seine beyond, from their bedroom.

It was also close to Whitfield's, which Sarah liked, and to some of her favorite shops. And this time, they had brought Phillip with them. He was furious not to be at the château, or somewhere else, or even Whitfield, and he claimed that being stuck in Paris was boring. Sarah had hired a tutor for him, a young man who could take him to the Louvre and the Eiffel Tower, and the zoo, when she couldn't. And she had to admit that for the past two weeks, ever since he'd been home, she could barely move. The baby seemed to have taken over her entire existence.

And Phillip was annoyed about that too. They had told him about the baby during his spring break, and he had looked at them with dismay and horror. And afterwards Sarah heard him tell Emanuelle he thought it was disgusting.

He and Emanuelle were very close, and the one thing Phillip did like was to go to the shop to visit her, and look at the things, as he did that afternoon when Sarah dropped him off with Emanuelle so she could do some errands. He thought some of the jewelry very nice, he admitted. And she tried to tell him the baby would be nice, too, but he said that he thought babies were stupid. Elizabeth hadn't been, he said sadly, but that was different.

'You weren't stupid,' Emanuelle said gently as they ate madeleines and sipped hot chocolate in her office, after Sarah had gone to do some errands before she had to go into the clinic. 'You were a wonderful little boy,' Emanuelle said gently, wishing she could soften him. He had grown up to be so hard, and so brittle. 'And your sister was too.' Something now crossed his face as she mentioned her, and Emanuelle decided to change the subject. 'Maybe it'll be a little girl.'

'I hate girls . . .' And then he decided to qualify it. 'Except you.' And then he startled her completely. 'Do you think you might marry me one day? I mean, if you're not married yet by then.' He knew she was already pretty old. She was twenty-eight, and he knew that by the time he could marry her she'd be almost forty, but she was the most beautiful woman he'd ever seen, he thought, even prettier than his mother. His mother had been pretty good-looking, too, until she got big and fat with her dumb baby. Emanuelle told him he was too old to feel that way, at his age, he shouldn't be jealous of a baby, he should be excited about it, and about being a big brother. But he clearly wasn't. He wasn't excited at all. Emanuelle could tell he was very angry.

'I'd love to marry you, Phillip. Does this mean we're engaged?' She beamed at him and offered him another madeleine.

'I guess so. But I can't buy you a ring. Father never lets me have any money.

'That's all right. I'll borrow one from the store in the meantime.'

He nodded and glanced at some of the things on her desk, and then he surprised her by what he said next, and he would have surprised his mother even more.

'I'd like to work here with you one day, Emanuelle . . . when we're married.'

'Would you?' She looked amused, and then teased him a little bit. 'I thought you wanted to live in England.' Maybe he'd discovered Paris wasn't so bad after all. She wondered.

'We could open one there. In London. I'd like that.'

'We'll have to tell your parents that sometime,' she said as she put her cup of tea down, just as Sarah walked into the room, looking absolutely huge but still very pretty, in a dress Dior had made for her that summer.

'Tell me what?' Sarah asked as she sat down, looking incredibly uncomfortable to Emanuelle, who hoped she never had a baby, and was fully prepared to make every possible effort not to. She had seen enough of Sarah's deliveries to know that children were not something she wanted. She didn't know how Sarah did it.

'Phillip wants to open a store in London. A Whitfield's,' Emanuelle said proudly, and sensed instantly that he didn't want her to tell his mother about their engagement, so she didn't.

'That sounds like a nice idea.' Sarah smiled at him. 'I'm sure your father would be pleased. I'm not sure I'd survive it however.' The last year, since their opening exactly a year before, had been absolutely exhausting.

'We'll have to wait till Phillip is old enough to run it.'

'And I will.' He said with a stubborn look Sarah knew well. She offered him a drive through the Bois de Boulogne, and he grudgingly left Emanuelle with a kiss on both cheeks, and a squeeze of the hand to remind her of their engagement.

They had a nice walk in the park after that, and he was more talkative than usual, chatting about Emanuelle, and the shop, and Eton and Whitfield. And he was patient with Sarah's slow, cumbersome pace. He felt sorry for her, she looked so uncomfortable all the time now.

William was waiting for them when they returned to the apartment, and they had dinner at the Brasserie Lipp that night. Phillip always loved it. And for the next two weeks Sarah devoted herself to him, because she knew she wouldn't have as much time once she had the baby. They were planning to go back to the château as soon as it was born, and the doctors said she could travel. They had even wanted her in the clinic a week before the baby was due, and she flatly refused, and told William that in the States people just didn't do that. In France people went into private clinics a week or two before the baby was born, to be pampered and wait, and then they stayed another two weeks after. But she wasn't going to sit in a clinic, no matter how fancy, and do nothing.

They stopped in at the shop every day, and Phillip was very excited when a new emerald bracelet came in, and on another afternoon when Emanuelle told them they had sold two enormous rings in one morning. What was even more amazing was that she had sold one of them to Jean-Charles de Martin, her lover. He had bought it for her, and had teased her mercilessly, pretending it was for his wife when he bought it. And then, as she grew angrier and angrier at him, he took the ring from the box, and slipped it on her finger. It was there now, and Sarah raised an eyebrow.

'Does this mean something serious?' Sarah asked, but she also knew how much jewelry he bought for his wife and girlfriends, at other jewelers.

'Only that I have a beautiful new ring,' Emanuelle said realistically. She had no illusions. But she had a few very interesting clients. Many of the men who bought from them, bought for their mistresses as well as their wives. They had complicated lives, and all of them had come to know that Emanuelle Bourgois was the soul of discretion.

They went back to the apartment late that afternoon, and Phillip went to the movies that evening with his tutor. He was a fine young man, a student at the Sorbonne, and was fluent in both English and French, and fortunately Phillip liked him.

It was already July by then, and Paris was hot and steamy. They had been there for two weeks, and Sarah was anxious to go home again. It was so beautiful at the château at that time of year. It seemed a shame to waste the summer in Paris.

'I wouldn't call it "wasted",' William mused with a smile as he watched her. She looked like a beached whale as she lay on their bed in an enormous pink satin nightgown. 'Aren't you hot in that thing?' he asked, it made him uncomfortable just looking at her. 'Why don't you take it off?'

'I don't want to make you sick, having to look at me like this.' But he rolled slowly toward the bed as she said it.

'Nothing about you ever makes me sick.' He was a little sad this time, not to be there when she had the baby. He felt a little left out of it, with her fancy Paris doctor, and the clinic, but it was William who wanted her there, because it was so much safer.

She fell into a deep, deep sleep that night, as he slept fitfully in the heat, and she woke him at four in the morning, when the pains came. He dressed carefully, and called the maid to help her, and then he drove her to Nevilly, to the clinic they had chosen. She seemed to be in considerable pain by the time they left, and she said very little to him on the short drive in his Bentley. And then they took her away from him, and he waited nervously until noon, fearing that things might be going as badly as they had the first time. They had promised to give her gas this time, and they had assured her that everything would be easy and modern. As easy as it could be for a woman having a nine-pound baby. And finally, at one-thirty, the doctor came out to him, looking very neat and prim, and smiling broadly.

'You have a handsome son, Monsieur.'

'And my wife?' William asked worriedly.

'She worked hard,' the doctor looked serious for a moment, 'but it went very well. We have given her a little something to sleep now. You may see her in a few moments.' And when he did, she was draped in white sheets, and very pale, and very groggy, and she seemed to have no idea where she was, or why she was there. She kept telling him that they had to go to the shop that afternoon, and not to forget to write to Phillip at Eton.

'I know, my darling . . . it's all right.' He sat quietly next to her for hours, and about four-thirty, she stirred and looked at him, and glanced around the room in confusion. He moved closer to her again then, and kissed her cheek and told her about their baby. William still hadn't seen him yet, but all the nurses said he was lovely. He weighed nine pounds, fourteen ounces, almost as big as Phillip, and William could only imagine from the look of her that it hadn't been easy.

'Where is he?' she asked, looking around the room.

'In the nursery, they'll bring him in soon. They wanted you to sleep.' And then he kissed her again. 'Was it awful?'

'It was strange . . .' She looked at him dreamily, holding his hand, and still trying to focus. 'They kept giving me gas and it made me feel sick . . . but all it really did was make me woozy, it seemed like everything was very faraway, and I still felt the pain, but I couldn't tell them.'

'Maybe that's why they like it.' But at least they were both safe, and nothing dreadful had happened.

'I liked it better when you did it,' she said sadly, this was all so odd, and so foreign, and so antiseptic, and they hadn't even showed her the baby.

'Thank you. I'm afraid I'm not much of a surgeon.'

But they brought the baby in to them then, and all the pain was suddenly forgotten. He was beautiful and round, he had dark hair and big blue eyes, and he looked just like William. And Sarah cried when she held him. He was so perfect, such a wonderful little boy. She had wanted a little girl, but she didn't mind now that they had him. All that mattered was that he was there, and he was all right. They had decided to call him Julian, after a distant cousin of William's. And she insisted on William as his middle name, which his father said was foolish, but he reluctantly agreed. Sarah cried when they took him away again. She couldn't understand why they had to do that. She had her own nurse and her own room. She even had her own sitting room and her own bathroom, but they said it wasn't sanitary to leave him there for too long. He belonged in the nursery with sterile conditions. Sarah blew her nose and looked at William after Julian was gone, and the emotions of the day overwhelmed her. And he suddenly felt guilty for bringing her here, but he promised to take her home quickly.

He brought Phillip to see her the next day, and Emanuelle, who proclaimed Julian beautiful when she saw him through a window. They wouldn't let the infants visit with guests, and Sarah hated the place more than ever. And Phillip stared at him through the glass and then shrugged and turned away, visibly unimpressed, as Sarah watched in disappointment. He looked angry about the baby, too, and he wasn't very kind to his mother.

'Don't you think he's sweet?' Sarah asked hopefully.

'He's all right. He's awfully small,' Phillip said disparagingly. And his father laughed ruefully, knowing what Sarah had been through.

'Not to us, young man. Nine pounds, fourteen ounces is a monster!' But there was nothing else monstrous about him, whenever they brought him to Sarah to feed, she could see he had the sweetest disposition. And after he nursed, he would lie nestled next to her, and as though a bell had rung, a nurse arrived instantly to remove him from her.

By the eighth day, Sarah was waiting for William when he arrived with a fresh bouquet of flowers, and she was standing in her sitting room with her eyes blazing.

'If you don't get me out of here in the next hour, I'm going to take Julian and walk out of here in my nightgown. I feel perfectly well, I'm not ill. And they won't let me get near my baby.'

'All right, darling,' William said, knowing this would come, 'tomorrow, I promise.' And the next day, he took them both back to the apartment, and two days later they all went back to the château, as Sarah held Julian in her arms, and he slept happily in the warmth of his mother.

By her birthday, in August, Sarah was her old self again, thin and well and strong, and enchanted with her new baby. They had closed the shop for the month, Emanuelle was on a yacht in the South of France, and Sarah didn't even have to think of business. And in September when Phillip went back to school, they went to Paris for a few days, and Sarah took the baby with her. He went everywhere with them and sometimes he slept peacefully in a little basket in her office.

'He's such a good little boy,' everyone commented about him, he was always smiling and laughing and cooing, and on Christmas eve, he was sitting up and the whole world was in love with him. The whole world except Phillip. He looked angry each time he saw him. And he always had something disagreeable to say about him. It cut Sarah to the quick, she had been so hopeful that he would come to like him. But the brotherly affection she had hoped would come never had, and he remained distant and unpleasant.

'He's just jealous,' William said, accepting what was, as

he always did, unlike Sarah, who railed over what wasn't. 'That's the way it is.'

'But it's not fair. He's such a sweet baby, he doesn't deserve that. Everyone loves him, except Phillip.'

'If only one person dislikes him for the rest of his life, he'll be a very, very lucky man,' William said realistically.

'But not if that one person is his brother.'

'Sometimes that's the way life is. No-one ever said brothers had to be friends. Look at Cain and Abel.'

'I don't understand it. He was crazy about Lizzie.' She sighed. 'And Jane and I adored each other when we were young.' And they still did, although she never saw her. Jane had remarried after the war, and moved to Chicago, and then Los Angeles, and they never came to Europe, and Sarah never went to the States, let alone California. It was hard to believe Jane was married now, to someone Sarah didn't even know. It was just one of those things. As close as they had been, they had drifted apart. But she still loved her, and they wrote each other frequently, and Sarah always urged her to come to Europe.

But no matter what his parents thought of it, Phillip never warmed up to his baby brother. And when Sarah had tried to talk to him about it, he brushed her off, until she pressed him, and then he exploded at her. 'Look, I don't need another baby in my life. I've already had one.' It was as though he couldn't try again, couldn't open himself up to the risk and the loss and the caring. He had loved Lizzie, maybe too much, and he had lost her. And he had decided, as a result, never to love Julian. It was a sad thing for both children.

William and Sarah had taken Julian to meet his only grandmother, at Whitfield, shortly after he was born, and now they were together at Christmas. And the dowager duchess was enchanted with him. She said she had never seen a happier baby. He just seemed to radiate sunshine, and he made everyone laugh and smile who watched him.

It was a particularly nice Christmas at Whitfield that year, with all of them there. William's mother was ninety-six now, and in a wheelchair, but always in remarkable spirits. She was the ultimate good sport, the kindest woman Sarah had ever known, and she still doted on William. He brought her a beautiful diamond bracelet that year, and she murmured that she was far too old for such a lovely thing, but it was obvious that she loved it and she never took it off the whole time they were there. And when they left after the New Year, she held William tightly to her and told him what a good son he had always been, he had always, always made her happy.

'Why do you suppose she said that?' William asked, with tears in his eyes as they left. 'She's always been so incredibly good to me,' he said, turning away, embarrassed to have Sarah see him cry, but his mother had really touched him. She had kissed Julian's chubby little cheek as well, and Sarah, and thanked her for all the lovely presents from Paris. And two weeks later, she died quietly in her sleep, gone to meet her husband and her Maker, after a lifetime of happiness at Whitfield.

William was very shaken by her loss, but even he had to admit that she had had a good life, and a very long one. She would have been ninety-seven that year, and she had enjoyed good health all her life. There was much to be thankful for, as they all stood at the cemetery at Whitfield. King George and Queen Elizabeth came, her surviving relatives and friends, and all those who knew her.

Phillip seemed to feel her absence most acutely. 'Does this mean I can't come here anymore?' he asked, with tears in his eyes.

'Not for a while,' William said sadly. 'It will always be here for you. And one day, it will be yours. We'll try to come over for a bit every summer. But you can't come here on holidays and weekends, as you did when

Grandmother was alive. It wouldn't be right for you to be here alone with the servants. You can come to La Marolle, or Paris, or stay with some cousins.'

'I don't want to do any of that,' he said petulantly, 'I want to stay here.' But William didn't see how he could do that. In time, he could come here on his own, when he was at Cambridge. But that was still seven years away, and in the meantime, he'd have to be satisfied with occasional visits in the summer.

But by the spring, it had become obvious to William that he was not going to be able to be away from Whitfield as much as he expected. Not having any member of the family present there any more suddenly meant that there was no-one to watch over things and to make immediate decisions. He was startled to realize how many things his mother had actually done, and it was suddenly very difficult to run the place without her.

'I hate to do this,' he admitted to Sarah one night, as he read page after page of complaints from his estate managers. 'But I really think I need to spend more time there. Do you mind terribly?'

'Why should I?' She smiled. 'I can take Julian anywhere right now.' He was eight months old and still very portable. 'And Emanuelle has the shop perfectly in control.' She had hired two more girls to work there, so all in all they were four now, and the business was extremely successful. 'I don't mind spending some time in London.' She had always liked it. And Phillip could join them at Whitfield for the weekends, which she knew would please him.

They spent the entire month of April there, except for a quick trip to Cap d'Antibes at Easter. They saw the Windsors at a dinner party, and Wallis made a point of mentioning that she had just bought some very pretty pieces from Sarah's shop in Paris. She seemed very impressed with their things, particularly their new designs. All over London, people seemed to be talking about Whitfield's.

'Why don't you open one here?' William asked her one night as they left a party where three women had practically devoured her with questions.

'In London? So soon?' They had only had the shop in Paris for two years, and it worried her a little to spread herself so thin, and she didn't want to be forced to spend a lot of time in London. It was one thing if she was here with him, but an entirely different matter if she had to spend all her time dashing back and forth across the English Channel. And she wanted to spend most of her time now with the baby, before he grew up and walked out of her life like Phillip. She had too strong a sense now of how fleeting were the moments.

'You'd have to find someone very good to run it. Actually' – William looked pensive, as though he was trying to dredge up a distant memory – 'there used to be a marvelous man at Garrard's. Very discreet, very knowledgeable, he's young but a bit old-fashioned perhaps, but just what the English love, full of good manners and old traditions.'

'Why do you think he'd ever want to leave them? They're the most prestigious jewelers here. He might be shocked by a new venture like Whitfield's.'

'I always got the impression that he was a bit underrated there, sort of the forgotten man, but a very good one. I'll stop in next week and see if I see him. We can take him to lunch if you like.'

Sarah grinned at him, unable to believe what they were doing. 'You're always trying to get me into more trouble, aren't you?' But she loved it. She loved the way he encouraged her, and helped her do the things she really wanted. She knew that without him she could never do it.

True to his word, William stopped in at Garrard's the

334

following afternoon, and bought her a lovely antique diamond ring. It was very old and very pretty. And while he did, he had spotted his man. Nigel Holbrook. They had an appointment for lunch with him at noon, at the Savoy Grill on the following Tuesday.

And the moment they walked into the restaurant, Sarah knew exactly who he was from William's earlier description. He was tall and thin and very pale, with blondish gray hair, and a small, clipped mustache. He wore a well-tailored pinstripe suit, and he looked like a banker or a lawyer. There was something very elegant about him, distinguished and discreet, and he was extremely reserved as William and Sarah told him what they were thinking. He said that he had been at Garrard's for seventeen years, since he'd been twenty-two, and it would be difficult to think of leaving them, but he had to admit that the prospect of a new venture like theirs intrigued him greatly. 'Particularly,' he said quietly, 'given the reputation of your shop in Paris. I've seen some of the work you do there, Your Grace,' he said to Sarah, 'and it's very fine indeed. I was quite surprised actually. The French can be' – he hesitated, and then went on – 'shoddy sometimes . . . if you let them.' She laughed at the chauvinism, but she knew what he meant. If she didn't watch the work-rooms she used, they would be inclined to cut corners, and she never let them. She was pleased with what he'd said, and the reputation they were obviously earning.

'We'd like to be around for a long time. We want to do things right, Mr Holbrook.' He was the second son of a British general, and had grown up in India and China. He'd been born in Singapore, and had become entranced with the jewels in India as a boy. And as a young man, he'd worked briefly in South Africa, with diamonds. He knew his business well. And Sarah agreed with William completely. He was exactly the man they needed in London. It was a totally different atmosphere here, and she sensed instinctively that they would have to move into it with more grace, less panache, and the kind of dignity that Nigel Holbrook had to offer. They asked him to call them when he'd thought about it, and a week later, Sarah was dismayed that he still hadn't called them.

'Give him time. He may not call for a month. But you can be sure he's thinking about it.' They had made him a very handsome offer, and no matter how loyal he was to Garrard's, it was difficult to believe that he wouldn't be tempted. If not, William was prepared to be truly impressed by how faithful he was to his current employers. Because he knew that he couldn't possibly be making a salary anything like the one he'd just been offered.

As it happened, he called them at Whitfield, the night before they left. Sarah waited impatiently while William took the call, and he was smiling when he hung up. 'He'll take it,' he announced. 'He'd like to give Garrard's two months notice, which is damn decent of him, and then he's yours. When do you want to open?'

'Good Lord . . . I hadn't even thought of it . . . I don't know . . . end of the year . . . Christmas? Do you think we really should do it?'

'Of course you should.' He always insisted on giving her all the credit. 'I have to come back in a few weeks anyway, we can look for a location then, and speak to an architect. I know a good one.'

'I'd better start buying some new pieces.' She had been using the money she'd been making in the Paris shop to buy new pieces, and have new designs made, but now she'd need some capital, and she planned to use the money she still had from the sale of her parents' house on Long Island. And if London was anything like Paris, she knew they'd be making money quickly.

And then William said something she hadn't even thought about. 'Looks like Phillip's got his shop,' he said with a slow smile as they made plans for their return to London.

'It does, doesn't it? Do you suppose he'll really ever do it?'

'He might.'

'Somehow I can't imagine him coming into the business with us. He's so independent . . .' And so cool, and so distant . . . and so angry about Julian . . .

'He might surprise you one day. You never know what children will do. Who ever thought I'd become a jeweler?' He laughed and she kissed him, and the next day, they went back to Paris.

Nigel flew to Paris several times in the next few months to meet with them, and talk to Emanuelle, and see the way the operation worked in Paris. They were actually talking about moving to a new store, business was so good, but Sarah didn't want to press her luck, particularly now with the opening in London.

Nigel was extremely impressed with everything they were doing in Paris. He even began to grow rather fond of Emanuelle, who had accurately guessed long since that ladies were not entirely his passion. In fact, she didn't think they were at all, and she was right, but she admired his impeccable taste, his excellent business sense, and his good breeding. She had spent the last several years trying to acquire more polish herself, and she particularly admired Nigel's quiet elegance and incredibly good manners. They had dinner together whenever he came to town, and she introduced him to some of her friends, including a very important designer, who became someone very important in Nigel's life. But most of the time, they turned their full attention to business.

They had found a beautiful little store on New Bond Street, and William's architect came up with some wonderful ideas. They were going to do everything in navy-blue velvet and white marble.

It was to open on December first, and they had to work like demons to do it. Emanuelle came over from Paris to help, leaving the best of her girls in Paris in charge of the store there. But the shop on Faubourg-St Honoré took care of itself now. It was the shop in London that was the new baby.

The week before they opened they worked till midnight every night with a crew of tireless workmen, laying marble, adjusting lights, installing mirrors, tacking velvet. It was an incredible scene, and Sarah had never been so tired in her life, but she had never had so much fun either.

She had brought Julian to London with her, and they were staying at Claridge's again, with a nanny. They were too tired at night to make the long drive to Whitfield.

Everyone wanted to give parties for them, but they never had time. They never stopped for an instant, until their doors were finally open. They had invited four hundred relatives and friends, and another hundred of Nigel's very best customers from Garrard's. It was a gathering of the titled and the elite, and it made their opening in Paris two and a half years before dim by comparison. It was glittering beyond words, and the jewels Sarah had bought to open with absolutely staggered the people who saw them. She was, in fact, frightened that she had gone overboard, that the pieces she had bought were too important and too expensive. Whereas she had some chic pieces in Paris that you could own without hiring an armed guard, in London she had pulled out all the stops, and stopped at nothing. She had spent every penny left to her from the estate on Long Island, but as she looked around her as the first guests arrived, she knew it was worth it.

And the next day, when Nigel came to her looking stunned and pale, she thought something terrible had happened. 'What's wrong?'

'The Queen's secretary has just been here.' She wondered if they had committed some ghastly *faux pas*, and she looked at William with a worried frown, as Nigel went on to explain his visit. 'Her Royal Highness wishes to purchase something her lady-in-waiting saw here last night. We sent it over to the palace this morning, and she likes it very much.' Sarah listened in amazement. They had made it. 'She'd like to buy the large pin with the diamond feathers.' It looked very much like the insignia of the Prince of Wales, and she had bought it from a dealer in Paris for an absolute fortune. The price tag she'd put on it herself had embarrassed her when she wrote it.

'Good Lord!' Sarah said, impressed by the sale, but what had impressed Nigel was something far more important.

'This means, Your Grace, that on our very first day in business, we have become Jewelers to the Crown,' which meant they had sold something to the Queen. Crown Jewelers were Garrard's, who were the Queen's official jewelers, and annually restored the Crown Jewels kept in the Tower of London. But this was a very important feather in their cap in London. 'If the Queen wishes it, after three years, she can bestow a royal warrant on us.' He was overwhelmed, and even William raised an eyebrow. They had pulled off a major coup without even trying.

The Queen's purchase got them off to a royal start, and the rest of the items they sold that month could have kept them in business for a year. Sarah was satisfied that she could go back to Paris and leave everything in Nigel's capable hands. She could hardly believe it when they flew back to Paris after the New Year. Emanuelle had returned to Paris long since, after the London opening, and her Christmas figures were astounding.

Sarah also noticed that there was a friendly rivalry between the two stores, each one trying to outdo the other. But there was no harm in that. Nigel and Emanuelle genuinely liked each other. Besides which, Sarah wanted the two stores to be similar but different. In London, they sold fabulous antique jewels, many of them of royal provenance from the royals of Europe, and also a smattering of modern designs. They sold antique jewelry in Paris, too, but they also sold a great many new pieces that were both chic and striking.

'What new frontier now?' William teased her as they drove back to the château. 'Buenos Aires? New York? Cap d'Antibes?' The possibilities were limitless, but Sarah was satisfied with what they had. It was manageable, and fun. It kept her busy, but she could still enjoy her children. Julian was eighteen months old by then, and keeping everyone around him very busy, as he climbed on to tables, and teetered on chairs, fell down stairs, and disappeared out the door into the garden. Sarah kept an eye on him constantly, and he was a handful for the local girl who came to help her. They always took her to Paris with them, and in London they hired temporary nannies. But most of the time Sarah liked taking care of him herself, and he loved to sit on William's lap and speed around in the wheelchair.

'*Vite! Vite!*' he squealed, urging his father to go faster. It was one of his few words, but for him it was a good one, and he liked to use it often. It was a happy time for them. All of their dreams had come true. Their lives were busy and full and happy.

Chapter 20

For the next four years, Julian and both shops kept William and Sarah extremely busy. Business in both places grew, Sarah gave in and agreed to enlarge the Paris store eventually, but they kept the London store the way it was in spite of their excellent business. It was elegant, discreet, and extremely important, and it suited the British. And both Emanuelle and Nigel had continued to do a splendid job of it. Sarah was well pleased as she blew out the candles on her cake on her thirty-ninth birthday. Phillip was at the château with them then, he was just turning sixteen, almost as tall as his father, and itching to get back to Whitfield. He was going to visit friends, and he had stayed on for Sarah's birthday only because his father said he had to. She wanted him to stay and celebrate his own birthday with them, but he wasn't interested in that. And he had managed to forget Julian's fifth birthday in July as well. Family did not appear to be of major importance to Phillip. In fact, he seemed careful to avoid it. It was almost as though he had to put a barrier up, and he never let anyone cross it. When he left again, Sarah was philosophical this time. Over the years, she had slowly learned something from William.

'I suppose we're lucky he comes here at all,' she said to William the day he left. 'All he ever wants to do is play polo, be with his friends, and stay at Whitfield.' They had finally agreed to let him go there alone on weekends and occasional holidays, and he could take friends, as long as he invited one of his teachers to go with him. It was an arrangement that seemed to suit everyone, most especially Phillip. 'Isn't it funny, how he's so British, and Julian is so French?' Everything about the little boy was incredibly Gallic. He preferred to speak French with them, he loved his life at the château, and he much preferred Paris to London.

'Les Anglais me font peur,' he always said. 'English people scare me.' Which Sarah told him was silly, since his father was an Englishman, and he was English, too, although as the second son, he would never inherit the title. He would be merely Lord Whitfield when he grew up. Sometimes British traditions seemed incredibly quixotic. But she didn't think Julian would ever care. He was so happy and good-natured, nothing ever bothered him, not even the indifference of his older brother. He had learned as a very little boy to steer clear of him, and keep to his own doings, and that seemed to suit them both to perfection. He adored his parents, his friends, his pets, the people who worked at the château, he loved visiting Emanuelle. Julian loved everyone and everything, and in return, absolutely everyone who knew him loved him.

Sarah was thinking about it one afternoon in September, as she tended the flowers over Lizzie's grave. She still went there regularly, kept it looking tidy, and she couldn't help herself, she always cried when she went there. It was incredible that after eleven years she still missed her. She would have been fifteen by then . . . so loving, and so sweet . . . She had been a little bit like Julian, only softer, not as strong . . . Sarah's eyes were filled with tears as she cut back some of the flowers and patted the soft earth they grew on, and she didn't hear the wheels of William's wheelchair approaching. He hadn't been quite as well recently. His back had been bothering him a great deal, and he never complained, but Sarah knew that the rheumatism in his legs had gotten worse during the past winter.

She felt his hand on her shoulder, and turned, the tears streaming down her cheeks, and she reached out to him, as he gently brushed the tears from her cheeks and kissed them. 'My poor darling . . .' He looked at the well-tended grave, '. . . poor little Lizzie . . .' He was sorry, too, that Sarah had never had another daughter, to bring her comfort, although Julian was a great source of joy to both of them, and he accepted Phillip for what he was. But he had never known his only little girl, and without ever having seen her face, he missed her.

Sarah turned, and finished her work, and then came to sit next to him on the ground, accepting his perfectly pressed handkerchief from him.

'I'm sorry . . . I shouldn't, after all this time . . .' But always, always, she felt the little warm body next to hers, the little hands around her neck, until she had grown so still and had stopped breathing . . .

'I'm sorry too.' He smiled gently at her. 'Maybe we should have another baby.'

She knew he was only joking and she smiled at him. 'Phillip would really love that.'

'It might do him good. He's a very self-centred young man.' Phillip had annoyed him this time, being so impatient and unkind with his mother.

'I don't know who he takes after, you're certainly not like that, I hope I'm not . . . Julian adores everyone . . . and your mother was so sweet. My parents were pretty nice too, and my sister.'

'There must have been a Visigoth king somewhere in my past, or a savage Norman. I don't know. But Phillip is certainly Phillip.' All he cared about now was Whitfield, Cambridge, and the shop in London. That fascinated him, and whenever he was there, he always asked Nigel ten thousand questions, which amused the older man. He answered all of them, taught him what he knew about the stones, and showed him all the important points about the size, quality, clarity, and the settings. But Phillip had a lot of other things to do before he could think about going to work at Whitfield's.

'Maybe we ought to go away somewhere this year.' Sarah was looking at William, and she thought he looked tired. At fifty-two, he had weathered a lot in his lifetime, and there were times when he looked it. He chased after her tirelessly, from Paris to London and back again. But the following year, when Julian started school in La Marolle, they would have to spend more time at the château. This was the last year they could really travel. 'I'd really like to go to Burma and Thailand and look at some stones,' she said thoughtfully.

'You would?' William was surprised. She had gotten incredibly knowledgeable about stones in the six years since they'd started the business, and she was very choosy about what she bought and from whom. But because of that, Whitfield's had an impeccable reputation. Business had grown in both London and Paris. In London, the Queen had bought from them again several times, as had the Duke of Edinburgh, and soon they were hoping to be able to hang a sign with the royal warrant.

'I'd love to go away. We could even take Julian with us.'

'How romantic,' William teased. But he knew full well that she always liked to have him near her. 'Why don't I organize something for the three of us then? And we should probably take a girl with us to help with Julian. We could probably get out to the Orient and back before Christmas.' It would be a long, long trip, and she knew it would be tiring for him, but it would do them both good too.

They left in November, and arrived back in England on Christmas Eve, when they met Phillip at Whitfield. They had been gone for more than six weeks, and they had endless tales to tell him about tiger hunts in India, and visits to the beach in Thailand, and Hong Kong, and temples, and rubies . . . and emeralds . . . and fabulous jewels. Sarah had brought an absolute fortune of beautiful stones back with her. And Phillip was fascinated by them, and all the tales they had to tell him. For once he was even agreeable to his little brother.

The following week, when Sarah showed all her treasures to Nigel, he was in awe of them and assured her that she had bought well. And Emanuelle was thrilled with some of the Indian maharaja's jewels she took back to Paris, and so were the ladies who bought them.

It had been a fabulous trip, and a productive autumn for them, but they were all happy to return to the château. The girl they'd taken with them had wonderful stories to tell her family, and Julian was thrilled to be back home, with his friends, as was Sarah. She had said very little about it, but while William's health had improved on the trip, she had picked up a bug in India and just couldn't shake it. It ravaged her stomach continually, and she did her best not to complain, but by the time they got back to the château she was worried. She didn't want William to be concerned, and she tried to make light of it, but even once they were home she could barely eat. And finally, the next time they were in Paris in late January, she went to the doctor. He ran a few tests, and saw nothing serious and then he asked her to come back again. But by then, she was feeling a little better.

'What do you suppose this thing is?' she asked, truly annoyed by then. She hadn't enjoyed a meal since November.

'I believe it's very simple, Madame,' the doctor said calmly.

'That's comforting.' But she was still annoyed at herself for catching it in the first place. Thank God Julian hadn't gotten it, but she'd been careful about what he ate and drank. She didn't want him to get sick there. But for herself, she had been a good deal less careful.

'Have you any plans for next summer, Madame?' he asked, with a small smile, and Sarah began to panic. Was he suggesting surgery? But that was seven months away, and then suddenly, she wondered. But it couldn't be. Not again. Not this time.

'I don't know . . . why . . . ?' she said vaguely.

'I believe you will be having a baby in August.'

'I am?' At her age, she couldn't believe it. She was going to be forty in August. She had heard of stranger things before, and she was hardly over the hill. She still looked as she always had, but one couldn't lie to the calendar. And forty was forty. 'Are you sure?'

'I believe so. I would like to run one more test to be certain it is positive.' He did, and it was, and she told William as soon as the doctor called her.

'But at my age . . . isn't that absurd?' Somehow, this time, she was faintly embarrassed.

'It's not absurd at all.' He looked thrilled. 'My mother was much older than you are when she had me, and I'm perfectly fine, and she survived it.' He looked happily at her. 'Besides, I told you we should have another child.' And this time, he, too, wanted a daughter.

'You're going to send me to that dreadful clinic again, aren't you?' Sarah looked at him ruefully and he laughed. There were times when she still looked like a young girl to him, she was a beautiful woman.

'Well, I'm not going to deliver it myself again – not at your age!' he said teasingly, and she screeched at him.

'See! You think I'm too old too. What will people think?'

'They'll think we're very lucky . . . and not very well behaved, I'm afraid,' he teased, and she had to laugh at herself. Having a baby at forty seemed a little foolish, but she had to admit, she was pleased too. She had enjoyed Julian so much, but he was hardly a baby any more at five, and he would be starting school in September.

Emanuelle was a little startled when Sarah told her in

March, and Nigel was faintly embarrassed by the news, but congratulated them very politely. Both shops were doing so well that they really didn't need Sarah's constant attention. She spent much of that year at the château, and as always, Phillip joined them there for the summer. He made very little comment about his mother's pregnancy. He thought it was too nauseating to even mention.

This time Sarah prevailed on William not to make her go away. They compromised and he let her go to the new hospital in Orléans, which wasn't as fancy as the clinic was, but it was very modern, and he was satisfied with the local doctor.

They managed to celebrate her birthday and have a good time, and this time even Phillip was very pleasant. He left for Whitfield the next day, for the last of his vacation before he went off to Cambridge. And the night he left, Sarah got very uncomfortable and after Julian went off to bed, she looked at William very strangely. 'I'm not sure what's happening, but I'm feeling strange.' She thought maybe she should warn him.

'Maybe we should call the doctor.'

'I feel silly doing that. I'm not having pains. I just feel . . .' She tried to describe it to him as he watched her nervously. 'I don't know . . . kind of heavy . . . more than heavy . . . and like I want to move around all the time or something.' She had an odd sensation of pressure.

'Maybe the baby's pressing on something.' This baby wasn't quite as big as the others had been, but it was large enough to make her uncomfortable, and it had for weeks. And it never seemed to stop moving. 'Why don't you take a warm bath and lie down, and see how you feel then.' And then he looked at her firmly. He knew her too well, and he didn't entirely trust her. 'But I want you to tell me what's going on. I don't want you to wait till the last second, and then not make it to the hospital. Do you hear me, Sarah?'

'Yes, Your Grace,' she said demurely. He smiled at her, and left her to take her bath. And an hour later, she was lying on their bed, still feeling the same pressure. But by then, she'd decided that it was indigestion and not labor.

'Are you sure?' He questioned her when he came back to check on her again. There was something about the way she looked that made him nervous.

'I promise.' She grinned.

'Right. See that you keep your legs crossed.' He went back to the other room to look at some balance sheets from the stores, and Emanuelle called her from Monte Carlo to see how she was and they chatted. Her affair with Jean-Charles de Martin had ended two years before, and she was engaged in a far more dangerous one now, with the Minister of Finance.

'Darling, be careful,' Sarah scolded her, and her old friend laughed.

'Look who's talking!' Emanuelle had teased her a little bit this time about being pregnant.

'Very funny.'

'How are you feeling?'

'I'm fine. Fat, bored. And I think William is getting a little nervous. I'll come in to the shop as soon as I can after you get back from your holiday.' As they were every year, they were closed for August, but they were going to reopen again in September.

They chatted on for a little while, and when they hung up, Sarah walked around the room again. She seemed to be making endless trips to the bathroom.

But each time she came out of the bathroom, she seemed to walk around the room again, and then she went downstairs and came back, and she was still pacing when William came back to their bedroom.

'What are you doing, for heaven's sake?'

'It's too uncomfortable to lie down, and I'm restless.' By then she had a sharp pain in her back, and she felt as

though she were dragging her stomach along the floor. She
went to the bathroom again and suddenly as she walked
back into their bedroom, a huge pain roared through her,
starting at her back, and making her want to bear down.
All she suddenly wanted to do was stop where she was and
push out the baby. The pain never stopped, it just kept
pressing down on her, from her back to her stomach and
downward. She could barely stand as she clutched a chair,
and William instantly rushed to her as he saw her expression. He pulled her on to his wheelchair and lay her
down on the bed with a look of terror.

'Sarah, you're not doing this to me again! What
happened?'

'I don't know.' She could barely speak. 'I thought . . . it
was indigestion . . . but it's pushing so hard . . . it's . . .
oh, God . . . William . . . the baby's coming!'

'No, it's not!' He absolutely refused to let it happen
again, he left her for an instant, and wheeled across the
room to call the hospital and ask them to send an
ambulance. She was forty years old this time, not twenty-
three, and he was not going to play games again with
another ten-pound baby. But she was screaming for him
when he hung up, and they had assured him they would
come at once. They were twenty minutes away, and the
doctor was going to come with them.

She clutched at his shirt as he reached her again, and
clung to his hand. She wasn't crying, but she seemed to be
in terrible agony, and she looked surprised and frightened.
'I know it's coming . . . William . . . I can feel it!' She was
shouting at him, it was all happening so hard and so fast
and she had had no warning. Or at least, precious little. 'I
can feel the baby's head . . . it's coming now!' She
screamed, and as she lay there, she was alternately pushing and screaming, and he quickly pulled up her nightgown, and saw the baby's head just crowning, as he had
seen before. Only the last time it had taken hours, and so

much work, and this time, nothing seemed to stop it. 'William . . . William . . . no! I can't do this . . . make it stop!' But nothing was stopping this baby. Its head was pushing its way relentlessly out of its mother, and a moment later there was a small face looking at him, and two bright eyes, and a perfect pink mouth shouting, as they both watched it. And instantly, William reached down to help her. He tried to get Sarah to relax and then to push again a moment later, and suddenly the shoulders were free and the arms, and then in a burst of speed, the rest of her body. It was a beautiful little girl, and she looked absolutely furious with both of them, as Sarah lay back on their bed with a look of amazement. They were both stunned by the sheer force of it. It had been so powerful and so quick. One minute she'd been talking to Emanuelle, and then suddenly, she was having the baby. And the whole delivery had taken less than ten minutes.

'Remind me never to trust you again,' William said huskily as he looked at her and then kissed her. He waited for the doctor to cut the cord, and wrapped them both in clean sheets and towels. Their brand-new daughter was slightly mollified by then, suckling at her mother's breast, and giving her an occasional angry look about how rudely she'd been expelled from her cozy quarters.

They were both smiling and laughing when the doctor came twenty minutes later. He apologized profusely, explaining that he had come as fast as he could. But she was Sarah's fourth child, after all, and there had been no way of knowing she would come so quickly.

He congratulated both of them, pronounced the baby to be perfect, cut the cord that William had neatly tied with a clean piece of string he'd found in his office. He complimented them on how well they'd both done, and offered to take Sarah to the hospital, but admitted that she didn't need it.

'I'd much rather stay home,' Sarah said quietly, and William looked at her, still pretending to be angry.

'I know you would. Next time I'm taking you to the hospital in Paris two months early!'

'Next time!' she said. '*Next* time! Are you joking? Next time I'll be a grandmother!' She was laughing at him, and suddenly feeling more herself. It had been shocking, and briefly terribly painful, but it had actually been very easy.

'I'm not sure I'd trust you at that either,' he retorted, and went to let the doctor out. And then he brought her a glass of champagne, and sat watching her for a long moment with their new daughter. 'She's so beautiful, isn't she?' He stared at her, at her mother's breast, as he rolled slowly toward them.

'She is.' Sarah smiled, looking up at him. 'I love you, William. Thank you for everything . . .'

'Anytime.'

He leaned over and kissed her. They called the baby Isabelle. And in the morning, Julian announced that she was 'his' baby, entirely his, and they would all have to ask him if they could hold her. He held her all the time, with all the tenderness of a new father. He had all the emotions that Phillip never showed now, all the gentleness, all the love. He adored his baby sister. And as he grew, there was a bond between the two that no-one could tamper with. Isabelle adored Julian, and he remained her loving brother, and fiercest protector. Even their parents could never come between them, and in a very short time, they learned not to even try. Isabelle belonged to Julian, and vice versa.

Chapter 21

When Phillip graduated from Cambridge in the summer of 1962, no-one in the family was surprised when he announced that he wanted to go to work at Whitfield's, London. The only startling thing was that he announced to all of them that he was going to run it.

'I don't think so, darling,' Sarah said quietly. 'You have to learn the business first.' He had taken courses in economics, and gemology during the summertime, and he felt he knew everything he needed to know about Whitfield's.

'You're going to have to let Nigel show you the ropes at first.' William added his voice to hers, and Phillip was livid.

'I know more now than that dried-up old fruit will know in his entire lifetime,' he spat at them, and Sarah got very angry.

'I don't think so. And if you don't take a backseat to him, and treat him with the utmost respect, I won't let you work at Whitfield's at all, is that clear? With your attitude, Phillip, you will not be an asset to this business.' He was still furious with her after several days, but he agreed to work for Nigel. For a while at least, and then he wanted to review the situation.

'That's ridiculous,' Sarah stormed afterwards. 'He's a twenty-two-year-old boy, almost twenty-three, all right, but how dare he think he knows more than Nigel? He should kiss the ground he walks on.'

'Phillip has never kissed anything,' William said truthfully, 'except if it got him what he wanted. He sees Nigel as no use to him. I'm afraid Nigel is going to have a hard time with Phillip.' They warned Nigel, before Phillip started working there in July, that he had full control, and that if he felt that their son was unmanageable, he had their permission to fire him. He was deeply appreciative of their vote of confidence for him.

His relationship with Phillip was certainly tenuous over the next year, and there were moments when he would have gladly killed him. But he had to admit that the boy's business sense was excellent, some of his ideas good, and although he didn't think much of him as a human being, he thought that in the long run he would be very good for the business. He lacked the imagination and the sense of design that his mother had, but he had all his father's business acumen, he had already shown that in helping him to run Whitfield.

William's health in the past six or seven years had been anything but good. He had developed rheumatoid arthritis where all his old wounds were, and Sarah had taken him to every specialist she could. But there was very little they could do for him. He had suffered so much, and been tortured for so long, that there was very little they could do now. William was brave about it. But he looked ten years older on his sixtieth birthday in 1963, and Sarah was worried. Isabelle was seven years old by then, and she was a little fireball. She had dark hair like Sarah, and the same green eyes, but she had a mind of her own, and a disposition that defied any possible contradiction. What Isabelle wanted was law, as far as she was concerned, and no-one was going to tell her anything different. The only one who was ever able to change her mind about anything was her brother Julian, who adored her. And she loved him with the same unqualified passion, too, but she still did exactly what she wanted.

Julian was thirteen, and he still had the same easygoing disposition he had had as a baby. Whatever Isabelle did, to him, or anyone else, it amused him. When she pulled his hair, when she screamed at him, when she took the things he held most precious and broke them in a temper, he kissed her, he calmed her, he told her how much he loved her, and eventually she calmed down again. Sarah always marvelled at his patience. There were times when Sarah herself thought she might strangle her daughter. She was beautiful, and enchanting at times. But she was most emphatically not an easy person.

'What did I do to deserve all this?' she asked William more than once. 'What did I ever do to get such difficult children?' Phillip had been a thorn in her side for years, and Isabelle made her furious sometimes. But Julian made everything better for everyone, he spread the balm that soothed everyone's ruffled feathers, he loved and he kissed, and he cared, and he did all the right things. He was just like William.

Their businesses were still prospering. Sarah kept busy with both of them, and somehow she managed to be with her children, too, while working on jewelry designs, and combing the market for fine stones, and still buying occasional rare and very important antique pieces. They had become the Queen's favorite jeweler by then, and that of many illustrious people in both cities. And it amused her how Julian studied her sketches now, and made little changes here and there, suggestions that actually worked very well. And from time to time, he designed an original piece, completely different from her style, and yet really lovely. Recently, she had had one of his designs made, and wore it, and Julian had been absolutely thrilled. As much as Phillip had no interest in design, and concentrated on the business side of what they did, Julian had a real passion for jewelry. They might make an interesting combination one day, William often said; if they didn't kill each other first, Sarah added. And she had no idea where Isabelle would fit into the plan, except that she would have to have a very rich, tolerant husband, who would let her spend part of every day throwing tantrums. Sarah always tried to be firm with her, and tried to explain to her why she couldn't do everything she wanted, but it was always Julian who finally made sense to her, who got her to calm down and listen.

'How is it possible I only have one reasonable child?' Sarah complained to William one afternoon in late November.

'Maybe it was some vitamin you were missing during pregnancy,' he teased, as she flipped on the radio in the kitchen at the château. They had just come back from seeing another doctor for him in Paris. He suggested a warm climate, and a lot of tender loving care, and she was about to suggest a trip to the Caribbean, or maybe even to California to see her sister.

But they were both startled when they heard the news. President Kennedy had been shot. And as they listened, and followed the news for the next few days, like the rest of the world, they found it deeply depressing. It all seemed so incredible, and that poor woman with her two little children. Sarah cried for them as they watched the news later on, on the television, and they marvelled at a world that could do a thing like that. But they had seen worse in their lifetime, the war, the tortures in the concentration camps . . . but still, they mourned the loss of this one man, and it seemed to cast a pall on both of them, and the world, almost until Christmas.

They went to visit the shop in London during the holidays, to see how Phillip was doing there, and they were pleased that he was getting along with Nigel. He was smart enough to have learned how valuable Nigel was to them, and now he argued with him less, and seemed to have made his own niche at Whitfield's. He wasn't exactly running it yet, but he was getting there. And their Christmas figures were beyond excellent, just as they were in Paris.

And then finally, in February, Sarah and William took the trip they had planned. They went away for a month, to the South of France. It was cool at first, but they went on to Morocco from there, and came back via Spain to see friends, and everywhere they went Sarah teased William about opening a Whitfield's. She was worried about him most of the time. He looked so tired, and so pale, and he was so often in so much pain now. And two weeks after they got back, in spite of their pleasant holiday, William was feeling tired and weak, and absolutely terrified Sarah.

They were at the château when he had a mild heart attack. He had said he wasn't feeling well after dinner, a little mild indigestion, he thought, and then he started having chest pains, and Sarah called the doctor. He came from the hospital at once, far more quickly than he had when Isabelle was born, but by then William was feeling a little better. And when they checked him the next day, they said it had been a small heart attack, as the doctor said, 'a kind of warning'. He explained to Sarah that William had been through so much during the war, that it had strained his entire system. And that the pain he was experiencing now only served to strain it further.

He said that William had to be very, very careful, lead a quiet life and take very good care of himself. Without hesitating, she agreed, although William didn't.

'What nonsense! You don't suppose I survived all that in order to spend the rest of my life sitting in a corner, under a blanket. For heaven's sake, Sarah, it was nothing. People have heart attacks like that all the time.'

'Well, you don't. And I'm not going to let you wear yourself out. I need you around for the next forty years, so you'd damn well better settle down and listen to the doctor.'

'Balls!' he said, looking annoyed, and she laughed at him, relieved that he was feeling better, but she wasn't going to let him overdo it. She made him stay home all though April after that, and she was so worried about him most of the time, it actually made her feel sick. She was also sick about Phillip's behavior to his father. The other two children had doted on him, and Isabelle absolutely adored him. She sat with him every day after school, and read to him, and Julian did everything he could to entertain him. Phillip had flown over from England to see him once, and only called once after that. According to the newspapers, he was much too busy chasing debutantes to be bothered with his father.

'He is the most selfish human being I know,' Sarah railed about him to Emanuelle, who always defended him. She had loved him so much as a child that she saw his faults less clearly than everyone else did. Nigel could certainly have catalogued a few of them, but nonetheless he seemed to have worked out a relationship of sorts with him, and the two worked very well together. Sarah was grateful for that, but she was still upset about his lack of attention to his father. And when he had come, he had looked at her in dismay, and told her that she looked worse than he did.

'You're looking dreadful, Mother dear,' Phillip said coolly.

'Thank you.' Sarah was really hurt by his comment.

Emanuelle told her the same thing, the next time she came to Paris. She was practically green, she was so pale. It really worried Emanuelle to see her. But William's heart attack had really frightened her. The one thing she knew in her life was that she couldn't live without him.

By June, outwardly anyway, everything seemed to be back to normal. William was still in pain, of course, but he was resigned to it, and he seldom complained, and he seemed healthier than he had been before what he referred to as 'his little problem'.

But Sarah's problems seemed larger these days. It was one of those times when nothing went right and you never felt well. She had backaches, and stomachaches, and for the first time in her life terrible headaches. It was one of those times when the stress of the past months caught up with her with a vengeance.

'You need a vacation,' Emanuelle said to her. And what she really wanted to do was go to Brazil and Colombia and look at emeralds, but she didn't think William was well enough to do it. Nor did she want to leave him.

She mentioned it to him the next afternoon and he sounded noncommittal. He didn't like the way she looked, and he thought it was too much of a trip for her too. 'Why don't we go to Italy instead? We can buy someone else's jewelry for a change.' She laughed, but she had to admit, she liked the suggestion. She needed a fresh start these days, she had been depressed lately anyway. Her change of life had come, and it made her feel old and unattractive. The trip to Italy made her feel young again and they had a wonderful time remembering when he proposed to her in Venice. It all seemed so long ago. Life had been good to them, for the most part, and the years had flown. Her parents were long gone, her sister had moved on to a new life, and Sarah had heard years before that Freddie had been killed in a car accident in Palm Beach, after he got back from the Pacific. It was all part of another life, a life of closed chapters. For years now William had been her whole life. William . . . and the children . . . and the stores . . . She felt renewed when she returned from the trip, but annoyed at the weight she'd put on after two weeks of eating pasta.

She continued to gain weight for another month, and she wanted to go to the doctor about it, but she never seemed to find time, and she felt well otherwise, a lot better than she had two months before, but suddenly as she lay in bed with William one night, she felt a strange but familiar feeling.

'What was that?' she asked him, as though he might have felt it.

'What was what?'

'Something moved.'

'I did.'

And then he turned over and smiled at her. 'What are you so nervous about tonight? I thought we took care of that this morning.' At least that hadn't changed, even though she had. She was feeling better about things now. Thanks to William, the time in Italy had been incredibly romantic.

She didn't say anything more to him, but she went to see the doctor in La Marolle immediately the next morning. She described her symptoms to him, all of them, and the fact that she had been certain she'd gone through the change of life four months before, and then she described the sensation she'd had the night before as she lay beside William.

'I know this sounds crazy,' she explained, 'but it felt . . . it felt like a baby . . .' She felt like one of those old men with amputated legs who think they feel their knee itch.

'It's not impossible. I delivered a baby last week to a woman fifty-six years old. Her eighteenth child,' he said encouragingly and Sarah groaned at the prospect. She loved the children that she had, handful that they were, and there was a time when she would have wanted more, but that time was no longer. She was about to be forty-eight years old, and William needed her, she was just too old to have another baby. Isabelle was turning eight that summer, and she was her baby.

'Madame la Duchesse,' the doctor said formally as he stood up to look at her after his examination, 'I have the pleasure of informing you that you are indeed having a baby.' For a moment, he had even thought it might be twins, but now he was sure it wasn't. It was only one, but a good-sized one. 'I think perhaps at Christmas.

'You're not serious.' She looked shocked and for a moment she went pale and felt dizzy.

359

'I am very serious, and very sure.' He smiled at her. 'Monsieur le Duc will be very pleased, I'm sure.' But she wasn't even sure of that this time. Maybe after his heart attack he would feel differently. She couldn't even imagine it now. She would be forty-eight years old when this child was born, and he would be sixty-one. How ridiculous. And suddenly, she knew with absolute certainty, that she couldn't have this baby.

She thanked the doctor and drove back to the château, thinking of what she was going to do about it, and what she was going to tell William. The whole thing depressed her profoundly, even more than thinking she was going through the change of life had done. This was ridiculous. It was wrong at their age. She couldn't do this again. And she suspected that he'd probably feel the same way. It might not even be normal, she was so old, she told herself. For the first time in her entire life, she considered an abortion.

She told William after dinner that night, and he listened quietly to all her objections. He reminded her that his parents had been exactly the same age when he was born and it hadn't done him or them any harm, but he also understood how upset Sarah was. More than anything she was startled. She had had four children in her life, one had died, one had come as a late surprise . . . and now this, so unexpected, so late, and yet in his eyes so great a gift, at any time, he didn't see how they could refuse it. But he heard her out, and he lay next to her that night and held her. He was a little shocked by how she felt, but he wondered, too, if she was just frightened. She had been through a lot before, and perhaps now it would be even harder.

'Do you really not want this child?' he asked sadly, as he lay next to her that night, holding her in his arms as he always did when they went to sleep. He was sad that she didn't seem to want it, but he didn't want to press her.

'Do you?' She answered his question with one of her own, because there was a part of her that wasn't sure either.

'I want whatever is right for you, my love. I'll stand by whatever you decide.'

Hearing him say that brought tears to her eyes, he was always so good to her, so there for her, it made him even more precious. 'I don't know what to do . . . what's right . . . part of me wants it . . . and part of me doesn't . . .'

'You felt that way the last time too,' he reminded her.

'Yes, but I was forty then . . . now I'm two hundred.' He laughed gently at her, and she smiled through her tears. 'It's all your fault. You're really a menace to the neighborhood,' she said, and he laughed. 'It's a wonder they even let you walk the streets.' But he loved hearing it, and she knew it. The next day they took a long walk around the grounds, and inadvertently they reached Lizzie's grave, and they stopped, and she swept some of the leaves away. She knelt for a moment, tidying things, and then suddenly she felt him very near her. She looked up and William was looking down at her sadly.

'After that . . . can we really take a life, Sarah? . . . Do we have a right to?' Suddenly she remembered the feel of Lizzie in her arms again, twenty years later . . . the child that God had taken away from them and now He was giving her another. Did she have a right to question the gift? And after almost losing William, who was she to decide who lived or died? Suddenly, with a wave of feeling, she knew what she wanted, and she melted into his arms and began to cry, for Lizzie, for him, for herself, for the baby she might have killed . . . except deep down, she knew she couldn't. 'I'm so sorry . . . I'm so sorry, darling . . .'

'Shhh . . . it's all right . . . everything is all right now.' They sat together for a long time, talking about Lizzie, and how sweet she had been, this new child, and the children they had, and how blessed they were. And then they went slowly back to the château, she beside him and he in his wheelchair. They felt strangely at peace, and filled with hope for the future.

'When did you say it was again?' he asked, feeling very proud suddenly, and very pleased, as he smiled at Sarah.

'The doctor said Christmas.'

'Good,' he said happily. And then he chuckled. 'I can hardly wait to tell Phillip.' They both laughed and they went back to the château, laughing and talking and teasing, just as they had for twenty-five years now.

Chapter 22

This time Sarah stayed close to the château for most of her pregnancy, she could do her business from where she was, and she didn't want to make a spectacle of herself in London or Paris. No matter what William said about how old his parents were, she still felt self-conscious about being pregnant at her age, although she had to admit, she enjoyed it.

And predictably, Phillip was absolutely outraged when they told him. He said it was the most vulgar thing he'd ever heard, and his father laughed out loud at him. But the other children were both pleased. Julian genuinely thought it was wonderful news, and Isabelle could hardly wait to play with the baby, and neither could Sarah.

She designed a few pieces of special jewelry before Christmastime, and was very pleased with the way they were made, and Nigel and Phillip bought some excellent new stones, and she was extremely impressed with their choices.

And this time, she didn't argue with William about having the baby at home. They went to Paris, and she checked into the clinic in Neuilly two days before her due date. After her performance in ten minutes with Isabelle, William told her she was lucky he let her wait that long. She was extremely bored staying there, and she insisted she was twice the age of any of the other mothers. But in a funny way, it amused both of them, and William sat with her for hours and played cards, and talked about the business. Julian and Isabelle had stayed at the château with the servants. And it was already almost a week after Christmas.

On New Year's Day, Sarah and William drank champagne, she had been there for five days then, and she was so tired of it, she told him that if the baby didn't come the next day, she was going to Whitfield's. He wasn't even sure it would do her any harm, but her water broke that afternoon, and by that night, the pains were strong and she was looking very distracted. They had just come to wheel her away from him, when she reached out and took his hand, and looked at him. 'Thank you . . . for letting me have . . . this baby . . .' He wanted very much to stay with her, but the doctors had balked at that. It wasn't the policy of the hospital, and given Madame's age and the high risk involved, they thought it would be better if he waited elsewhere.

By midnight he hadn't heard anything, and by four in the morning, he was beginning to panic. She had been gone for six hours by then, which seemed odd after Isabelle had come so quickly, but each baby seemed to be very different.

He went to the desk and asked the nurse again if she'd heard anything, and he wished he could go to find Sarah and see for himself. But they told him there was no news, and they would let him know when his wife had had the baby.

And by seven o'clock in the morning when the doctor finally came, William was frantic. He had done everything he could think of to pass the time, including pray. And he suddenly wondered if he had been mad to let her have this baby. Maybe it was too much for her. What if it killed her?

The doctor looked serious as he entered the room, and William's heart sank when he saw him.

'Is something wrong?'

'No.' He shook his head firmly. 'Madame la Duchesse is

doing very well, as well as can be expected. You have a fine son, Monsieur. A very big boy, more than ten pounds. I'm afraid we had to perform a cesarean. Your wife tried very hard to deliver him, but she simply couldn't.' It was just like when Phillip had been born, and he remembered how awful it had been. The doctor had threatened her with a cesarean then. And she had managed to escape it, and have five children. And now, finally, at forty-eight, Sarah's baby days were over. It was a respectable career, William smiled in relief, and then looked at the doctor.

'Is she all right?'

'She's very tired . . . There will be some pain from the surgery . . . We will do what we can for her, of course . . . to make her comfortable. She can go home in a week or two.' He left the room, and William sat thinking about her then, about how much she meant to him, and the children she had borne . . . and now this baby.

It was later that afternoon when he finally saw her again, and she was half asleep, but she smiled at him, and she knew about the baby.

'It's a boy,' she whispered to him, and he nodded, and smiled, and kissed her. 'Is that all right?'

'It's wonderful,' he reassured her, and she drifted off to sleep again, and then she opened her eyes suddenly. 'Can we call him Xavier?' she asked.

'All right,' he agreed, and she had absolutely no recollection of it afterwards, but said she had always loved the name. They called him Xavier Albert, for his cousin the late king, Queen Elizabeth's father, whom William had always been very fond of.

She stayed at the hospital for a full three weeks, and they brought the baby home triumphantly, although William teased her mercilessly about not being able to have another baby. He told her it upset him terribly, and that he had hoped she would have their sixth child on her fiftieth birthday. 'We could adopt, of course,' he said on the way back to the château, and she threatened to divorce him.

The children were enchanted with Xavier, he was a huge, happy child with an easy disposition. Nothing seemed to bother him, and he liked everyone, but he still didn't have the magic of his brother Julian. What he had was an open, happy nature. But he seemed to have a mind of his own, although fortunately, not such an extreme one as his sister.

And by the following summer, Xavier was constantly being dragged everywhere by everyone. He was always being held or taken somewhere by Julian or Isabelle or his parents.

But Sarah was less focused on the baby than she would have liked to be. William wasn't well, and by the end of summer, he took up all her attention. His heart was giving him trouble again, and the doctor in La Marolle said he didn't like the way he looked. And his arthritis was rampant.

'It's such nonsense to be such a burden to you,' he complained to her, and when he could he took Xavier to bed with him, but the truth was that much of the time, he was in too much pain to enjoy him.

Christmas was sad and strained that year. Sarah hadn't been to Paris in two months, or to London since before the summer. But she just couldn't tend to her business then, and she had to trust Nigel and Phillip and Emanuelle to do it for her. All she wanted to do now was give William her full attention.

Julian spent every moment of his vacation with him. And Phillip even flew in from London on Christmas Eve, and they had a lovely dinner in the dining room, and even managed to go to church, although William wasn't well enough to join them. Phillip noticed that he seemed to have shrunk somehow, he looked frail and gaunt, yet the spirit was still there, the strength, the grace, the sense of humor. In his own way, he was a great man, and for a brief moment that day, Phillip saw it.

Emanuelle drove down from Paris on Christmas Day, and she didn't tell Sarah how shocked she was at the way William looked, but she cried all the way back to Paris.

Phillip left the next morning. And Julian was going skiing in Courchevel, but he hated to leave, and he told his mother that if she needed him, he would return immediately. All she had to do was call him. Isabelle went to spend the rest of her holiday with a friend in Lyon that she had met the previous summer. It was a big adventure for her, and the first time she'd been away from home for so long. But at nine, Sarah thought she was old enough to do it. She'd be back in a week, and maybe by then her father would be feeling better.

But he seemed to fail day by day. And on New Year's Day, he was too weak to celebrate Xavier's first birthday. They had a little cake for him, and Sarah sang happy birthday to him at lunch, and then she rushed back upstairs to be with William.

He had been sleeping most of the time for the past few days, but he opened his eyes when he heard her enter the room, no matter how quiet she tried to be. He just liked knowing she was somewhere near him. She thought about taking him to the hospital then, but the doctor said it would do no good, they could do nothing for him. The body that had been so battered twenty-five years before was finally wearing down, its parts broken beyond repair once and only pasted together for a time, and now that time was drawing to an end. But Sarah couldn't bear the thought of it. She knew how strong his spirit was, and that eventually he would recover.

The night of Xavier's birthday, she lay quietly next to William in their bed, and held him in her arms, and she felt him clinging to her, almost like a child, just the way

Lizzie had, and then she knew. She held him close to her, and covered him with blankets, and tried to give him all the love and strength she could. And just before dawn, he looked up at her, and kissed her lips, and sighed. She kissed him gently, on the face, as he took his last breath and died quietly in the arms of the wife who had loved him.

She sat there like that, holding him, for a long time, the tears pouring down her face. She never wanted to let him go, to live without him. For a long moment, she wanted to go with him, and then she heard Xavier wail in the distance, and knew she couldn't. It was almost as though he knew his father was gone. And what a terrible loss it was for him, for all of them.

Sarah laid him gently down, and kissed him again, and as the sun came up and long fingers of light crossed the room, she left him, and closed the door silently as she cried. The Duke of Whitfield was gone. And she was a widow.

Chapter 23

The funeral was somber and serious, in the church at La Marolle, as the local choir sang the 'Ave Maria', and Sarah sat beside her children. Close friends from Paris had come, but the principal memorial service was to be held in London five days later.

She buried him beside Lizzie at the Château de la Meuze, and she and Phillip had argued about it all night, because he said that for seven centuries the dukes of Whitfield had been buried at Whitfield. But she wouldn't agree to it. She wanted him there, with her, and their daughter, in the place he had loved, and where he had lived and worked with Sarah.

They filed silently out of the church, as she held Isabelle's hand, and Julian put an arm around her. Emanuelle had come down from Paris, and she walked out of the church on Phillip's arm. They were a small group, and Sarah served lunch at the château afterwards for everyone. The locals had come to pay their respects, too, and Sarah invited them in to lunch as well, those who had served him, and known him, and loved him. She couldn't even begin to imagine a life now without him.

She looked numb as she walked around the living room, offering people wine, or shaking their hands, or listening to their stories about Monsieur le Duc, but this had been his real life, the life they had built and shared, over twenty-six years. It was impossible to understand now that it was over.

Nigel had flown over from London too. And he cried as

they buried him, as Sarah did, and Julian held her in his arms as she cried. It was more than she could bear, seeing him there next to Lizzie. It seemed only yesterday that they had come here and talked about it . . . about her . . . and about having Xavier, who was such a joy to her now. But the tragedy was, he would never know his father. He would have two brothers to care for him, and a mother and sister who adored him, but he would never know the man William had been, and it broke her heart to know that.

Two days later they all travelled to London together for the memorial service. It was filled with pomp and ceremony. All of his relatives were there, and the Queen was, too, and her children. Afterwards they all drove to Whitfield, where they had four hundred people to tea. Sarah felt like an automaton as she shook hands with everyone, and she turned suddenly when she heard someone say behind her, 'Your Grace,' and heard a man's voice answer. For a crazed moment, she thought William had entered the room, but she gave a start when she saw that it was Phillip. And for the first time she realized that her son was the duke now.

It was a hard time for all of them, a time she would always remember. She didn't know where to go, or what to do to escape the anguish of what she felt. If she went to Whitfield, he would be there, and at the château even more so. If she stayed at the hotel in London, all she could do was think of him, and the apartment in Paris filled her with dread, they had been so happy there, and they had stayed at the Ritz on their honeymoon . . . there was nowhere to go, and nowhere to run to. He was everywhere, in her heart, in her soul, in her mind, and in each of them, whenever she looked at her children.

'What are you going to do?' Phillip asked her quietly as she sat at Whitfield one day, staring out the window. She had absolutely no idea at all, and suddenly she didn't give a damn about her business, she would have given it to him gladly. But he was only twenty-six years old, he still had a lot to learn, and Julian was only fifteen, even if one day he wanted to run the shop in Paris.

'I don't know,' she said honestly. He'd been gone for a month by then, and she still couldn't think straight. 'I keep trying to figure it out, and I can't. I don't know where to go, or what to do. I keep wondering what he would have wanted me to do.'

'I think he would have wanted you to go on,' Phillip said honestly, 'with everything . . . the business, I mean . . . and everything you used to do with him. You can't just stop living.' But there were times when she was tempted.

'Sometimes I'd like to.'

'I know, but you can't,' he said quietly. 'We all have an obligation.' And his were heavier than most now. He had inherited Whitfield, Julian would never have any share in it. He would in the château, which he would share with Isabelle and Xavier, but that was the injustice of the English system. And Phillip had the burden of the title on his shoulders now, too, and all that that carried with it. His father had worn it gracefully and well, and Sarah was not quite so sure about Phillip.

'What about you?' she asked him gently then. 'What are you going to do now?'

'The same things I've been doing,' he answered hesitantly, and then he decided to tell her something he hadn't yet. 'One of these days there's someone I'd like you to meet.' It seemed an odd time to tell her, which was why he hadn't. He had wanted to tell them about Cecily at Christmas, but his father had been so ill, he never mentioned it.

'Someone special?'

'More or less.' He blushed and answered vaguely.

'Maybe we could have dinner together, before I leave England.'

'I'd like that very much,' he said shyly. He was different

371

from the rest of the family, yet she was still his mother.

She reminded him of it again two weeks later, when she was thinking about going back to Paris. Emanuelle had had some problems with the shop, and Isabelle had to go back to school. She had kept her at Whitfield with her, although Julian had returned weeks before, to go back to school.

'What about the friend you wanted me to have dinner with?' she prodded gently, and he was vague.

'Oh that . . . you probably don't have time before you leave.'

'Yes, I do,' she contradicted him. 'I always have time for you. When would you like to do it?' He was sorry he had ever mentioned it, but she made him as comfortable as she could, as they made a date to go to the Connaught for dinner. And the girl she met there the following night didn't surprise her at all, she only wished she had. She was so typically English. She was tall and spare and pale, and she almost never spoke. She was extremely well-bred, and totally respectable and the most boring girl Sarah thought she had ever met. She was Lady Cecily Hawthorne. Her father was an important Cabinet minister, and she was a very nice girl, incredibly proper and well-bred, but Sarah couldn't help wondering how Phillip could stand her. She had absolutely no sex appeal, there was nothing warm and cozy about her, she was certainly not a person you could ever laugh with. And Sarah tried to mention that to him gently before she left the next morning.

'She's a lovely girl,' she said over breakfast.

'I'm glad you like her.' He seemed very pleased, and Sarah found herself wondering how serious this was and if she should worry. Here she had a baby in diapers on her hands, and now she had to worry about daughters-in-law, and William was gone. There was no justice in the world, she moaned to herself, as she tried to look casual to Phillip.

'Is it serious?' she asked, trying not to choke on a piece of toast when he nodded. 'Very serious?'

'It could be. She's certainly the kind of girl you'd want to marry.'

'I can see why you think that, dear,' she said, trying to sound calm to him, and wondering if he believed her. 'And she's a lovely girl . . . but is she enough fun? That's something to think about. Your father and I always had such a good time together. That's an important thing in a marriage.'

'Fun?' he said, with a look of astonishment. 'Fun? What difference could that possibly make? Mother, I don't understand you.'

'Phillip.' She decided to be honest with him, and hoped she wouldn't regret it. 'Good breeding isn't enough. You need something more . . . a little character, someone you want to jump in and out of bed with.' He was old enough to hear the truth from her, and it was 1966 after all, not 1923. Young people were going to San Francisco and wearing bedspreads and flowers in their hair, surely he couldn't be that stuffy. But the amazing thing was that he was. He seemed appalled as he looked at his mother.

'Well, I can certainly see you and Father did a lot of that, but that doesn't mean I intend to choose my wife by those standards.' She knew at that exact moment that if he married this girl, he would be making a terrible mistake, but she also knew that if she told him that, he'd never believe her.

'Do you still believe in a double standard, Phillip? That you play with one kind of girl, and marry another? Or do you really like the serious, well-bred ones? Because if you like playing with the sexy, fun ones, and you marry a proper one, you could be in for a lot of trouble.' It was the best she could do under the circumstances, but she could see he got it.

'I have my position to think of,' he said, sounding very annoyed with her.

'So did your father, Phillip. And he married me. And I don't think he regretted it. At least, I hope not.' She smiled sadly at her eldest son, feeling as though he were a total stranger.

'You were from a perfectly good family, even if you were divorced.' She had told them all long ago, so no-one else would. 'I take it you don't like Cecily then?' he asked icily, as he stood up and prepared to leave the table.

'I like her very much. I just think that if you're thinking about marrying her, you need to think seriously about what you want in a wife. She's a very nice girl, but she's very serious, and not very outgoing.' Sarah had always known he had a passion for racier girls 'on the side', from tales she'd heard in London and Paris. He liked to be seen and photographed with the 'right' kind of girls, but at the same time, he enjoyed the others. And there was no doubt that Cecily was one of the 'right' ones. But she was also a very dull one.

'She'd make an excellent Duchess of Whitfield,' Phillip said austerely.

'I suppose that's important. But is it enough?' she felt compelled to ask him.

'I think I'm the best judge of that,' he said, and she nodded, hoping he was right, but convinced that he wasn't.

'I only want what's best for you,' she told him as she kissed him, and he went into the city then, and she went back to Paris that afternoon with her two younger children. She took them back to the château, and left them with Julian, and then she went back to Paris for a few days to attend to business, but her heart wasn't in it anymore, and all she wanted to do was go back to the château and visit his grave, which Emanuelle told her was morbid.

It took her a long time to feel like herself again, and it

was only that summer that she felt halfway normal. And then Phillip announced to them that he was marrying Cecily Hawthorne. Sarah was sorry for him, but she would never have said so. They were going to live in his London flat, and spend a great deal of time at Whitfield. She would keep her horses there, but Phillip assured his mother that she could use the hunting box whenever she wanted. He and Cecily were taking over the main house, of course. He never even mentioned the other children.

Sarah didn't have to make any wedding plans. The Hawthornes did all that, and the wedding was held at their family seat in Staffordshire. The Whitfields arrived en masse, and Sarah took Julian's arm. It was a Christmas wedding, and she had worn a beige wool Chanel suit for the wedding breakfast.

Isabelle was wearing a sweet white velvet dress, with a matching coat trimmed in ermine, and Xavier was wearing a little black velvet suit from La Châteleine in Paris. Julian looked incredibly handsome in his morning coat, as did Phillip. And the bride looked very nice in her grand-mother's lace dress. She was a little too tall for it, and the veil sat oddly on her head, and if Sarah had had someone to gossip with, like Emanuelle, who hadn't come, she would have admitted that she looked awful, like a great dry stick of a girl, with no charm and no sex appeal whatsoever. She hadn't even bothered to wear makeup. But Phillip seemed very pleased with her. The wedding was the week before Christmas, and they were spending their honeymoon in the Bahamas.

Sarah couldn't help wondering what William would have thought of them. It depressed her as she went back to Claridge's that night, that she didn't like the first daughter-in-law she had, and she suddenly wondered if she'd have any better luck with the others.

It was an odd life. These children, who did such strange things. Who led their own lives, in their own way, with people who appealed to no-one but themselves. It made her even lonelier for William as they flew back to Paris, and drove to the château. It was the first Christmas they'd spent without him . . . a year since he'd died . . . and Xavier would be two years old on New Year's Day. Her mind was full of memories as they drove home. But as she pulled up slowly in front of the château at dusk, she saw a man standing there, who looked so familiar to her and yet so different. She wondered if she was dreaming, as she stared at him. But she wasn't. It was he . . . and for a moment he looked as though he had barely changed. He walked slowly toward her with a gentle smile, and she could only stare at him . . . It was Joachim.

Chapter 24

As Sarah stepped out of the Rolls in front of the château, she looked as though she had seen a ghost, and in some ways, she had. It had been almost twenty-three years since she'd seen him. Twenty-three years since he'd kissed her goodbye, and taken his troops back to Germany. She had never heard from him again, or known if he had lived or died, but she had thought of him often, particularly when she thought of Lizzie.

She stepped slowly out of the car, and he looked at her long and hard. She had changed very little. She was still a beauty. She looked more dignified now, her hair was only a little gray. She had turned fifty that year, but looking at her, it was hard to believe it.

'Who is that?' Julian whispered. The man looked very strange. He was thin and old and he was staring at their mother.

'It's all right, darling. He's an old friend. Take the children inside.' He picked Xavier up, and took Isabelle with him, and they went into the château, looking over their shoulders, as Sarah slowly approached him. 'Joachim?' she whispered, as he came slowly toward her with the smile she knew so well. 'What are you doing here?' He had waited so long to come. And why now? There was so much to tell him, and to ask him.

'Hello, Sarah,' he said quietly, taking her hands in his own. 'It's been a long time . . . but you look very well.' She looked much more than well. Just seeing her again made his heart beat faster.

'Thank you.' She knew he was sixty years old then, but the years hadn't been kind to him. Yet they had been kinder to him than to William. He was still alive, and William was gone now. 'Would you like to come inside? We've just come back from England,' she explained, sounding suddenly like a hostess with a long-expected houseguest, 'from Phillip's wedding.' She smiled, their eyes still searching each other beyond what she was saying.

'Phillip? Married?'

'He's twenty-seven now,' she reminded him, as he opened the door for her, and he followed her in. They were both suddenly painfully aware that he had once lived here.

'And you have had other children?'

'Three,' she nodded, and then she smiled. 'One very recently, Xavier will be two next week.'

'You have a baby?' He looked visibly startled and she laughed.

'You don't look nearly as surprised as I did. William was quite a good sport about it.' She didn't want to tell him William had died, not yet at least. And then she realized that Joachim didn't know William had ever returned. There was so much she had to tell him.

She invited him to sit down in the main salon, and he looked at the room, so full of memories for him. But looking at her was even more remarkable, and he couldn't stop himself from staring. It stunned him to realize that if he had come the day before, she might still have been in England.

'What brings you here now, Joachim?'

He wanted to say 'you', but he didn't. 'I have a brother in Paris. I came to see him for Christmas. We are both alone, and he asked me to come.' And then, 'I have wanted to see you for a long time, Sarah.'

'You never wrote to me,' she said softly, and she hadn't written to him. But looking back now, she wasn't sure she would have, even if she had known where to find him. Perhaps once, but it would have seemed unfair to William.

'Things were very difficult right after the war,' he explained. 'Berlin was a madhouse for a long time, and when I was able to make my way back this way, I read in the newspapers of the remarkable survival of the Duke of Whitfield. I was very happy for you then, I knew how much you had wanted him to return. I didn't think it was appropriate for me to write to you after that, or to come to see you. I thought about it sometimes. I was in France several times over the years, but it didn't seem right, so I never came to see you.' She nodded. She understood only too well. In some ways, it would have been very strange to see him. There was no denying what they had both felt for each other then. They had managed to keep it in check, fortunately, but one couldn't pretend that the feelings hadn't existed.

'William died last year,' she told him sorrowfully. 'Or actually, this year, on January second.' Her eyes told him how lonely she was without him. And again, he couldn't pretend ignorance. It was why he had finally come now. He had never wanted to interfere with her life with him, knowing how much she loved her husband, but now that he knew he was gone, he had to come, to satisfy the dream of a lifetime.

'I know. I also read that in the paper.'

She nodded, still not understanding why he had come, but nonetheless happy to see him. 'Did you remarry eventually?'

He shook his head. 'Never.' She had haunted him for more than twenty years, and he had never met another woman like her.

'I'm in the jewelry business now, you know.' She looked amused, and he raised an eyebrow.

'Are you?' This time he seemed genuinely surprised. 'That's something new, isn't it?'

'Not any more. It was after the war.' She told him about all the people who had come to them to sell their jewelry and how the business had grown after that. She told him about the Paris store, and Emanuelle running it, and about the store in London.

'That sounds quite amazing. I'll have to go and see Emanuelle when I'm in Paris.' And then, as he said it, he thought better of it. He knew she had never really liked him. 'I imagine the prices are a little rich for my blood. We lost everything,' he said matter-of-factly. 'All of our land is in the East now.'

She felt sorry for him. There was something desperately sad about this man. There was something beaten and terribly lonely about him. She offered him a glass of wine, and went in to check on the children. Isabelle and Xavier were having dinner in the kitchen with the serving girl, and Julian had gone upstairs to call his girlfriend. She wanted to introduce them to Joachim, but she wanted to talk to him for a while first. She had the odd feeling that there was a reason why he had come to see her.

She went back into the living room to see him again, and when she did, he was looking over the books. And after a moment she saw that he had found the book he had given her, twenty years before, for Christmas. 'You still have it.' He looked pleased, and she smiled at him. 'I still have your photograph, on my desk, in Germany.' But that seemed sad to her too. It was so long ago. There should have been someone else on his desk by now, and not Sarah.

'I have yours too. It's put away.' But his photograph had had no place in her life with William, and Joachim knew that. 'What do you do now?' He looked distinguished, and not poor, but he didn't look either as though he had a great deal of money.

'I am a professor of English literature at the University of Heidelberg.' He smiled, as they both remembered long conversations about Keats and Shelley.

'I'm sure you're very good at it.'

He set down his wineglass then and moved closer to her.

'Perhaps it's wrong of me to have come, Sarah, but I have thought of you so often. It seems only yesterday since I left here.' But the truth was, it wasn't yesterday, it was a lifetime. 'I had to see you again . . . to know if you remember, too, if it means as much to you still, as it did to both of us then.' It was a lot to ask, and her life had been so full, and apparently his so empty.

'It's been a long time, Joachim . . . I have always remembered you.' She had to be honest with him. 'And I loved you then. I did, and perhaps if things had been different, if I hadn't been married to William . . . but I was . . . and he came home. And I loved him very much. I can't imagine loving another man again, ever.'

'Even one you had loved before?' His eyes were filled with hope and lost dreams, but she couldn't give him the answer he wanted.

She shook her head sadly. 'Even you, Joachim. I couldn't then, and I can't now . . . I am married to William forever.'

'But he is gone now,' he said gently, wondering if he had merely come too early.

'Not in my heart, just as he wasn't then. I was grateful then, and I am now . . . I can't be any different, Joachim.'

'I'm sorry,' he said, looking like a broken man.

'So am I,' she said softly.

The children came in to them then. Isabelle looked adorable as she curtsied to him, and Xavier raced around the room, happily destroying whatever he could, and eventually Julian came down, too, to ask if he could go out with friends, and she introduced him to Joachim.

'You have a beautiful family,' he said when they left again. 'The little one looks a little like Phillip.' Phillip had been just that age during the Occupation, and she could

381

see his fondness for her son in his eyes . . . and for Lizzie
. . . She knew he was thinking of her then, too, and she
nodded. 'I think of her sometimes, too . . . in some ways,
she was like our baby.'

'I know.' And William had thought so too. He had told
her that he'd been jealous of Joachim, because he had
known Elizabeth, and he hadn't. 'She was so sweet . . .
Julian is a little bit like that. And Xavier once in a while
. . . Isabelle is her own person.'

'She looks it.' He smiled. 'And so are you, Sarah. I still
love you. I always shall. You are exactly as I thought you
might be now . . . except perhaps more beautiful . . . and
still as good. Perhaps I wish you were not quite so much
so.'

She laughed softly in answer. 'I'm sorry.'

'William was a very lucky man. I hope he knew it.'

'I think we both did. It was too short a time . . . I only
wish he'd had longer.'

'How was he after the war? The newspapers said his
survival was miraculous.'

'It was. He was very badly damaged, and he was
tortured.'

'They did terrible things,' he said, without hesitation.
'For a time, I was ashamed to say I was a German.'

'All you did was help your men while you were here.
The rest was done by other people. You have nothing to be
ashamed of.' She had loved him, and respected him, in
spite of their divergent positions.

'We should have all stopped it long before. The world
will never forgive us that we didn't, and they're not
wrong. The crimes were inhuman.' She couldn't disagree
with him, but at least they both knew that his conscience
was clear. He was a good man, and he had been an
honorable soldier.

Eventually, he stood up and looked around the room
again, as though wanting to remember every inch, every

detail, when he left her. 'I should go back to Paris now. My brother will be waiting.'

'Come back again,' she said as she walked him outside, but they both knew he wouldn't. She walked him slowly to his car, and when they reached it, he stopped and looked at her again. The hunger in his heart was etched in his eyes as he longed to touch her.

'I'm glad I came to see you again . . . I have wanted to for so long.' He smiled, and gently touched her cheek as he had once before, and she leaned forward and kissed him on the cheek, touched his face, and then slowly took a step backwards. It was like taking a last step from the past back to the present.

'Take care of yourself, Joachim . . .'

He hesitated for a long moment, and then nodded. He got back into his car, with a small salute, and she didn't see the tears in his eyes as he drove away. All she could see was his car . . . and the man he had once been. All she could think of were her memories of William. Joachim had left her life years before. He was gone. And there was no place for him any more. There hadn't been in years. And when she couldn't see the car any more, she turned and went back inside to her children.

Chapter 25

When Julian graduated from the Sorbonne with a degree in philosophy and *lettres* in 1972, Sarah was extremely proud of him. They all went to the ceremony, except Phillip, who was busy in London buying a famous collection of jewels, which included an important tiara. Emanuelle went to the graduation, looking very dignified in a dark-blue Givenchy suit, and a wonderful set of sapphires from Whitfield's. She had become an important woman by then. Her affair with the Minister of Finance had long since been an open secret. They had been together for several years, and he treated her with respect and affection. His wife had been very ill for years, his children were grown, and they weren't doing anyone any harm. They were discreet, he was very kind, and she truly loved him. He had bought her a beautiful apartment on the Avenue Foch several years before and she entertained with him, and people begged to be invited to their parties. All the most interesting people in Paris seemed to go there, and her position as the manager of Whitfield's was an object of fascination and great interest. She dressed impeccably, and her taste was glorious, as were the jewels she had carefully acquired herself over the years, as well as those he gave her.

Sarah was grateful that she was still working for her, particularly now that Julian was coming into the business. He had great taste and a wonderful sense of design, and a fine eye for extraordinary jewels, but there were many things he didn't know about running the business.

Emanuelle was no longer working on the floor selling, and hadn't been in a long time; she had an office upstairs, she was the *directrice générale*, and her office was directly across from Sarah's. They left their doors open sometimes, and shouted across the hall, like two girls in a dormitory doing homework. They had remained close friends, and only their friendship, her children, and her ever-increasing workload had helped Sarah survive William's death. It had been more than six years, and for Sarah, they had been brutally lonely.

Life wasn't the same without him, in countless major ways, and all the small ones. All the laughter they had shared, all the thoughtful little gestures, the smiles, the flowers, the deep understanding, the shared or even diametrically opposed points of view, his endless good judgment, and limitless wisdom, they were all gone now, and the ache she felt was almost physical, it was so painful.

The children had kept her busy over the years, Isabelle was sixteen, and Xavier seven. He was into everything, and Sarah often wondered if he was going to survive his childhood. Sarah found him on the roof of the château, or in caves he created near the stables, testing electric wires, and building things that looked as though they might easily kill him. But somehow he managed to get through it, and his energy and ingenuity intrigued her. He had a passion for rocks, too, and he always thought he had just found gold or silver or diamonds. The moment anything glimmered in the soil, he would pounce on it and proclaim he had found a bijou for Whitfield's.

Phillip had children of his own, a boy of five and a girl of three, Alexander and Christine, but Sarah admitted only to Emanuelle that they were so much like Cecily, they were of very little interest to her. They were sweet, but very wan and pale, and they were not very exciting, or very endearing. They were distant and shy, even with Sarah. Sarah brought Xavier to play with them at

Whitfield sometimes, but he was far more enterprising than they were, and always got into too much mischief, and it was obvious eventually that Phillip wasn't anxious to have him.

In fact, Phillip wasn't fond of any of his brothers or his sister, nor was he interested in them, except Julian, whom Sarah sometimes feared Phillip hated.

He was unreasonably jealous of him, so much so that she worried that with Julian entering the business, Phillip might do something to hurt him. She suspected that Emanuelle feared it, too, and she had already urged her to watch him. Phillip had once been her friend, her charge when she was young and her life had been less sophisticated than it was now, and in some ways she knew him even better than Sarah. She knew what viciousness he was capable of, what slights he feared, and what revenge he wrought when he thought someone had crossed him. In fact, it amazed Emanuelle that after all these years, Phillip was still getting on with Nigel. It was an unusual union between them, a marriage of convenience of sorts, but it was very obviously still working.

But Phillip hated how much Julian was loved, by his family, by his friends, even by his women. He took out the most attractive girls in town, they were always beautiful and fun and glamorous, and they adored him. Even before Phillip was married the women he took out were always a little bit sleezy. And Emanuelle knew he was still attracted to that kind of woman when his wife wasn't around. She had seen him in Paris with one of them once, and he had pretended she was his secretary and they were there on business. They were staying at the Plaza Athénée, and he borrowed some of their flashiest jewelry to let her wear for a few days, and he had asked Emanuelle if she would be good enough not to tell his mother. But the jewelry looked pale on her, she looked tired and used, and the ridiculously short clothes she wore were not even stylish. She just looked cheap, and Phillip didn't seem to notice. Sarah was sorry for him. It was obvious to her by then that he wasn't happy in his marriage.

But Phillip was not missed at Julian's graduation.

'So, my friend,' Emanuelle asked Julian as they all left the Sorbonne, 'how soon do you begin work? Tomorrow, *n'est-ce pas?*' He knew she was teasing, because she was coming to the party his mother was giving for him that night at the château, and all his friends were going to be there.

The boys were staying in the stables and the girls were sleeping in the main house and the cottage, and the additional guests were staying in local hotels. They were expecting about three hundred people. After the party, he was going to the Riviera for a few days, but he had promised his mother he would go to work on Monday.

'Monday, I promise.' He looked at Emanuelle with huge eyes that had already melted many hearts. He looked so much like his father. 'I swear . . .' He held up a hand officially, and Emanuelle laughed. It would be fun to have him at Whitfield's. He was so handsome, women would buy anything from him. She just hoped he didn't buy for them. He was incredibly generous, as William had been, and terribly kindhearted.

Sarah had offered him her Paris flat, until he could find his own, and he was looking forward to staying there. She had just given him an Alfa Romeo as a graduation present, which would surely impress the girls. He offered to drive Emanuelle to the château in it that day, after they had lunch at the Relais at the Plaza, but she had promised to go with Sarah.

Isabelle rode down to the château with him instead, and he teased her about her long legs and her short skirts, as she piled into the car, looking more like twenty-five than sixteen.

And as Julian often said about her, she was trouble. She

flirted with all his friends, and had gone out with several of them. He was always amazed that his mother didn't take a stronger position with her. But ever since his father had died, she was softer with all of them. It was almost as though she didn't have the strength or the desire to fight them. Julian thought she let Xavier run wild, too, but all he ever did was set firecrackers off in the stables and frighten the horses, or chase the farm animals into the vineyards. Isabelle's misdeeds were far more discreet, and a lot more dangerous, if what his friend Jean-François said was true. She had driven him to a frenzy recently on a ski weekend in St Moritz, and then she had slammed the door in his face, a fact for which Julian was grateful, but he also knew that soon she wouldn't be slamming doors, she would be leaving them open.

'So,' he said, as they drove south on Route 20, toward Orléans. 'What's new with you, any new boyfriends?'

'No-one special.' She sounded very cool, which was unusual for her. Normally, she loved to brag to him about her latest conquests. But she was more secretive these days, and she was getting prettier by the hour. She looked like their mother, but in a more sultry, smoky way. Everything about her suggested passion and immediate gratification. And her underlying innocence only served to make the invitation more tempting.

'How's school?' She was still going to school in La Marolle, which he thought was a mistake. He thought she should go away to school, perhaps to a convent. At least he had been smart enough to be discreet when he was her age; he looked all innocence, and pretended to play tennis after school, while he was actually having an affair with one of his teachers. No-one had ever discovered them, but eventually she had gotten serious, and she had threatened to commit suicide when he finally left her, which really upset him. And after that it was the mother of one of his friends, but that had been complicated, too, and after that, he realized it was easier chasing virgins than dealing with the complications of older women. But they still intrigued him anyway. He was totally omnivorous when it came to women. He adored them all, old, young, beautiful, simple, intelligent, and sometimes even ugly. Isabelle accused him of having no taste, and his friends said he was always horny, which was true, but no great sin as far as Julian was concerned. He was, and happy to oblige at any moment.

'School is stupid and boring,' Isabelle answered him, looking petulant, 'but it's over for the summer, thank God.' And she was furious they weren't going anywhere till August. Her mother had promised her a trip to Capri, but she wanted to stay at the château until then. She had things to see about there, alterations they wanted to make on the Paris store, and repairs that needed to be made on the farm and the vineyards.

'It's so boring being here,' she complained, lighting a cigarette, taking a few puffs and tossing it out the window. He didn't think she really smoked, she was just trying to impress him.

'I used to love it at your age. There's so much to do, and Mother always lets you have friends to stay.'

'Not boys.' She glowered at him. She adored him, but sometimes he didn't understand anything, especially lately.

'Funny,' he teased her mercilessly, 'she always let me have boys over.'

'Very funny.'

'Thank you. Well, at least it won't be boring tonight, my dear. But you'd better behave yourself, or I'll spank you.'

'Thanks a lot.' She closed her eyes and slid down in the seat of his Alfa Romeo. 'I like your car, by the way.' She smiled at him. Sometimes she really liked him.

'So do I. It was nice of Mother to do that.'

'Yeah, she'll probably make me wait till I'm ninety.' Isabelle thought her mother was unreasonable with her.

But anyone who stood in the way of what she wanted, in her eyes, was a monster.

'Maybe you'll have passed your driver's license by then.'

'Oh, shut up.' There was a joke in the family about what a terrible driver she was. She had already damaged two of the old junk heaps at the château, and she claimed it was because they were so impossible to drive, and it had nothing to do with her driving. But Julian knew better, and he wouldn't have let her touch the steering wheel on his precious Alfa Romeo.

They reached the château long before his guests, and Julian went for a quick swim, and then went to see if he could help his mother. She had hired a local caterer and there were long buffet tables everywhere, several bars, and a canopy over an enormous dance floor. There were two bands, a local one, and a big fancy one from Paris. Julian was thrilled and touched that his mother was giving him such a fabulous party.

'Thank you, Maman,' he said, and put an arm around her, still wet from his swim. He stood tall and handsome beside her, dripping wet in his swim trunks. Emanuelle was standing next to her, and she pretended to swoon when she saw him.

'Cover yourself, my dear. I'm not at all sure I can handle having you at the office.' And neither would anyone else. She made a mental note to watch her girls. She wasn't at all sure that Julian wouldn't take them off to his apartment after lunch. She knew he had a bit of a naughty reputation. 'We're going to have to do something very imaginative at work to make you look ugly.' But the truth was that it couldn't be done, he oozed charm and sex appeal. As restrained and repressed as his brother was, Julian was everything he wasn't.

'You should get dressed before your guests arrive.' His mother smiled at him.

'Or perhaps not,' Emanuelle whispered. She always enjoyed an attractive body and enjoyed teasing him a little bit. It was harmless after all, she was an old friend, and he was just a child to her. She had just turned fifty.

Julian was back downstairs long before the guests, having spent half an hour with Xavier while he was getting dressed explaining to him about cowboys in the Wild West. For some reason Xavier was obsessed with Davy Crockett. He was fascinated by American things, and had told someone in school that he was really from New York, and only in France for a year while his parents did business.

'Well, my mother *is!*' He had defended himself afterwards. He wanted to be American more than anything. Having never known his father, and seeing very little of Phillip these days, he seemed to feel no kinship whatsoever with the British. And while Julian was clearly French, Xavier found it far more exciting to pretend he was from New York, or Chicago, or even California. And he talked constantly about his Aunt Jane and the cousins he didn't even know, which amused Sarah. She often spoke English to him, and he spoke it very well, as did Julian, but nonetheless with a French accent. Julian's English was better than his, but still one could tell that he was French, unlike Phillip, who sounded so relentlessly British. And Isabelle didn't care where she was from, as long as it was somewhere far removed from all her relations. She wanted to be separate from all of them, so she could do exactly what she wanted.

'I want you to be a good boy tonight,' Julian warned Xavier as he went to join his friends. 'No wild tricks, no getting hurt. I want to have fun at my party. Why don't you go watch TV?'

'I can't,' he said matter-of-factly. 'I don't have one.'

'You can watch the one in my room.' Julian smiled at him, impossible as he was, he really loved him. Julian had been like a father to him, and he really enjoyed being with him. 'I think there's a soccer game on.'

'Great!' He shouted as he headed back to his brother's room, humming Davy Crockett.

Julian was still smiling to himself when he ran into Isabelle on the stairs. She was wearing a white, almost see-through dress that barely reached her crotch and covered her stomach with chain mail.

'Cardin?' he asked, trying to sound cool.

'Courrèges,' she corrected, looking arch and far more dangerous than she knew. She was walking trouble.

'I'm learning.'

But so was Sarah. When she saw her, she sent her back upstairs to put something else on. And Isabelle slammed every door in the house on the way, as Emanuelle watched her, and Sarah sighed and helped herself to a glass of champagne.

'That child is going to kill me. And if she doesn't, Xavier will.'

'You said that about the others too.' Emanuelle reminded her.

'I did not,' Sarah corrected. 'Phillip disappointed me because he was so distant and so cool, and Julian worried me because he slept with the mothers of all his friends and thought I didn't know. But Isabelle is an entirely different creature. She refuses to be controlled, or to behave herself or listen to reason.' Emanuelle couldn't disagree with her. She would have hated to be the girl's mother. Seeing Isabelle always made her grateful she had never had children. Xavier was another story though, he was impossible but so warm and cuddly that you couldn't resist him. He was like Julian, but freer and more adventuresome. They were an interesting bunch, the Whitfield crew. And none of them saw Isabelle emerge again in a zebra-striped leotard and a white leather skirt that was even worse than what she'd worn the first time.

392

But fortunately for her, this time Sarah didn't see her.

'Having fun?' Sarah asked Julian hours later when she saw him. He looked a little drunk, but she knew no harm would come to him. No-one was driving anywhere, and he had worked so hard to graduate from the Sorbonne. He deserved it.

'Maman, you're terrific! This is the best party I've ever been to.' He looked happy and dishevelled and hot. He'd been dancing for hours with two girls who were causing him to make an impossible decision. It was an evening filled with blissful dilemmas.

And for Isabelle too. She was stretched full-length in the bushes near the stables with a boy she had met that night. She knew he was a friend of Julian's and she couldn't remember his name. But he was the best kisser she had ever met, and he had just told her he loved her.

Eventually, one of the servants saw her there, and whispered something discreetly to the duchess, who suddenly appeared miraculously on the path to the stables, with Emanuelle, pretending to stroll along and enjoy a casual conversation. And when Isabelle heard her, she scurried away and the two women looked at each other and laughed, feeling both old and young at the same time. In August, Sarah was going to be fifty-six, although she didn't look it.

'Did you ever do things like that?' Emanuelle asked. 'I did.'

'You only did them with Germans during the war,' Sarah teased her and Emanuelle corrected her firmly.

'That was to get information from them,' she said proudly.

'It's a wonder you didn't get us all killed,' Sarah scolded her thirty years later.

'I would have liked to kill all of them,' she said with feeling.

Sarah told her then about Joachim turning up just after

Phillip's wedding. She had never told her that before, and Emanuelle was annoyed.

'I'm surprised he's still alive. A lot of them were killed when they went back to Berlin. He was pretty decent, as Nazis went, but a Nazi is a Nazi is a Nazi . . .'

'He looked so sad, and so old . . . and I guess I disappointed him bitterly. I think he thought he'd come back, with William gone, and everything would be different. But it could never have been.' Emanuelle nodded. She knew how much Sarah had loved William. She had never looked at another man since he died, and she didn't think she would again. She had tried discreetly to introduce her to a few friends after a few years had gone by, but it was obvious that she had no interest. She was only interested now in her business and her children.

The party ended at four a.m. with the last of the young people falling into the swimming pool as the bands left, and finally winding up in the château kitchen at dawn while Sarah cooked them scrambled eggs and served them coffee. It was fun having them there, she liked having them around, and lately she was glad that she had had some of her children so late in life. So many of her friends were lonely and alone, instead she would have them around her forever. They would drive her crazy probably, but those who knew her well, knew that she enjoyed it.

She went to her own room at eight o'clock, and smiled when she saw Xavier sleeping soundly on Julian's bed. The television was still on and there was nothing on the screen but snow, and a continuing recording of the 'Marseillaise'. She went in and turned it off, took off the Davy Crockett hat and smoothed his hair, and then she went to her own room and slept till noon.

Sarah and Emanuelle had lunch before she went back to Paris. They had a lot to talk about. They were expanding the Paris store again, and lately Nigel had been saying they should think of doing that in London. They still had their royal warrant, and were officially Jewelers to the Crown. In fact, in recent years, they had sold to many heads of state, several kings and queens, and scores of Arabs. Business was excellent, in both stores, and Sarah was excited about Julian coming into the business.

He started, as promised, the following week, and everything went smoothly until they closed in August. He went to Greece then with a bunch of friends, and she took Xavier and Isabelle to Capri. They loved it there. They loved the Marina Grande and the Marina Piccola, and the square, and going to the beach clubs like Canzone del Mare, or some of the more public ones. Isabelle had been studying Italian in school, and with a smattering of Spanish under her belt, too, she considered herself a great linguist.

They all had a good time, staying at the Quisisana, and eating ice cream in the square, and Sarah couldn't restrain herself from checking out the jewelry shops. She found the prices high, but some of their pieces very pretty. There wasn't much for her to do there, except eat and read and relax, and spend time with the children. And she felt there was no harm in letting Isabelle go down to the beach club by herself in one of the beach taxis everyone took. She met her there later in the morning with Xavier, who always wanted to visit the little donkeys.

And one morning, when Isabelle went on ahead, Sarah and Xavier stopped a little longer on their way to the square, to do some shopping. They reached the Canzone del Mare just in time for lunch, and Sarah looked everywhere for her daughter, but she couldn't find her. She was beginning to panic until Xavier found her sandals under a chair, and followed her trail into a little cabana. They found her there, with the top of her swimsuit off, with a man twice her age holding her breast, moaning, as she held the ominous bulge in his bikini.

For an instant, Sarah only stared, and then without

thinking she grabbed Isabelle by the arm and dragged her out of the cabana.

'What in God's name do you think you're doing in there?' She raged at her and Isabelle burst into tears, as the man emerged trying to regain his composure as he wrapped himself rather unsuccessfully in a towel. 'Do you realize my daughter is sixteen years old?' she said to him in a venomous voice, trying to keep control of herself with difficulty. 'I could call the police.' But she knew that the one she should give them was her daughter. She was only trying to frighten him so he didn't do it again, and she saw that she had hit her mark from his expression. He was a very attractive man, from Rome, and he looked like something of a playboy.

'*Signora, mi dispiace* . . . she said she was twenty-one. I am so sorry,' he apologized profusely and looked regretfully at Isabelle, sobbing hysterically as she stood next to her mother. They went back to the hotel, and Sarah suggested in icy tones that she spend the rest of the afternoon in her room, and then they would talk about it again. But as she went back to the beach with Xavier she knew she had to do more than talk now. Phillip and Julian were right. Isabelle needed to go away to school. But where? That was the question.

'What were they doing in there?' Xavier asked with curiosity as they passed the same cabana again, and Sarah shuddered at what she'd seen.

'Nothing, darling, they were playing silly games.'

She kept a short rein on Isabelle after that, and the rest of the holiday wasn't quite as much fun. But by the next day, Sarah had made several phone calls. She had found a wonderful school for her, near the Austrian border, close to Cortina. She could ski all winter there, speak both Italian and French, and learn to control herself a little better. It was an all-girl school, and there was no brother school nearby. Sarah had asked very clearly.

She told Isabelle about it on the last day of the vacation, and she went through the roof predictably, but Sarah stood her ground, even when Isabelle cried. It was for her own good. If she didn't do it, she knew that Isabelle was going to do something very stupid before too long, and maybe even get pregnant.

'I won't go!' she raged. She even called Julian at the shop in Paris. But he stood behind his mother this time. And after Capri, they went to Rome to buy her what she needed. The school term was starting in a few days, and there was no point taking her back to France to get into more trouble. Sarah and Xavier delivered her there, and she looked mournful as she saw the place. It was very pretty, and she had a big, sunny room of her own. The other girls looked very nice. They were French and English and German and Italian, two Brazilians, an Argentine girl, and one from Tehran. It was an interesting group, and there were only fifty girls in the school. Isabelle's school in La Marolle had given it the highest recommendation, and the headmaster had congratulated Sarah for her good judgment.

'I can't believe you're leaving me here,' she wailed, but Sarah couldn't be moved. They left her there, and Sarah herself cried all the way to the airport. And then she and Xavier flew to London to visit Phillip. After leaving her son with his nephew and niece for lunch, she went directly to the London store. Everything seemed fine. She had lunch with Phillip, and she was startled to hear him make several nasty remarks about his brother.

'What's that all about?' Sarah asked candidly. 'What's he done to get you so annoyed?'

'He and his damn stupid ideas about design. I don't understand why he has to meddle in that sort of thing,' he ranted on at her, and she answered quietly.

'Because I asked him to. He's very talented with design. Far more than you and I, and he understands important stones and what you can and can't do with them.' He had recently set a maharaja's emerald that had been over a hundred carats, and anyone else would have cracked it. But Julian understood exactly what to do with it, and had overseen every single moment it spent in the workroom.

'There's no harm in his doing that. You're good at other things,' Sarah reminded him. He was wonderful at dealing with the royals, and keeping them foremost in that market. Stuffy as he was, they loved him.

'I don't know why you defend him all the time,' Phillip said irritably.

'If it's any consolation, Phillip,' she said, refusing to rise to the bait, but disappointed at how jealous he still was. He was worse than ever. 'I always defend you too. I happen to love both of you.' He didn't answer her, but he looked slightly mollified as he asked about Isabelle, and told her he'd heard very good things about the school.

'Let's hope they work a miracle,' Sarah said softly.

And as they walked back to his office, she noticed a very pretty girl leaving the building. She had long, shapely legs, and wore a very short skirt, that looked like something Isabelle would wear, and she gave him a knowing glance that concealed very little. He looked furious with her while trying to pretend not to know her. The girl was new and had no idea that Sarah was his mother. Stupid bitch, he thought to himself, but in an instant, Sarah had seen the look that passed between them, although she didn't say anything to him. But he felt obliged to explain it to her, which made their situation even more obvious to Sarah.

'It doesn't matter, Phillip. You're thirty-three years old, what you do is your affair.' And then she decided to be brazen anyway. 'Where does Cecily stand these days?' He looked shocked and actually blushed at the question.

'I beg your pardon. She's the mother of my children.'

'Is that all?' Sarah eyed him coolly.

'Of course not, I . . . she . . . she's away at the moment.

For heaven's sake, Mother . . . that was just a joke, that girl flirting with me.'

'Darling, never mind.' But he was still obviously up to his old tricks, sleeping with tarts, the girls with whom he had 'fun', as he used to say, while being married to the other. She was sorry for him that he hadn't been able to find both in one, but he never complained to her, so she let the matter drop, and he was relieved.

And the next day, she and Xavier flew back to Paris, where Julian met them at the airport. On the short trip Sarah told her son about seeing the Crown Jewels in the Tower of London with his father when she first met him.

'Was he very strong?' Xavier asked, always fascinated to hear about his father.

'Very,' she assured him. 'And very good, and very smart and very loving. He was a wonderful man, sweetheart, and you'll be like him one day. You already are, in some ways.' And so was Julian.

They had dinner with Julian in Paris on the way home, and he was happy to see them and hear about Isabelle, and the store in London. She said nothing about her encounter with Phillip, or his comments about Julian. She didn't want to stoke the fires that already raged between them. Eventually Sarah drove back to the château with the car she had left in Paris. Xavier slept during the trip in the car, and she looked at him from time to time, asleep beside her, thinking how lucky she was to have him. While other women spent occasional Saturdays with their grandchildren at her age, she had this enchanting little boy to share her life with. She remembered how distressed she had been when she first found out she was pregnant, and how reassuring William had been . . . and her late mother-in-law, who had called William a great blessing. And so he had been to everyone who had known him for his entire life, and now this child was to her . . . her own very special blessing.

Chapter 26

Isabelle wrote to them as seldom as she could, and only when her preceptors forced her to, and she complained bitterly about the school when she did write. But the truth was, after the first few weeks, she loved it. She loved the sophistication of the girls she met there, the places they went, and she loved skiing in Cortina. She met even more interesting people there than she did in France, and although the school kept a short rein on her, she managed to make a lot of friends in the racier Roman set, and she was always getting letters and phone calls from men, which the school made every effort to discourage, but couldn't stop completely.

But by the end of her first year, Sarah saw a marked change in her, and Emanuelle saw it too. Isabelle wasn't necessarily better behaved, but she was a little more reasonable and a great deal more worldly. She had a better idea of what she could and couldn't do, and how to behave with men without giving them an open invitation. In some ways Sarah was relieved, and in others she was worried.

'She's a dangerous girl,' she said to Julian one day, and he couldn't disagree with her. 'She always reminds me of a bomb about to go off. But now it's a much more complicated one . . . maybe a Russian one . . . or a very delicate missile . . .'

Julian laughed at the description of his sister. 'I'm not sure you'll ever be able to change that.'

'Neither am I. That's what scares me,' his mother admitted. 'And what about you?' She had been waiting for weeks to see him. 'I hear you're doing a little business with one of our best customers.' They both knew who she meant, and he wondered if Emanuelle had told her. 'La Comtesse de Brise is a very interesting woman, Julian, and much more dangerous than your sister.'

'I know,' he confessed with a grin, 'she scares me to death, but I adore her.' The late comte had been her third husband in fifteen years, and she was thirty-four years old, and she devoured men. And all she wanted now was Julian. She had bought half a million dollars in jewels in the past month, and she could certainly afford to pay for them, but she was still coming back for more, and the biggest jewel she wanted was him, as her plaything.

'Do you think you can manage that?' she asked him honestly. She was afraid he might get hurt, but so was he, so he was careful.

'For a while. I play very carefully, Mother, I assure you.'

'Good.' She smiled at him. They were a busy lot, all of them, with their mischief and their mates, and their affairs. She only hoped Isabelle would make it through the second year of her finishing school in Switzerland. And in fact, she finished the year, and flew home on the day of Whitfield's twenty-fifth anniversary party, which Sarah was giving at the château, for seven hundred guests from all over Europe. Every possible kind of press would be there, there would be fireworks, and most of Europe's crowned heads, absolutely everyone who was anyone had been invited. Emanuelle and Julian had helped her organize everything. And Phillip and Nigel and Cecily were flying in for the party.

It was glorious. Everyone who was supposed to came, the food was exquisite, the fireworks extraordinary, and the jewels beautiful, most of them theirs. It was an absolutely perfect evening, and a major victory for Whitfield's. The press raved, and even before they left, they all came to congratulate Sarah for her major coup, and she in turn thanked and congratulated all the people who helped her to put on the party.

'Has anyone seen Isabelle?' Sarah asked, already late into the night. She hadn't been able to pick her up at the airport herself, but she had sent someone to pick her up and bring her to the party. She had seen her and kissed her when she arrived, before she was dressed, but she hadn't seen her since then. The crowd was simply too large and she had too much to do to go and look for her. She had barely been able to find Phillip and Julian for most of the evening. Phillip had deserted his wife as the evening began, and seemed to spend a lot of time with a model who had done several ads for them, and he had been telling her how much he liked them, while dancing with her, and Julian had been very busy chasing some of his latest conquests, one of them married, and two of them slightly overaged, and all the others dazzling girls that every man in the place envied him, especially his brother.

They had sent Xavier to stay with friends for the night, so he wouldn't get into too much mischief, although at nine and a half he was behaving better. Davy Crockett was no longer the thing. But James Bond was what really made him happy. Julian bought him every gimmick he could find, and had already snuck him into two of the movies.

Sarah had left a dress out for Isabelle. She had bought her a diaphanous pink organdy gown from the Emanuels in London, and she was sure that Isabelle would look like a fairy princess in it. She hoped that she wasn't lying under a bush somewhere in that dress. She laughed to herself at the thought. But when she finally found her, there was no bush in sight, and she was dancing very sedately with an older man, and deep in conversation. Sarah glanced at her approvingly, and then waved to her and moved on. Her entire family looked wonderful that night, even her daughter-in-law, wearing a dress by Hardy

Amies, and a hairdo by Alexandre. The Château de la Meuze looked like a fairyland. More than ever, she wished that William could see it. He would have been so proud of them, and maybe even of her . . . they had worked so hard on the château for so long. It was impossible to believe that it had ever been less than perfect, let alone ramshackle and rundown, as it had been when they found it. But that was all so long ago. Twenty-five years since Whitfield's had begun . . . thirty-five since they had found the château on their honeymoon. Where did the time go?

The reviews of the party in the press were extraordinary the next day. Everyone agreed that it was the party of the century, and wished Whitfield's another hundred years, as long as they were invited to the next anniversary party. And for the next few days, Sarah basked in the glory of the party. She saw very little of Isabelle during those days, who was catching up with old friends. At eighteen she could drive, and enjoy greater freedom than she had in earlier years. But Sarah still wanted to keep an eye on her, and she was worried one afternoon when she couldn't find her.

'She went out in the Rolls,' Xavier explained when she saw him.

'She did?' Sarah looked surprised. She was supposed to drive the Peugeot station wagon they kept for her, and other people at the château. 'Do you know where she went, sweetheart?' Sarah asked him, thinking probably just to the village.

'I think she was going to Paris,' he said, and sauntered off. There was a new horse in the stables and he wanted to see it. He still liked to pretend he was a cowboy sometimes, when he felt like it. The rest of the time he was an explorer.

She called Julian at the store and asked him to keep an eye out for her in case she came in. And sure enough, an hour later, she walked in, looking like a customer, in a very pretty emerald-green dress, and dark glasses.

Julian saw her on the camera in his office upstairs, and came downstairs to the shop as soon as he saw her.

'May I help you, Mademoiselle?' he asked in his most charming voice, and she laughed. 'A diamond bracelet perhaps? An engagement ring? A little tiara?'

'A crown would be very nice.'

'But of course.' He continued to play the game with her. 'Emerald, to match your dress, or diamond?'

'Actually, I'll take both.' She beamed at him, and he asked her casually then what she was doing in town.

'Just meeting a friend for a drink.'

'You drove two hours and ten minutes for a drink?' he asked. 'You must be very thirsty.'

'Very funny. I had nothing to do at home, so I thought I'd come up to town. In Italy, we used to do it all the time. You know, go to Cortina for lunch, or to go shopping.' She looked extremely sophisticated and very beautiful. She was truly a knockout.

'How chic,' he teased. 'It's a shame people aren't as amusing here.' But he knew she was going to the South of France in a few weeks, and stay with one of her friends from school, in Cap Ferrat. She was still very spoiled, but undeniably very grown-up now. 'Where are you meeting your friend?'

'The Ritz, for a drink.'

'Come on,' he said, coming around the counter. 'I'll drop you off. I have to take a diamond necklace to a viscountess.'

'I have my car,' she said coldly, 'well, actually, Mother's.' And he didn't ask any questions.

'Then you can drop me off. I don't. Mine is sick. I was going to take a taxi,' he lied, but he wanted to see who she was meeting. He went to the wrapping desk and picked up a very impressive box and put it in an envelope and followed Isabelle outside, and got in her car before she could object. He chatted as though it were perfectly normal for her to come to town to see a friend, and he kissed her when he left her at the front desk, and pretended to talk to the concierge, who knew him well and went along with the pretense.

'Can you pretend to take this box from me, Renaud? Just throw it away after I leave, but don't let anyone see you.'

'I should give it to my wife,' he whispered back, 'but maybe she'd expect more than the box. What are you doing today?'

'Following my sister,' he confided, still pretending to give his instructions. 'She's meeting someone at the bar, and I want to make sure it's OK. She's a very pretty girl.'

'So I saw. How old is she?'

'Just eighteen.'

'Oooh laaa . . .' Renaud whistled sympathetically, 'I'm glad she's not my daughter . . . sorry . . .' he apologized quickly.

'Do you suppose you could go in and check if she's sitting with anyone yet? And then I can go in and pretend to run into them by mistake. But I don't want to waste it before he gets there.' He assumed she was meeting a man, it was unlikely she would drive two hours each way to meet a girlfriend.

'Sure,' Renaud agreed readily, just as a large bill slipped into his palm for good measure, but he was happy to help this time. Lord Whitfield was a nice guy, and a great tipper.

Julian pretended to write an extensive note at the concierge's desk, and Renaud was back in a minute. 'She's there, and my friend, you got trouble.'

'*Merde*. Who is it? Do you know him?' He was beginning to fear it was some mafioso.

'Sure do. He's here all the time, or at least a couple of

times a year, working on some woman. Old women sometimes, young ones other times.'

'Do I know him?'

'Maybe. He bounces checks at least twice a trip, and never tips anyone unless someone else is looking.'

'He sounds charming.' Julian groaned.

'He's poor as dirt. And I think he's looking for money.'

'Great. Just what we needed. What's his name?'

'You'll love it. The Principe di Venezia e San Tebaldi. He says he's one of the Princes of Venice. He probably is. There are about ten thousand of them over there.' Not like the British, or even the French. The Italians had more princes than dentists. 'He's a real jerk, but he looks good, and she's young. She doesn't know the difference. I think his first name is Lorenzo.'

'How distinguished.' Julian was anything but encouraged by what he had just heard.

'Just don't expect a tip,' his friend reminded him, and Julian thanked him again, and sauntered into the bar, looking distracted and very businesslike, and incredibly aristocratic. He was the Real Thing, Renaud always said, and he knew. He was right of course, and Julian looked it. Not like the Prince of Pasta, as he called him.

'Oh, there you are . . . sorry . . .' Julian said as he pretended to bump into her with a huge grin. 'I just wanted to kiss you goodbye.' He glanced over at the man she was with, and smiled broadly, pretending to be absolutely thrilled to meet him. 'Hello . . . terribly sorry to interrupt . . . I'm Isabelle's brother, Julian Whitfield,' he said easily, extending a hand, looking comfortable and relaxed, as his sister squirmed slightly. But the prince wasn't bothered at all. He was charming and unctuous and oily.

'*Piacere* . . . Lorenzo di San Tebaldi . . . I'm so happy to meet you. You have a most charming sister.'

'Thank you. I completely agree.' He kissed her lightly

then, and apologized for leaving, but he had to get back to the shop for a meeting. He left without ever looking back, and despite his brilliant performance, Isabelle knew instantly that she was in big trouble.

Julian winked at the concierge on his way out and then he hurried back to the office. He called his mother as soon as he got in, but the conversation was not reassuring.

'Maman, I think we may have a bit of a problem.'

'What is it? Or should I say who?'

'She was with a gentleman, of I'd say about fifty years, whom according to the concierge at the Ritz, is well known to him, and a fortune hunter of sorts. He's very pretty, but he ain't much, as they say.'

'*Merde*,' Sarah said bluntly at the other end. 'Now what do I do with her? Lock her up again?'

'She's getting a little old for that. It won't be easy this time.'

'I know.' She gave an exasperated sigh. Isabelle had been home for all of two days and she was already in trouble. 'I really don't know what to do with her.'

'Neither do I. But I don't like the looks of this guy.'

'What's his name?' As though that mattered.

'Principe Lorenzo di San Tebaldi. I think he's from Venice.'

'Christ. Just what we need. An Italian prince. My God, she's such a fool.'

'I can't disagree with you there. But she sure is a knockout.'

'More's the pity,' her mother exclaimed in despair.

'What do you want me to do? Go back and drag her out of there by the hair?'

'I probably should ask you to do that. But I think you should leave her alone. She'll come home eventually, and I'll try to reason with her.'

'You're a good sport.'

'No.' Sarah confessed. 'I'm just tired.'

'Well, don't be discouraged. I think you're terrific.'

'Shows what you know.' But she was touched by the kind words, she needed them to fuel herself for the battle she knew would come when Isabelle came home, which she did, with the Rolls at midnight. It meant she had left Paris at ten o'clock, which was pretty reasonable for her. But still, her mother was far from pleased as Isabelle walked across the main floor of the château, and Sarah came downstairs to meet her. She had heard her come in, and she had been waiting.

'Good evening, Isabelle. Did you have a nice time?'

'Very, thank you very much.' She was nervous, but cool, as she faced her mother.

'How's my car?'

'Very nice . . . I . . . sorry, I meant to ask. I hope you didn't need it.'

'Actually,' Sarah said calmly, 'I didn't. Why don't you come into the kitchen for a cup of tea. You must be tired after all that driving.' All of which scared Isabelle even more. This was fatal. Her mother wasn't screaming, but her tone was frigid.

They sat down at the kitchen table, and Sarah made her an infusion of mint, but Isabelle didn't give a damn about it, as she sat there. 'Your brother Julian called me this afternoon,' Sarah said after a moment, and then looked into her daughter's eyes.

'I thought he would,' Isabelle said nervously, playing with the cup with her fingers. 'I was just meeting an old friend from Italy . . . one of the teachers.'

'Really?' Her mother said. 'What an interesting story. I checked the guest list, and he was here the other night, as someone's guest. The Principe di San Tebaldi. I saw you dancing with him, didn't I? He's very handsome.' Isabelle nodded, not sure what to say to her. She didn't dare argue with her this time, she just waited to hear what her punishment was, but her mother had more to say to her, which was agony for Isabelle as she waited.

'Unfortunately,' Sarah went on, 'he has a rather unattractive reputation . . . He comes to Paris from time to time . . . looking for ladies with a bit of a fortune. Sometimes he does very well, and sometimes not so well. But in any case, my dear, he is not someone you want to go out with.' She didn't complain about his age, or the fact that Isabelle had gone to town without permission, she tried to talk to her reasonably and point out that her friend was a fortune hunter, and Sarah thought that might impress her, but it didn't.

'People always say things like that about princes, because they're jealous,' she said innocently, but still too frightened to enter into armed combat with her mother. Besides, she knew instinctively that she would lose this one.

'What makes you think so?'

'He told me.'

'He told you *that*?' Sarah looked horrified. 'Doesn't it occur to you that he is saying that to you to cover himself, in case people say things about him? That's a smoke screen, Isabelle. For God's sake, you're not stupid.' But she was about men, she always had been, and particularly this one.

Julian had made several more phone calls that afternoon, and everyone said the same thing about Isabelle's new friend. He was trouble.

'This is not a nice man, Isabelle. You have to trust me this time. He's using you.'

'You're jealous.'

'That's ridiculous.'

'You are!' She shouted at her, 'Ever since Daddy died you don't have anyone in your life, and it makes you feel old and ugly and you are . . . and you just want him for yourself! . . .' It was a torrent of words, and Sarah stared at her in amazement, but she spoke to her calmly.

'I hope you don't believe that. Because we both know it's not true. I miss your father terribly, every moment, at every hour of the day' – tears filled her eyes at the thought of it – 'but not for a moment would I replace him with a fortune hunter from Venice.'

'He lives in Rome now,' Isabelle corrected, as though it mattered, as her mother pondered the overwhelming stupidity of youth. Sometimes it absolutely staggered her what a mess they made of their lives. But on the other hand, at the same age, she hadn't done much better with Freddie, she reminded herself, trying to be reasonable with her daughter.

'I don't care where he lives.' Sarah was beginning to lose her temper. 'You will not see him again. Do you understand me?' Isabelle did not answer. 'And if you take my car again, I'll call the police next time to bring you back. Isabelle, behave yourself, or it won't go well with you! Do you hear me?'

'You can't tell me what to do any more. I'm eighteen.'

'And a fool. That man is after your money, Isabelle, and your name, which is much more powerful than his. Protect yourself. Stay away from him.'

'And if I don't?' she taunted her. But Sarah had no answer. Maybe she should send her to stay with Phillip at Whitfield for a while, with his incredibly boring wife and children. But Phillip would be no better an influence on his sister, with his secretaries, and his tarts, and his little games. What was wrong with all of them? Phillip was married to a woman he didn't care about, and probably never had, except that she was respectable, and Julian slept with absolutely every woman and her mother, if possible, and now Isabelle was half crazy over this four-flusher from Venice. What had she and William done, she asked herself, to create such unreasonable children?

'Don't do it again,' she warned Isabelle. And then she

went upstairs to her room, and a little while later she heard Isabelle's door slam.

Isabelle behaved herself for a week, and then she disappeared again, but this time in the Peugeot. She insisted she went to see a friend in Garches, and Sarah couldn't prove otherwise, but she didn't believe her. The atmosphere was tense until she left for Cap Ferrat, and after she did, Sarah heaved a sigh of relief, though she didn't know why. The Côte d'Azur was hardly on another planet. But at least she was staying with friends, and not with that cretin from Venice.

And then Julian sent her the newspapers from Nice and Cannes and Monte Carlo when he was there for a weekend. They were full of stories about the prince of San Tebaldi and Lady Isabelle Whitfield.

'What are we going to do with her?' Sarah asked him in despair.

'I don't know,' Julian answered her honestly. 'But I think we'd better go down there.' They did the following week, when they both had time, and they tried to reason with her together. But she refused to listen, and she told them bluntly that she was in love with him, and he adored her.

'Of course he does, you little fool,' her brother tried to explain to her. 'He can only guess at what you're worth. With you in his hand, he can sit on his ass forever.'

'You make me sick!' she screamed. 'Both of you!'

'Don't be so stupid!' he shouted back. They took her to stay at the Hotel Miramar with them, and she ran away. She literally disappeared from the face of the earth for a week, and when she returned, Lorenzo was with her. He apologized profusely to both of them for being so thoughtless, for not calling them himself . . . as Sarah's eyes shot daggers at him. She had been sick with worry, and didn't dare call the police, for fear of the scandal. She knew Isabelle had to be with Lorenzo . . .

'Isabelle was so upset . . .' he went on . . . and now he humbly begged their forgiveness . . . But Isabelle interrupted him, and addressed her mother directly.

'We want to get married.'

'Never,' her mother said bluntly.

'Then I'll run away again. And again. Until you let me.'

'You're wasting your time. I never will.' And then she turned her attention to Lorenzo. 'And what's more, I will cut off every cent she has.' But Isabelle knew better.

'You can't. Not all of it. You know that what Daddy left me comes to me when I'm twenty-one, no matter what.' Sarah was sorry she had ever told her, but Lorenzo looked extremely cheered by the news, and Julian looked sick. It was so obvious to everyone except Isabelle, who was too young to understand it. She was an eighteen-year-old girl with no experience about life, and hot pants, it was a hell of a combination. 'I'm going to marry him,' she announced again, and Sarah was intrigued that Lorenzo said nothing. He was letting his bride-to-be fight her own battles and his, an omen of things to come, Sarah wanted to remind her.

'I will never let you marry him.'

'You can't stop me.'

'I'll do everything I can,' Sarah vowed, and Isabelle's eyes blazed with anger and hatred.

'You don't want me to be happy. You never did. You hate me.' But Julian deflated her balloon this time.

'Try that on someone else. That's the dumbest thing I've ever heard.' And then he turned to his future brother-in-law, hoping to appeal to his reason, or his sense of decency, if he had either, but clearly he didn't.

'Do you really want to marry her this way, Tebaldi? What's the point?'

'Of course not. It tears at my soul to see you all like this.' He rolled his eyes, and looked ridiculous to everyone but Isabelle. 'But what can I say . . . I adore her. She

412

speaks for both of us . . . we *will* be married.' He looked as though he were about to break into song and Julian didn't know whether to laugh or cry.

'Don't you feel foolish? She's eighteen years old. You could be her grandfather, or almost.'

'She is the woman of my life,' he announced. And actually the only remarkable thing about him was that he had never been married. It had always paid to keep moving until now. This time the profits were a lot bigger, if he could land little Lady Whitfield, whose family owned the biggest jewel business in Europe, as well as their lands, and titles, and original holdings. It was quite a purse. No prize for an amateur. But Lorenzo wasn't.

'Why don't you wait, if you're both so sure?' Julian tried again, but they both shook their heads.

'We can't . . . and the disgrace . . .' Lorenzo looked as though he were about to cry. 'I just spent a week with her. Her reputation . . . and what if she gets pregnant?'

'Oh, my God.' Sarah sat down heavily in a chair. The mere thought of it almost made her sick. A child of his in her family would be even worse than poor Cecily's two colorless children. 'Are you pregnant now?' she asked Isabelle directly.

'I don't know. We didn't take any precautions.'

'How wonderful. I can hardly wait to hear the result of that in a few weeks.' There was always abortion, of course, but that wasn't the issue now. The issue was marriage.

'We want to get married this summer . . . or at the very latest, at Christmas. At the château,' she said, as though he had schooled her, and he had. He wanted a big lavish wedding, so they couldn't get rid of him easily. And they couldn't anyway. Once they were married, it was forever. He was Catholic, and he was going to marry Isabelle in the Catholic Church in Rome, after they were married at the château. He had already told her it was his only condition. The only thing that mattered to him, he said, was

413

to be truly married in the eyes of God, and he had even cried when he said it. Fortunately, Sarah hadn't had to hear him.

They had fought and discussed and argued and shouted well into the night, until Julian was hoarse, Sarah had a headache the size of the hotel, and Isabelle almost fainted as Lorenzo called for ice and smelling salts and damp towels. And finally Sarah gave in. There was no choice. They would elope anyway, if she didn't. She was sure of it. And Isabelle swore they would. She tried to get them to wait a year, but they wouldn't do that either. And Lorenzo kept insisting that it was better to do it now, in case she really was pregnant.

'Why don't we wait and find out?' Sarah suggested calmly. But they wouldn't even agree to wait till Christmas, by the end of the evening. Lorenzo had accurately gauged the full measure of their hatred, and he knew that if he didn't force the issue soon, they would find some way to get rid of him and it wouldn't happen.

So before the night was out, they all agreed to late August, at the château, with a handful of close friends, no-one else, and no press. Lorenzo was disappointed not to have the big wedding they deserved, but he promised her a fabulous party in Italy, which her mother assured her he wouldn't pay for.

It was a bitter night for her, and for Julian. But Isabelle left the room, and went to stay at Lorenzo's hotel with him. There was no stopping her now. She was hellbent on her own destruction.

The wedding was small, but tastefully done, at the Château de la Meuze, with only their close friends in attendance. And Isabelle looked lovely in a short white dress by Marc Bohan at Dior, and a big picture hat to go with it. And Sarah was deeply grateful for the fact that she wasn't pregnant.

Phillip and Cecily came from England for the wedding, Julian gave her away, and Xavier carried the ring, while Sarah wished he would lose it.

'You looked thrilled,' Emanuelle said in an undertone, as they sipped champagne in the garden.

'I may throw up before lunch,' Sarah said mournfully. She had watched them be married in her own garden, by a Catholic priest and an Episcopal bishop. It was doubly official then, and doubly disastrous for Isabelle. And throughout the day, Lorenzo gushed, and grinned, and charmed everyone, and made toasts, and talked about how he wished he could have met the great Duke, Isabelle's father.

'He's a bit much, isn't he?' Phillip said, for once making his mother laugh with his understatements. 'Pathetic.'

'And then some.' In comparison to him, Cecily was Greta Garbo. That was two now she didn't like. But Cecily only bored her. Lorenzo she hated, which broke her heart as well, because it meant that she would never be close to Isabelle while she was married to Lorenzo. It was no secret how they felt about her husband.

'How can she even think she loves him?' Emanuelle asked in despair. 'He's so obvious . . . so greasy . . .'

'She's young. She doesn't know about men like that yet,' Sarah said with infinite wisdom. 'Unfortunately, she's going to learn a great deal in a very short time now.' It reminded her again of her experience with Freddie Van Deering. She would have liked to spare Isabelle that, and she had tried, but it was no use. Isabelle had made her choice, and everyone in the world but Isabelle knew it was a poor one.

The wedding party stayed till the end of the afternoon, and then Isabelle and Lorenzo left. They were going to Sardinia for their honeymoon, to a new resort there, to see his friend the Aga Khan, or so he said. But Sarah imagined there were a lot of people whom he said he knew who were going to disappear into thin air over the next few years, if he lasted that long. And she hoped he wouldn't.

After they left for the airport, in a hired Rolls-Royce with a driver, the family sat gloomily in the garden, thinking of what she'd done, and feeling that they'd lost her forever. Only Phillip seemed not to care too much, as usual. He was chatting quietly with a woman who was a friend of Emanuelle and Sarah. But for the rest of them, it was more like a funeral than a wedding. Sarah felt somehow as though she had failed not only her daughter, but her husband. He would have been devastated if he could have seen Lorenzo.

Sarah heard from her very briefly when they reached Rome, and then not a sound from her until Christmas. Sarah called once or twice and sent several letters, and Isabelle never answered. She was clearly angry at all of them. But Julian spoke to her once or twice, so at least Sarah knew she was all right, but none of them had any idea if she was happy. She didn't come home at all the following year, and she didn't want Sarah to go there, so she didn't. Julian flew to Rome to see her once. He said she looked very serious and very beautiful, and very Italian, and according to their mutual bank, she was spending an absolute fortune. She had bought a small palazzo in Rome, and a villa in Umbria. Lorenzo had bought a yacht, a new Rolls and a Ferrari. And as far as Julian could see, there was no baby on the horizon.

They came back to the château for Christmas after the first year, but grudgingly, and Isabelle said nothing to any of them, but she gave her mother a very pretty Buccellati pearl-and-gold bracelet. She and Lorenzo left on Boxing Day to go skiing in Cortina. It was difficult to fathom what was happening with them, and she didn't even open up with Julian. But it was Emanuelle who finally ferreted out the truth. She flew to Rome, after a business trip to London to see Nigel and Phillip, and afterwards she told

Sarah that she thought Isabelle looked dreadful. She had circles under her eyes, she was rail thin, and she never laughed any more. And each time she saw her, Lorenzo wasn't with her.

'I think there's trouble there, but I'm not sure she's ready to admit it to you. Just be sure to leave the door open, and eventually she'll come home. I promise.'

'I hope you're right,' Sarah said sadly. The loss had weighed on her terribly. For all intents and purposes, in the past two years she had lost her last surviving daughter.

Chapter 27

It was an agonizing three years later, before Isabelle came back to Paris again. They came when Sarah invited them to Whitfield's thirtieth-anniversary party at the Louvre. They had taken over part of it for a party. It had never been done before, and Emanuelle had had to use her government connections to get permission. The entire area around it was going to be closed, and it was going to take hundreds of museum guards and gendarmes to make it work. But Sarah knew it would. And Lorenzo knew it was an event not to miss. Sarah was stunned when they accepted. Isabelle and Lorenzo had been married for five years by then, and Sarah had almost resigned herself to the distance between them. She concentrated her energies and her affection on Xavier and Julian, and Phillip to some extent, as little as she saw him. He'd been married to Cecily for thirteen years by then, and his affairs were hinted at in the press, but never confirmed, usually, Sarah suspected, out of respect for his position. The Duke of Whitfield, according to some, was allegedly pretty dicey.

The party Sarah gave was the most dazzling Paris had ever seen. The women there were so beautiful it took your breath away, and the men so important, you could have run five governments from her central table. The President of France was there, the Onassises, the Rainiers, the Arabs, the Greeks, every possible important American, and all the crowned heads of Europe. Everyone who had ever worn jewelry was there, and a lot of young women who hoped to. There were courtesans and queens, the very rich and the very famous. It made the party five years before look paltry in comparison. No expense was spared, and Sarah herself was thrilled when she saw it. She sat back quietly in victory, looking at all of it, as a thousand people dined and danced and drank and cavorted for each other's benefit and that of the press, and undoubtedly many misbehaved in assorted ways, although no-one knew it.

Julian had brought a very pretty girl, an actress Sarah had read about in a recent scandal, which was an interesting change for him. He had recently been going out with a startlingly pretty Brazilian model. He never lacked for girls, but he always behaved well. They loved him when they arrived and when they left. One couldn't ask for more. Sarah would have liked to see him choose a wife, but at twenty-nine, there seemed to be no sign of it, and she didn't press him.

Phillip had brought his wife, of course, but he spent most of the evening with a girl who worked for Saint Laurent. He had met her in London the year before, and they seemed to have a lot in common. He always cast an eye on Julian's girls, and he had noticed the actress, too, but never got around to introducing himself, and then they got lost in the crowd. It took him ages to find Cecily afterwards, chatting happily to the King of Greece about her horses.

Isabelle was one of the most beautiful women there, Sarah was pleased to note. She was wearing a skintight black Valentino dress that revealed her figure dazzlingly, her long black hair cascaded down her back, and she wore a remarkable diamond necklace and bracelet, with matching earrings, that Julian had loaned her. But she didn't even need the jewels. She was simply so beautiful that people stared at her, and Sarah was pleased that she had come home for the party. She had no delusions about why

419

they'd come. Lorenzo worked the crowd that night, chasing royals, and constantly posing for the papers. Sarah noticed, as did his wife, who eyed him quietly, but Sarah said nothing. She sensed easily that something was wrong there, and she waited for Isabelle to say something, and she never did. She stayed late and danced with old friends, particularly a well-known French prince, who had always liked her. There were so many men who would have loved to pursue Isabelle, she was twenty-three years old, and so beautiful, but she had been gone for five years, married to Lorenzo.

Sarah took them all to lunch the next day at Le Fouquet's, to thank them all for helping her with the party. Emanuelle was there, of course, and Julian, Phillip and Cecily, Nigel, his designer friend, and Isabelle and Lorenzo. Xavier was already away by then. He had begged for months for Sarah to let him visit old friends of hers in Kenya. She had resisted him at first, but he was so persistent, and she was so busy with their anniversary party plans, that she had finally let him go, and he had thanked her profusely. At fourteen, all he wanted was to see the world, and the farther away the better. He loved being with her, and he loved France, but he had a constant craving for the exotic and the unknown. He had read Thor Heyerdahl's book four times, and he seemed to know everything about Africa, and the Amazon, and every possible place in the world no-one else in his family ever wanted to go to. He was definitely his own man, a bit of William in some ways, a bit of Sarah in others, he had some of Julian's warmth, and a lot of William's fun. But he had a sense of adventure, and a passion for the rugged life that no-one else in his family shared with him. The rest of them much preferred Paris and London and Antibes, or even Whitfield.

'We're a very dull group compared to him.' Sarah smiled. He had already written her half a dozen letters

420

about the fabulous animals he'd seen. And he was already begging to go back, if she'd let him.

'He certainly doesn't get it from me.' Julian grinned. He was far happier on a sofa than a safari.

'Or me.' Phillip laughed at himself for once, and Lorenzo immediately launched into an endless tale that bored everyone, about his dear friend the Maharaja of Jaipur.

They had a nice time at lunch, in spite of him, and afterwards they all went their separate ways, and the Whitfields all said goodbye to their mother. Julian was going to Saint-Tropez with friends for a few days to rest after all their work on the mammoth party, and Phillip and Cecily were flying back to London. Nigel was staying in Paris for a few days with his friend. Emanuelle was going back to work, as Sarah was eventually. Only Isabelle lingered after lunch. Lorenzo said he had to pick up something at Hermès, and wanted to see friends. They weren't leaving for another day, and for the first time in years, Isabelle seemed to want to talk to her mother. She hesitated when they were finally alone, and Sarah asked her if she'd like another cup of coffee.

They both ordered espresso, and Isabelle came to sit next to her. She had been at the other end of the lively table, but there was something deeply unhappy in her eyes, and she looked at her mother miserably finally, as tears filled her eyes and she tried to fight them.

'I don't suppose I have the right to say anything now, do I?' she asked ruefully, and Sarah gently touched her hand, wishing she could take away her pain, that she could have shielded her from it from the beginning. But she had long since learned the hard lesson that she couldn't. 'I can't really complain, since you all warned me.'

'Yes, you can.' Sarah smiled. 'One can always complain.' And then she decided to be honest. 'You're unhappy, aren't you?'

'Very,' Isabelle admitted, wiping a tear from her cheek. 'I had no idea what it would be like . . . I was so young and so stupid . . . you all knew. And I was so blind . . .' It was all true, but it made Sarah sad anyway. There was no consolation in being right this time. Not at her child's expense. It broke her heart to see her so unhappy. She had tried to resign herself for years to barely seeing her any more, but nonetheless it had always been painful. And now, seeing how unhappy she had been, her estrangement from them seemed even more wasted.

'You were very young,' Sarah excused her. 'And very stubborn. And he was very shrewd.' Isabelle nodded miserably, she knew that only too well now. 'He played you like a violin to get what he wanted.' He had played all of them, he had forced their hand, and enticed Isabelle to marry him. It was easy to forgive Isabelle, but not as easy to forgive Lorenzo. 'He knew what he was doing.'

'More than you know. As soon as we got to Rome, and he got what he wanted, everything was different. It seemed like he already had the palazzo picked out, he said everyone had them there, everyone of any consequence, and we'd need it for all our children, and the villa in Umbria too. And then he bought the Rolls . . . and the yacht . . . and the Ferrari . . . and then all of a sudden I never saw him any more. He was always out with his friends, and I started seeing things in the paper about him and other women. And every time I asked him about it, he just laughed and said they were old friends, or cousins. He must be related to half of Europe,' she said grimly, looking straight at her mother. 'He's cheated on me for years. He doesn't even hide it any more. He does what he wants, and he says there's nothing I can do. There's no divorce in Italy, and he's related to three cardinals, he says he will never divorce me.' She looked hopeless as she sat there. Sarah had no idea that it had come to that, or that he had dared to be so blatant. And how dare he come here, and sit with all of them, come to her party, pursue her friends, after abusing her daughter. She was livid.

'Have you asked him for a divorce?' Sarah looked worried as she stroked her daughter's hand, and Isabelle nodded.

'Two years ago, when he had a passionate affair with a well-known woman in Rome. I just couldn't take it any more. They were all over the papers. I just couldn't see the point of playing the game any more.' She started to cry openly then. 'I've been so lonely.' Sarah hugged her then, and Isabelle blew her nose and went on with her sad tale. 'I asked him again last year. But he always says no, that I must resign myself to the fact that we're married forever.'

'He wants to be married to your bank account, not you.' He always had, and according to Julian, he had been very lucky. He had stashed a lot of the money Isabelle had given him and continued to make her pay for everything. But she wouldn't have cared about that so much if she'd loved him. But she hadn't loved him in years. When their first passion burned away, and it had quickly, there had been absolutely nothing left, except ashes. 'At least you haven't had children with him. If you can get out of it at all, it will be less complicated this way. And you're still young, you can have them later.'

'Not with him,' Isabelle said bleakly, lowering her voice still further as they sat at the table, and the waiters kept a discreet distance. 'We can't even have children.'

This time Sarah looked stunned. Up until then, nothing had really surprised her. 'Why not?' He had even threatened that Isabelle might be pregnant when he wanted to marry her, it had been his main reason for not waiting until Christmas. And he wasn't that old. He was fifty-four then, William had been older than that when they had Xavier, and not even in good health, Sarah thought warmly. 'Is there something wrong with him?'

'He had severe mumps as a child. And he's sterile. His uncle told me. Enzo had never told me anything. And when I asked him, he laughed. He said I was very lucky, it was built-in birth control. He lied to me, Maman . . . he told me we would have dozens of children.' The tears spilled over on her cheeks again and again. 'I think I could even stand being married to him, no matter how much I hated him, if we had children.' There was a longing in her heart that nothing would fill now. For five long years she had had no-one to love, and no-one to love her. Not even her family, whom he had caused her to fight with.

'That's no way to have children, dear,' Sarah said quietly. 'You don't want them to grow up in misery.' But she didn't want her own daughter living in it either.

'We don't sleep with each other any more anyway. We haven't in three years. He never comes home any more except to pick up his shirts, or get money.' But something Isabelle had said had caught Sarah's attention, and she made a mental note of it for later. The Principe di San Tebaldi was not quite as slick as he thought, but almost. 'I don't care any more,' Isabelle went on. 'I don't care about anything. It's like being in prison.' And she looked it. In the daylight, Sarah saw that Emanuelle had been right when she went to Rome, and now she knew why. Isabelle looked wan and pale, and desperately unhappy, and with good reason.

'Do you want to come home? You could probably get a divorce here. You were married at the château.'

'We married again in Italy,' Isabelle said hopelessly. 'In the church. If I got a divorce here, it wouldn't be legal in Italy, and I could never get married again anyway. It would be illegal. Lorenzo says I just have to resign myself to my fate. He's not going anywhere.' Once again, as he had before, he really had them over a barrel, and Sarah didn't like it. It was worse than her first marriage had been, by far, or certainly similar to it. And her father had gotten her out of it. She knew she had to find a way now to help her daughter.

'What can I do to help you? What do you want, my darling?' Sarah asked sadly. 'I'll speak to my attorneys at once, but I think you may have to bide your time with him. Eventually there will be something he wants more than you, and maybe we can bargain with him.' But she had to admit, it wouldn't be easy. He was a tough one.

Isabelle looked at her oddly then. There was something she wanted very much. Not as much as a divorce, or a child, but at least it would give her life some meaning. She had been thinking of it for a long time, but given the estrangement between them, she felt she couldn't ask her.

'I'd like a store,' she whispered, and Sarah loked surprised.

'What kind of store?' Sarah imagined she meant some kind of boutique. But she didn't.

'Whitfield's.' She was absolutely certain.

'In Rome?' Sarah had never even thought of it. The Italians had Buccellati and Bulgari. She had never even considered opening in Rome, but it was certainly an intriguing idea, although Isabelle was a little young to run it. 'It's an interesting idea. But are you sure?'

'Absolutely.'

'What if you succeed in divorcing him, or you simply decide to leave, divorced or not, then what do we do?'

'I won't. I like Italy. It's Lorenzo, and my life with him, that I hate. But it's wonderful there.' Her face lit up for the first time. 'I have terrific friends, and the women are so chic, they wear tons of great jewelry. Mother, it would be a huge success, I promise.' Sarah couldn't disagree with what she said about the Italian women, anyway, but it was a new idea to her, and she had to digest it.

'Let me think about it. And you think about it too. Don't enter into this hastily. It's an enormous amount of work, and a tremendous commitment. You'll work very hard, endless hours. There's more to this than dressing up. Talk to Emanuelle . . . talk to Julian . . . You have to be very sure before you do this.'

'It's all I've wanted for the last year, I just didn't know how to ask you.'

'Well, you have.' Sarah smiled at her. 'Now let me think about it, and talk to your brothers.' And then she grew serious again. 'And let me think about how I can help you with Lorenzo.'

'You can't,' Isabelle said sadly.

'You never know.' In her heart of hearts, Sarah suspected that all it would take was money. In the right way, at the right time. She just hoped the moment would come soon, so Isabelle didn't have to be married to him for much longer.

They sat and talked for another hour and then walked slowly back to the store arm in arm. It warmed Sarah's heart to feel close to her again, she hadn't in years, not since she was in her teens and losing her had been so painful. In its own way, it had been almost as sad as losing Lizzie, because in many ways, Isabelle had been dead to her. But she was back now, and Sarah's heart felt lighter.

Isabelle left her outside the shop, and went to have tea with an old friend, a girl she had gone to school with who was just getting married. Isabelle envied her her innocence. How nice it would have been to start over. But she knew there was no hope of that for her. Her life, empty as it was, would end with Lorenzo. At least if her mother let her open the store, it would give her something to do, and she could concentrate on that, instead of sitting at home and hating him, and crying every time she saw a baby, as she thought of the babies she would never have. She could have lived without children if she loved him, or without his love if she had a child to console her, but to have neither was a double punishment, and sometimes she wondered what she'd done to deserve this.

'She's too young,' Phillip said absolutely when Sarah called him. She had already discussed it with Julian and he thought it was an intriguing idea. He liked some of the old Buccellati things, and many of the new designs young Italian designers were doing. He thought they could do something very exciting in Rome, different from both Paris and London, each of which had their own style, and their own clients. London had the Queen and the old guard, and Paris had the flash and the dash, the chic and the very rich, and the nouveau riche. And Rome would have all the greedy stylish Italians who devoured jewelry.

'We could get someone to help her run it, that's not important.' Sarah brushed his objections aside. 'The real question is if Rome is the right market.'

'I think it is,' Julian said quietly, on the same call with them.

'I think you don't know what you're talking about, as usual,' Phillip snapped, and Sarah's heart ached. He always did that. Julian was everything he wanted to be, and everything he wasn't. Handsome, charming, young, adored by everyone, and particularly by women. Phillip had become increasingly stuffy over the years, so much so that he almost seemed to dry up, and instead of being sensual, he was sneaky. He was forty years old, and much to her chagrin, Sarah thought he looked more like fifty. Being married to Cecily hadn't helped anything, but it had been his choice, and she was still the kind of wife he wanted, respectable, dull, well-bred, and usually absent. She spent most of her time in the country with her horses. And she had just recently bought a horse farm in Ireland.

'I think we should get together on this,' Sarah said matter-of-factly. 'Can you and Nigel come here, or do you want us to come to London?'

In the end, they decided that it was simpler if Nigel and Phillip came to Paris. Isabelle and Lorenzo were gone by then, and the five of them argued for three days, but in the end, Emanuelle won. She pointed out that if William and Sarah hadn't been courageous enough to try something new and different, and almost outrageous then, there would be no Whitfield's. And that if they didn't continue to grow and expand, one day there wouldn't be again. They were entering the eighties, an era of expansion. She felt they had to look to Rome, maybe even Germany . . . New York . . . the world did not begin and end in London and Paris.

'Point well taken,' Nigel said. He was looking well these days, distinguished as he always had, and Sarah dreaded thinking that he would retire one day. By then, he was in his late sixties. But unlike her son, Nigel was still thinking ahead, reaching out into the world, trying out new ideas, and daring to move forward.

'I think she's right,' Julian added. 'We can't just sit here being self-satisfied. That's the surest way to kill the business. Actually, I think we should have thought of this long ago, without Isabelle. This is just very good timing.'

By nightfall they had agreed, although Phillip only grudgingly. He thought another branch somewhere in England made more sense than Rome, which all of the others vetoed. Somehow he never really believed that there was any other place worth a damn, except England.

Sarah called Isabelle herself that night, and gave her the news, and you would have thought she had given her the moon. The poor child was starving, for life, for love, for direction, for affection. Sarah promised to come to see her the following week, to discuss their plans. And when she did, she was intrigued that for the entire five days of her stay, she never saw Lorenzo.

'Where is he?' Sarah finally dared to ask.

'In Sardinia with friends. I hear he has a new mistress.'

'How nice for him,' Sarah said tartly, suddenly remembering Freddie coming across the lawn at their anniversary party with his hookers. She told Isabelle about it for the first time, and her daughter stared at her in amazement.

'I always knew you were divorced. But I never really knew why. I don't think I ever thought of it when I was growing up. I never thought that you could make a mistake or be unhappy . . .' Or be married to a man who would bring prostitutes to her parents' home. Even forty years later it was quite a story.

'Anyone can make a mistake. I made a big one. So did you. But eventually, I got out of it, with my father's help. And I met your father. You'll meet someone wonderful one day too. Wait.' She kissed her gently on the cheek and went back to the Excelsior, where she was staying.

For the next year they worked frantically on the space they rented on the Via Condotti. It was larger than the two other stores, and extremely glamorous. It was a real showplace, and Isabelle was so excited, she could hardly stand it. It was almost like having a baby, she said to friends. It was all she could eat, think, drink, talk about, and she didn't even care any more that she never saw Enzo. He made fun of it, and told her she was going to fall flat on her face. But he hadn't reckoned with Sarah.

She hired a PR firm to woo the Italian press, she had Isabelle give parties, get involved in Roman society in countless ways she had never thought of. She gave to charities, gave lunches, and attended important events in Rome, Florence, Milan. Suddenly Lady Isabelle Whitfield, the Principessa di San Tebaldi, became one of the most sought-after people in Rome. And by the time they were ready to open, even her husband was paying attention. He was telling his friends about the store, talking about the fabulous jewels he was selecting himself, and the people who had already bought from him. Isabelle heard the tales, but she paid no attention. She was too busy working night and day, checking plans, talking to architects, hiring staff. Emanuelle had come to Rome for the last two months to help her, and they had hired a capable young man, a son of an old friend of hers who had worked for Bulgari for the last four years in a position of importance. They stole him easily, and he was going to help Isabelle run it. He couldn't believe his good fortune, and he was in awe of her, but in a short time they became good friends, and Isabelle liked him. He was smart, he was good, he was nice, and he had a great sense of humor. He also had a wife and four children. His name was Marcello Scuri.

The opening party they gave was the hit of Rome, and absolutely *everyone* in Italy was there, and several of their loyal customers from London and Paris. People came from Venice, Florence, Milan, Naples, Turin, Bologna, Perugia. They came from all over the country. Her year of carefully laid groundwork had paid off, and Sarah's foresight had been brilliant. Even Phillip had to grudgingly admit that it was a fabulous store, and Nigel said when he saw it that if he died at that exact moment, he would die happy. It was so totally perfect for Rome, the jewelry so beautiful and so stunning, the perfect mix of old and new, showy and discreet, merely expensive and truly astounding. Isabelle was thrilled with the success of it, and so was her mother.

The young director, Marcello, did a splendid job, and so did Isabelle. Emanuelle was very proud of both of them. And both of Isabelle's brothers praised her for her excellent results. She had done a wonderful job. And three days later when they left her to return to their own stores, the shop was off and running.

Emanuelle had already gone back the day before, to deal with a minor crisis in the Paris store. There had been a break-in, but miraculously, due to the remarkable security system of bullet-proof glass and locking doors, nothing was taken. But Emanuelle had felt she should be there to bolster everyone's spirits. The staff at the store had been pretty shaken. Protecting their stores from theft was becoming more and more complicated. But so far, in both of their shops, they had excellent security, and had been very lucky.

Sarah was still thinking of how well the opening in Rome had gone as she and Julian boarded the plane to Paris. She asked him if he'd had a good time, and he said he had. She had seen him talking to a very pretty young principessa early on, and later a well-known Valentino model. The women in Rome were certainly beautiful, but she'd had the feeling for a while that Julian was slowing down. He was about to turn thirty, and there were times when Sarah suspected that he was actually behaving. He had been quite wild for a while, but according to what she read about him in the newspapers, not lately. And as they prepared to land at Orly, he expained why.

'Do you remember Yvonne Charles?' he asked innocently and Sarah shook her head. They had been talking about business a moment before, and she couldn't remember if the woman he mentioned was a client.

'Only the name. Why? Have I met her?'

'She's an actress. You met her at the anniversary party last year.'

'Along with perhaps a thousand other people. At least I know I'm not slipping.' But then suddenly she did remember her, not from the party, but from something she'd read in the papers. 'Didn't she have a very scandalous divorce a few years ago . . . and then marry again later? Seems to me I read something about her . . . Why?'

He looked very uncomfortable for a moment as the plane came in for a landing. It was unfortunate his mother still had such a good memory. But at sixty-four she was as sharp as she had ever been, as strong, and in a softer way, just as pretty. He was crazy about her, but there were times when he wished she didn't pay such close attention to details.

'Something like that . . .' he answered vaguely. 'Actually, she's getting divorced again right now. I met her between two marriages' – or possibly during, knowing him – 'and we just ran into each other again a few months ago.'

'What good timing.' Sarah smiled at him, sometimes he still seemed so young to her. They all did. 'How lucky for you.'

'Yes, it is.' There was something in his eyes suddenly that scared her. 'She's a very special girl.'

'She must be, with two marriages under her belt already. How old is she?'

'Twenty-four. But she's very mature for her age.'

'She must be.' She didn't know what to say to him, or where he was leading her, but she had a feeling she wasn't going to like it.

'I'm going to marry her,' Julian said quietly, and Sarah felt as though the bottom had just dropped out of the plane as the wheels hit the runway.

'Oh?' She tried to look nonplussed, but she could feel her heart beating too hard as they landed. 'When did you decide this?'

'Last week. But we were all so busy with the opening, I didn't want to say anything until after it was over.' How considerate of him. How wonderful for him to marry a girl who was already twice divorced, and tell her. 'You're going to love her.' She hoped he was right, but she hadn't liked any of their mates so far. She was beginning to give up on the hope that she would ever have in-laws she could even tolerate, let alone be fond of. So far she hadn't done well at all.

'When am I going to meet her?'

'Soon.'

'How about Friday night? We could have dinner at Maxim's before I leave Paris.'

'That would be fine.' He smiled warmly.

And then, she dared to ask him something she knew she probably shouldn't. 'Have you made up your mind?'

'Absolutely.' She'd been afraid of that. And then he saw her face and laughed. 'Mother . . . trust me . . .' She wished she could, but she had a feeling deep in the pit of her stomach that he was making a mistake. And when they met at Maxim's on Friday night, she was certain of it.

There was no denying that the girl was beautiful, she had the cool, icy blond beauty one imagines the Swedes have. She was long, tall, thin, with creamy skin, big blue eyes, and pale blond hair that hung straight to her shoulders. She said she had been a model at fourteen, but then she got into the movies, and she had been acting since she was seventeen. She had been in five movies in seven years, and Sarah remembered vaguely that there had been a scandal involving her sleeping with a director when she was underage. And then there had been something about her first divorce, from an equally naughty young actor. Her second husband had been a more interesting choice. She had married a German playboy and she had been trying to take him for a great deal of money. But Julian insisted that a settlement had just been made. And they would be able to marry by Christmas.

Sarah did not find herself anxious to celebrate. She wanted to go home and cry. It was happening again. One of her children was blindly walking into someone else's trap and absolutely refused to see it. Why couldn't he have an affair with her? Why did he have to delude himself that this was a girl to marry? It would have been obvious to Helen Keller that she wasn't. She was beautiful, and incredibly sexy, but her eyes were cold, and everything about her was calculated and planned. There was nothing spontaneous or sincere or warm, or caring about her. And Sarah suspected from the way she looked at him, that she liked him, she wanted him, but she didn't love him. Everything about the girl suggested that she was a taker

433

and a user. And Julian deluded himself that she was an adorable little girl, and he loved her.

'Well?' he asked happily when Yvonne went to powder her nose at the end of dinner. 'Isn't she terrific? Don't you love her?' He was so blind, it exhausted her. They all were. She patted his hand, and said she was a beautiful girl, which was true. And the next day, when he picked up some papers from her, she tried to talk about it discreetly.

'I think marriage is a very serious thing,' she began, feeling four hundred years old and incredibly stupid.

'So do I,' he said, looking amused by his mother being so pedantic. It wasn't like her. Usually she was pretty direct, but she was afraid to be now. She had learned that lesson once, no matter how right she had been, and she didn't want to lose him. But with Julian, she knew, it was different. Isabelle had been hot-headed and young, and Julian adored his mother, and was less likely to reject her completely. 'I think we're going to be very happy,' he said optimistically, which gave Sarah the opening she needed.

'I'm not as sure. Yvonne is an unusual girl, Julian. She's had a checkered career, and she's been taking care of herself for ten years.' She had run away from home at fourteen, she'd explained, and had given up school to model. 'She's a survivor. She's looking out for herself, maybe more than even for you. I'm not sure she really wants what you do, when you think of marriage.'

'What does that mean? You think she's after my money?'

'Possibly.'

'You're wrong.' He looked angry at her. She had no right to do this, as far as he was concerned. But she thought she did, because she was his mother. 'She just got half a million dollars from her husband in Berlin.'

'How nice for her,' Sarah said coolly. 'And how long were they married?'

'Eight months. She left him because he forced her to have an abortion.'

'Are you sure? The newspapers say that she left him for the son of a Greek shipping tycoon, and he then dumped her for some little French girl. Complicated group of people you run with.'

'She's a decent girl, and she's had a tough time. She's never had anyone to take care of her. Her mother was a whore, and she never even knew her father. He left before she was born, and her mother ditched her when she was thirteen. How can you expect her to have gone to some prissy little finishing school, like my sister?' His sister had made her own mistakes in spite of that, but this girl wasn't making mistakes. She was making intelligent, calculating decisions. And Julian was one of them. You could see it.

'I hope you're right. I just don't want you to be unhappy.'

'You have to let us lead our own lives,' he said angrily. 'You can't tell us what to do.'

'I try not to.'

'I know.' He forced himself to calm down. He really didn't want to fight with her. But he was sad that she hadn't been more impressed by Yvonne. He'd been crazy about her from the first moment he saw her. 'It's just that you always think you know what's right for us, and sometimes you're wrong.' Though he hated to admit it, not often. But still, he had a right to do what he wanted.

'I hope I'm wrong this time,' she said sadly.

'Will you give us your blessing?' That meant a lot to him. He had always adored her.

'If you want it.' She leaned forward and kissed him, with tears in her eyes. 'I love you so much . . . I don't ever want you to suffer.'

'I won't.' He beamed. He left then, and Sarah sat alone in her apartment for a long time, thinking of William, and her children, and wondering miserably why they were all so stupid.

Chapter 28

Julian and Yvonne were married in a civil ceremony performed at the *mairie* of La Marolle at Christmas. And then they all went back to the château, and had a sumptuous lunch. There were about forty guests, and Julian looked blissfully happy. Yvonne wore a short, beige lace dress by Givenchy, which reminded Sarah vaguely of a short modern version of her own when she married William. But all similarities ended there. There was a hardness to the girl, and a coldness that genuinely frightened Sarah.

It was obvious to Emanuelle, too, and the two women stood and laughed together ruefully in a quiet corner. 'Why does this keep happening to us?' Sarah said, shaking her head and looking at her old friend, who put a gentle hand on her shoulder.

'I told you . . . every time I look at you, I count my lucky stars that I never had children.' But it wasn't entirely true. There were times when she envied her, particularly now as she got older.

'They certainly make me wonder sometimes. I don't understand it. She's like ice, and he thinks she adores him.'

'I hope he never sees the truth,' Emanuelle said quietly, and she didn't tell Sarah that he had bought her a thirty-carat canary diamond ring for their wedding, and he had two matching bracelets on order. She was doing very well, and Emanuelle was sure that this was only the beginning.

Isabelle had come to the wedding, too, without Lorenzo

this time, and she was full of tales of the store in Rome. Everything was going brilliantly, and she was only annoyed that they had to spend so much money on guards. The situation in Italy, with the terrorists and the Red Brigade, made things difficult. But business was booming. Phillip had even had the grace to admit he'd been wrong, but not the spirit to come to his brother's wedding. But Julian didn't mind. All he saw, all he knew, all he wanted was Yvonne. And now he had her.

They were going to Tahiti for their honeymoon. Yvonne had said she'd never been and always wanted to go there. And they were going to stop in Los Angeles on the way home, to see his Aunt Jane, Sarah's sister. Sarah hadn't seen her in years, but they still kept in close touch, and Julian always maintained a family spirit. And conveniently, Yvonne wanted to go to Beverly Hills to go shopping.

Sarah saw them off, with the rest of the guests. And Isabelle stayed at the château until New Year's, which pleased Sarah. They celebrated Xavier's sixteenth birthday with him, and Isabelle said it seemed difficult to believe that he was so grown-up, she still remembered when he was a baby, which made Sarah laugh.

'Think how I feel when I look at you and Julian and Phillip. It seems like only yesterday when you were all small . . .' Her mind drifted off for a minute then, as she thought of William and those years. They had been so happy.

'You still miss him, don't you?' Isabelle asked softly, and Sarah nodded.

'It never goes away. You just learn to live with it.' Like losing Lizzie. She had never stopped loving her, or feeling the loss, she had just learned to live with the pain day by day, until it became a burden she was used to. But Isabelle knew something about that too. The absence of children in her life was a constant pain in her heart, and her hatred for

Lorenzo weighed on her whenever she let herself think of it, which lately, was less and less often. Mercifully, she was too busy with the store now to think of much else. And Sarah was thrilled they had opened a store in Rome for Isabelle to run.

She was sad to see her go, and life went on peacefully after that. That year seemed to fly by, as it always did. And then suddenly, it was summer, and they were all coming to visit for her birthday. She was going to be sixty-five, and for some reason she dreaded it, but they had all insisted on coming to the château, and helping her to celebrate it, which was her only consolation.

'I can't bear thinking I'm so old,' she admitted to Isabelle when they arrived. Lorenzo had come, too, this time, which seemed too bad. Isabelle was always more tense when he was around, but they had a lot to talk about, about the store, which kept her distracted.

Phillip and Cecily came, too, of course. She was in high spirits, and talked endlessly about her new horse. She was involved with the English Olympic equestrian team, and she and Princess Anne had just gone hunting together in Scotland. They were old friends from school, and Cecily seemed not to even notice the fact that Phillip neither listened nor spoke to her. She just went on talking. Their children had come too. Alexander and Christina. They were fourteen and twelve, and Xavier was a good sport about keeping them amused, although he was older. He took them swimming in the pool, played tennis with them, and teased them by making them call him 'Uncle' Xavier, which amused them.

And then finally, Julian and Yvonne arrived, in his brand-new Jaguar. She was looking prettier than ever, and rather languid, and Sarah couldn't decide if it was due to the heat, or boredom. It wasn't likely to be an exciting weekend for any of them, she mused, and she felt guilty for bringing them there. At least she could tell them about her trip to Botswana with Xavier. It had been fascinating, and she'd even visited relatives of William in Cape Town. She'd brought home small presents for everyone, but Xavier had brought home some extraordinary fossils and rocks, some rare but rough-cut gems, and a collection of black diamonds. He had a real passion for stones, and an eye for them, an immediate instinct for their value, in the roughest state, and how they would have to be cut to preserve them. He had particularly loved the diamond mines they'd visited in Johannesburg, and had tried to talk his mother into bringing home a tanzanite the size of a grapefruit.

'I had no idea what to do with it,' she explained, after telling them the story.

'They're very popular in London now,' Phillip said, but he was not in the best mood. Nigel had been ill recently, and was talking about retiring at the end of the year, which was bad news for him. He told his mother that he would be impossible to replace after all these years, and she didn't remind him of how much he'd hated him at first. They would all miss him, if he left, and she still hoped he wouldn't.

They went on talking about the trip to Africa for a while, over lunch on their first day there, and then she apologized for boring them. Enzo was staring at the sky, and she could see that Yvonne was restless.

Cecily said she wanted to see the stables after lunch, and Sarah informed her that there was nothing new there, just the same old tired horses, but Cecily went anyway. Lorenzo went to take a nap, Isabelle wanted to show her mother some sketches she'd designed, and Julian had promised to take Xavier and Phillip's children for a ride in his new car, which left Phillip and Yvonne on their own, feeling somewhat awkward. He had only met her once before since they'd been married, but he had to admit she was a smashing-looking girl. Her blond hair was so pale, it looked almost white in the midday sun, as he offered her a tour of the gardens. And as they strolled, she referred to him as 'Your Grace', which he didn't seem to mind or find inappropriate, but then again, she loved being Lady Whitfield. She told him about her one brief experience in Hollywood, and he seemed fascinated, and as they walked and talked, she seemed to move closer to him. He could smell the shampoo in her hair, and as he looked down at her, he could see right down the front of her dress. It was almost all he could do to control himself suddenly as he stood next to her, she was an incredibly sensuous young woman.

'You're very beautiful,' he said suddenly, as she looked up at him almost shyly. They were at the very back of the rose garden by then, and the air was so hot and still, she wished they could take their clothes off.

'Thank you.' She lowered her eyelids then, her long lashes brushing her cheek, and unable to stop himself, he suddenly reached out and touched her. It was almost more powerful than he, a desire so great that he couldn't control it. He slipped a hand into her dress, and she moaned, moving closer to him until she leaned against him. 'Oh, Phillip . . .' she said softly, as though she wanted him to do it again, and he did. He took both her breasts in his hands, and fondled the nipples.

'My God, you're so lovely,' he whispered, and then slowly he pulled her down on the grass next to him, and they lay there, feeling each other's passion mount until they were both frenzied.

'No . . . we can't . . .' she said softly, as he pulled her thin silk underwear down past her knees. 'We shouldn't here . . .' It was the location she was objecting to, but not the act, or the person. But he couldn't stop himself by then. He had to have her. He was exploding with desire for her, and at that exact moment, as they lay there in the brilliant sun, nothing could have stopped him. And as he entered her slowly, achingly, and then with overwhelming force, she pressed hard against him, urging him on, enticing him, torturing him with desire and then teasing him until he shouted in the still air, and then it was over.

They lay panting side by side afterwards, and he looked at her, unable to believe what they'd done, or how extraordinary it had been. He had never known anyone like her. And he knew he'd have to have her again . . . and again . . . As he looked at her he wanted her yet again, and he felt himself harden, and plunged into her without a word. The only sound he heard was her delicious moaning, until they came again, and he held her.

'My God, you're incredible,' he whispered to her, wondering finally if anyone had heard them, but no longer caring. He was impervious to everything except this woman who drove him to near madness.

'So are you,' she breathed at him, still feeling him throb inside her. 'It's never been like this for me,' she said, and he believed her, and then something occurred to him, and he pulled himself slowly away to see her better.

'Not even with Julian?' She shook her head, and something in her eyes told him that there was something she wasn't saying. 'Is something wrong there?' He looked hopeful and she shrugged and clung adoringly to his older brother. She had figured out long since that a lord was not a duke, and a second son was not his older brother. And she liked the idea of being a duchess, and not merely a lady.

'It's . . . it's not the same thing . . .' she said sadly. 'I don't know.' She shrugged, looking distressed. 'Maybe there's something wrong with him . . . we have no sex life . . .' she whispered. Phillip looked at her in astonishment, with a happy smile.

'Is that right?' He looked so pleased. Julian was a sham. His reputation meant nothing. All these years of hating him. For nothing. 'How amazing.'

'I used to think that . . . maybe he was gay.' She looked ashamed, and her extreme youth touched him. 'But I don't think he is. I think he's just nothing.' Several thousand women would have screamed with laughter at what she had just said, but she was a better actress than any of them thought, particularly Phillip.

'I'm so sorry.' But he wasn't sorry at all. He was thrilled. And he hated to pull away from her, and put their clothes on. He had merely unzipped his own, but they had to look for a moment in the rose bushes for her silk panties, and as they did, they laughed, wondering what his mother would think if she ever found them. 'I daresay she'd think the gardener was having some fun.' He grinned, and Yvonne laughed so hard at what he said that she fell on the ground again, and rolled in the soft grass, her long lean thighs beckoning him, and he took her again without hesitation. 'I daresay we should go back,' he said eventually, with regret. But his whole life had just changed, in the past two hours. 'Do you suppose you could get away from him tonight for a while?' he asked, wondering where they would go. Maybe a local hotel. And then he had a better idea. The old barracks in the stables. There were still dozens of mattresses there, and blankets they used for the horses. But he couldn't bear the thought of spending a night without her, and the forbiddenness of it made it even more enticing.

'I can try,' she said hopefully. This was the most fun she'd had since she'd gotten married . . . this time. And it was her specialty. The Double Entendre Extraordinaire. She loved it. Her first husband had been a twin. And she had slept with his brother, and his father, before he left her. Klaus had been more complicated, but very amusing. And Julian was sweet, but so naive. She had been bored since May. And Phillip was the best thing that had happened to her all year . . . possibly ever.

They walked back by the road, side by side, brushing

hands, seeming to make normal conversation, but in an undertone she kept telling him how much she loved him . . . how good it had been . . . how wet she was . . . and how she could hardly wait until that night . . . By the time they got back to the house she had driven him into a frenzy. He looked flushed and vague as Julian drove into view in the Jaguar.

'Hi there!' He waved. 'What have you two been up to?'

'Looking at the rose gardens,' she said sweetly.

'In this heat? You're brave.' The young people got out of his new car then, and he noticed how hot and miserable his brother looked and he almost laughed at him, but he didn't.

'Poor baby, did he bore you to death?' he asked, after Phillip left. 'It's just like him to drag you around the property to look at gardens on the hottest day of the year.'

'He meant well,' she whispered, and they went upstairs to make love before dinner.

Dinner that night was a jolly affair. Everyone had had a good day and was in high spirits. Cecily had managed to find some old German military saddles in the barn which fascinated her, and she even asked Sarah if she could take one back to England, and Sarah said she was welcome to anything she liked. Xavier had gotten to drive Julian's new car, the younger children had had a good time, too, and in spite of Lorenzo being there, Isabelle looked relaxed and happy. The newlyweds seemed in fine spirits too. Phillip was a little quiet, which wasn't unusual for him. And even the birthday girl seemed to have made her peace with what she referred to as 'those appalling numbers'. But she was so happy to see them all, that suddenly the birthday seemed less important. And she was sorry they would all be leaving again the following afternoon. Their visits were always so short, but at least nowadays, with Isabelle having returned to the fold, they were fairly pleasant.

They sat in the drawing room for a long time that night,

Julian asking her questions about the Occupation during the war, and he was fascinated with some of her stories. Cecily wanted to know how many horses they'd had quartered there and what kind, and Yvonne kept standing behind Julian and rubbing his shoulders. Enzo was dozing in a comfortable chair, and Isabelle played cards with her youngest brother, as Phillip drank brandy and smoked cigars and stared out the window at the stables.

And then, eventually Julian understood what Yvonne had in mind, and they disappeared upstairs quietly, with a last kiss to his mother. Cecily was the next to leave. She said she was still exhausted after her recent trip to Scotland. And eventually Phillip disappeared too. Enzo dozed on, and Isabelle and Sarah chatted for a long time, after Xavier went to bed. The house was quiet, and there was a full moon. It was a beautiful night for her birthday. They had eaten cake and drunk champagne, and she loved being surrounded by her children.

And all the while, upstairs, Yvonne was using all her most exotic tricks to torture her husband. There were things she had learned in Germany that she loved to do to him that absolutely drove him crazy. And half an hour later, he was so exhausted and so sated that he was sound asleep, and she slipped quietly out of the room with a smile. She was wearing jeans, and a very skimpy T-shirt, as she ran to the stables.

Cecily was also asleep by then. She had taken sleeping pills, which she liked to do, to ensure that she slept well. She thought it was worth the occasional hangover in the morning. And she was already snoring by the time Phillip left the room, still wearing the same clothes he had worn at dinner. He knew the back paths well, and only a few twigs crunched beneath his feet, but there was no-one to hear him, and he entered the stables through the back door, pausing for a moment to adjust his eyes in the darkness. And then he saw her, only a few feet away from him, beautiful and shimmering pale in the moonlight, like a ghost, totally naked, as she sat astride one of the German saddles. He got up behind her then, and pulled her close to him, and he ground against her that way, for a short time, feeling the satin of her flesh, as his desire mounted, and then he pulled her off her seat and carried her to one of the mattresses in the stalls. It was where the German soldiers had lived, and where he made love to her now, pounding into her, and begging her never to leave him. They lay together for hours, and as he held her he knew his life would never be the same. It couldn't be. He couldn't let her go . . . she was too extraordinary . . . and too rare . . . too powerful . . . like a drug he needed to survive now.

Isabelle went up to bed after one o'clock, after finally waking Lorenzo. He apologized, and walked sleepily up the stairs, as Sarah sat alone in her living room, wondering what would happen.

They couldn't go on forever like that. Sooner or later, he would have to let her leave him. He was holding her hostage, and Sarah didn't intend to let him do that forever. Just thinking of it made her angry. Isabelle was such a beautiful girl, and she had a right to more of a life than he was willing to give her. He had been every bit as bad as they feared, and worse. And as Sarah thought of it, she let herself out on to the patio in the moonlight. It reminded her of some of the summer nights during the war, when Joachim was still there, and they had talked late into the night about Rilke and Schiller and Thomas Mann . . . trying not to think of the war, or the wounded, or whether or not William was still alive. As she thought of it, she began to walk instinctively toward the cottage. No-one lived there any more. It had been unused for a long time. The new caretaker's cottage was closer to the gate, and a good deal more modern. But she let the old one stand, out of sentiment. She and William had lived there first, while they worked on the château, and Lizzie had been born and died there.

She was still thinking of that time, as she took a little stroll before going to bed, when she heard a noise as she passed the stables. It was a low moan, and she wondered if an animal was injured. They kept half a dozen horses there, in case anyone wanted to ride, but most of them were old and not very exciting. She quietly opened the door, and there didn't seem to be anything there, the animals were all quiet again, but then she heard noises again, coming from the old barracks. They sounded like weird unearthly sounds, and she couldn't fathom what they were, as she made her way slowly toward them. It didn't even occur to her to be afraid, or to pick up a pitchfork or something to protect herself with if it was an intruder or a rabid animal. She just walked into the stall it came from and snapped on the light, and found herself staring at the entwined bodies of Phillip and Yvonne, both of them entirely naked, and there was no question in anyone's mind what they were doing. She stared at them in amazement for an instant, and saw the look of horror on Phillip's face, before she turned away to let them dress, but then she turned back to them in total fury.

She addressed herself to Yvonne first, and without an instant's hesitation. 'How dare you do this to Julian? How *dare* you, you tramp, with his own *brother*, in his own *home* under *my* roof! How *dare* you!' But Yvonne only tossed her long, blond hair over one shoulder and stood there. She hadn't even bothered to get dressed, and she stood there without shame in all her naked beauty.

'And you!' She turned to Phillip then. 'Always sneaking around . . . always cheating on your wife, and consumed with jealousy for your brother. You make me sick. I am filled with shame for you, Phillip.' And then she looked at both of them as she stood there shaking, for Julian, for

446

herself, for what they were doing to each other's lives and their complete lack of respect for everyone around them. 'If I discover that you are continuing this, that this happens again, *anywhere*, I will tell Cecily and Julian immediately. And I will have you both followed in the meantime.' She had no intention of doing it, but nor did she intend sanctioning their infidelities, particuarly not in her own home, and at the expense of Julian, who didn't deserve it.

'Mother, I . . . I'm terribly sorry.' Phillip had managed to cover himself with a horse blanket by then, and he was mortified at having been discovered. 'It was one of those unusual things . . . I don't know what happened . . .' he blustered, on the verge of tears.

'She does,' Sarah said brutally, looking straight at her. 'Don't ever let it happen again,' she said, looking deep into her eyes. 'I warn you.' And then she turned on her heel and left. And once she had left them, and was outside again, she leaned against a tree and cried, out of grief and shame and embarrassment for them, and herself. But as she walked slowly back to the château, all she could think of was Julian and the pain he had coming to him. How foolish her children were. And why was she never able to help them?

Chapter 29

Yvonne was unusually quiet with Julian on the ride home from the château. She didn't seem upset, but she just didn't talk much. There had been an odd atmosphere in the air the day they left, almost like a storm, Xavier had said innocently to his mother after they were gone. But the weather was hot and relentlessly sunny. Sarah had said nothing to anyone about what she'd seen, but Phillip and Yvonne knew. That was enough. And the others just moved along, oblivious to what had happened the night before in the stables, which was just as well. Everyone would have been stunned, except maybe Lorenzo, who would have been amused, and Julian who would have been devastated.

And when they got to Paris, Julian asked Yvonne gently if anything had happened to upset her.

'No,' she shrugged. 'I was just bored.' But when he tried to make love to her that night, she resisted.

'What's wrong?' He persisted in asking her, she had been so enthusiastic about it the night before, and now suddenly she was so cool. She was unpredictable all the time, mercurial, but he liked that. Sometimes he liked it best when she resisted him, it only made her more exciting. He reacted that way to her resisting him now, but this time she wasn't playing.

'Stop it . . . I'm tired . . . I have a headache.' She had never used that excuse before, but she was still annoyed about the performance the night before, with Sarah acting like she owned the world and threatening them, and

Phillip grovelling to her like a child. She had been so angry, she had slapped him afterwards, hard, and he had gotten so excited they'd made love again. They hadn't left the stables until six o'clock that morning. And now she was tired and annoyed that all of them were so affected by their mother. 'Leave me alone,' she repeated to him. They were all nothing but mama's boys, and their damn snob of a sister. She knew that none of them approved of her. But she didn't care. She was getting what she wanted. And now maybe she'd get more of it, if Phillip did what he said he would, and came to see her from London. She could still use her old studio on the Île Saint Louis, or go to the hotel where he stayed, or make love to him right here in Julian's bed, if she wanted, no matter what the old bitch said. But she was in no mood for any of them just then, least of all her husband.

'I want you now . . .' Julian was teasing her, excited by her refusal, and sensing something animal and strange, like a predator who had somehow come too near him. It was as though he sensed someone else's scent on her, instinctively, and he wanted her now to make her his again. 'What's wrong?' he kept asking, trying to excite her with his deft fingers, but she kept him away this time, which was rare for her.

'I forgot to take the pill today,' she said, and he whispered huskily as he brushed against her.

'Take it later.' But the truth was that she had run out the day before, and now she wanted to be careful for a few days. She'd had enough abortions to last a lifetime, and the one thing she didn't want was brats, Julian's or anyone else's. And when he pressed her about it eventually, she was going to quietly go and get her tubes tied. That would make things easier, but for right now things weren't quite that easy. 'Never mind the pill.' He played with her, and turned her over to face him, and then as he did, just as his brother had the night before, he was overwhelmed with desire for her, just as men always had been, since she was twelve and she began to learn just exactly what it was they wanted. She knew what Julian wanted now, but she didn't want to give it to him. She preferred torturing him. She lay with her legs open, and her eyes wide, and if he came near her, she was going to hit him. But he couldn't stop himself by then. She had pushed him too far, denying him, and lying there, naked and lovely, with her legs apart, her body calling to him, while she pretended not to.

He took her quickly and hard, and she was surprised by the force of it, as she shuddered with pleasure, too, and then afterwards groaned at how stupid she had been. But she always was and this time she was really angry.

'Shit!' she said, as she rolled away from him.

'What's wrong?' He looked hurt, she was behaving very strangely.

'I told you I didn't want to do it. What if I get pregnant?'

'So?' He looked amused. 'We have a baby.'

'No, we don't,' she spat at him. 'I'm too young . . . I don't want a baby now. We just got married.' She wasn't ready yet to tell him more than that, and she knew how much he wanted children.

'All right, all right. Go have a hot bath, or a cold shower, or a douche or something, or take the pill. I'm sorry.' But he didn't look it as he kissed her. He would have liked nothing better than to get her pregnant.

But three weeks later, he came home unexpectedly in the afternoon, and found her retching over the toilet.

'Oh, poor baby,' he said, helping her to bed. 'Is it something you ate, or flu?' He had never seen her so sick, as she looked at him with eyes filled with hatred. She knew it too well. It was the seventh time for her. She'd had six abortions in the last twelve years, and she was going to have another one this time. She got sick from the first

450

moment, the first hour, and she always knew, as she did this time.

'It's nothing,' she insisted, 'I'm fine.' But he hated to leave her again, to go back to the office. He made her soup that night, and she threw that up too. The next morning she wasn't much better, so he came home early without warning to take care of her. She was out when he answered the phone, and the receptionist at her doctor was calling to confirm that her abortion was the following morning.

'Her *what*?' He shouted into the phone. 'Cancel it! She won't be there.' He called his office then, cancelled the rest of his afternoon, and waited for her. She came back at four, and she was in no way prepared for his fury when she walked back into the apartment.

'Your doctor called,' he explained, and she looked at him, wondering if he knew, but only for an instant. After that, there was no doubt at all as to what he knew or how he felt about it. He was livid. 'Why didn't you tell me you were pregnant?'

'Because it's too soon . . . we're not ready for it . . . and . . .' She looked at him and wondered if he'd believe her. 'The doctor said it was too soon after the abortion Klaus forced me to have.'

He almost bought it for an instant and then he remembered. 'That was last year.'

'I haven't fully recovered yet.' She started to cry. 'I want our baby, Julian, but not yet.'

'Sometimes these choices aren't ours to make, and we have to make the best of it. I don't want you to have an abortion.'

'Well, I do.' She looked at him stubbornly. She wasn't going to let him talk her out of it. Besides, this was no time for her to be pregnant. Phillip was coming over to see her and she didn't want a big belly now, or a baby at the end of it, or any of it. She wanted it out of her body, now, or at the very least by the next morning.

'I'm not going to let you do this.' They fought about it all night, and he refused to go to work the next day, for fear that she'd go to her doctor, and then when she realized how serious he was, she really got nasty. She was fighting for her life, or she thought she was, and she cut him to the quick as he listened.

'Listen, dammit, I'm going to get rid of it no matter what you do . . . it probably isn't even your baby.' Her words stunned him, like a knife to his heart, and he backed away from her as though he'd been shot, unable to believe her.

'Are you telling me this is someone else's child?' He stared at her in horror and amazement.

'It could be,' she said, without expression or feeling.

'Do you mind if I ask whose? Has that little Greek shit been back again?' He had seen him twice before they were married and he knew Yvonne thought he was very sexy. But suddenly she thought it was all a big joke. His baby was probably actually the next Duke of Whitfield, not the son of the second son at all, but the son of His Grace, the Duke of Whitfield. She started laughing until she couldn't stop, she was hysterical, and then, beside himself, he slapped her. 'What's happening to you? What have you been doing?' But she had given up by then, she knew that she had lost with Julian the moment she refused to have his baby. There was nothing more to get from him now. The game was over. It was time to concentrate on Phillip.

'Actually' – she grinned evilly at him – 'I've been sleeping with your brother. The baby is probably his, so you don't need to worry about it any more.' But as Julian stared at her in horror and grief, he sat down on the bed and started to laugh at the same time he started to cry, as she watched him.

'That's really very funny.' He wiped his eyes, but he was no longer laughing.

'Isn't it? Your mother thought so too.' She decided to tell him everything now. She didn't care. She had never loved him. It had been good for a while, but now they both knew it was over. 'She found us in the stables at the château. Fucking.' He reeled at the word she used and the image it conjured.

'My mother knows about this?' He looked horrified. 'Who else knows? Does Phillip's wife?'

'I don't know.' She shrugged. 'I suppose we should tell her if I'm going to have his baby.' She was taunting him with that, because she wasn't going to have anyone's child, unless, of course, Phillip agreed to divorce Cecily and marry her, then she might agree to have his baby. It was called marrying up, and as an incentive, she might agree to have the baby.

But Julian was looking at her with broken eyes. 'My brother had a vasectomy years ago, because his wife didn't want any more children,' he said tonelessly. 'Did he tell you that? Or didn't he bother?' Julian knew just when it had happened and that it was his child. It had happened the night she had forgotten to take the pill and he had forced her. But then something else occurred to him, and he looked up at her with anger and hatred. 'I don't understand how you could do this to me, or why. I would never have done something like this to you.' He wouldn't have because he was a decent person. 'But I'll tell you one thing now and you'd better believe me. If you married me for my money, you will not get one red cent from me unless you have this baby. If you get rid of it, I'll see that you never get a penny from me, or my family, and don't fool yourself, my brother won't help you. That child inside you is a person, a real life . . . and it's mine. And I want it. You can leave after that. You can go to Phillip if you want. He'll never marry you. He hasn't got the guts to leave his wife. But you can do anything you want, and I'll give you a decent settlement. Maybe even a big one. But kill my baby, Yvonne, and it's all over. You'll never see a penny from me. And I mean that.'

'Are you threatening me?' She looked at him with such hatred that it was hard to believe he had ever thought she loved him.

'Yes, I am. I'm telling you that if you don't have that baby, if you even accidentally lose it, I'm not giving you one cent. Keep it, have it, give it to me, and you can have a divorce from me, and a settlement . . . with honors . . . Is that a deal?'

'I'll have to think about it.' He walked across the room toward her, feeling violent about a woman for the first time in his life, grabbed her long blond hair, and pulled it. 'You'd better think fast, and if you kill my baby, I swear I'll kill you.'

He threw her away from him, then, and left the house. He was gone for hours, and he drank and cried, and when he came back he was so drunk he had almost forgotten what he was upset about, but not quite. And in the morning, she told him that she would go through with it, and have the baby. But she wanted a settlement from him first. He told her he'd call his lawyers as soon as he got to the office. But he made it clear to her that he wanted her living with him, she could move into the guest room, but he wanted to know that she was taking care of herself, and he wanted to be there when she had the baby.

She looked at him venomously and spoke in a hard, vicious tone that left no doubt in anyone's mind how she felt about him, or his baby.

'I hate you.'

And she hated every single moment of being pregnant. Phillip came over to visit her for the first few months, but eventually after Christmas it just got too awkward. She was no fun for him then any more, and the situation was too complicated. He didn't mind Julian knowing what he was about, in fact he rather liked it. But he knew his

454

mother did as well, and he didn't want to run into her. He told Yvonne they'd go for a holiday in June after she had the baby. And she hated Julian even more after that. As far as she could see, he had ruined everything, and was costing her everything she wanted. She wanted Phillip more than anything in life, and she wanted to be his duchess. He had said he might leave his wife eventually, but just then it wasn't the right time as her mother was very ill, and she was deeply upset, and with the baby . . . He urged her to wait and stay calm, and hearing that only made her more hysterical and angrier at Julian. And then she began calling Phillip every day, taunting him, teasing him on the phone, in the office, at home, at all the most awkward moments possible, reminding him of the things they'd done, and suddenly he was begging for her again, throbbing, pounding, aching, and he could hardly wait till June. She had made him crazy for her again, and now the wait till June didn't seem quite as painful. They spoke on the phone every day, usually several times, and always sexually, as she told him the things she was going to do to him when they went away after she had the baby. It was what Phillip wanted from her, and he loved it.

She and Julian barely spoke to each other. She had moved to another room, and she looked almost as bad as she felt. She threw up for six months, and then began again two months later. Julian thought that half of it was her resentment and her anger. And he saw the constant calls to Phillip on his bill, but he said nothing. He had no idea what would happen between them and he tried to tell himself he didn't care, but he did, the whole experience had been incredibly painful. And the only thing that cheered him was the baby she had agreed to have and give him. She wanted no custody, no visitation rights, no claim on the child at all. The baby was Julian's entirely. For a mere million dollars. Play or pay. And he agreed to pay it. *After* she had the baby.

He had only one conversation with his mother about the whole affair, if only to explain to her why he would be selling some of his stock in the company. Paying off Yvonne was going to completely wipe out his savings, but he knew it was worth it.

'I'm sorry I got myself into this mess,' he apologized to Sarah one day, which she told him was absurd. It was his life, and he owed her no apologies and no explanations.

'You're the only one who's been hurt by it. I'm just so sorry it all happened,' she told him.

'So am I . . . but at least I'll have the baby.' He smiled ruefully, and went back to the cold war in his apartment. He had already hired a nurse for the child, set a room aside for it, and Isabelle had even promised to come from Rome to help him. He had no idea how to care for a child, but he was willing to learn. Yvonne had already said she was going straight from the hospital to her own apartment. Their deal would be complete then. And her bank account a million dollars richer.

The baby wasn't due till May, but in late April she started packing up her things, as though she couldn't wait to leave, and Julian watched her in fascination.

'Don't you feel anything for this child?' he asked sadly, let alone for him. But he knew the answer to that question long since. All she cared about was Phillip.

'Why should I? I've never seen it.' She had no maternal instincts, no feelings of remorse for him. The only thing she was interested in now was continuing her affair with Phillip. He told her he had made reservations in Mallorca for the first week in June. And she didn't care where they went, just so she was with him. She was going to see to it that she got everything she wanted.

On the first of May, Julian got a call at his office. Lady Whitfield had just checked into the clinic in Neuilly, it was the same one where he had been born, unlike his more enterprising brother and sister who had been delivered by their father at the château.

Emanuelle saw him leave and asked if he'd like her to come with him, but he shook his head and hurried outside to his car, and half an hour later he was at the hospital, pacing up and down, waiting for them to let him into the delivery room, and for a moment he was afraid that Yvonne wouldn't let him. But the nurse came in to him a few minutes later, handed him a green cotton suit and what looked like a shower cap, told him where to change, and then guided him to the delivery room, where Yvonne glanced up at him between pains with open hatred.

'I'm sorry . . .' He felt instantly sorry for her, and tried to take her hand, but she pulled it away from him and clutched the table. The contractions were terrible, but the nurse said it was going very well, very quickly for a first baby. 'I hope it's fast,' he whispered to Yvonne, not knowing what else to say to her.

'I hate you,' she spat out between clenched teeth, trying to remind herself that she was being paid a million dollars for this and it was worth it. It was a hell of a way to build a fortune.

Things slowed down then for a while, they gave her a shot, and it dragged on, as Julian sat nervously, wondering if everything was all right. It was so strange being here with this woman whom he no longer loved, and who clearly hated him, as they waited for their baby. It seemed very surreal, and he was sorry he hadn't asked someone to come with him after all. He felt suddenly very lonely.

Her labor finally picked up again, and Julian had to admit he felt desperately sorry for her, it looked awful. Nature knew nothing of her indifference to this child, or the fact that she wasn't keeping it, and it was making her pay a price for it nonetheless. She worked long and hard and momentarily even forgot her hatred of Julian and let him help her. He held her shoulders and her hands, and

457

everyone in the room encouraged her until dark, and then suddenly, finally, there was a long, thin wail, and a tiny red face appeared angrily as the doctor held him. Yvonne's eyes filled with tears as she looked at him, and she smiled for an instant, and then she turned her face away from him, and the doctor handed him to Julian, who cried openly, unashamed, and nuzzled the little face next to his own, as the baby stopped crying the moment he heard him.

'Oh God, he's so beautiful,' he said in awe of his son, and then he gently held him toward Yvonne, but she shook her head and turned away again. She didn't want to see him.

They let Julian take the baby back to the room with him, and he held him there for hours until they brought Yvonne back. And she asked him if he would leave, so she could call Phillip. She told the nurse to take the baby to the nursery, and not to bring him to her again, and then she looked at the man whose son she had just borne, and whom she had married, but her face was without emotion.

'I guess this is goodbye then,' she said quietly, but she held out no hand, no arms, no hope, and Julian felt sad for both of them, despite the arrival of the baby. It was an emotional day for him, and he cried easily as he looked at her and nodded.

'I'm sorry things worked out the way they did for us,' he said sadly. 'The baby is so beautiful, isn't he . . .'

'I guess so.' She shrugged.

'I'll take good care of him,' he whispered, and then took a step closer to her and kissed her cheek. She had worked so hard for him and now she was giving him up. It tore at Julian's heart, but not at Yvonne's. He was the only one crying.

She looked at him matter-of-factly before he left. 'Thanks for the money.' That was all he had ever meant to her. And he left her then, to her own life.

She left the hospital the next day. The funds were already in her bank account since that morning. True to his word, he had paid her a million dollars for their baby.

Julian took the baby home with the nurse. He had named him Maximillian. Max. And the baby looked it. Sarah drove up from the château with Xavier that afternoon to see him, and Isabelle flew in from Rome that night, and held him for hours in the rocking chair. In his short life, he had already lost his mother, but he had gained an adoring family who had waited for him lovingly. And Isabelle thought her heart would break with longing as she held him.

'You're so lucky,' she whispered to her brother that night as they looked down at Max as he slept.

'I wouldn't have thought so six months ago,' Julian said to her, 'but I do now. It was all worth it.' He wondered where Yvonne had gone, how she was, if she was sorry, but he didn't think so as he lay in bed that night, thinking of his son, and how lucky he was to have him.

Chapter 30

The family reunited for Sarah's birthday again that year, although not all of them. Yvonne was gone, of course, and Phillip had discreetly stayed away, after making excuses that he was just too busy in London. Sarah had heard a rumour from Nigel, who was still at work, that Phillip and Cecily were having a trial separation, but she didn't say anything to Julian.

Julian came with Max, of course, and a nurse, but he did most of the work himself, and it was obvious that he loved it. Sarah watched admiringly as he changed Max, bathed him, fed him, dressed him. The only painful thing was seeing Isabelle watching him. There was still a longing in her eyes that cut Sarah to the core. But they were freer to talk now, she had come to the château that summer without Lorenzo. It was also a special summer for all of them, because it was Xavier's last one at home. He was starting Yale a year early, in the fall, at seventeen, and Sarah was very proud of him. He was majoring in political science with a minor in geology. And he was talking about doing his junior year somewhere in Africa, as a special project.

'We're going to miss you horribly,' Sarah admitted to him, and everyone agreed with her. She herself was going to spend more time in Paris and less at the château, so she wouldn't be so lonely. At sixty-six, she liked to claim that they all ran the business entirely, but she still kept a strong hand in it, as did Emanuelle, who had just turned sixty, which Sarah found even harder to believe than her own age.

Xavier was very excited about going to Yale, and Sarah couldn't blame him. He would be coming back at Christmastime, and Julian had promised to go over and visit him when he had to go to New York on business. The two were chatting about it, as Sarah and Isabelle drifted off to the garden for a chat, and Isabelle asked her discreetly what was happening with Phillip. She had heard the rumour of his separation, too, and echoes of his affair with Yvonne had reached her through Emanuelle the previous summer.

'It was an ugly business,' Sarah said with a sigh, still shaken by it. But Julian seemed to have come out of it pretty well, especially now with the baby.

'We don't make life easy for you, Mother, do we?' Isabelle asked ruefully and her mother smiled. 'You don't make life easy for yourselves.' But Isabelle laughed as she said it.

'There's something I want to tell you.'

'Oh? Has Enzo finally agreed to move out?'

'No.' Isabelle shook her head slowly, and her eyes met her mother's. But Sarah saw that she looked more peaceful than she had in a long time. 'I'm pregnant.'

'You're what?' This time Sarah was stunned, she had thought there was no hope of it. 'You are?' She looked amazed and then thrilled as she put her arms around her. 'Why darling, how wonderful!' And then she pulled away from her again, a little puzzled. 'I thought . . . what did Lorenzo say? He must be beside himself.' But the prospect of cementing the marriage further wasn't entirely good news to Sarah.

Isabelle laughed again in spite of herself at the absurdity of the situation. 'Mother, it's not his.'

'Oh dear.' Things were getting complicated again. She sat down on a little wall and looked up at Isabelle. 'What have you been up to now?'

'He's a wonderful man. I've been seeing him for a year

461

'. . . Mother . . . I can't help it . . . I'm twenty-six years old, I can't lead this empty life . . . I need someone to love . . . someone to talk to . . .'

'I understand,' she said quietly, and she did. She had hated knowing how lonely Isabelle was and how little hope there was for her. 'But a baby? Does Enzo know?'

'I told him. I was hoping it would make him so angry he'd leave, but he says he doesn't care. Everyone will think it's his. In fact, he told two of his friends last week and they congratulated me. He's crazy.'

'No, greedy,' Sarah said matter-of-factly. 'And the baby's father? What does he say? Who is he?'

'He's German. From Munich. He's head of a very important foundation there, and his wife is very prominent and she doesn't want a divorce. He's thirty-six, and they had to get married when he was nineteen. They lead totally separate lives, but she doesn't want the embarrassment of a divorce. Yet.'

'How does he feel about the embarrassment of an illegitimate baby?' she asked bluntly.

'Not great. Neither do I. But what choice do I have? Do you think Lorenzo will ever leave?'

'We'll try. And what about you?' She looked at her daughter searchingly. 'Are you happy? Is this what you want?'

'Yes, I really love him. His name is Lukas von Ausbach.'

'I've heard of the family, not that that means anything. Do you think he'll ever marry you?'

'If he can.' She was honest with her mother.

'And if he can't? If his wife won't let him go? Then what?'

'Then at least I have a baby.' She had wanted one so badly, especially when she saw Julian with Max.

'When is it due, by the way?'

'February. Will you come?' Isabelle asked softly, and her mother nodded.

462

'Of course.' She was touched to be asked, and then suddenly she wondered. 'Does Julian know about all this?' The two were always so close, it was hard to believe he didn't. Isabelle said that she had just told him that morning. 'What does he say?'

'That I'm as crazy as he is.' She smiled.

'It must be genetic,' Sarah said as she stood again, and they walked back to the château. One thing was certain, at least. Her children were never boring.

In September, Xavier left for Yale, as planned, and Julian went to New Haven in October to see him. He was doing well, loved the school, and had two very nice roommates, and a very attractive girlfriend. Julian took them out to dinner, and they had a good time. Xavier loved his American life, and he was planning to go to California to visit his aunt for Thanksgiving.

When Julian went back to Paris he heard that Phillip and Cecily were getting a divorce, and at Christmas he saw a photograph of his brother and his ex-wife in the *Tatler*. He showed it to Sarah when she was at the shop, and she frowned. She was not pleased to see it.

'Do you suppose he'll marry her?' she asked Emanuelle when they talked about it later.

'It's possible.' She no longer had the faith in him she once had had, especially lately. 'He might even do it just to upset Julian.' His jealousy for him had never abated, it had grown worse over the years instead of better.

Xavier came home at Christmas and the days flew by, as usual. And when he left to go back to school, Sarah went to Rome, to keep an eye on the store and help Isabelle get ready for the baby.

Marcello was still there, working very hard, as Isabelle prepared to leave. And as it had been from the first, business was booming. Sarah smiled when she saw her daughter, rattling off instructions to everyone in Italian.

She looked beautiful, and prettier than she ever had before, but she was absolutely enormous. It reminded her of when she'd been pregnant with her own children, who were always so large. But Isabelle seemed sublimely happy.

Sarah invited her son-in-law to lunch shortly after she arrived. They went to El Toulà, and shortly after the first course, Sarah got to the point. She didn't mince words with Lorenzo this time.

'Lorenzo, we're grown-ups, you and I.' He was very close to her age, and Isabelle had been married to him for nine years now. It seemed a high price to pay for a youthful mistake, and she was anxious to help her end it. 'You and Isabelle haven't been happy for a long time. This baby is . . . well, we both know the situation. It's time to call it a day, wouldn't you say?'

'My love for Isabelle will never end,' he said, sounding melodramatic as Sarah made a supreme effort not to lose her temper.

'I'm sure. But it must be very painful for both of you, and you certainly.' She decided to change tack with him and treat him as the wounded party. 'And now this terrible embarrassment to you, with the baby. Wouldn't you think it a good time to make some wise investments, and agree to leave Isabelle to a new life?' She didn't know how else to say it. 'How much' seemed a little blunt, though it was tempting. She was sorrier than ever that William wasn't there to help her. But Enzo had gotten the point.

'Investments?' he asked, looking hopeful.

'Yes, I was thinking that American stock might be important for you to have, in your position. Or Italian, if you prefer it.'

'Stock? How much stock?' He had stopped eating in order to listen to every word she was saying.

'How much do you think?'

464

He made a vague Italian gesture as he watched her. '*Ma* . . . I don't know . . . five . . . ten million dollars?' He was trying her out and she shook her head.

'I'm afraid not. One or two perhaps. But certainly no more than that.' Negotiations had begun, and Sarah was pleased with the way things were going. He was expensive, but he was also greedy enough to do what she wanted.

'And the house in Rome?'

'I'd have to discuss it with Isabelle, of course, but I'm sure she could find another one.'

'The house in Umbria?' He wanted everything.

'I really don't know, Lorenzo. We'll have to discuss that with Isabelle.' He nodded, not disagreeing with her.

'You know, the business, the jewelry store, it is going very well here.'

'Yes, it is,' she said vaguely.

'I would be very interested in becoming partners with you.' She wanted to stand up and slap him, but she didn't.

'That will not be possible. We are talking about a cash investment, not a partnership.'

'I see. I will have to think about it.'

'I hope you do,' Sarah said quietly as she paid for the check, he made no move to take it from her. And Sarah said nothing to Isabelle about the lunch. She didn't want to raise false hopes in case he decided not to take the bait, and maintain the status quo instead. But Sarah fervently hoped he wouldn't.

The baby was still a month away, and Isabelle was anxious to introduce her to Lukas. He had taken an apartment in Rome for two months, looking into a project there, so he could be with her when she had the baby. And Sarah had to agree with her. She had done well this time. His only flaw was his wife and family in Munich.

He was tall and angular and young, with dark hair like Isabelle's, he loved the outdoors, and skiing, and children, and art and music, and he had a wonderful sense of humor. And he tried to talk Sarah into opening a store in Munich.

'That's not my decision any more,' she said, laughing, but Isabelle wagged a finger at her.

'Oh, yes, it is, Mother, and don't you pretend it isn't.'

'Well, not mine alone at least.'

'What do you think then?' her daughter pressed her.

'I think it's too soon to make that decision. And if you go to open a store in Munich, who will run Rome?'

'Marcello can run it blindfolded without me. And everyone loves him.' Sarah did, too, but opening yet another store was still a very big decision.

They spent a wonderful evening together, and Sarah told Isabelle afterwards that she was crazy about Lukas. She had another lunch with Lorenzo after that, but so far, he had made no final decision. Sarah had asked her discreetly how she felt about their two houses, and Isabelle had admitted that she hated them both, and didn't care if Enzo took them, as long as she got the escape she wanted.

'Why?' she asked her mother, and Sarah was vague with her. But this time, at lunch, she pulled out her ace card and reminded Lorenzo that it would be grounds for an annulment in the Catholic Church, if Isabelle sought one on the basis of fraud, citing that he had entered into marriage knowing that he was sterile, but having concealed it from Isabelle. Sarah eyed him quietly but firmly, and almost laughed as she waited for him to panic. He tried to deny that he had known, but Sarah held her ground and didn't let him. She reduced the cash offering from two million dollars to one, and offered him both houses. And he said he'd let her know, as he left her with the check and vanished.

Julian called them every few days to see how Isabelle was and if the baby had come, and by mid-February, Isabelle was going crazy. Lukas had to go back to Munich in two weeks, and the baby hadn't come, and she was getting bigger by the minute. She had stopped work and she had nothing to do, she said, except buy handbags and eat ice cream.

'Why handbags?' her brother asked her, mystified, wondering if she had developed a new fetish.

'They're the only thing that fit. I can't even wear shoes any more.'

He laughed at her, and then sobered when he told her that Yvonne had called him to tell him she was marrying Phillip in April. 'That ought to be interesting in years to come,' he said ruefully to his sister. 'How do I explain to Max that his aunt is really his mother, or vice versa?'

'Don't worry about it. Maybe you'll have found him a new mother by then.'

'I'm working on it,' he said, trying to sound light-hearted, but they both knew he was still deeply upset about Yvonne and Phillip. It had been a terrible blow to him, and a terrible slap in the face from Phillip, which was really why he'd done it. That and the fact that Julian's wife had literally driven him crazy. 'He must have always hated me a lot more than I realized,' he said sadly to his sister.

'He hates himself most of all,' she said wisely. 'I think he's always been jealous of all of us. I don't know why. Maybe he liked having Mother to himself during the war or something. I just don't know. But I can tell you one thing. He's not a happy person. And he's not going to be happy with her. The only reason she's marrying him is so that she can be the Duchess of Whitfield.'

'Do you think that's really it?' He wasn't sure if that made it better or worse, but at least it was some explanation.

'I'm sure of it,' Isabelle said without hesitation. 'The minute she met him you could hear bells going off that this was the big time.'

'Well, he's getting a great piece of ass anyway.' He laughed, and she chuckled.

'You sound like you're feeling better.'

'I hope you feel better soon too. Get rid of that baby,' he teased her.

'I'm trying!'

She did everything she could. She walked miles with Lukas every day, she went shopping with her mother. She did exercise, she went swimming in a friend's pool. The baby was three weeks overdue and she said she was going to go crazy. And then finally, one day, after an endless walk, and a bowl of pasta in a trattoria, she started to feel things happen. They were at Lukas's place, where she was staying. She hadn't even spoken to Lorenzo in two weeks and she had no idea what he was up to, nor did she care now.

Lukas made her get up again as soon as she said something to him that night, and made her walk around the apartment, insisting that it would get things going. She called her mother at the hotel, and she came over in a taxi, and they sat around until midnight, drinking wine and talking, and by then Isabelle was starting to look distracted. She wasn't laughing at their jokes, or paying much attention to what they said, and she started getting irritable with Lukas when he asked her how she was feeling.

'I'm fine.' But she didn't look it. Sarah was trying to decide whether to go or stay, she didn't want to intrude on them, and just when she had decided to leave, Isabelle's water broke, and the pains suddenly got much worse. It made Sarah think of the past and when Isabelle herself had been born with such force and such speed, but she had been Sarah's fourth child, and this was her first. It wasn't likely to be as speedy.

But when they called the doctor at the Salvator Mundi Clinic he said to come then, and not wait much longer. And as they all left for the via delle Mura Gianicolensi in Lukas's car, Sarah looked at her daughter with excitement.

She was finally going to have the baby she had wanted for so long. She only hoped that one day she would have Lukas too. She deserved him.

The nurses at the hospital were very kind, and they settled Isabelle in their birthing room, which was all very modern. It was a big, friendly suite, and they offered Sarah and Lukas coffee while they got Isabelle settled. Isabelle was feeling very uncomfortable by then, and an hour later she said she was feeling terrible pressure. And through it all, Lukas talked to her, and held her hands, and wiped her forehead with damp cloths, and her lips with Chapstick. He never left her alone or stopped talking to her for a moment, as Sarah watched them. It was wonderful to see them so close and so much in love, and once or twice, he almost reminded her of William. He wasn't as distinguished, or as handsome, or as tall. But he was a good man, and a kind, intelligent one, and it was obvious that he loved her daughter. She liked him more every time she saw him.

And then finally, Isabelle began to push, as she crouched on the bed with Lukas holding her, and then she lay back again and he held her shoulders and rubbed her back. He was tireless, and Sarah felt useless, and then suddenly Isabelle worked even harder and the whole room seemed to buzz with action and encouragement, and then they saw the head. Sarah saw the baby come out herself. It was a little girl and she looked just like Isabelle, as Sarah began to cry, and looked at her daughter. Isabelle had tears of joy streaming down her face, as Lukas held her and she held her baby. It was a beautiful sight, an unforgettable moment, and when Sarah went back to her hotel at dawn, she felt bathed in love and tenderness for them.

The next morning when she called Lorenzo and asked him to come to see her, she resolved to pay him anything he wanted. But he had gotten the point at their last lunch. He wanted both houses, and they settled for three million dollars. It was a high price to pay to get rid of him, but Sarah didn't doubt for a moment it was worth it.

She told Isabelle that afternoon when she went back to the hospital, and a huge grin of relief broke out on her face. 'Do you mean it? I'm free?' Sarah nodded as she bent to kiss her. Isabelle said it was the best gift she could have given her. And Lukas smiled at her as he held their baby.

'Maybe you'd like to come back to Germany with me, Your Grace,' he said hopefully, and Sarah laughed.

Lukas extended his stay in Rome by another two weeks, but then he had to go back to Germany and attend to his business. Sarah stayed until Isabelle came home from the hospital and helped her find a new house. And Sarah fell in love with the baby. Her two latest grandchildren had been a huge hit with her, she raved to Emanuelle, little Max was the cutest thing she'd ever seen since Julian was running around, and little Adrianna was a real beauty.

And this year, on Sarah's birthday, there was a most interesting group present. Isabelle came alone with the baby. And Julian with Max. Xavier was in Africa again for the summer, but he had shipped home two extraordinary emeralds for her, with exact instructions about how to cut them. They were going to make two huge, square rings, and he thought it would be fabulous if she wore one on each hand. She explained the whole idea to Julian when she showed him the stones and he was impressed. They were beauties.

Phillip came with Yvonne, which wasn't easy for Julian, but they were married now. And Sarah sensed that there was a certain meanness which made Phillip come to the château with her, and shove it in Julian's face. But Julian handled it very well, as he did everything. He was such a decent person that it would have been hard for him not to. And interestingly, Yvonne showed absolutely no interest whatsoever in the child she had borne the year before. She never even looked at him while she was there. She spent most of her time getting dressed and putting on her makeup, and complaining about her room, it was either too warm or too cold, or the maid hadn't helped her. And she wore an inordinate amount of jewelry, Sarah thought, which was intriguing. She was obviously making Phillip spend his pennies on her, and she made everyone call her Your Grace, constantly, which amused them, especially Sarah, who called her that, too, and Yvonne seemed not to notice that everyone was laughing, even Julian.

But as usual, it was Isabelle who really surprised her, as she and Sarah played with Adrianna one afternoon on the lawn. She was six months old and just crawling, and she was very busy trying to eat a blade of grass when Isabelle told her mother that she was pregnant again, and the baby was due in March this time.

'I assume it is Lukas's baby, isn't it?' she asked calmly.

'Of course.' Isabelle laughed. She adored him, and she'd never been happier. He was spending about half of his time in Rome and the other half in Munich, and it seemed to be working out pretty well, except for the fact that he was still married, though barely.

'Is there any chance he'll be getting divorced soon?' her mother asked, but Isabelle shook her head honestly.

'I don't think so. I think she's going to do everything she can to resist it.'

'Does she realize he has a family somewhere else? With two children? That might get the point across.'

Isabelle nodded. 'Not yet. But he says he'll tell her, if he has to.'

'Isabelle, are you sure?' Sarah asked. 'What if he never leaves her, if you're alone with these children forever?'

'Then I'll love them, and I'll be happy to have them, just like you when you had Phillip and Elizabeth, and Daddy was away during the war, and you never knew if you'd see him again. Sometimes there are no guarantees,'

471

she said wisely. She was getting smarter. 'I'm willing to accept that possibility.' Sarah respected her for it, her life was certainly not conventional, but it was honest. And even Roman society seemed to have swallowed what had happened. She was back at the shop part-time, and designing jewelry, too, and things were going extremely well. She was still talking about a branch in Munich. Maybe if she ever married Lukas they would open a store there. There were some very knowledgeable people there and a real market for good jewelry.

Her divorce was due to come through by the end of the year, which meant that this baby would not have Enzo's name, which was another obstacle for her to overcome, but Isabelle seemed ready to face it. Sarah wasn't worried about her when she flew back to Rome with Adrianna. And after they all left, she found herself thinking, as she often did, what interesting lives they led. Interesting, but not easy.

Chapter 31

Xavier graduated from Yale three years later with honors, and his family was there to see him do it, or most of them anyway. Sarah and Emanuelle had arrived together. Julian had come to Yale, of course, and he'd brought Max, who was four, and busily embarking on destroying his surroundings wherever he went, and Isabelle had come, but she hadn't brought the children. She was pregnant again, and they were used to seeing her that way by then. This was her third child in four years. And Adrianna and Kristian were in Munich with Lukas. He still hadn't divorced his wife, but Isabelle seemed at peace with the situation. And predictably, Phillip and Yvonne hadn't bothered to come. She was at a spa in Switzerland, and he said he was too busy, but he sent Xavier a watch from their new line at Whitfield's. Julian had designed it.

It was a lovely ceremony at Yale, and afterwards they all went to New York and stayed at the Carlyle. Julian kept teasing Xavier that it was time for him to open a shop in New York, and his brother diplomatically said maybe he would one day, but they all knew that he wanted to roam the world first. He was going back to Botswana the minute he left New York. He was flying to London and then straight down to Cape Town. And all he wanted for the next few years was to find rare stones for Whitfield's. After that, maybe he'd settle down, but he made no promises to anyone that he ever would. He was far too happy in a jungle with a pick and a gun and a backpack to ever want the responsibility of a store like the ones in Paris and London and Rome. He much preferred being their man on the prowl, out in the wilderness somewhere. It suited him far better, and they respected him for that, although he was certainly different.

'I think it was that Davy Crockett hat you had when you were a kid,' Julian teased him. 'I think it went to your brain or something.'

'It must have.' Xavier smiled, always unruffled by them. He was a handsome boy, and of all of them he looked the most like William, yet in all other ways he was the least like him. He had had a very interesting girlfriend at Yale. She was going to Harvard Medical School in the fall, but in the meantime, she had agreed to join him in Cape Town. But nothing was serious with him for the moment, except his travels, and his passion for stones. Sarah had worn the two enormous emerald rings that he'd found for her, to his graduation. She wore them almost every day, and she loved them.

Isabelle and Julian got a sitter for Max, and managed to have a drink in the Bemelmans Bar that night, as Bobby Short played in the next room, where Sarah and Emanuelle were. Xavier had gone to Greenwich Village with his girlfriend to have dinner.

'Do you think he'll ever marry you?' Julian asked her honestly, looking at her big belly, but she only smiled and shrugged.

'Who knows? I'm not sure I care any more. We're as good as married. He's there whenever I need him and the children are used to his coming and going.' She spent a lot of time in Munich with him now, whenever she could. It was a totally comfortable arrangement, and even Sarah had adjusted to it. Lukas's wife had known about Isabelle for the past two years, but she still refused to divorce him. They had some very complicated family business dealings together, and some land holdings in the north they'd invested in, and she was doing everything she could to tie up his money and stop him from divorcing her. 'Maybe one day. In the meantime, we're happy.'

'You look it,' he had to admit. 'I envy you all these kids.'

'What about you? I've been hearing little rumors in Rome,' she teased him.

'Don't believe everything you read.' But he blushed as he said it. At nearly thirty-six, he had never remarried, but there was a woman he was very much in love with.

'OK, then tell me the truth. Who is she?'

'Consuelo de la Varga Quesada. Mean anything to you?'

'Vaguely. Wasn't her father the ambassador to London a few years ago?'

'Right. Her mother's American, and I think she might be a vague cousin of Mother's. Consuelo's wonderful, I met her last winter when I went to Spain. She's an artist. But she's also Catholic, and I'm a divorced man. I don't think her parents were too thrilled when she told them.'

'But you were never married in the Catholic Church, so in their eyes you were never married.' She was an expert on all that, after divorcing Lorenzo. At least that part of her life was over.

'That's true. But I think they're being cautious. She's only twenty-five years old, and oh, Isabelle, she's such a sweet girl, you'd love her. She adores Max, and she says she wants dozens of children.' She looked like a little girl herself, when Julian showed his sister a picture of her. She had huge brown eyes and long brown hair, and a smooth olive complexion that made her look faintly exotic.

'Is this serious?' If it was, it was the first really serious affair he'd had since Yvonne. For a long time, he had gone back to just playing.

'I'd like it to be. But I really don't know how her parents are going to feel about me. Or how she will.'

'They should feel very lucky. You're the nicest man I

know, Julian,' she said, and kissed him gently. She had always loved him dearly.

'Thank you.'

The next morning they all flew away again, like birds to their own destinations. Julian to Paris, and then to Spain, Isabelle to Munich to be with Lukas and her children, Sarah and Emanuelle back to Paris too. And Xavier to Cape Town with his girlfriend.

'What a migratory bunch we are, spread all over the world, like nomads,' Sarah said as they took off on the Concorde.

'I wouldn't call it that.' Emanuelle smiled at her. She and the Minister of Finance were about to go on a long vacation. His wife had finally died that year, and he had just asked her if she would marry him. It had actually come as a shock to her after all these years. But she was sorely tempted. They had been together for so long and she really loved him.

'You should marry him,' Sarah urged her as they drank champagne and ate caviar.

'After all these years, the aura of respectability might be too great a shock to my system.'

Sarah patted her hand and grinned. 'Try it.'

When they landed, Sarah went back to the château, thinking about all her children. She only hoped that Isabelle didn't wait as long to get married as Emanuelle had. It amused her to think of Emanuelle married now . . . how long they had been friends . . . how far they had come . . . how much they had learned together.

Chapter 32

Sarah moved slowly back toward the window again, to watch them. How funny they were . . . how different . . . how beloved. It made her smile to watch them as they emerged from their cars. Phillip and Yvonne from the Rolls, she looked beautiful and overdressed and over-jewelled, as usual. At thirty-five, she was aging well, she still looked like a girl of twenty, but she worked hard at it, as she did everything she did. She thought of herself, and no-one else, and what she wanted. Phillip had learned that lesson a long time since. He was still enthralled with her after nine years, but his duchess was most emphatically a mixed blessing. There were times when he wondered if Julian had actually been glad to be rid of her. It disappointed him to think so.

Isabelle arrived just after them, in an absurd van they had rented at the airport. She and Lukas unloaded prams and bicycles and baby things. There were their three children, and two by his former marriage. She looked up at the upstairs window then, as though sensing that Sarah was there, but she didn't see her. Isabelle smiled at Lukas briefly as he handed her the baby and took their bags into the château. Their children were chattering loudly as they ran upstairs, wondering where their grandmother was, and then growing distracted before they found her. Isabelle stood for a moment and smiled at Lukas, as the noise echoed in the halls around them. Her marriage to him finally had been fruitful.

Julian arrived in the Mercedes 600 his father-in-law had

insisted on giving him. It was an impossible car, in need of constant repair, but beautiful, and it held all his children. Consuelo held the two little girls' hands as Julian helped her out, and they followed her, giggling, and looking just like their father. He was teasing Max, who was nine and very handsome. And as Consuelo turned you could see the full belly she carried well on her small frame. The new baby was due in the fall. Their third in four years. Julian and Consuelo had been busy.

And then at last, Xavier, his backpack over his arm, in an old jeep he had borrowed somewhere. He had a deep tan, and he had grown to be a strong, powerful man. She looked at him, overwhelmed with memories as she saw him. If she closed her eyes just a tiny bit, it was William coming toward her.

As she looked at them, she thought of him, the life they had shared, the world they had built, the children they had loved, who had stepped out into the world on their own, stumbled, and then righted themselves again. They were all strong, good, loving people. Some more than others, some were easier to understand, or easier to love. But she loved all of them. And as she again passed the table where the photographs were, she stopped to look at all of them . . . William . . . Joachim and Lizzie . . . they were still there in her heart too. They always would be. And then there was one of her, in her mother's arms . . . brand-new . . . newborn . . . seventy-five years ago tomorrow.

Remarkable. It was amazing how fast it all went, how the moments flew . . . the good with the bad, the weak, the strong, the tragedies, the victories, the wins and the losses.

She heard a soft knock on the door of her room then. It was Max with his two little sisters.

'We were looking for you,' he said excitedly.

'I'm so glad you've come.' Sarah smiled at him, as she

walked toward him, looking proud and tall and strong. She pulled him quickly into her arms and gave him a big hug, and then kissed both of his sisters.

'Happy Birthday!' they said, and as she looked up, she saw Julian in the doorway, and Consuelo . . . and Lukas and Isabelle, Phillip and Yvonne, and Xavier . . . and if she closed her eyes, she could still see William. She could feel him there with her as he had always been, at her side, in her heart, every moment.

'Happy Birthday!' they all shouted in unison, and she smiled at them, unable to believe that seventy-five precious years had passed so quickly.

THE END

OTHER DANIELLE STEEL TITLES
PUBLISHED BY CORGI AND
BANTAM PRESS

THE PRICES SHOWN BELOW WERE CORRECT AT THE TIME OF GOING
TO PRESS. HOWEVER TRANSWORLD PUBLISHERS RESERVE THE RIGHT
TO SHOW NEW PRICES ON COVERS WHICH MAY DIFFER FROM THOSE
PREVIOUSLY ADVERTISED IN THE TEXT OR ELSEWHERE.

☐ 13526 7	**VANISHED**	£4.99
☐ 13525 9	**HEARTBEAT**	£4.99
☐ 13522 4	**DADDY**	£5.99
☐ 13524 0	**MESSAGE FROM NAM**	£5.99
☐ 13746 4	**MIXED BLESSINGS**	£5.99
☐ 13523 2	**NO GREATER LOVE**	£5.99
☐ 13747 2	**ACCIDENT**	£4.99
☐ 14245 X	**THE GIFT**	£4.99
☐ 13748 0	**WINGS**	£5.99
☐ 02263 7	**LIGHTNING** (Hardback)	£15.99
☐ 03892 4	**FIVE DAYS IN PARIS** (Hardback)	£9.99
☐ 14395 2	**FIVE DAYS IN PARIS** – Audio	£12.99
☐ 14374 X	**THE GIFT** – Audio	£9.99
☐ 14401 0	**LIGHTNING** – Audio	£12.99*
☐ 14362 6	**VANISHED** – Audio	£8.99*

* including VAT

All Transworld titles are available by post from:

Book Service By Post, PO Box 29, Douglas, Isle of Man IM99 1BQ

Credit cards accepted. Please telephone 01624 675137, fax 01624 670923 or
Internet http://www.bookpost.co.uk for details.

Please allow £0.75 per book for post and packing UK.
Overseas customers allow £1 per book for post and packing.